# Praise for Ellen Hart and her Sophie Greenway mysteries

## THIS LITTLE PIGGY WENT TO MURDER

"Strong characters and a rich Lake Superior setting make this solidly constructed mystery hard to put down. Another winner for Ellen Hart!"

—*M. D. Lake*

"There are some good, nail-bitingly-tense scenes and lots of red herrings."

—*Publishers Weekly*

## FOR EVERY EVIL

"A dilly . . . A fair-play plot and contemporary characters that leap off the page . . . Stir in Martha Grimes with P. D. James and add a dash of Christie and Amanda Cross and you begin to get the idea: a cosy with a brain."

—*Alfred Hitchcock Mystery Magazine*

"Another splendid specimen of the classical mystery story, nicely updated and full of interesting and believable characters."

—*The Purloined Letter*

*Please turn the page
for more reviews . . .*

# Praise for Ellen Hart and her Jane Lawless series

## HALLOWED MURDER

"Hart's crisp, elegant writing and atmosphere [are] reminiscent of the British detective style, but she has a nicer sense of character, confrontation, and sparsely utilized violence . . . . *Hallowed Murder* is as valuable for its mainstream influences as for its sexual politics."

—*Mystery Scene*

## VITAL LIES

"This compelling whodunit has the psychological maze of a Barbara Vine mystery and the feel of Agatha Christie. . . . Hart keeps even the most seasoned mystery buff baffled until the end."

—*Publishers Weekly*

## STAGE FRIGHT

"Hart deftly turns the spotlight on the dusty secrets and shadowy souls of a prominent theater family. The resulting mystery is worthy of a standing ovation."
—*Alfred Hitchcock Mystery Magazine*

## A KILLING CURE

"A real treat . . . Secret passageways, a coded ledger, a mysterious group known only as the Chamber, experimental drugs, blackmail, sexual assault, betrayal: all the ingredients of a good whodunit."
—*Lambda Book Report*

## A SMALL SACRIFICE

"A smart and shocking thriller."
—*The Minnesota Daily*

By Ellen Hart
*Published by Ballantine Books:*

The Jane Lawless mysteries:
HALLOWED MURDER
VITAL LIES
STAGE FRIGHT
A KILLING CURE
A SMALL SACRIFICE

The Sophie Greenway mysteries:
THIS LITTLE PIGGY WENT TO MURDER
FOR EVERY EVIL
THE OLDEST SIN

# THE OLDEST SIN

## Ellen Hart

BALLANTINE BOOKS • NEW YORK

Copyright © 1996 by Ellen Hart

All rights reserved under International and Pan-American Copyright Conventions. Published in the United States by Ballantine Books, a division of Random House, Inc., New York, and simultaneously in Canada by Random House of Canada Limited, Toronto.

http://www.randomhouse.com

Library of Congress Catalog Card Number: 96-97129

ISBN 0-345-40202-2

Printed in Canada

First Edition: December 1996

10   9   8   7   6   5   4   3

For Gregory Johnson,
one of the greatest gifts of my college years and beyond,
and also for all those long-ago friends who survived
their membership in the Worldwide Church of God.

## Cast of Characters

**SOPHIE GREENWAY:** Managing editor of *Squires Magazine*; wife of Bram; mother of Rudy.

**BRAM BALDRIC:** Radio talk-show host for WTWN Radio in Minneapolis; husband of Sophie.

**RUDY GREENWAY:** Sophie's son; student at the University of Minnesota; part-time employee at the Maxfield Plaza.

**LAVINIA FIORE:** Founder of the Daughters of Sisyphus Society (D.O.S.S.); originator of *The Daughters of Sisyphus Society Cookbook*; fashion designer.

**BUNNY HUFFINGTON:** Founding member of D.O.S.S.; author; professor of Women's Studies at White Rock College in Bar Harbor, Maine.

**GINGER POMEJAY:** Student at Purdis Bible College in 1971.

**CINDY SHIPMAN:** National Treasurer of the D.O.S.S.; owner of Shipman Trucking in Norman, Oklahoma.

**ADELLE PURDIS:** Wife of Hugh Purdis; mother of Joshua.

**HUGH PURDIS:** Son of Howell; vice-chancellor of Purdis Bible College; husband of Adelle; father of Joshua; head of the Church of the Firstborn's field ministry.

**HOWELL PURDIS:** Founder and chancellor of Purdis Bible College; ordained leader of the Church of the Firstborn.

**ISAAC KNOX:** Evangelist-rank minister in the Church of the Firstborn; onetime dean of students at Purdis Bible College; pastor of the church in St. Louis, Missouri.

**PETER TRAHERN:** New husband of Lavinia Fiore; real-estate agent.

In Eden lived a serpent foul,
for when he heard Eve's stomach growl,
he said by way of greeting:
"I've cookies, beer, and pretzels, too.
Deep-fried cheese and chicken stew.
I've cake and candy just for you."

The serpent coiled around her side,
and said, although he knew he lied,
"An apple isn't cheating."

The serpent looked Eve in the eye,
and said "A teeny piece of pie?
Remember, life is fleeting."
Eve passed the apples and the chips.
She held a doughnut to her lips.
She never thought about her hips.

Though some say greed or lust or pride,
the hungry know down deep inside,
the oldest sin is eating.

KATHLEEN KRUGER
ELLEN HART

# Prologue

*Purdis Bible College*
*Los Angeles, California*
*Spring 1971*

Sophie paused next to a palm tree and looked both ways down Terrace Lane. When she was sure there was a suitable break in the traffic, she tucked her schoolbooks under her arm and rushed across the street.

It had been a hectic day. Starting just after sunup, she'd begun work on an outline of the main prophecies in Isaiah and Jeremiah, with classes filling her afternoon hours. Her four o'clock class, Harmony of the Gospels, had gone long. The paper she'd written two weeks ago on the Sermon on the Mount had finally been returned to her, the grade a disappointing C-. Later, at her job in the dining-hall kitchen, three men's club meetings had been scheduled instead of the normal two. That meant an extra hour on prep and another on cleanup. Now, nearly nine, she desperately needed to get back to Terrace Lane, to the apartment she shared with five other women students. She had to check on her ailing friend, Ginger Pomejay.

Ginger hadn't been feeling well for almost a month. No one spoke the words out loud, but everyone feared the worst. Ginger's mother had died of ovarian cancer in her late twenties, several years after giving birth to her last child. Ginger, while trusting in the Lord, secretly feared she would suffer the same fate. Not that anyone at Purdis Bible College believed in fate. God's plan for His firstborn of the spirit

1

was far more sophisticated than that. Even so, as Sophie bounded up the steps to the second-floor apartment, she couldn't help but worry.

Last night, as she'd been preparing dinner—it was her week to cook the low-calorie meals the dean of women had prescribed for their "weight problems"—Ginger had walked in, looking flushed and sweaty. Lavinia Fiore, one of the other women in the dorm, had helped her to bed and stayed by her side the entire night. By morning, Ginger's color looked terrible. She was still lucid, but refused to eat anything offered to her. Sophie felt a growing sense of panic as she watched her friend lying there, in such obvious pain. All anyone could do now was pray.

Even though there was an infirmary on campus, the doctor didn't do much more than treat minor injuries. Bruises. Cuts. Sprained ankles. The biblical injunction was clear. If someone became ill, it was the elders of the church who must be summoned to pray over the sick, anointing them with oil and asking God to heal. If a person's faith was strong, all would be well. Modern medicine was little more than Satan's attempt to undermine faith. Ginger's roommates had been praying for her for weeks. Now, since the entire student body had been told of her condition, it would become a vigil.

As Sophie passed by the front windows, she could see that a dozen or so of the other students had begun to gather in the living room. Most were quietly reading from the Bible, while some were engaged in silent prayer. Entering the apartment, she noticed that the door to Ginger's bedroom was closed. In the kitchen, Lavinia was preparing herbal tea. Sophie could smell the spicy scent of cinnamon.

Slipping up next to her, Bunny Huffington, another dorm mate, whispered, "She's pretty bad. I was just in to see her. I don't think she'll last the night."

"Who else is with her?" asked Sophie, setting her books down on a table by the door. She removed a yellow plastic band from her long, reddish-gold hair.

"Adelle."

"What about Cindy?"

Bunny shook her head. "I haven't seen her all day. I can't believe she isn't here."

"I guess she's still pretty angry with Ginger."

"*Angry* hardly covers it, Soph," snorted Bunny. "After what Ginger did to her, I wouldn't be surprised if they never spoke to each other again. But right now"—her eyes darted to the closed door—"I think a little forgiveness is in order."

Lavinia walked up carrying a mug. "What are you two whispering about?" She glanced over her shoulder as two more students entered the apartment. The small, sparsely decorated living room was becoming crowded.

"Cindy's noticeable absence," said Bunny, brushing a lock of dark hair away from her eyes. Bunny was eighteen, the youngest of them all, and the most athletic. Even though her body was solid, her muscles firm, she didn't precisely fit the womanly image Purdis Bible College was trying to achieve in its female students. Hence, she'd been banished to the fat-girl dorm.

"Forget Cindy," said Lavinia, blowing on the tea. "It's Ginger who needs our thoughts and prayers now."

"Do you think I could go in and see her?" asked Sophie. Lavinia seemed to have taken charge. Since she was Ginger's closest friend, it felt right. Ginger's only living relative, a cousin in Montana, had made it abundantly clear that he had no interest in her at all. In the time Sophie had known Ginger, the guy had written only once, calling Ginger a religious freak and saying he wanted nothing to do with her. No, Ginger's family was on this campus now, and even more specifically, in this apartment. The regular students lived in dorms, eating their meals at the dining hall. But for the six women of Terrace Lane, this off-campus, three-bedroom apartment was home. If Ginger was going to die, it should be here, surrounded by the people who loved her most.

"Sure," said Lavinia. "Come on. But be quiet. Loud noises upset her."

Sophie and Bunny followed Lavinia into the room. Adelle, the only senior woman in the group, was sitting on the bed next to Ginger, holding her hand and gently stroking her cheek. Since the outside light was fading fast and the interior light was dim, Sophie couldn't really get a good view of Ginger's face. Her eyes appeared to be closed. Even so, Sophie smiled a greeting. She felt awkward, not knowing quite what to do or say. Ginger was lying on her back, blankets a tangled mess around her middle. Sophie's eyes opened wide as she noticed a dark stain on the sheets. "What's that?" she whispered.

Adelle put a finger to her lips. "She's bleeding," she said, her voice barely audible. "Has been since this afternoon."

Sophie was appalled. At nineteen, she'd never been around someone who was dying before. It was one thing to view death in the abstract, to think of God's plan and what awaited the firstborn of the spirit during the resurrection. But it was another matter entirely to see death at work right in front of her eyes. She swallowed back a wave of revulsion and then perched on a cracked red Naugahyde chair by the window. As much as she didn't want to stay, she couldn't leave.

Lavinia bent over Ginger and offered her the tea.

The young woman's eyes fluttered and then burst open. "He's coming," she shouted, her voice clear and strong. A look of tension spread over her face.

"Who's coming?" asked Lavinia.

When Ginger didn't respond, Bunny said, "Maybe she's talking about the Second Coming."

Lavinia nodded. "Could be." She attempted to straighten the blankets.

"The fire and the wood!" cried Ginger, her voice once again rising to a shout.

"It's okay," soothed Lavinia, touching her on the shoulder. "You're here with us. We're all going to stay and take care of you."

"Agh," cried Ginger, wincing in pain. "The ram," she coughed. "Moriah. Send them . . ." The end of the sentence was mumbled.

"What did she say?" asked Bunny. She'd moved over next to Sophie, settling her solid frame against a desk under the window.

"Something about a ram," said Adelle. She felt Ginger's forehead. "She's got a fever."

"My fault," mumbled Ginger again. "My . . . but how—" She kicked her feet, as if she were trying to get away from something.

"She's not making any sense," said Lavinia.

"Isaac," called Ginger, knotting the sheets and blankets around her stomach.

"Isaac?" repeated Bunny. "Maybe she wants us to call Mr. Knox."

Isaac Knox was the dean of students. In emergencies, medical, personal, or otherwise, he was always the one who was called on to visit the student dorms. Most everyone liked him. Since he was in his late twenties, he didn't seem so far above the rest of the students. And he was so passionate about his commitment to the church and the college that most assumed, one day, he would become an evangelist-rank minister right alongside his best friend, Hugh Purdis. Hugh was the heir apparent. The firstborn son of Howell A. Purdis, God's apostle to a godless nation. "Is that what you want, Ginger? Should we call Isaac Knox?"

"Yes," she wailed, tears streaming down her cheeks. "He'll get the ram."

"She must be in terrible pain," whispered Sophie, her voice low and thick. She felt her own eyes burn with tears.

"Go call him," said Lavinia, looking over at Adelle.

Adelle immediately left the room.

"Don't care about . . . stars." Ginger continued to mumble. A few words here and there were intelligible, though mostly, she just seemed out of it. It didn't appear she was going to leave this world peacefully.

A good half hour later Isaac Knox entered the room, followed closely by Adelle, carrying his briefcase. He was tall and skinny, with a sandy-blond crew cut and intense gray eyes. His manner was normally very sober and reserved. *Lean and hungry* was how he liked to describe himself. It was meant to be humorous, but it was too accurate to be funny.

He nodded to everyone and then knelt down next to Ginger. In the light of the one dim lamp, his face looked utterly serious. He focused every ounce of his attention on the young woman before him. Removing a small vial of oil from his coat pocket, he unscrewed the cap and dabbed some onto his right index finger. Then, touching it gently to Ginger's forehead, he closed his eyes and prayed out loud, "Father in heaven, we ask that You would heal Ginger Pomejay of her sickness. She is Your child, the first fruits of Your spirit, a faithful member of Your church, and a loving friend to everyone here."

As Sophie bowed her head she felt her body begin to quake. Sensing someone move up next to her, she looked up and saw Adelle backing away from the bed. Their eyes locked for only an instant, but in that brief second Sophie could see a startling hopelessness in her friend's expression.

Isaac continued, "Heal Ginger of her sins. We know that our faith in You and the power of Your might will bless our lives. We humbly ask Your help. We are weak and sinful, and fall short of Your glory. Forgive us, Father. Show us the strength of Your mercy. Ginger accepts Your will for her life, as do we all. We ask for Your help and for the blessing of Your profound love. In Jesus' name, Amen." Except for the twitching of a small muscle in his cheek, he didn't move for almost a minute. Finally, removing his hand from her forehead, he leaned back on his heels and asked, "How long has she been like this?" His tone had grown more demanding. Even a little anxious.

"She's been really sick since last night," answered Lavinia. "She'd told me she'd gone to Pastor Heim twice last week. He anointed her both times. But . . . tonight, when she stopped making sense, we didn't know what else to do. So we phoned you."

Knox nodded and then stood up. "You did the right thing."

"She was calling for you," said Adelle.

He jerked his head around. "She what?"

"She said the name Isaac. We assumed she meant you."

From her chair, Sophie watched his reaction. Mr. Knox seemed truly surprised. Well, not surprised exactly. If she didn't know better, she would have thought he was frightened.

"What else did she say?" His posture had become ramrod straight.

"Just some mumbling," said Lavinia.

"She talked about a ram," said Bunny.

"A ram," he repeated, a confused look on his face.

"We couldn't make much of it out," said Adelle, shrugging apologetically.

He rubbed the back of his neck, giving himself a moment to think. "I understand. She looks feverish. Nothing she says now will have much meaning."

Sadly, everyone agreed.

In the presence of death, Sophie felt mute. Even so, she needed to ask, "Is there something else we should be doing for her?" She felt so helpless. So utterly useless.

"Just pray," said Isaac. He glanced back down at Ginger, then checked his watch. "I'm needed elsewhere, but—" He paused. "Perhaps I should stay."

"Oh, could you?" said Lavinia, her face brightening. "That would mean so much."

"Can I get you something to drink?" asked Bunny. "Some tea?"

"That would be fine," said Isaac, pulling a chair up close to the bed.

Bunny scurried out.

Sophie moved over to a small desk chair in the far corner of the room. Cindy should be here, she thought to herself. There were rules. Women students weren't supposed to be out unescorted after dark. As she sat back and watched Isaac Knox, his kindness and concern focused completely on Ginger, an almost fatherly look on his face, she felt an acute sense of guilt. Unlike her friends, she would have preferred that he leave. She was selfish and would have to ask God to forgive her. Bowing her head and closing her eyes, she offered up the most heartfelt prayer she'd ever prayed. Ginger had to get well. She just had to.

Two hours later Ginger opened her eyes and smiled.
And then she was gone.

# 1

*The Present*

Hildegard O'Malley gazed across her desk at the elderly
man who had been shown into her office just a few minutes
before. Even though he looked vaguely familiar, perhaps
someone she'd seen on TV, someone she was supposed to
like, his rather abrupt, almost imperial manner instantly put
her off. He had snow-white hair and a pleasant, even kindly
face, but thirty-two years spent in hotel management had
taught her not to trust first impressions. Hildegard prided
herself on her sixth sense about people. It was a must in her
line of work. And the bottom line was, this man wasn't what
he appeared to be.

For one thing, he hadn't mentioned money. Most people
who came to the Maxfield Plaza in downtown St. Paul to
discuss holding a convention on the premises always talked
money up front. After all, if you couldn't afford the price,
there was no point wasting each other's time.

"So, if I understand you correctly," she continued,
leaning forward and touching the tips of her fingers
together, "you'd like to see our conference facilities."

"One of your larger meeting rooms." His voice was deep
and formal. A briefcase and a narrow-brimmed man's fedora
rested on the chair next to him. "I represent God's church.
The Church of the Firstborn." He said the words proudly, as

if she should know the organization. And to be honest, it did ring a faint bell somewhere in the back of her mind.

"That brings me to my next question, Mr.—"

"Purdis. Howell Purdis."

"Yes . . . Mr. Purdis. The Maxfield Plaza is a rather expensive hotel in which to hold a week-long meeting. Will your membership be staying here?"

"Some will. Most won't. I don't have all the particulars."

"I see."

"Besides, money is no object." He said the words dismissively.

So that was it, thought Hildegard. He was wealthy. Or his church was. She glanced at his leather briefcase. It did look expensive. So did his dark suit, immaculate white shirt, and striped silk tie.

"Our area membership is only about two hundred people."

"And, may I assume then that you are a minister?"

"I am an *apostle*."

She had no particular problem with ministers, but apostles were a new one. Her uncle had been the pastor of the Lutheran church in the small southern Minnesota town where she'd grown up. Even though she was in her early sixties now, she still remembered how much she'd adored him. Religious nuts, on the other hand, were another matter. She wasn't quite sure where Mr. Purdis fit on the spiritual continuum. Adjusting her sweater, she said, "Let me show you the Lindbergh Room. It's just across the lobby in the north wing. I believe it will handle your needs quite nicely."

Silently, Hildegard led the way down a wide corridor and through the red marble, Art Deco lobby. The Maxfield Plaza had an unabashedly theatrical quality to it. Sleek lines were mixed together with jazzy zigzag ornamentation. The bold geometric sunbursts and lightning bolts had always been a bit much for the more conservative locals, though everyone seemed to enjoy a periodic foray into its glamorous interior. Streamlined club chairs and couches were scattered in small conversational clusters throughout the lobby. The Maxfield was an exclusive four-star hotel, and on the National Register of Historic Places. Kings and queens had stayed within its walls.

Passing Scotties, the Maxfield's first-floor bar—and a favorite haunt of the downtown St. Paul theatre crowd—Hildegard made a sharp turn and then headed into another hallway, which led to a spacious banquet room near the rear of the building. She removed a set of keys from her sweater pocket and unlocked the door.

Howell Purdis stepped inside, adjusted his rimless spectacles, and gave the room a thorough once-over. His eyes came to rest on the Deco chandelier high above his head. "This will do," he pronounced, looking pleased. "I'll want to order a buffet lunch for our noon meals. We follow the Levitical laws of clean and unclean meats."

"I'll notify our food-and-beverage manager. He can help you with the particulars."

"Splendid." Even though his movements were slowed by age, Purdis walked around the room with the ease of a man used to giving orders. After setting his briefcase and hat down on the front stage, he turned around to face her. "I will need a podium. The larger the better."

"That's no problem. Now that you've seen the space, why don't we go back to my office and I can get the paperwork started for you. I'll need to know the date—"

"This weekend."

"Oh . . . dear," she said, shaking her head. "That will be a problem." She began paging through the scheduling book. "That's rather short notice, I'm afraid. I'm not usually the one who sets up these events, but I'm pretty sure we're booked. There's a large convention in town this weekend. The meetings are being held over at the Civic Center, but most of our rooms will be taken since we're so close. It's the Daughters of Sisyphus Society. Have you ever heard of the group?" She was attempting to be pleasant, though she could see he had little interest in anything but his own agenda.

"No," he said, his tone both annoyed and abrupt. "And you can stop pawing through your notes. Our meeting has already been scheduled by my assistant, Isaac Knox."

"Oh. I see," she said, looking up. "Well, that does change matters. I assume you've been apprised of the cost."

"Cost? We're not paying."

"Then, can you tell me who we should bill?"

His eyes flashed at her. "Didn't you hear me say I represented God's church on earth? God doesn't have to pay. You're giving this to me free of charge."

She stared at him, dumbfounded. In all her years at the Maxfield, this was a new one. Of course, as the general manager, she'd been asked to donate space to various organizations and causes over the years, but to simply walk in and demand charity, well, this was a new one.

"I have been given a commission, Miss O'Malley. 'Go ye therefore into all the world, preach the gospel unto everyone.' My job as God's anointed is to be a witness to a sinful society. I am to preach His word. Your job is to help me!" His face had grown flushed.

"You *are* part of a cult," she murmured, more to herself than to him. So, her instincts had been right.

"You didn't hear me!"

"Oh, but I think I did." She backed toward the exit. "I'm sorry, Mr. Purdis, but this hotel does not give its services away free of charge." An inner sense told her that the longer they talked, the more upset he would become. He already looked angry enough to eat glass. The smart thing to do was to get back out to the lobby. At least there, she wouldn't be alone with his temper tantrum.

"You are refusing me?" he said, his voice a mixture of astonishment and frustration.

"I'm afraid so." Thinking one more comment was in order, she added, "I'm going to have to ask you to leave."

He held her eyes. " 'Whosoever shall not receive you, nor hear your words, when ye depart out of that house, shake off the dust of your feet. Verily I say unto you, it shall be more tolerable for the land of Sodom and Gomorrah in the day of judgment, than for that house.' " He picked up his briefcase and hat and walked slowly toward her.

"I'm sorry you feel that way, Mr. Purdis." She was put

off by his pomposity, and yet she felt rooted to the floor by the intensity of his eyes.

"You think the day of judgment is a long way off, don't you, Miss O'Malley? Well, you're wrong. The day of judgment is right now. It's all around us. This hotel will not be spared. You may not believe me, but from this day forward, the Maxfield Plaza is *cursed*."

This was ridiculous, thought Hildegard. The man was clearly unbalanced. Even so, his words carried a frightening impact. She knew it was his intent to frighten, and much to her dismay, his fear tactic was working. She was about to answer his threat with one of her own when he charged past her out the door.

# 2

Much like twins raised together, Minneapolis and St. Paul had always been rivals. While St. Paul capitalized on its historic charm, Minneapolis projected a slick, more cosmopolitan image. Sophie often likened the two cities to loaves of bread. St. Paul was a hearty, old-world rye, while Minneapolis was an upscale French baguette. Both towns had pretensions, yet each was a singularly beautiful northern city, filled with lakes and a rich social history, and as the inhabitants liked to point out, good, solid, clear-thinking Midwestern folks. Sophie's husband, Bram Baldric—a local radio talk-show personality—was periodically heard to comment that these stalwart folks were the same people who prided themselves on their independence as they lined up to gush hosannas at Rush Limbaugh on national radio and utter that battle cry of independent thought: "Ditto!"

Whether residents of Minneapolis or St. Paul, or that vast Minnesota never-never-land known simply as *outstate*, Minnesotans and their independent thought sometimes gave Sophie and Bram a bad case of indigestion.

A dear friend of Sophie's once observed that if you traveled to say, Cleveland, for instance, you knew immediately if someone in town hated your guts merely because you were black, red, green, fat, liberal, gay, poor, or any other social class or color that didn't quite cut the current societal mustard. Yet, in the Twin Cities, all the good citizens merely smiled. Smiled and smiled. And then smiled some more. Thus, a person never really knew where he stood. But, as Minnesotans were quick to point out, that didn't matter as long as everyone was pleasant about it.

Remember your manners and be sure to smile as you twist the knife. Otherwise, your Sons of Norway membership might be revoked. Not that there wasn't a lot of good in Minnesota. More good than bad. And that was the dilemma.

Both Sophie and Bram had deep roots in the Twin Cities, and yet each had begun to feel a certain strain with the relationship. Recently, they had begun to talk of getting away. Not just a vacation this time, but of trying someplace new. Of course, it was just a pipe dream. Bram was at the beginning of another two-year contract at the station. And Sophie was entrenched at her job as well. It was hardly the time to think about such a drastic life change.

As they walked the two blocks from their favorite downtown parking garage to the Maxfield Plaza, the hotel Sophie's parents had owned for over thirty years, Bram and Sophie continued their running conversation. It was late September. The maples and elms in the park across the street had already turned colorful shades of red and gold, scattering their bright confetti onto the grass.

"I suppose moving to Key Largo and making a living selling sand candles on the beach is out of the question," said Bram as he slowed his pace so that his wife wouldn't have to sprint. He was nearly a foot taller. The height difference was never more apparent than when they went for walks together. What was a leisurely stroll for him was a mad dash for her.

She slipped her arm through his, looking up into his handsome face. "You know what this restlessness is all about, don't you?"

"No, but I have a feeling you're going to tell me."

"This is a midlife crisis, darling. The fact that we're headed to my birthday celebration tonight only proves my point."

"Your big forty-four finger birthday."

"Exactly. And you'll be forty-eight next month."

"Don't remind me."

Stopping at the light, Sophie grabbed her sun hat as a gust of wind nearly blew it away. A late-summer thunderstorm was approaching from the west. The humidity was high, and so was the temperature.

When the light turned green, they continued on across the street.

"Are you really that tired of your job?" asked Bram, his voice growing serious.

Sophie had been the managing editor of an arts magazine for several years. It was a good living. Reasonably inter-esting work. But her real love was her part-time job as a restaurant reviewer for the *Minneapolis Times Register*. Not that it paid many bills. Yet cooking, eating, reviewing restaurants, writing about food—that had always been her passion. Working for *Squires Magazine* was moderately lucrative, and the arts had always been an interest, though less so in the past year. "I've got nothing to gripe about," she said, turning the corner and seeing the Maxfield come into view. It was an impressive gray-brick building with black streamline trim, rounded corners, and high, twin towers overlooking a center courtyard garden. A terra-cotta sunburst frieze surrounded the main entrance. To Sophie it had always seemed like something from another century. Since it was built in 1930, it just about was.

"Did you remember to bring your mother's present?" asked Bram, his right hand shooting into the pocket of his suit coat.

"It's right here," she assured him, patting the strap of her large sack purse.

"When you were a kid, you must have hated having the same birthday as your mom."

"True. That's why we're planning our own private party when we get home." She squeezed his hand, giving him her best come-hither look.

He grinned back. "The champagne is on ice even as we speak."

They entered through one of the front glass doors just as an elderly man barreled out the door directly next to them. Sophie did a double take, watching as he climbed with some difficulty into a waiting limousine. The door was immediately shut. "Nuts," she said under her breath.

"Something wrong?" asked Bram, noticing the rapt expression on her face.

"I don't know." She felt a bit disoriented. "That man looked so familiar. Just like—" She stopped and then shook her head. "But . . . he'd be so old now. It couldn't be him."

"Couldn't be who?"

She watched the limo pull away from the curb and slip into traffic. Wouldn't that be a coincidence? Tomorrow night, Sophie was planning to attend a reunion with four of her best friends from her days at Purdis Bible College. They hadn't all been together in the same room in over twenty years. Wouldn't it be strange if the head of the church she once belonged to was in town? Shaking off a feeling of déjà vu, she said, "My eyes must be playing tricks on me." She looked up at Bram with a pained expression and added, "It comes with age."

"Hey, you're not so old."

"You mean I'm not as old as you are."

"I mean," he said, putting a finger under her chin and tipping her face up to his, "that you're as beautiful today as the day I first met you. And you always will be." He kissed her, right there in the middle of the lobby, with everyone watching.

As he stepped back one of the bellboys began to clap. "Go for it, Mr. Baldric."

Bram gave a small bow.

"Come on," said Sophie, hoping no one had seen her blush. "We're going to be late."

Two hours later, after finishing the birthday dinner catered by the Zephyr Club, the four-star restaurant located near the top of the Maxfield's south tower, Sophie and Bram took their after-dinner coffee and strolled into the living room. They stood for a moment next to the windows, looking out at the sprawling Mississippi River fifteen stories below them. An occasional burst of lightning illuminated the darkening sky, though the storm was still a fair distance away.

"Time to open presents," called Henry Tahtinen, Sophie's father, herding everyone into the living room.

After singing "Happy Birthday"—some singing in Finnish and some in English—and blowing out all the candles, Sophie and her mother sat down on the couch to open presents. The entire family had been invited to the Tahtinens' private residence at the top of the south tower. There was Bram's daughter, Margie. Her boyfriend, Lance. Rudy, Sophie's son, had skipped one of his classes at the university in order to attend. His friend and lover, John Jacobi, was also in attendance. And Sophie's aunt Ida, her uncle Harry, and her cousin Sulo had all driven down from Bovey, a small town in northern Minnesota.

As the gifts were opened, Henry and Pearl beamed at each other across the brightly wrapped presents. After forty-five years of marriage, they were still very much in love. Pearl and Sophie were the same height—five-foot-two—and both had roundish figures that tended to overweight. Pearl's hair had gone completely gray many years ago, while her husband's had remained brown, with just a bit of salt and pepper around the temples. They both looked radiantly happy tonight. Too radiantly happy, thought Sophie. She wondered what was up.

Finally, after all the presents were oohed and aahed over and the hilarity had died down, Sophie's father called for quiet. Making his usual grand birthday gesture, he walked up and handed his wife an envelope. Then, stepping over to his daughter, he dropped a similar envelope into her lap.

"Your turn first," he said, nodding to his wife.

Pearl blushed. "Oh, Henry. You shouldn't have. I just know it's much too expensive."

"If a man can't buy his wife a damn fine present on her sixty-fifth birthday, what good is he?" He winked at Bram.

Pearl slipped a brochure out of the envelope. "What is it?" She gasped as she read the writing on the front cover. "Henry! This is too much!"

"It's what we've talked about for years, Pearlie. We're not waiting any longer." He stuck his cigar back into his mouth.

"What is it?" asked Sophie, attempting to restrain her curiosity. It wouldn't be appropriate to rip the paper out of her mother's hand, not that it hadn't occurred to her.

"It's"—Pearl's eyes grew round with wonder as she looked from face to face—"a round-the-world trip!"

"We'll be gone four months," said Henry, blowing smoke out of the side of his mouth. "Four wonderful, relaxing months."

"But . . . how can you do that, Henry?" protested Cousin Sulo. "You've got a hotel to run."

Henry's eyes gleamed at his wife. "Oh, I'm a resourceful man."

"Open your present now, Sophie," suggested Pearl, smiling amiably.

Sophie didn't need coaxing. She slid a legal-looking document out of the envelope.

"What's it say?" asked Sophie's son, Rudy. He was standing behind the bar, sipping from a can of Coke. John stood next to him, a look of intense interest on his face.

As she read the cover sheet Sophie's jaw dropped open. She looked up, handing it across to Bram.

Bram studied it for only a second before his own jaw dropped. "I don't understand, Henry."

"What don't you get?" He flicked ash somewhat impatiently into an ashtray.

"You're giving Sophie and me the hotel?"

"For tax purposes, I'm selling it to you," he corrected. "For the sum of one dollar. You've got a buck between you, don't you?" His smile was sly.

"But, Dad?" said Sophie. "You can't just—"

"I can do anything I damn well please! I'm sixty-nine next January. I've got plenty of money in the bank. So I asked myself, what am I still working for? It's time to retire. Your mom and I deserve to spend some time having fun. Kicking up our heels. Not that this hotel doesn't still mean the world to both of us. That's why we're giving it to you two. Soph, you grew up here. This place is in your blood."

It wasn't that she disagreed. It was just that the idea of owning the Maxfield was a little *rich* for her blood. She always assumed that when the time came for her parents to retire, they would sell.

"You worked here until you went to college," continued Sophie's father. "And Rudy's already working part-time in the kitchen helping our pastry chef. From what I hear, he's a natural. Think of it as the family business. Bram will learn. Running the place will be a piece of cake. Besides, we've got the best staff in the business. I've talked to Hildegard O'Malley. She's going to take over for me until you're both up to speed."

This was so much like her dad, thought Sophie. Impetuous. Generous. Imperious. He always figured he knew what was best—for everyone.

"Day after tomorrow, your mother and I are off for Helsinki. From there, it's wherever the wind takes us."

"Ah, dear, I believe we go to St. Petersburg next," said Pearl Tahtinen, glancing at the brochure.

"Whatever," he grunted. "I have absolute confidence that, if we keep this a family affair, the Maxfield will be in competent hands."

Sophie caught Bram's eye. She wasn't sure how he was taking all this, but his good humor seemed to be holding. Even so, he couldn't help looking a bit bemused.

"I'm sure you two have a lot to talk about," said Sophie's mom in a kindly tone. "While your dad and I set up the projector so that we can show our slides of the trip we took to Florida last April, why don't you two step outside for a breath of fresh air?"

"Good idea," said Bram, shooting to his feet.

Sophie followed him out through the French doors onto a balcony that overlooked the Mississippi River.

The evening air was heavy with the threat of rain. The sky had turned a funny yellow-gray, pretornadic light in Sophie's lexicon of Minnesota weather lore. Severe weather this late in the year was rare, though not impossible. As she sank into one of the metal patio chairs, she could hear the rumble of thunder. The storm was close now. She waited a few moments more as Bram paced in front of her, giving him some time to think. Finally, she asked, "What are we going to do?"

"Your father has quite a talent for turning lives upside down." His good humor was gone.

"I agree," she said softly. "This doesn't exactly fit into our dream of someday moving away." She paused, then added, "You know, someplace romantic. Like the oil fields of Iraq. The crocodile-infested Everglades."

"Very funny."

"The peaceful hills and vales of Afghanistan?" Even her humor had grown tentative.

He stopped and looked down at her. "We'd be crazy, Sophie, to turn this down."

"I know."

"Very few people have ever been handed a multimillion-dollar hotel."

"True."

"Then why do I feel like I've just been hit by a truck?"

She shook her head. "Ditto."

"Don't say ditto. It gives me heartburn."

"Sorry."

"I won't quit my job at the station, Sophie. You need to understand that up front."

"Of course not. You wouldn't have to."

He stared at her. "You want this, don't you?" It was less a question than a perception.

Looking up into his deep green eyes, she realized how much she really did want it. "Yes," she said, taking hold of his hand. She left it at that, waiting.

Without a moment's hesitation, he pulled her up into his arms and whispered close to her ear, "Maybe *this* is our adventure. We'll never know where the train is going unless we hop on for the ride." He nuzzled her hair. "I love you, Sophie. Happy birthday."

She hugged him with all her might, then stood back and gently brushed a lock of his chocolate-brown hair away from his forehead. "How did I get so lucky?"

"You paid your dues with your first husband, remember? Anybody would look good compared to Norman Abnormal."

"Not true." Again, she eased into his warm embrace, feeling his strong arms wrap around her. They were good together. Both of them smart, able to stand alone, but both also knowing the value of tenderness, of someone to lean on when times got rough. As she looked over his shoulder toward the north tower, she saw a figure move out onto the balcony directly across from them. Her breath caught in her throat as she realized it was the same man she'd seen coming out of the Maxfield only a few hours before.

"Bram, look!" she said, drawing away from him. She stepped over to the railing.

Bram walked up beside her just as a lightning flash illuminated the man's face.

"It *is* Howell Purdis," she whispered. "I'm sure of it."

"The head of that church you used to belong to?"

"Yeah. This is too amazing."

As the thunder cracked loudly over their heads the man,

his expression austere and unsmiling, lifted his hat in greeting.

# 3

Across the way, inside one of the luxury suites at the top of the north wing, Adelle Purdis emerged from the bathroom wearing a thick white cotton robe—compliments of the Maxfield Plaza—and drying her long red hair on one of the equally thick bath towels. The flight in from L.A. had been tiring. Now, moving slowly about the elegant living room, she noticed her father-in-law, Howell Purdis, standing outside on the balcony. From the sound of thunder, she assumed the storm that had been threatening for several hours was just about on top of them. Perhaps it was already raining. Adelle had no confidence at all that Howell Purdis had the sense to come in out of the rain. As far as she was concerned, the old guy was losing his marbles. She found it a pity that not one of the spineless wonders who called themselves ministers in the Church of the Firstborn had the guts to point that little problem out to him.

As she passed in front of the sofa on her way to the wet bar, there was a loud rap on the door.

"Will you get that?" called Hugh Purdis. Her husband was sitting on the bed in the bedroom typing something into his laptop computer. It was a standard issue. All evangelist-rank ministers were given the same one. Although Hugh looked like he was working, he was probably playing one of his many computer games. It was what he did for relaxation these days—and for escape. She couldn't blame him. Over the years the stress of being Howell Purdis's firstborn son and heir to the church leadership had taken its toll. While Adelle wanted her own firstborn son to one day assume his rightful place as spiritual head of the church, she'd developed a plan to shield him from the worst of the pressure.

The Church of the Firstborn was clearly the work of one periodically egomaniacal man. Even so, deep in her heart, where only God the Father could enter, she'd felt the hand of God. For all the evil and human weakness inherent in this worldwide work, she truly believed she'd found God's one true church on earth.

Since its beginning in 1933, Howell Purdis had created a stunningly Machiavellian organization, full of secrets and ever-changing alliances. The governing principle was power: hierarchical, authoritarian, absolute. The members of the ministry, from lowly church elders all the way up to evangelist-rank ministers, were constantly vying for favor and status. As far as Howell Purdis was concerned, he *was* the Church of the Firstborn. He set the tone, made the rules, and meted out the rewards and the punishment. Yet as he had begun to sink into a kind of madness, so had the organization.

Pulling open the door, she was surprised to find Isaac Knox, pastor of the church in St. Louis, standing before her, a furious look on his face.

"I need to speak to your husband," he said curtly. He didn't wait for an invitation but instead pushed past her into the room.

"Hello, Isaac. It's nice to see you again, too," said Adelle, her smile a little too cheerful to be anything other than snide.

"Sorry," said Isaac. "This is important." The years had treated Isaac Knox rather badly, thought Adelle. Gone was the lean build and rugged face. At fifty-one, he had the ancient, weary eyes of a man who had seen far too much strife in his life. Even though most women would probably find him attractive, even distinguished, Adelle saw only wreckage.

Hugh Purdis breezed out of the bedroom, his smile at high beam. "Isaac," he said, moving into his deep ministerial voice. "Great to see you again. It was good of you to stop by. I left a message for you at the front desk just after we arrived. I don't think you'd checked in yet." His gaze swept over the room. "This is a wonderful place. Father's very impressed. I'm glad you suggested this hotel and set everything up. You did a wonderful job. Top-notch. The adjoining suites are quite large and comfortable."

Isaac didn't move. Instead he whispered, "Where *is* your father?"

"He's out on the balcony," said Hugh, looking confused. "Why?"

Isaac took a few steps farther into the room. "I need to talk to you. Alone."

"What about?" asked Hugh.

"About what happened this afternoon!"

Adelle assumed by his tone that her presence had already been dismissed as meaningless. As a woman in the church, she was used to being invisible. Stepping over to the bar, she quickly selected a bottle of twelve-year-old Scotch, pulled up a bar stool, and poured herself a drink. She might as well be comfortable as she watched this latest drama unfold.

"Just keep it down and tell me what happened," said Hugh, perching on the edge of the desk. He was a large, barrel-chested man, much taller and heavier than his dad.

Isaac lowered his voice. "Your father talked to a woman named O'Malley here at the hotel this afternoon. He insisted she give him the meeting room for the Sabbath festival free of charge. She left a message for me which I received as soon as I got here. She was ready to cancel the entire event!"

Hugh put a hand on the back of his shaggy gray mane. "I don't believe it."

"He's going to ruin us," said Isaac, sinking into a chair. "He can't pull a stunt like that and expect people to just go on as if nothing's happened. You can't bully people into believing the way you do."

"I agree," said Hugh, narrowing his eyes in thought.

Adelle had seen her husband's concerned act before—and she wasn't buying it. "Say, Isaac," she said sweetly. "Did Hugh tell you what his father did last week?"

Hugh shot her a cautionary look.

"No. What?" said Isaac.

"I don't think we need to hear that right now, Adelle." Hugh gave her another hard look.

Adelle ignored him. "He walked into a car dealership in Glendale and demanded that the owner give him a brand-new luxury sedan. He is, after all, the head of God's church on earth. When the man said he'd call the police if he didn't leave, he stood his ground, cursed the dealership, and threatened the man with eternal damnation."

Isaac closed his eyes. "I think I'm going to be sick."

"Be sick somewhere other than our bathroom," said Adelle, adding some club soda to her drink. If Isaac was going to treat her as if she wasn't in the room, she was hardly going to view *his* discomfort with much sympathy.

"I won't accept that there's nothing we can do to put a stop to this kind of behavior," continued Isaac, erupting out of his chair.

"What behavior?" demanded a voice from the balcony. Howell Purdis pushed through the French doors just as a crack of thunder rumbled across the sky behind him.

Yup, thought Adelle, watching him drip water onto the carpet. No sense at all.

Both of the younger men attempted to excise the guilty looks from their faces.

The strained silence was finally broken by Hugh. "Well, ah"—he stammered, smiling at his dad—"it seems one of the deacons in St. Louis has been creating some problems. Isaac was just asking me what he should do about it."

"Problems?" repeated Purdis, easing his elderly frame onto the sofa as if he were trying it on for size. He picked up the remote and turned on the TV.

"He throws temper tantrums," said Adelle with a completely straight face. "And he's obnoxious. He goes around threatening people."

"Sounds like a matter for the ministerial committee," said Purdis absently, switching to one of the shopping channels. "Point him out to me at Sabbath services."

"Will do," said Isaac, jumping visibly as the phone on the desk next to him gave a sudden, jarring ring.

"I'll get it," said Hugh. He picked it up and said hello. Listening for a moment, he covered the mouthpiece with his hand. "It's for you, Isaac."

"Me? That's odd. I didn't tell anyone I was coming up here." He took the receiver, turned his back to the room, and walked toward the balcony doors. "Yes," he said, his voice regaining some of its confidence.

Adelle sipped her drink, retreating into her own thoughts. She couldn't help but conclude once again that ministers were a strange bunch. Since she'd spent her entire life around them, she'd had a lot of time for intimate observation. Early on, when she was a student at Purdis Bible College back in the early Seventies, she was much too awed by the thought of their spiritual status to even view them as human. But, over the years, she'd come to the conclusion that they were very human indeed. Some of them were good, some bad. Some weak and some strong. Some committed to the work, and some, *more* than a few, embarrassingly lazy. Yet to a man, they all craved flattery, attention, and when they could get it, even adoration. If they had an Achilles' heel, that was it.

"Speak up," said Isaac testily. "And slow down. I can't understand you." He stuck a finger in his other ear and lowered his head.

Popping a pretzel into her mouth, Adelle wondered who was on the line.

"No, I don't. And this isn't a very good time for—" He paused, listening. After almost a minute he said, "I see. Yes, I suppose you're right." As he turned around, Adelle noticed a slight loss of focus in his eyes. "Yes . . . I, ah, won't forget."

Everyone was now watching him.

"No, that won't be necessary. You've made yourself perfectly clear." Nervousness rose off of him in waves. "We'll have to continue this conversation later. Yes . . . thank you. Goodbye." He replaced the receiver in its cradle.

"Problems?" asked Hugh curiously.

"Nothing I can't handle," said Isaac. "Just a little local church matter. Nothing to worry about."

"Good." Hugh smiled.

Isaac reached for the handkerchief in his pants pocket and wiped the sweat off his face. "Well, I guess I'll get going. I suppose I'll see you both tomorrow. Everything's all set for the beginning of the festival on Saturday."

"Thanks," said Hugh, nodding cordially.

"Night," called Isaac as he got to the door.

"Good night," repeated Howell Purdis from the couch. "Oh, and one more thing. I want that limousine kept at my disposal for the entire weekend." His attention was so caught by the jewelry being advertised on the shopping channel that Isaac's rather sudden departure had barely registered. Still, he had enough brainpower left to issue an order.

"I'll see to it," said Isaac. He gave Adelle a last, uncertain look, and then left in such a hurry, he forgot to shut the door.

# 4

Lavinia Fiore struck a dramatic pose in front of the mirror in her hotel suite, critically appraising the evening dress she was planning to wear to the opening ceremonies of the Daughters of Sisyphus Society's annual Upper Midwest convention tomorrow night. Her mahogany hair was piled carelessly on top of her head as she gazed admiringly at the lush image she would present. As founding mother of the organization, and author of the best-selling *D.O.S.S. Cookbook*, she was expected to give the keynote address. Lavinia wasn't the least bit concerned about the speech. She was a good public speaker. Some might even call her inspirational. Yet tonight she felt jumpy, a ball of unfocused energy.

Normally, when she felt agitated, she would try on every piece of clothing in her closet just to get her mind off her problems. Eyeing the graceful lines of the hand-dyed silk gown, she did feel better. She smiled at her stylish image, knowing the dress she was wearing was one of her own creations.

After graduating from Purdis Bible College back in the early Seventies, Lavinia spent a short time as a secretary in the registrar's office. Every morning she would attempt to squeeze her square-peg mind and body into a very uncomfortable round hole. And every night, she came home to her tiny apartment, bruised and depressed. Finally, after a particularly nasty run-in with the assistant registrar, a man whose hair always struck her as so bizarre that the only way she could figure he achieved the look was by sleeping with a funnel on his head, she switched off her typewriter, threw the report she was working on in the trash, grabbed the jelly doughnut she was hiding in her bottom desk drawer, and stomped out. Forever. In a matter of days she was packed and on her way back home. Lavinia was a New York woman, born and bred. California, with all its crazy inhabitants, might have seduced her temporarily, but they could never keep her permanently. Still, it was a big step. She'd not only left her job behind, but for all practical purposes, her faith as well.

After knocking around Manhattan for a few months, she enrolled in a fashion-design class at NYU. From that day forward she never looked back. Fashion became her passion. She worked her way through several New York houses, her brain soaking up every last detail of the business. One basic fact became apparent quite quickly. A fat woman was never going to get hired as a fashion designer.

The year her aunt died and left her a hefty inheritance, she took a dangerous leap and started her own small design shop. Everyone predicted immediate insolvency. Lavinia persevered. This tiny hole in the wall was going to be her ticket to the big leagues. As she failed, as her designs were rejected, she learned. Eventually, her ideas began to catch on, to command attention. Today, the House of Fiore was internationally known and respected.

Lavinia's special interest, since she was a large woman herself, had been the creation of a fashion line especially suited to the so-called larger woman. In fact, the most compelling reason she'd gotten into the fashion industry in the first place was because she loved fabulous, gorgeous, outrageous, extravagant, beautifully designed clothing, but no matter how hard she looked, she was never able to find the kind she craved in a size that fit.

In 1984, Lavinia and a handful of other overweight women began to meet one evening a week at her apartment to discuss their success—or lack thereof—with current dieting fads. She was living in the Village at the time. Her longtime friend, Barbara—Bunny—Huffington, was finishing her doctorate in American Studies at Columbia, and would attend when she wasn't buried under a mound of schoolwork. During that summer and the following fall, some startling, even life-changing conclusions were reached by this small cadre.

To each of the women, eating and then dieting had taken on the quality of obsession. They were so fixated on food, and their failure to control their appetites and thus achieve the proper female image in the world, that most of them went around in a permanent state of gloom.

Bunny was the first one to connect this struggle with women's equally profound struggle for identity in the last half of the twentieth century. As women moved from the home into positions of power and authority in the world, the ambivalence they felt over their newfound status, and the anxiety they experienced over their equally newfound responsibilities, were often played out in their relationship to food. Always the philosopher at heart, Bunny wrote several papers—eventually even a book—on the issues of overweight, food addiction, and society's physical expectations of women. After all, as she pointed out, at least ninety-two percent of the anorexics in America today were female, and one out of five college-age women supposedly suffered from bulimia. Clearly, women were in a life-and-death struggle with their bodies.

Lavinia read the papers with interest, yet her approach to the matter was far more pragmatic. Theory might be great, but why not start a support group for women who refused to fight the battle any longer. The image of Sisyphus, that sorry man in Greek myth who spent his entire life pushing a boulder up a mountain only to have it roll back down again, instantly sprang to mind. The boulder, in Lavinia's scenario, was dieting. Hence, the organization became the Daughters of Sisyphus Society.

Lavinia wanted to emphasize personal acceptance. She told women, through speeches and in the pages of her now famous cookbook, that they needed to look at themselves in the mirror and love what they saw. Fat or thin. Tall or short. Young or old. They were all beautiful and unique. And even more important, she encouraged women to grow and develop their talents and skills. Only through accomplishment would they come to love and appreciate themselves fully. There were no overnight successes in her book, only hard work.

While Lavinia made it clear that it was important to be as healthy as possible, fad dieting was public enemy number one. She urged the women of the country to throw away their diet books and stop fixating on every last morsel they put into their mouths.

Finally, Lavinia insisted that, in our efforts to be trim and healthy, we'd lost something fundamental from our lives. Eating was one of life's greatest pleasures. Pleasure was good, not bad. To infuse the simple act of eating with such guilt, with such convoluted mental and emotional anguish, was draining our society of joy. And the loss of joy, she pointed out with a fervor bordering on a holy crusade, was a far too terrible price to pay.

Unzipping her gown, Lavinia slipped it off and then sat down on the bed. She felt a sense of pride when she thought of what she'd created. The D.O.S.S. had grown from a membership of seven to just over seven hundred thousand women worldwide. And it was still growing. To be sure, many were now joining as a means of networking with other like-minded, aggressive, achievement-oriented women. Housewives, mothers, poets, cabdrivers, businesswomen, athletes, academics, anyone and everyone interested in a better, more satisfying relationship with food and their own bodies, had become a part of the organization—some, no doubt, for the sheer pleasure of thumbing their noses at society's feminine imperatives. But whatever the reason, *The Daughters of Sisyphus Society Cookbook* and the first D.O.S.S. chapter in New York City had captured the imagination of the nation. And Lavinia, from the first, was at the head of the parade, leading the battle charge.

Glancing at the clock next to her on the nightstand, she saw that it was nearly nine-thirty. Bunny Huffington was supposed to stop by before ten to go over the revisions for tomorrow night's speech.

Bunny was now a tenured professor of Women's Studies at White Rock College in Bar Harbor, Maine. She was a no-nonsense New Englander by birth, so Maine suited her just fine. She also remained the philosopher for the organization, writing most of Lavinia's speeches. Her usual traveling companion, Iris Quinn, hadn't come along this time. Iris and Bunny had been together for almost twelve years, though Lavinia had recently heard rumors of a breakup. Since Bunny was a very private person, Lavinia knew better than to press her on the subject. Lavinia's own love life had been something less than stellar. Mainly, she'd had a series of ill-fated love affairs, mostly with totally unsuitable men. She just couldn't seem to get a handle on personal happiness—that is, until now.

Hearing a loud rap, Lavinia pulled on her bathrobe, unpinned her hair, and swept into the living room. She expected to see Bunny's smiling face when she answered the door, but instead, a young man in a bellboy's uniform greeted her.

"Good evening, Ms. Fiore. I was told you had a package you wanted me to deliver downstairs to the safe."

Of course, thought Lavinia. Where was her mind? She'd called the concierge right after dinner, asking that they send someone up. But that was two hours ago. She raised a carefully plucked eyebrow at the young fellow, about to protest the miserable service. Lavinia was a stickler for punctuality. She also expected to get what she paid for. Part of the price of staying at an exclusive hotel was the special service it could provide. To her mind, at this moment she wasn't getting it.

"I'm sorry for the delay, Ms. Fiore. There are so many people checking into the hotel right now, it took me an extra hour to get all the bags delivered."

A poor excuse, thought Lavinia, but then, she didn't have any difficulty believing him. "See that this doesn't happen again." She whipped a hundred-dollar bill out of her bathrobe pocket and handed it to him.

His eyes opened wide. "Yes, ma'am!"

"What's your name?"

"Elvis."

She did a double take. "Well, Elvis, I expect to be taken care of while I'm here. I'll call for you directly if I need anything."

"Yes, ma'am." He grinned.

"I believe in paying for what I get. But I have high expectations. I expect fresh ice in my room every evening."

"Of course, Ms. Fiore."

"Make sure the refrigerator is restocked daily. I drink a lot of grapefruit juice, and I don't want to run out."

"Will do."

"And *three* chocolates on my pillow when the maid comes in to turn the bed down. Not just one."

"I'll inform the housekeeping staff."

"Oh, and speaking of pillows, I have very serious allergies, Elvis. I travel with my own pillows instead of using the standard feather variety that hotels provide. Please see to it that they are aired and replaced on the bed every morning. I won't tolerate any slipups on this."

"I understand, Ms. Fiore. Don't give it another thought."

She nodded approvingly. "Also, those little butter cookies I found in my room tonight when I arrived were wonderful."

"We make them in our kitchen."

"I assumed as much. You know, Elvis, as I think about it I wouldn't mind having an extra plate of those, too."

"Your wish is my command, Ms. Fiore." He stuffed the hundred into his pants pocket.

"I thought it might be." She smiled back at him. "I think we understand each other now, Elvis. I expect my stay here at the Maxfield Plaza to be a joy." Bending down, she picked up a sealed, document-sized manila envelope resting next to the door and handed it to him. "I want this put under lock and key as soon as you get downstairs."

"Yes, ma'am."

"If anyone asks, I gave you nothing. You don't remember any package."

"But"—he looked unsure—"there'll be a record of it downstairs. And you'll receive a receipt with your name on it."

Hmm. That was a problem. Giving it a few moments' thought, she said, "All right, here's what we're going to do. I want you to put another name on the hotel record."

"Oh, Ms. Fiore, that could get me in real trouble."

She pulled another hundred from her pocket. "Will this take care of the inconvenience?"

He stared at it for only an instant before plucking it from her hand. "Yes, ma'am. I believe it will. What name do you want me to use?"

Lavinia allowed herself a private smile. "Martha Finchley," she said without missing a beat. As she watched him jot it down on a notepad, she heard the elevator doors open. Peeking out of her doorway, she saw Bunny at the other end of the hall, steaming in her direction.

"Get out of here," she whispered, pushing him away. "Don't use the elevator. Take the stairs down to the floor below us."

He tipped his cap and disappeared into the stairwell.

"Bunny!" cried Lavinia, throwing her arms around her friend as soon as she'd come within reach. "It's great to see you!"

Bunny gave Lavinia several thumps on her back and then pulled away. "You look fabulous."

"As always." She smiled, standing aside and allowing Bunny to enter.

Bunny Huffington was a short, square woman in her mid-forties, with close-cropped brown hair and a kindly bulldog face. The dark, horn-rim glasses made her look distinctly intellectual, though she was also quite the athlete, engaging in everything from rock climbing to scuba diving. Setting her leather briefcase down on a small end table, she dumped herself wearily into a chair. "I'm exhausted. And you look as fresh as an Oregon peach. Life isn't fair." Eyeing her a moment longer, she said, "It's none of my business, but have you lost weight?"

"Almost thirty pounds."

"A new diet?"

They both laughed at the absurdity of the notion. Lavinia moved over to the bar to pour drinks. "What do you want? I've got Scotch, gin, champagne, brandy, several wines, and the usual sodas and fruit juices."

"Make it a brandy," said Bunny, lifting her feet up on a footstool. She was wearing her usual well-worn jeans and chambray shirt. Fashion had never been high on her list of personal imperatives. She continued to stare. When Lavinia handed her the drink she remarked, "Pardon me, but one does not *lose* thirty pounds without a modicum of effort."

"I suppose you're right. Would you believe I've given up chocolate?"

"Not unless you've had a lobotomy." Bunny opened up her briefcase and removed a stack of papers. Dropping them in her lap, she continued, "I've highlighted the changes I made in your speech. Maybe we could go over them now."

Lavinia nodded, unable to wipe the grin off her face.

"What's so funny?" asked Bunny, clearly not getting the humor in the situation.

"Nothing."

"Then why are you smiling like such an idiot?"

"Oh, don't ask so many questions."

"That's not an answer," said Bunny. "Come on, give. What's going on?"

"You'll see."

"I'll see *what*?" Her exasperation was showing.

"It's a surprise," said Lavinia, sitting down on the couch and leaning back expansively against the cushions.

Any good humor remaining on Bunny's face was now gone. "I don't like surprises. You know that."

"You'll love these."

"More than one?"

Lavinia lowered her eyes seductively. "Two."

"Jeez, Lavinia. Why do we always have to play these silly games. Just tell me what's going on so I can brace myself for the worst."

"Oh, come on, Bun. You're ruining my fun. Besides, timing is everything, you know that. And this is neither the time nor the place."

"For what!"

"Revelation, Bunny dear."

In exasperation, Bunny downed several gulps of the brandy. "You're giving me an ulcer, you know that? More than twenty thousand women have signed up for the convention this weekend. We've got to give them a good show. Surprises are the last thing we need."

"Maybe. Maybe not. You'll just have to wait and see."

Bunny groaned. "And you know what else? I don't have a clue why you insisted the Upper Midwest convention be held in St. Paul this year. We've always done it in Chicago. It's been a nightmare to reorganize."

"St. Paul is better. It's prettier."

"*That* was your reason?"

"We needed a change. Otherwise, things get stale." Lavinia switched on the light next to her. "Give me the revisions."

Bunny handed one set of papers over. "You know, not to belabor the point, but you weren't the one who had to do the grunt work of reorganizing the event."

"Meaning you were."

"Among others, yes."

"Have I failed to say thank you?"

"Jeez, Lavinia." She tipped her head back and stared at the ceiling. "Sometimes I'm not sure I even like you anymore. You're so frustrating!"

"I've always been frustrating."

"True."

"It never stopped us from being friends before."

"There wasn't so much at stake before."

"Bunny, listen to me for a minute. When you think of all we've accomplished together, all the years we've been friends, you can't get angry with me just because I want to keep a couple of secrets."

"But—"

"Admit it, Bunny. I'm simply too lovable to stay mad at." She flipped her mahogany hair behind her back and mugged a wounded expression.

Bunny shook her head, her anger dissolving into resignation. "All right. You win."

"I don't need to win."

"Funny, I thought you did."

"No," said Lavinia, pulling her robe more snugly around her body. "But it would hurt me a great deal if I thought you were really upset with me."

Bunny gave a deep sigh. "Good. I'd like to think I provide some sort of check and balance to your shoot-from-the-hip style of leadership."

"Is that how you see me?" She was intrigued. Bunny had never said anything like that before.

"Let's just get down to business," said Bunny, adjusting her glasses and shuffling the pages in front of her.

"First things first," said Lavinia with a mischievous glint in her eye. "I'm hungry. What do you say we order something to eat? I just had a bite in the coffee shop a couple of hours ago. Not enough to keep a bird alive."

"What do you have in mind?"

Lavinia tapped a long red nail to her cheek. "We could start off with some shrimp? Then maybe some nice pâté and crusty French bread. For dessert, how about some fresh strawberries and cream?"

"Sounds great."

"Fabulous." As she walked over to the phone she said, "Say, what about *after* the opening ceremonies tomorrow night? Have you arranged with the others from the old college gang to meet here for our reunion?"

Bunny laughed. "It's amazing, isn't it? After all these years, so many of us in the same city at the same time. What a coincidence."

"Yeah, amazing."

"What's it been? Twenty-three years? How did we get so old? Yes, I talked to Sophie and Cindy last night. They're both planning to come. Sophie's even booked us a small room off the main lobby. She said it was usually used as a hospitality suite, but she's reserved it for the evening and is having a meal catered for us."

"Good old Soph." Turning her back to Bunny, she added, "Oh, by the way, Adelle Purdis is coming, too."

"Adelle?" Bunny sounded truly shocked. "She's *here*?"

"Another coincidence. It seems the entire Purdis clan is in town for Tabernacles Week. Remember that?" Lavinia's look was amused.

"It's so weird. All that religious stuff seems so long ago now."

"Not for Adelle. She married the apostle's son. The hall they rented for services is right downstairs. I, ah—" As she picked up the receiver she once again turned her back to Bunny. "I saw it posted on a list of weekend events as I was walking through the lobby earlier. I thought, what the hell. I'll check and see if they're staying here. And sure enough, they are. I called her just a little while ago to see if she'd like to attend."

"You actually talked to her?"

"Why not? We used to be pretty close." She began punching in the number for room service.

"But we were thrown out of the church. Officially disfellowshipped. She can't talk to us."

Lavinia put her hand over the mouthpiece. "She didn't seem to think it was a problem."

"But—"

"She said she'd be delighted to attend. Maybe she's planning to get some sort of papal dispensation."

"Wrong church, Lavinia."

Laughing, Lavinia placed the order. After hanging up, she returned to the bar to freshen her drink. "Come on, Bunny. Lighten up. I think this little reunion of ours may just prove to be a real night to remember."

"You mean like the sinking of the *Titanic*?" Bunny set her empty glass down on the table and stared bleakly into the melting ice.

Mona Lisa's enigmatic smile paled next to Lavinia's.

# 5

"You mean we'd actually live here free of charge?" said Bram, drawing back the curtains and peering at the downtown skyline. September-morning sunlight streamed in through the high, wide windows, creating pools of light on the beautifully polished hardwood floors.

Sophie tapped him on the shoulder. "We own the hotel now, dear. Remember? Or at least we will after we sign the papers later this morning." To be fair, both she and Bram were having trouble getting their minds around the notion that they were now in the hospitality business.

Ethel, the ancient black mutt who shared their home in south Minneapolis, lumbered out of the kitchen, her head lowered, her expression dour. After casting a baleful eye at the series of windows in the living room, she lurched slowly toward the bathroom.

"Cute dog," said Hildegard, patting her immaculate blonde bun. Hildegard O'Malley was a cultured, elegantly turned-out St. Paul matron in her early sixties. Sophie assumed that all of her clothing came from Dayton's Oval Room. Unfortunately, Hildegard also had the permanently surprised expression of a woman who'd undergone one too many face-lifts. "Is she part basset hound?" she asked, staring at the dog incuriously.

Sophie shrugged. "Actually, we think she's part tortoise."

Bram laughed. "Yeah, she's a real ball of fire. We keep her around because living with *her* makes *us* feel motivated."

Sophie walked silently through the spacious rooms, feeling an understandable sense of déjà vu. She'd spent all of her teenage years at the Maxfield. Living here once again would feel like . . . well, like coming home. Glancing tentatively at her husband, she asked, "Are you sure you'd like it, Bram? We wouldn't have a yard or a garden."

Bram sat down on one of the radiators and smiled serenely. "Oh, that *would* be a hardship. If I didn't have to mow grass or shovel snow, what would I do for aggravation?"

Last night, after the birthday party, the two of them had gone home, uncorked the champagne, and then spent the rest of the evening taking stock of their lives. Being presented with such an amazing gift was too incredible for words, yet, like most life-changing events, it had its downside. Even though Bram had sounded positive at the birthday party, Sophie still wasn't convinced he thought her desire to run the hotel was such a hot idea. They'd stayed up until nearly three, talking and planning, and finally falling exhausted into bed.

This morning, as Bram was showering and getting dressed, Sophie had spent some time in the backyard. As she walked around admiring the mums and sipping from a mug of French roast, she realized she was certain of only one thing. Whatever ownership of the historic Maxfield Plaza would mean, she wanted it. Bram might not have any interest in quitting his job, but Sophie did. First thing next week that's just what she was going to do. She was grateful her father and mother had surrounded themselves with such a varied and competent staff. Hildegard would be her rock until she could get a handle on the daily operations.

"I have a question," said Bram, raising a finger.

"Yes?" said Hildegard, studying him for a moment. "You know, you look a lot like that old actor. I'm terrible with names, but I think he starred in *Arsenic and Old Lace*."

"Peter Lorre?" offered Sophie, watching Bram wince. "Or, maybe you mean Raymond Massey."

"No," said Hildegard, closing her eyes in thought. "Cary Grant," she pronounced. "That's it. You look just like Cary Grant—especially in his middle years."

"Oh? Do you think so?" said Bram. He straightened his tie.

He was shameless, thought Sophie. And a hopeless flirt. He should rot in hell. "Is this apartment laid out the same as Mom and Dad's?"

"They're similar, though this one is a bit smaller." Hildegard stepped into the kitchen and switched on the overhead light, allowing a better view of the cupboards. A pantry separated the kitchen from the formal dining room. "But don't forget, you have the maid's quarters in the back, with a private entry and an attached sitting room. Very cozy. And another small room off the living room which could easily be used as a study, or a family room. Even a library. Whatever you like."

Sophie leaned against the doorjamb, taking it all in. "My son, Rudy, has been living with us since he started at the university. We'd want to make sure we have enough room for him, too."

"Yes, he's a delightful boy," said Hildegard. "And he's really taken the Zephyr Club's kitchen by storm. You must have taught him well when he was a child. I've never seen anyone take to chefing the way he has."

Sophie nodded and then moved quickly down the hall. She would have loved to have taken credit for her son's expertise, but the truth was, she'd had very little contact with him as he was growing up. Her first husband, Norman

Greenway, had been awarded custody after their divorce. She and Norman had spent most of their married life in Montana, where he was the pastor of a local church. The custody battle had been a fait accompli from the outset. Since the town was small, and filled with loyal church members, Norm had no problem finding witness after witness to attest to Sophie's ungodly character. Lizzie Borden—*after* the ax murders—would have had an easier time gaining custody.

From the moment they were officially divorced, Norm took charge of Rudy. He refused almost all of Sophie's visitation requests. It had been the single most painful experience of her life. Even so, she could never resign herself to the notion that Rudy was gone from her life forever.

Two years ago, much to her surprise and delight, he had appeared on her Minneapolis doorstep, asking if he could stay with her while he attended the University of Minnesota. Sophie was thrilled. Yet, thinking back on that time now, she remembered their first few months together as terribly awkward. They were mother and son, but they knew virtually nothing about each other. It took her nearly the entire winter to get him to open up, to tell her the full story of why he'd left Montana.

It seemed that Rudy had defied his father's wish that he attend Purdis Bible College, and instead he'd come to Minnesota to pursue a degree in theatre arts. He wanted to be an actor. The real bottom line was, Rudy was gay. He knew if he stayed in Montana with his father, or attended the church's college, he'd have to hide that part of himself for the rest of his life. While he couldn't give up all his beliefs, he also couldn't see living a lie. So he'd come to Minnesota to get away, to think matters through, to find his own path. It had been a hard two years. Yet now Sophie felt she'd finally connected with her son. They were becoming closer all the time. Wherever she and Bram ended up living, there had to be room for Rudy, too.

"I know Rudy could get used to living here," said Bram, walking up behind her. He put a hand on her shoulder. "The fact is, I'm more worried about Ethel." He pulled a badly chewed green tennis ball out of his pocket, leaned down, and rolled it down the hall.

On cue, Ethel dragged herself out of the bathroom, sniffing the air.

"Say, I hadn't thought of that," said Sophie. "Would that be a problem? I know the Maxfield doesn't allow pets."

"I hardly think so," said Hildegard with a shrug. "After all, it *is* your hotel now. You make the rules."

True, thought Sophie. She liked this newfound power. Not that she wanted to abuse it. She was still the novice innkeeper. Even though she'd watched her parents running the place most of her life—even worked on the front desk when she was in high school—she still needed Hildegard's constant guidance. "It wouldn't cause a problem with the other guests?"

"I shouldn't think so. There are lots of hotels that have a house pet. The Algonquin in New York has a cat that sits in the lobby, but the hotel doesn't allow cats or dogs in the rooms. If you want Ethel to live with you, don't give it another thought. We could even enshrine her downstairs on her own pillow."

Ethel raised her head and gave Hildegard a suspicious look.

"I think she likes it here," said Bram. "Do you like it here, girl?" He bent down and scratched the short fur on her back. Ethel closed her eyes, giving in to the ecstasy of the moment. "See? She wants to stay."

"This penthouse apartment isn't quite as grand as the one your parents have," continued Hildegard. "But I have strict orders not to touch theirs while they're gone. When they get back from their trip, they'll have to decide if they want to continue to live here, or move somewhere else."

Sophie couldn't imagine her parents living anywhere but the Maxfield. Besides, if they wanted to continue to be world travelers, this would provide the perfect home base.

"The rest of the apartments are already rented."

"How many apartments are there?" asked Bram.

"Four in the north tower, and three in the south. The rest are regular hotel rooms and suites. Not many hotels offer apartment living anymore. It's more or less a thing of the past."

Sophie walked over to the front door, opened it, and then looked both ways down the hall. All was quiet. The guest suite at the opposite end of the hall was the same one she'd seen Howell Purdis enter from the balcony last night. She'd checked the hotel computer this morning just to make sure. Sure enough, Purdis was registered. Hugh and Adelle were in the connecting suite.

It was so incredibly strange, seeing Howell Purdis again after all these years. They'd stared at each other across the expanse that divided the towers until the rain had driven them indoors. Had he recognized her? It seemed unlikely he'd remember a student from so long ago. After doing a little further checking, she'd found that the Church of the Firstborn was holding its annual Tabernacles Week services downstairs in the Lindbergh Room. It was quite a coincidence when combined with the fact that this was the same weekend she and three other friends from Purdis Bible College had planned a reunion. Sophie hadn't stayed in regular contact with any of them. She'd kept all reminders of her onetime association with the church to a minimum. Yet now, since Rudy had returned to her life, she felt she'd be able to approach her old friends with some kind of equanimity. A little reminiscing might even be fun.

Closing the door, Sophie could see that Hildegard and Bram were now in one of the bedrooms, discussing the recent removal of the Maxfield Plaza's last Murphy bed. Stepping over to the doorway, she asked, "Hildegard, do you know who booked the Church of the Firstborn in here this weekend?"

Hildegard gave an involuntary shudder. "Alan Bergman. He's the banquet manager. But since he was ill yesterday, I ended up talking to the head of the group myself. Just between the three of us, that elderly man is a first-class nutcase. He wanted me to give him the room free of charge!"

This was a new one, thought Sophie. She never remembered Howell Purdis demanding charity before.

"And then," continued Hildegard, "when I said no, he started quoting scripture. Before he left, he cursed the hotel. Can you believe it?"

"He did what?" exclaimed Bram, easing his foot out from under the dog. "Isn't this just our luck? We inherit a perfectly normal hotel and now we find out someone's placed a curse on it."

Sophie could tell he was joking, but something about the story left her feeling uneasy. Surely she didn't put any stock in that old man's ravings anymore. Did she?

Hildegard continued, "Believe me, I told that man in no uncertain terms what he could do with his threats. I was ready to cancel the entire event when I got a call from a fellow named Knox."

"*Isaac* Knox?" asked Sophie.

"Yes. Late yesterday afternoon. He apologized so profusely, what could I do? And," she added, touching the pearls at her neck, "since I could tell this fellow had both his oars in the water—pardon my language—I told him I'd let it go, as long as it never happened again. My feeling is, another scene like that and he and his church can find another conference facility." She gave her head an annoyed twist. "You know, I had that older gentleman pegged right from the start. As soon as I set eyes on him, I knew he was part of a cult."

That cult, as Hildegard referred to it, was also one of the top money-grossing religious organizations in the country. Sophie felt it wasn't the time to mention she'd once been a member.

"Well," said Bram, hoisting Ethel into his arms, "we better shove off or we're going to be late. We don't want to keep the lawyers and your parents waiting."

Sophie gave a quick nod. "Right."

Hildegard walked them to the door. "We'll be repainting the apartment in the next couple of weeks. If you do decide to take it, you might want to sit down with our decorator and choose your own colors."

"Thanks," said Sophie. "I'll get back to you."

Breezing down the hall toward the elevators, Bram leaned

close to Sophie and whispered, "Say, honey, do you think your dad would reduce the price of this place if he knew it was cursed?"

She looked at him and rolled her eyes.

"No really. Maybe we should rethink our offer. What do you say we start by putting fifty cents on the table? We can always come up to seventy-five."

# 6

An annoying buzz pulled Hugh back to consciousness. Dropping a heavy hand over the alarm, he nearly knocked the small clock radio onto the floor. He hated mornings. He never rose rested and refreshed, only resigned that another day had begun. As he turned over on his back, hoping for a few more minutes of peace, a shadow fell across his eyes. Sensing a threat, he sat bolt upright in bed and peered around the darkened bedroom. His father was creeping soundlessly toward the curtains. An instant later the bright morning sunlight struck him square in the face.

Adelle sat up, too, grabbing a blanket and drawing it up to her chin. "Howell! What's going on?"

"A meeting! Now! This minute. My son and I need to talk." He said the words hurriedly and with an urgency that bordered on the comic. He was completely dressed, wearing his fedora pulled rakishly over his forehead. The hat made him look as if he'd come straight out of a 1930s cops-and-robbers movie. This morning, however, something new had been added. A series of feathers—short, long, fluffy, multi-colored, striped—had been tucked in all the way around the headband. Some looked as if they'd been found. Others could only have been bought.

Adelle and Hugh exchanged puzzled glances.

Just last week, Hugh had discovered his father outside his Glendale home, searching through the flower beds. When he'd asked him what he was doing, his father had replied that he was tracking birds. Now he understood why—at least, partially.

"Dad, you can't just come into our bedroom like this." He tried to keep his voice calm, though he was completely nonplussed.

"Keep it down," whispered Howell, pressing a finger to his lips.

"As long as I live, I'll never share a connecting suite with that man again," said Adelle, grabbing her bathrobe and yanking it on. "You do something about him. Nobody else can."

Howell quickly made himself comfortable in one of the leather armchairs. "Order us some breakfast," he said, watching her thin frame stomp out of the room.

"Order your own breakfast," she said, slamming the door.

Smoothing the brim of his hat, Howell removed it and placed it carefully on top of the table next to him. Then, leveling his gaze, he said, "Because she's a member of this family, I've made certain allowances for her over the years, but I will not stand for this blatant disrespect any longer. She's *your* wife. *You* do something about it!"

Hugh swung his feet out of bed and stared at the floor. Sometimes he felt as if his head were in a vise. Howell was on one side, his wife, the church, his own desires—or even his own sense of right and wrong—on the other. Absently, he wondered just how long a man could be squeezed before he burst.

"Look at me when I speak to you, Hugh."

Hugh's head popped up. "Yes, sir," he mumbled. He was nearly sixty years old, yet something about the look in his father's eyes always shrank his self-confidence to the size of a pea. "I'll talk to her."

"Good. Very good. Now. I just received information about a serious matter, something that needs our immediate attention." He removed a pack of papers from his suit-coat pocket. "The report I've been waiting for was delivered to me a few minutes ago."

"What report?" said Hugh, shuffling into the bathroom. Bracing his arms on the sink, he gazed up at his aging face, raking a hand through his gray hair. He didn't look much like his dad. He knew that in some odd way, his father held him responsible for that. Fathers and sons should look alike. The spirit of the boy came from his father, or at least that's what Howell Purdis taught. And the firstborn spirit was the strongest, the most holy. That's why God used only first-born males as ministers.

Hugh couldn't help but think of his own son, a remarkable young man whom he loved inordinately. One day Joshua Purdis would lead the Church of the Firstborn. Hugh believed with all his heart that Joshua was the best of them all. If there was hope for the church, it rested with him. Joshua had none of Hugh's weaknesses. He didn't see the world in confusing, infinitely frustrating shades of gray. Perhaps, even more important, Joshua wasn't always second-guessing himself, forever uncertain. "For he that wavereth is like a wave of the sea driven with the wind and tossed," whispered Hugh, quoting a favorite scripture. He had complete faith that one day that verse would be his epitaph.

"Quit mumbling to yourself and get out here," called Howell. "I don't have all day. We have to discuss this report, and we have to do it now."

Hugh splashed some cold water into his face and then grabbed a towel. Returning to the bedroom, he said, "I'm sorry, Father. I don't know what report you're talking about."

"Of course you don't. Nobody does—except the man I commissioned to write it. Do you remember Arthur Lebrasseur?"

"Sure. He worked in the Canadian office for several

years. You ordered me to send him to St. Louis a couple of months ago to help Isaac Knox. You said it was about time Arthur got some firsthand field experience."

"Exactly. Isaac's been in St. Louis now, for what? Four years? In that time he's developed a tiny congregation into the largest local church area in the country."

"He's done a wonderful job."

"Has he?"

"Of course he has, Father."

Howell nodded to the chair opposite him. "You're supposed to be the man monitoring the local church areas for problems. I put you in charge of the field ministry because that position is vital. I needed a man I could trust."

"And I've done my best. You know that."

"I know nothing of the kind. And Isaac Knox is living proof!"

"Look," said Hugh, sinking into the chair. "I told you from the first that I refused to use my authority within the church to conduct witch-hunts. It's bad for morale."

"Making sure the ministry remains doctrinally pure is not a witch-hunt. Now, I've heard rumblings about Isaac for nearly six months, but never from you. Why is that?"

"Rumblings about what?"

"Heresy!"

"Oh, Father, please. Isaac is one of our best ministers."

"What have I always told you, Hugh? Satan is wily. He appears as the angel of light. Perhaps in this case, he's even taken *you* in. I want you to look at the report Arthur Lebrasseur prepared for me. You may be surprised."

Hugh had no stomach for this conversation right now, but sat back in his chair and slipped on his reading glasses. He took the report and began to read through it.

"I'll tell you what it says," said Howell, tapping his fingers impatiently on the arm of the chair. "It says that Isaac Knox is a traitor. He's turned his back on God's truth and is preaching error!"

It did seem that Isaac was allowing his congregation a great deal of doctrinal license. Hugh was aware of some of the irregularities, but nothing like this. The first page of the report suggested that Isaac no longer insisted that his congregation adhere to the Levitical laws of clean and unclean meats. Also, he'd begun to look the other way while some of the membership openly celebrated birthdays. He even allowed women to come to church wearing makeup. On the second page, however, the situation deteriorated even further.

It appeared Knox had given up the preaching of God's law and the imminent fulfillment of Old Testament prophecy, and instead gave sermons almost exclusively revolving around relationships, how to have a more productive, happier life/marriage/career, and better, more rewarding friendships. His sermons were upbeat. Inspirational. Peppered with quotes not only from the Bible, but from famous men and women. As Hugh turned to the third page he found himself staring at the words in utter disbelief. He looked up, seeing his father's grim face.

"Read on," said Howell. "It gets worse."

According to the report, Knox had spoken privately with one of his deacons, telling the man that within the next month or two he was planning to announce to the entire congregation that they need no longer send their tithes and offerings to the headquarters church in Altadena. Instead, he would start collecting the money locally. In the next year the Church of the Firstborn in St. Louis would break ground on a new youth center. It was Knox's dream to build a space that not only the young men and women of the church could use, but one that would become a resource for any young person in crisis, or in need of guidance.

Hugh adjusted his glasses, and then placed the report down flat on the table. He had no idea Isaac had gone this far. There was no doubt about it. This was a bombshell. No minister of God had ever defied Howell Purdis like this before. And yet, no pastor had ever achieved quite the following or the popularity within the church that Isaac Knox had. Everyone loved him. This was a touchy situation, requiring a great deal of thought before any action was attempted. "What are you going to do?" asked Hugh.

"Do? I'm going to fire him! Disfellowship him! Throw him to the dogs of eternal damnation!"

Even though it might seem crass, Hugh felt it was important to point out to his father some realities they might have overlooked. "But . . . he may take a great many of our membership, even our ministers, with him if he goes."

Howell Purdis heaved himself up and stood looking down at his son, his face red with rage. "Not if I have anything to say about it!"

"But you may not. We have to *think* about this, Father. We can't act rashly."

Lately, Hugh found himself listening to his father's conversations for the off notes, the clues that would tell him whether or not his dad was truly losing his grip on reality. From Hugh's point of view, his father's bizarre behavior could just as easily be explained as an explosive, idiosyncratic personality altered by age and the perception of absolute authority. In other words, he wasn't crazy, he was just so old and powerful that he did what he pleased and didn't give a rip what anyone thought about it.

"You're a weak sister, Hugh. How a son of mine could have ended up with no backbone is beyond me. Thank the good Lord I'm still alive. I may be on my way out, but I'm not frightened of any man. Especially Isaac Knox. The work God began through me is my only concern. I made a mistake when I named you, Hugh *Abraham*. You're not the father of nations. You're the father of indecision. 'A double-minded man is unstable in all his ways.' "

"But—you're just going to walk up and fire him?" Hugh couldn't even imagine it.

Grabbing his feathery fedora, Howell gave his son a disgusted look and then jammed the hat down on his head. "What I decide to do will be between me and the Lord. He will advise. He will lead me in the path I should go. I suggest you get down on your knees and ask for a little guidance yourself. As of this moment you are no longer in charge of the field ministry."

# 7

Lavinia shut the door to her suite and then hurried down the hallway to the elevator. She'd spent the last half hour rushing through her morning coffee and jumping into her clothes, all in an effort to make it to a very important meeting. If everything went as planned, fifteen minutes from now, on a bench in front of the Mississippi River about two blocks away, she'd finally find the answers to a mystery that had haunted her for the better part of a year. Meeting away from the hotel was imperative. There were simply too many curious eyes around the Maxfield.

She'd been planning this particular meeting for months, going over in her mind all the questions she needed to ask. No matter what happened today, she was determined to discover the truth. Not that Lavinia didn't already think she had the truth. What she didn't have was proof.

After pushing the down button, she stood quietly readjusting her jewelry, gazing up at the light above the doors. She'd waited for the elevator last night for almost ten minutes. If it took that long this morning, she was in big trouble.

As she pushed the button several more times she felt someone move up next to her. Turning her head slowly to the side, she saw a paunchy, balding, middle-aged man standing very close to her, his eyes fixed straight ahead. Since he was fidgeting with his watch, she assumed he was also in a hurry. Normally, she wouldn't have given his presence another thought, except that he was standing *so* close. She didn't like to think she was a complete snob, but he wasn't the kind of man who looked as if he should be staying at the Maxfield. He was wearing jeans and an old polyester shirt, the middle button missing. Lavinia always noticed details like that. It was the curse of her profession.

She inched away.

Clearing his throat nervously, the man leaned in front of her and tapped the button. "Damn these hotel elevators. You never have enough of 'em. I got a friend who fixes elevators for a living. He says the old ones are the worst. They break down all the time."

"Really?" She covered the distaste in her voice with a cheery lightness.

"Yeah. Say." He shifted his weight toward her again. "There's a service elevator right off the main stairway. It ain't far. The only people usin' it are kitchen staff." He glanced at his watch again.

Lavinia's eyes rose to the light above the elevator, willing it to turn red.

After another minute he said, "I've had enough of this. I'm gonna take the other elevator down. I know it's off-limits to guests, but I used it last night and nobody arrested me. What do you say? You wanna join me?"

Lavinia was torn. If she was late for her appointment, she was afraid the person she was meeting would leave. She couldn't have that. "Okay," she said tentatively. "Why not?"

The man walked so quickly Lavinia had a hard time keeping up with him. From the back, he was even more of a mess than he appeared from the front. The heels of his boots were worn and lopsided, and the bottoms of his jeans were badly frayed. Worst of all, walking in his wake, Lavinia became aware of just how much he needed a bath.

Finally, after following him down several long hallways, they reached the small service elevator. Lavinia looked up at a sign above the doors: HOTEL STAFF ONLY.

The man pushed the button then turned to look at her.

"The name's Morton," he said, grinning and rocking back and forth on the balls of his feet.

She had no idea if it was a first or last name, and he didn't elaborate. She smiled at him briefly, and then returned her attention to the elevator doors. For whatever reason, she couldn't seem to rid herself of the feeling that something about this guy was a little off. Oh, stop it, she told herself. You don't need your New York City radar here. It's the Midwest.

"Here she comes," he said, continuing to grin. His teeth were yellowed by centuries of tobacco smoke.

Finally, the doors opened.

"Your carriage awaits, madam," said Morton with a slight bow and a wave of his hand.

Feeling a bit put off by his silly attempt at chivalry, Lavinia stepped on. Inside, the light was garish, the interior utilitarian. Still, it would get them where they wanted to go.

"The lobby?" he asked, his hand poised over the controls.

"Yes, thank you." She moved to the rear, her eyes drawn to her shoes. She should have worn her blue pumps. She could walk more quickly in those. Checking her watch, she saw that she was already five minutes late for her appointment.

Suddenly the elevator lurched to a stop.

Lavinia looked up and saw the man with his hand resting on one of the buttons. "What's going on?" she said, feeling her body tense.

"Don't you know?" he said, all innocence.

Oh, God, he *was* a crazy person. She could see it in his eyes. Why hadn't she listened to the alarms going off inside her head? "Know what?" she said, backing into the farthest corner. Her heart began to race.

"Didn't you recognize my name?" He repeated it again, this time more slowly.

"I've never heard of you," she said defensively, staring at a stain on his undershirt.

He seemed offended. "Sure you have. I sent you all them letters tellin' you how much I was lookin' forward to meetin' you in person when you got to the Twin Cities. I been a fan of yours for years. I use your cookbook all the time."

She swallowed back her fear and said timidly, "Do you? How . . . nice."

"Didn't you get my mail? Or the gifts?"

She rarely read her fan mail. She'd hired a secretary for that. And anything from potential weirdos went into a special file. Her lawyer took care of all those. "What gifts?" she said, steeling herself for the worst.

"The bonsai trees. They're my hobby. I just knew you'd like 'em."

"Oh . . . sure." She tittered. "The, ah . . . bonsai trees." Her voice sounded more strangled than thrilled as her eyes darted frantically around the small chamber. There was simply nowhere to run. She had visions of him chasing her around in a circle, like a couple of cartoon characters. "I . . . love bonsai trees." She lied.

"I knew it." He moved closer. "I could tell from your picture that we had lots in common. That's why I invited you."

"Ah . . . invited me?" She clasped her hands in front of her breasts, ready to scream her bloody head off if he made even the slightest move to touch her.

"Why, to my apartment, Lavinia. I can call you Lavinia, can't I? I feel like we been pals for years."

"Your apartment," she repeated.

"Sure. Tonight. For a late-night candlelight dinner. In my note I said that if you couldn't come, you should just write and let me know. I'm a reasonable man. We could of rescheduled. But since I ain't heard from you, that means you're comin'."

"It does?"

"Say," he said, narrowing his eyes. "You're not toyin' with me, are you? I hate women who toy with men's affections. My first wife did that, but"—his expression turned sad—"she ain't around no more, poor old gal. It was a terrible accident. I'll tell you about it sometime. You wouldn't never treat me like she did, would you, Lavinia?"

"Of . . . of course not." She added, gritting her teeth into a smile, "Morton."

He returned the smile. "That's good."

"So . . . would you push the button for the lobby again? I

have an important meeting I need to attend and I'm already late."

"Oh?" he said, his head dipping in disappointment. "I thought we might grab a cup of coffee downstairs. My treat."

"I'm sorry, Morton. But—" She took a chance. "I never agreed to that, you know. That wasn't on our schedule."

"No," he said, his eyes cast down. "But you don't wanna disappoint me too often, Lavinia. You wouldn't like how I get when I'm disappointed."

She began to inch ever so slowly toward the control panel. Squeezing her body against it, she reached behind her back and pushed the lobby button. She had to get the elevator moving again.

Still staring at the ground, Morton said, "Don't you want to know where I live?"

She watched the numbers above the door change as the elevator began to descend. "Well, sure I do," she said, realizing as she said the words that it was very important information. When she filed the police report, they'd be able to pick him up that much more quickly.

He looked up at her and grinned. "Nah. I'm gonna come get you in my car tonight, just like I said I would. I'm not havin' you takin' any crappy cabs. They can be dangerous. We wouldn't want nothing to happen to you."

"No," said Lavinia with heartfelt conviction. "We certainly wouldn't."

As the elevator doors opened and she edged away from him into the lobby, Morton said, his voice meek, "Did you enjoy your dinner last night in the coffee shop?"

"What?" She whirled around. "What did you say?"

"It was just a simple question. I heard the food's pretty good."

"But . . . you saw me?"

"Sure. I been watchin' you ever since you checked in. I loved what you were wearin' yesterday, Lavinia. It was"— his eyes took on a faraway look—"very sexy. I like big, sexy women." Grabbing a baseball cap from his back pocket, he said, "Eleven tonight. Don't forget."

In an instant he was across the lobby and out the front door.

Lavinia collapsed against the wall, her pulse racing. She took deep breaths until her breathing returned to normal. She had to inform the front desk about this right away. Unfortunately, it wasn't the first time a fan had gotten out of hand. But this was a close call. Even though he hadn't threatened her, or hurt her in any way, the encounter wasn't one she wanted to repeat. Lavinia had made up her mind years ago—after her first fan mishap—never to allow her fear of such rare occurrences to rule her life.

Glancing at an antique clock on the far wall, she suddenly remembered her appointment. Damn! If she talked to hotel security now, she might as well kiss that meeting goodbye. But what should she do? Feeling terribly conflicted, her mind raced ahead to the information she needed so desperately. She had to resolve this mystery. It had been eating away at her far too long.

Set priorities, she told herself. At this moment which was the most important?

The answer was obvious. Since she wasn't in any immediate danger, she would simply have to file her report when she got back to the hotel. Squaring her shoulders, she took one last deep breath, and then marched resolutely across the lobby and out the front door.

# 8

"Time for a toast," called Sophie, pouring the champagne into the last of the glasses. Handing the delicate flute across to Lavinia, she moved in front of the hearth in the Maxfield's Fireside Room and held her own glass high. "To our reunion," she said, her eyes washing affectionately over the small group. "To friendship and, as always, to good food."

"To friendship and to good food," repeated the five alumni of Purdis Bible College, clinking their glasses together.

"And to Terrace Lane," offered Bunny. "We can't forget that."

"As much as we'd like to." Adelle laughed.

Ever since breakfast, a nervous knot had been growing in the pit of Sophie's stomach as she thought about what it would be like to see her old friends again. What would they talk about? Would their conversations seem stiff, stilted? Would Adelle's presence stifle any real comments about the college and the church? And perhaps most important, would they even like each other anymore?

Before everyone arrived, Sophie had puttered around the suite she'd reserved for the evening, making sure all the pillows were fluffed, arranging the flowers ordered specially for the occasion, and stoking the fire one of the hotel staff had built in the fireplace. After last night's thunderstorm, the weather had turned chilly. A fire was just the right touch. This party, after all, was her way of honoring the people she'd once called her dearest friends on earth.

As everyone filtered into the room shortly after ten, Sophie watched in amazement as the years dropped away. They were back once again at Terrace Lane, laughing and poking fun at each other. The chemistry that had once made them close was still evident. It warmed Sophie deeply to see her friends again—everyone so animated, so clearly delighted to be in each other's company.

As she moved around the room making sure all the champagne glasses were full, Sophie couldn't help but be amazed by how little most of them had changed. Then again, perhaps this wasn't the best time for critical evaluation. Everyone was a little giddy with the wine and the reminiscing. Yet, as she stood looking across the room at Bunny, she couldn't help but smile.

Bunny still looked as solid as a rock. And Lavinia, still flamboyant as ever. Adelle had changed the most. She'd become as thin as the proverbial stick. Also, Sophie felt she detected a certain bitterness in her choice of words, and in the tight way she held her mouth. It made Sophie wonder if she was happy. Perhaps they'd have more time to talk later.

The last person to arrive tonight had been Cindy Shipman, the D.O.S.S. national treasurer. From what she'd been able to glean from their brief attempt at bringing each other up to date, Cindy had remained single. Two years ago, after the death of her father, she'd taken over as head of Shipman Trucking in Norman, Oklahoma.

Cindy and Lavinia had always looked a great deal alike. In college, one had often been mistaken for the other. Even though Sophie could still see the similarities, she was struck now by the differences. Lavinia looked wonderful. Healthy. Vibrant. And while both she and Cindy must have tipped the scales at well over two hundred pounds, everything about Lavinia smacked of glamour and class. Cindy, on the other hand, looked frumpy. She was clearly attempting to be fashionable, yet she missed the mark by miles. It was that failed effort that seemed most pathetic. Bunny had no fashion sense either, yet her jeans fit her personality to a tee. She projected the image of a woman comfortable with who she was and how she dressed. Cindy, on the other hand, projected a discomfort so strong it was almost palpable. Being the curious sort, Sophie couldn't help but wonder where all the discomfort was coming from.

"This food is fabulous," called Lavinia, popping another cream cheese ball nugget into her mouth. "These were always my favorites. I haven't had one in years."

"It's just like our Friday nights at Terrace Lane," declared Bunny. "Remember? Right after Bible study we'd all troop back to the apartment and have our own secret Sabbath celebration."

"It was the only time all week we allowed ourselves anything other than lettuce leaves," said Adelle, adjusting her harlequin glasses.

Sophie didn't want to belabor the fashion point tonight, yet there was something about the women in the Church of

the Firstborn that made them all look as if they'd just
stepped out of a 1950s Betty Crocker cookbook. Of course,
if you waited long enough, just about everything came back
into style. Sophie assumed that Adelle had no idea her
glasses and hairdo were now fashion's cutting edge.

"I went on a wine-and-popcorn diet once," announced
Bunny somewhat smugly.

"You're kidding," said Cindy. "I thought I'd tried them all."

"Oh, well, this one I invented myself. It lasted about as long
as it took to eat an entire turkey roaster full of popcorn."

"And that was?" asked Lavinia, an amused look on
her face.

"About two hours. After four glasses of wine it went
down so easily, it was all gone before I realized what I'd
done. It was supposed to last me several days. I couldn't
look a popcorn kernel in the face for years after that."

Everyone laughed.

"But getting back to *this* food," said Lavinia, turning
around and looking at the table laden with goodies. "It all
looks so familiar."

"That's because it is," said Sophie more than a little
proudly. "It's a compilation of our favorite Friday-night
treats."

Last weekend, Sophie had spent one entire afternoon digging through the junk in her attic, looking for her old college trunk. She'd finally found it pushed way back under
the eves, and much to her delight, when she opened it she
found her Home Management folder right on the top. She'd
already decided that she would have the Zephyr Club cater
the reunion party, but to set the right tone, she wanted to
provide the banquet chef with specific instructions. That
way, her old college chums could reminisce surrounded by
the food they once loved.

She'd begun planning the meal that night. At Terrace Lane,
she was the only genuine cook. Since she read cookbooks at
night to relax, she was forever coming up with new recipes.
The only problem was, the dean of women had put all the Terrace Laners on a restricted diet. That meant that Sophie

approached these clandestine Friday-night get-togethers with a gusto born of deprivation. Sometimes she'd cook for hours just preparing one small appetizer. But it was always worth it.

During the later half of her sophomore year, Sophie actually spent some time developing her own small cookbook based on the sweets and savories she'd prepared for those secret Friday-night Sabbath celebrations. She'd even xeroxed it and handed it out to other students. Several of the recipes were designed specifically for dorm cooking. If you didn't have an oven or a stove top, you had to be truly creative. Sophie's cream cheese balls became famous around campus. All you needed was a bowl and a few simple utensils, and presto, you had something really good to eat for those special dorm meetings, all-night study marathons, or . . . whatever.

Tonight, Sophie selected five dishes for the menu. While most of them couldn't be prepared in a dorm room, they'd all been favorites back at Terrace Lane. Of course, her own culinary tastes had moved on from many of these fairly simple recipes, yet she still had a warm place in her heart for them.

First, what would the reunion be without her favorite bite-sized cream cheese balls, all rolled in nuts? Three different varieties were placed carefully around the edge of an ornate silver platter, a nest of Breton wafers resting in the center of the tray.

Next came the chicken-stuffed mushrooms, a particular favorite of Bunny's. The addition of chopped toasted walnuts and slivers of sweet red grapes made the chicken salad truly memorable.

And then of course, no buffet was complete without Sophie's famous cold Torsk salad. It was a family recipe, and one of her very favorites. She assumed it was inspired by one of her Finnish relatives.

The fourth hors d'oeuvre was a spinach and Boursin cheese concoction she'd developed late one Friday afternoon. She simply started tossing together various leftovers she found in the refrigerator. After tasting it, she'd grabbed her purse and rushed over to El Rancho, where she bought some delicate phyllo dough. The result was a truly sublime, crisp buttery gem of an appetizer, especially good when served piping hot from the oven. A cold mustard dill sauce accompanied the dish.

And last but certainly not least came the fabulous Oriental chicken and cabbage salad that was a special favorite of everyone at Terrace Lane. Actually, Sophie had found that most people who tried it were hooked on the first bite.

"By the way," said Sophie, smiling expansively at her friends, "for those of you who might be interested in a piece of nostalgia, I've made copies of that cookbook I compiled back at college. If you want one, I've put some on the table next to the door."

"Great idea," said Bunny, selecting a plump mushroom from one of the silver trays. "You were always the gourmet. That must be because you grew up at the Maxfield."

"Must have been pretty soft having a four-star restaurant in the family," said Lavinia. "When I was a kid, my mom's idea of gourmet cooking was putting a piece of parsley between the fried pork chops and the applesauce."

"My mother thought *burning* the pork chop was decoration enough," offered Adelle, gazing at everyone over the tip of her champagne glass. "She always went that extra mile to make a meal memorable."

"I suppose you burn a lot of pork chops for Hugh," said Bunny, sitting down in a chair across from her. It was the first mention anyone had made of the Purdis family.

Adelle downed her last bit of wine before answering. "We don't eat pork, Bunny. Remember?"

Bunny seemed embarrassed by her forgetfulness. "Oh, I'm sorry. I didn't mean—"

"That's all right." Adelle waved the comment away. "I'm still part of the church and you're not. In other words," she added with a wry smile, "you're heathens and I'm ... unequally yoked together with unbelievers tonight."

"A heathen," repeated Lavinia, matching Adelle's sarcasm. "I've often wondered what I was. Now that I know, I can fill out all those government forms so much more easily. No more hesitating over the column marked 'religious affiliation.'"

"Come on," said Cindy with a nervous titter. "Adelle doesn't care about any of that. In fact, we've stayed close ever since college."

This was news to Sophie.

"Actually, not that it's anybody's business," continued Cindy, "but I've been attending a few Baptist services in my hometown recently. My beliefs mean as much to me as Adelle's do to her. But if we talk religion, we're only going to end up arguing."

"Funny how that works," said Sophie under her breath.

"So, where's the sweet stuff?" said Lavinia, rubbing her hands together hungrily. "Surely you're going to wow us with one of your fabulous desserts?"

Everyone seemed grateful for the change of subject.

Sophie made a quick phone call. Several minutes later a young man wearing a chef's uniform entered the room carrying a large round silver platter. In the center rested a cake decorated with beautiful swirls of whipped cream. Written on the top were the words WELCOME, TERRACE LANERS!

Sophie beamed at the young man as he set the cake down on a low table between the couch and the chairs. As he straightened up she placed a hand on his back and said, "I'd like you all to meet my son, Rudy."

"Your son?" said Lavinia, flashing him a delighted smile. "Norm's boy?"

"That's right," said Rudy. He shook her hand.

"So handsome," she said, sizing him up.

"He looks a lot like you did at that age, Soph," said Bunny wistfully. "Reddish-gold hair. Dreamy eyes."

"You never told me you thought I had dreamy eyes," said Sophie, elbowing her friend in the ribs.

Bunny blushed.

"I'll bet you've already broken more than one young girl's heart," said Cindy, gazing at him with interest.

Rudy cleared his throat. "Not really," he said, glancing at his mother.

"Oh, he's probably broken them," said Sophie. "But it wasn't intentional."

"Really," continued Cindy, her expression souring. "I've never met a handsome man yet who didn't enjoy his power over women."

Again, Rudy cleared his throat. "I think you finally met one," he said, looking her square in the eyes. "I'm gay."

Sophie watched everyone's response. Lavinia seemed fine with it, barely reacting at all. Bunny had already slipped Sophie the news that she was gay herself, so her smile only broadened. Cindy and Adelle, on the other hand, grew distinctly uncomfortable.

"Rudy's attending the University of Minnesota right now," continued Sophie, attempting to head off any awkward comments. She knew it was important to Rudy to be open about who he was, but she still had a mother's heart. If she could protect him from hurtful words, she had to try. "And he's working part-time in the Maxfield's kitchen."

"I made the cake myself," he said, smiling at everyone. "Of course, it was one of Mom's recipes."

"Not that milk chocolate jam torte," cried Lavinia, clasping her hands in front of her with all the melodrama of a silent-film actress.

"That's the one." Rudy smiled.

"You wonderful man," she said, giving him a hug.

"Let's dig in," suggested Bunny, eyeing Adelle and Cindy with barely concealed disgust.

"It was nice meeting all of you," said Rudy, backing toward the door. "I've got to get back to work."

"Thanks, honey," said Sophie. "I'll see you at home later."

Lavinia checked her watch. "You know, since we're making introductions, there's someone *I'd* like you to meet. It's a little surprise I've been looking forward to sharing with all of you. As a matter of fact, you're the first people I've told."

"Surprise?" said Bunny, her bulldog head jerking as if she were picking up a scent.

"That's right. Now, if you'll wait just one second." She moved over to the open doorway and waved into the lobby. A strikingly handsome young man entered the room a few moments later, pausing next to her to give her a kiss.

"Everyone," said Lavinia grandly, "I'd like you to meet Peter Trahern. My new husband."

"Your what?" said Bunny, nearly dropping her wineglass.

Husband? thought Sophie. Him? He was gorgeous. And young. Robert Redford and then some. In his Dockers and polo shirt, he looked as if he'd walked straight out of *GQ*.

Peter smiled at all the shocked faces, putting his arm around Lavinia's waist and drawing her close. "My plane just got in a couple of hours ago. Actually, I'm from the Twin Cities. My family's home is in Edina."

"Really?" said Sophie, her voice an octave too high. Clearing her throat, she tried again. "That's ... wonderful. Congratulations to both of you."

Bunny still hadn't moved.

Adelle rose and walked toward him, clearly wanting to get a closer look. "Where did you two meet?" she asked, extending her hand.

"In Monterey," said Lavinia, leaning her head on his shoulder and gazing up into his handsome face. "I needed to buy a home in California because so much of my business has moved out there."

"We met through the real-estate company I work for," said Peter, picking up the conversation.

"You were her real-estate agent?" said Bunny, at last regaining her ability to speak.

Sophie had the distinct impression that everyone wanted to pinch him to see if he was real. He was *so* good-looking. And of course, the unspoken question in everyone's mind was, what on earth was he doing with Lavinia? Sophie was ashamed of herself for even entertaining such a thought. But there it was, a niggling obnoxious little question that wouldn't go away.

"So I sold her a house," said Peter, flashing everyone his fabulous smile. "And then we started dating. One thing led to another—"

"We were married two months ago," said Lavinia. "It was a private ceremony. Just a couple of friends."

"Why didn't you tell me?" demanded Bunny. She poured herself another glass of wine and took several hefty swallows.

"Oh, well," said Lavinia, running her red nails across Peter's shirt. "We wanted to keep it a secret until we could announce it to his parents. We're going to do that on Sunday evening, right after the conference is done."

"Do you think they'll have some problem with your marriage?" asked Sophie. She hoped she wasn't being too nosy. People always said she asked too many questions.

"I don't know," said Peter. "Mom's always wanted to help plan my wedding. I'm sure she'll be disappointed. But she'll understand. So will Dad. We didn't want to wait. We're both spur-of-the-moment kind of people." He laughed.

"Really," said Adelle, her tone a tad too cheerful to be anything other than sarcastic.

Bunny seemed uncertain, and Cindy looked positively dumbfounded.

"Well, I'll keep my fingers crossed that everything goes well for you when you tell them," said Sophie, flailing for the right words. "Would you like some coffee and cake?"

"I'd love it," said Peter. "I know Lavinia has really been looking forward to this reunion." Turning to her, he added, "Did you tell them about your other surprise yet?"

Bunny nearly choked on her wine. "No," she said sternly, her eyes colliding with Lavinia's. "And what would that other surprise be?"

Lavinia sat down on the couch. Peter sat down next to her, wrapping his muscular arm around her shoulder. "Well," he began.

Placing a finger against his lips, Lavinia said, "Not here, honey. Tomorrow. At our business breakfast." Her eyes moved from face to face. "You're all welcome. Even Sophie and Adelle. I don't know why the two of you haven't joined my remarkable organization, but that doesn't prevent me from inviting you to this unveiling."

Bunny sank into a leather armchair. "What . . . unveiling?"

"Tomorrow," whispered Lavinia, giving her a confidential wink. "Now, I think my new marriage calls for another toast. Does everyone have champagne?"

Sophie walked over to the table and poured a glass for Peter.

"To our marriage," said Lavinia, smiling seductively at her new husband. "To the most wonderful man I've ever known."

As she took a sip of wine Sophie felt a tear come to her eye. Sometimes she was such a sucker for sentiment she even appalled herself.

"I'd like to propose another toast," said Bunny. Her face had grown flushed.

Sophie wondered if she wasn't a little drunk.

"I think we've forgotten someone tonight. Someone who should have been here."

"Who's that?" asked Cindy.

"Ginger Pomejay," said Bunny, spilling her wine as she held her glass aloft. "If it hadn't been for that horrible disease, we'd still have her with us."

"Ginger didn't die of any disease," said Lavinia, under her breath.

"Excuse me?" said Sophie. "What did you say?"

Lavinia straightened the neck of her dress and replied, "Ginger didn't die of cancer."

"But . . . of course she did. We all saw it. We were there."

"It wasn't cancer," said Lavinia flatly.

"Then what did she die of?" asked Adelle, looking visibly shaken.

"Look, I made a mistake. I shouldn't have said anything. Not yet."

"But you did," said Sophie, feeling more than a little indignant that Lavinia could let something like that slip, and then refuse to comment further.

Leaning back against the couch cushions, Lavinia said, "She was murdered. That's all I can tell you—for now."

Sophie was horrified. "But—"

"Listen," said Lavinia, cutting her off. She gave everyone a hard look. "I won't take back what I said. I can't, because it's the truth. Before I leave Minnesota, I'm going to find the proof I've been looking for. And when I do, I promise, you people will be the first to hear the real story."

# 9

Isaac Knox sat on a chair in his hotel room, feet propped up on the coffee table, staring out the window. It was nearly eleven. A few stars were visible in the night sky, though the downtown buildings obscured most of his view. He knew he should get out his laptop and begin preparing his notes for tomorrow morning's sermon, yet he couldn't seem to concentrate. Too much had happened today. Too many problems weighed heavily on his mind.

Isaac had been gone from the hotel since early morning. He'd been in meetings mostly. All over the city. Important contacts had to be made. Plans finalized. During these past few months, his life had take on the quality of a spy film. It wasn't a role that came naturally to him. He didn't like all the sneaking around, the whispered conversations. And yet Howell Purdis had left him no other choice.

Even though he felt a bit sorry for himself as he thought of his wife at home in St. Louis, he was still glad he hadn't allowed her—or his kids—to accompany him to the Twin Cities. Tabernacles Week, indeed, all of the church festivals, no longer held the same importance they once had. The next few days would be hard—probably the hardest of his life. He had to spend some time tonight in prayer, seeking God's guidance and strength. He knew he needed both desperately. He also needed a clear head and a pragmatic mind. The end didn't necessarily justify the means, yet he *had* to reach his goal. If someone got hurt along the way, well, perhaps it was God's will. Who could say?

Stretching his arms high above his head to release some of his pent-up tension, he rose and walked over to the bed, sitting down on the edge and switching on the light.

On the nightstand next to him, the phone rang.

This was entirely too late for anyone to be calling, thought Isaac. He'd already spoken to his wife. There wasn't a single other person on earth he wanted to talk to right now. Picking up the receiver, he said hello, knowing his voice sounded gruff and unfriendly.

"Isaac? Is that you?" asked another deep voice.

"Yes?"

"It's Hugh Purdis. I need to talk to you right away."

Leaning back against the pillow, he said, "It's kind of late, Hugh. Maybe we could talk in the morning."

"No. It has to be now." Silence. "Can I come up?"

"Where are you?" asked Isaac wearily. Surely there must be some way he could put him off until morning.

"Downstairs in the bar."

"It's the Sabbath, man. What are you thinking? There could be other church members around."

"I . . . had to get out of my hotel suite. The walls were closing in on me."

Isaac could well understand that. "Where are Adelle and your father now?"

"Dad's asleep. And Adelle had a reunion tonight. Some of her old friends from college are here."

Isaac's brow furrowed. "Okay. I'll meet you downstairs. But I want to make it quick."

"No. I think it would be better if I came up. I need to talk to you privately."

In other words, thought Isaac, he didn't want to be seen. A report might get back to his father. "All right," he said slowly, realizing he was curious what Hugh might have to say. "Do you know my room number?"

"I'll be right up."

The line clicked.

* * *

Ten minutes later Hugh and Isaac sat staring at each other across the dimly lit hotel room, each sipping somewhat uncomfortably from a glass of mineral water. Isaac didn't drink, though he knew just about everyone else in the Church of the Firstborn did. It was the one perceived vice Howell Purdis allowed his flock. If Jesus could turn water into wine, people should be allowed to drink it.

"So," said Isaac, deciding to get the ball rolling. "What can I do for you?"

Hugh didn't answer right away. Instead, he stared down into his glass, swirling the ice around and around. It was the only sound in the quiet room.

Isaac found the noise irritating. Why didn't he just get to the point?

"Have you talked to my father today?" asked Hugh finally, attempting to focus his eyes. His words sounded slurred.

So, thought Isaac. The game of cat and mouse had begun. As soon as Hugh had walked in the door, Isaac could tell he'd had too much to drink. "No," he said calmly, wondering in a vague, incurious sort of way whether people who drank too much knew how pathetic they seemed to people who didn't. "I was gone all day. Though I did get the messages he left for me at the front desk."

"Did he say what he wanted to talk to you about?"

Isaac shrugged. "Not really. Just that it was important. That I should contact him as soon as I got in."

"But you didn't."

"No, Hugh. I didn't."

Hugh's eyes shot to the minibar. "Have you got anything stronger than this?" He held up his drink.

Hugh had put on weight in the last few years. Isaac decided now that it was probably because of his drinking. "Help yourself," he said curtly. "The key's in the door."

Lurching slightly, Hugh pushed himself out of his chair and removed a small bottle of vodka from the refrigerator. After returning to his seat, he unscrewed the cap and dumped the entire contents into the mineral water. "That's better," he said, taking several long sips. His eyes seemed to lose focus again as his gaze drifted out the window.

Isaac was becoming impatient. "It's been a long day and I'm tired. If there's a point, get to it."

"Fair enough. I assume you know Arthur Lebrasseur?"

"Sure. He's my new assistant."

"This morning my father came to me with a report Arthur had just submitted to him. In it, he detailed all of your doctrinal heresy. Everything, Isaac. From your stand on the Levitical laws of clean and unclean meats, all the way down to your humanistic sermons. Nothing was left out."

Of course, thought Isaac. It was instantly clear to him what had been happening. When Lebrasseur had been transferred from the Canadian office so quickly and pressed upon him with such enthusiasm, Isaac smelled a rat. Or more specifically, he smelled the hand of Howell Purdis. Yet Arthur had played his part well. He'd convinced Isaac that he was a friend—even a potential ally. An infiltrator in the guise of an assistant was a masterstroke indeed.

"You knew, didn't you?" said Hugh, his voice dropping to a whisper.

"I suspected I was being watched. I didn't know it was Arthur. He's a good actor."

Hugh nodded. "There's no point in sugarcoating this. You're finished. As of tomorrow morning, you will no longer be a minister in God's church."

"You think so?"

"Absolutely. My father plans to disfellowship you. He would have done it today, but the two of you never connected." He pinched the bridge of his nose and looked down. "It's been coming for a long time. You and I both know that."

"As long as you were in charge of the field ministry, I thought I was safe."

Hugh's head popped up. His face hardened as he said the words, "I've been removed."

"I see. Daddy get sick of your management style? Benign neglect does smack of laziness. That was never Howell's way."

"I've saved your ass more than once," said Hugh angrily.

"As I've saved yours."

"Right. We've been friends. For a long time. I care about you. I always have. You're a good minister and I value that, you know I do. But there's no way I can help you now."

You may be surprised, thought Isaac, though he had the sense not to say it out loud. "What are you going to do now that your father no longer needs you to manage the field ministry?"

"I don't know," said Hugh, finishing his drink. "Knowing him, he'll probably give me the position back tomorrow morning."

"Or forget he ever fired you."

"Yeah. That's possible."

Isaac sat back, folding one leg over the other. He had to proceed with caution. "Hugh, as much as you may not want to admit this even to yourself, your father is losing it. You and I both know it's true. Sooner or later everyone else in the church will know it as well. It won't be long before he has to step down."

"He'll never do that. *Never.* They'd have to pry his hands off the pulpit."

"Maybe. Still . . ." He gave Hugh a second before continuing. "Have you ever thought of forcing him out? Taking over the reins of the church yourself? Forming a coalition with some of the other ministers who now see Howell Purdis as a liability?"

Hugh shook his head. "No," he said firmly.

"I don't believe you. In any case, if his behavior becomes too bizarre, and you really *do* care what happens to the church, you may have no other choice."

"I can't think about that."

"Why? Because you're a coward?"

"No! You of all people should understand. If I failed, if Father retained his position, my son would lose his chance to one day head the church. Father would be so angry at me, it would spill over onto Joshua. I can't do that to him. I simply can't."

So, thought Isaac. That was his answer. "Well," he said, rising and turning on the light next to him. "I think it's time we call it a night." He moved quickly over to the door, hoping Hugh would get the point. He wanted to be alone now. Time for talk was over.

Setting his glass down on the coffee table, Hugh stood. "I'm sorry I had to be the bearer of bad tidings. I . . . thought someone should at least warn you."

"I appreciate it." Isaac opened the door.

"Will I see you tomorrow?"

"Yes. Without a doubt."

"I hope this doesn't come as too big a blow."

"I'll survive."

Hugh held Isaac's eyes for a long moment and then peered carefully into the hallway, looking both ways down the silent corridor. "Night," he whispered with a jerky wave.

Isaac stood for another couple of seconds, watching his old friend's lumbering frame disappear around the corner. What a useless human being, he thought to himself, feeling a sudden sadness.

Then again, he had to be pragmatic. If someone needed to be sacrificed, better Hugh than him.

# 10

Lavinia woke the next morning to the sound of running water. Peter was humming in the bathroom as he took his shower. Easing back into the pillows, she closed her eyes and luxuriated in the remembrance of last night's love-making. Peter had been so passionate, saying how much he missed her during the few days they'd been apart. Lavinia felt the same way. To her, Peter was like a walking hot fudge sundae. She couldn't get enough of him. He was the best thing that had ever happened to her. She wondered if he knew how happy he'd made her. She hoped she made him feel the same way.

"Ah, you're awake," said Peter, breezing out of the bathroom, a towel wrapped around his waist.

Lavinia gave him a half-lidded smile, hoping it conveyed just that right note of lasciviousness. "Take that silly thing off and come back to bed."

He sat down next to her and gave her a long, lingering kiss. "Can't, honey. I've got to get dressed. I'm supposed to pick up my rental car by nine. You're keeping yours for a few days, right?"

The last thing she wanted to do was talk about rental cars. "I'm not ready for the day to start just yet." She ran her fingers lazily across his chest.

"You're incorrigible."

"I know. That's why you love me."

"I love you," he said, his voice turning serious, "because you're smart and competent. You're not a little girl."

"You left out gorgeous and sexy."

He grinned down at her. "Funny, I thought I made that part clear last night."

She could just eat him up.

"Come on," he said, whipping off her covers. "You've got to get ready for your morning meeting."

"Aren't you joining me?"

"Of course I am. I'll be there rooting you on."

She swung her feet out of bed as he tossed her a robe. "I wonder," she said softly, watching him slip into his crisp white shirt, "what the reaction will be to my little surprise."

"I'm sure everyone will be as excited as you are. Everything's all set. As soon as I got into town last night, I made sure the shipment had arrived. It's all ready to go."

"What would I do without you?"

He stopped buttoning his shirt and turned around to look

at her. "Oh, you'd be just fine. It's me you should worry about. If I ever lost you, I don't know what I'd do."

What a strange thing to say. "You're not going to lose me, Peter."

He stared at her a moment longer and then smiled. "Good."

As Lavinia was about to make another comment, the phone interrupted her. "I'll get it," she said, leaning over and grabbing it on the second ring. "This is Lavinia Fiore."

"Lavinia, hi. It's Cindy."

"Good morning, girl. Did you survive the reunion last night?" She noticed one of her red nails was chipped. She'd have to fix that.

"Yes . . . I, ah, think so. I called to ask if I could talk to you this morning before the meeting. I could come up right now."

Lavinia saw Peter looking at the room-service menu. He no doubt wanted to order breakfast. "Um, I don't think it's a good time. Maybe later today. What are you doing for lunch? I'm on a panel until one, but we could do it late."

"No, Lavinia. It has to be now." She sounded extremely agitated.

"Why? What's up?"

"I can't talk to you about this on the phone. It's . . . too complicated."

Peter drew a finger across his throat. He wanted her to get off so he could place an order.

"I'm sorry, hon. It just won't work for me now."

"But, Lavinia—"

"Whatever it is, it can wait."

"No, it can't!"

"Cindy, just get hold of yourself, girl. What's got you so upset?"

"It's . . . something I've done. I can't wait around for the other shoe to drop."

Peter was standing now with one hand on his hip, the other poised over the phone, about to cut off the call. "I'm starving," he mouthed, looking pitiful.

"We'll have to talk about whatever it is later. Are you coming to the breakfast meeting?"

No response.

"Cindy? Are you still there?"

"Yes."

"So, are you coming or not? In case no one told you, we're holding it in the Zephyr Club's private dining room. Sixteenth floor. South tower."

"I . . . suppose."

"Don't sound so enthusiastic."

"It's just—"

"Look, if the meeting doesn't go the full hour, maybe we can talk afterward."

"But—"

"Go have some steak and eggs, Cindy. Live a little. It's a convention. I'll talk to you later." Without waiting for any further pleas, she dropped the phone back on the hook.

"Thank you," said Peter, immediately picking up the receiver. "What do you want?"

"Oh, just some toast and coffee."

"Nothing else?"

"Maybe some orange juice."

He placed the order. Picking up his keys and pushing his wallet into his back pocket, he said, "I'm going to run downstairs and see if they have *The New York Times*."

"I'm sure you could phone for it," said Lavinia, looking him up and down, once again admiring his taste in clothes. Today he was wearing dark slacks and a designer herringbone sport coat. Not that he wouldn't have looked every bit as fabulous in dirty overalls. But Peter had expensive tastes. So did she. As far as she was concerned, they were a perfect match.

"Nah. I need to get a breath of fresh air. The food should be here in half an hour. I'll be back before that."

She followed him into the living room. After giving him a kiss goodbye, she stood in the doorway and watched as he got on the elevator. Before the doors closed, he called to her, "There's something on the floor next to your foot."

Lavinia's eyes dropped to the white envelope. Her name was printed in large block letters on the outside. Since no one had knocked, she knew a bellboy hadn't brought it up.

Returning quickly to the living room, she sat down on the couch and ripped it open. Inside was a piece of notebook paper. She read the words:

Dearest Lavinia,
   I don't like being stood up. I also didn't like seeing the police posted outside the hotel last night, waiting for me to call. I'm not sure what I'm going to do with you just yet, but, of course, I'll have to do something. What have I ever done to you to cause you to treat me this way? I'm just a simple fan, someone who adores you from afar and wanted to get to know you better. Now I see that's impossible. Nevertheless, you will be hearing from me.
   Till then, Lavinia.

Morton

"Oh, my God," she whispered. In all of last night's excitement, she'd completely forgotten about him. She'd filed her report with both hotel security and the police yesterday afternoon, and then she'd gone on about her business. The uniformed officer she'd talked to assured her the police would take care of everything. A squad car would be assigned to intercept him when he arrived at the hotel to pick her up. She'd have to come down to the station to file charges, but that would be the end of it. From then on, her lawyers could handle everything. She'd given the authorities a detailed description of what he looked like. The hotel representative and the police all sounded so confident, she'd walked out of that small conference room and hadn't given it another thought.

Until now. This minute. She felt as if someone had slapped her across the face. How had he gotten in? Surely hotel security was keeping an eye out for him. Since he didn't look like he belonged at the Maxfield, he'd be simple enough to spot. So what had happened? If he could get to her door to leave a message, what else could he do without being caught?

Feeling more frightened than she cared to admit, she got up

and moved unsteadily over to the phone. She had to alert security right away. Closing her eyes, she tried a few deep breaths first. That always helped center her. Move her to a more rational place. She'd be damned if she'd allow some screwball to scare her into a state of inertia. She still had too much to do. Too many clues to follow and people to interview.

She'd simply have to be extra careful. Peter was staying at his parents' home tonight. Since her new in-laws didn't know about their marriage, she was remaining here. Tomorrow, after the last convention panel was finished, she'd join him in Edina to break the news. But until then, she was on her own. Which was just the way she'd planned it. And Lavinia had no intention of changing her plans. Not even for Morton.

# 11

Sophie carried two mugs of coffee into the living room, glad that the new day had dawned mild and sunny. Her parents were leaving this afternoon for the first leg of their round-the-world tour. Since they both had a certain anxiety about flying—an anxiety Sophie shared—she didn't want them to take off in bad weather.

Sophie set her mug down on an end table and then paused for a moment to watch her husband. He was standing next to the fireplace, his expression faintly wistful as he gazed out the window at a row of mums in the back garden. She couldn't help but wonder if he was having second thoughts about moving to the Maxfield. All morning he'd been unusually quiet.

To be honest, Sophie was having some second thoughts about the move herself. They'd lived in this house for almost seven years, picked it out together before their marriage, and closed on it two weeks after they returned from their honeymoon. Bram's daughter, Margie, had lived with them until she'd left to attend college in St. Cloud, two years ago.

Walking up behind her husband, Sophie slipped her arm through his and handed him the mug.

"I haven't changed my mind," he said, drawing her close. Kissing the top of her head, he added, "I just have to spend some time saying goodbye. I've loved living here. And you know me. I don't like endings."

She leaned her head against his chest and understood. "We don't have to move."

"No. It's not that. I want to."

"The space we'd be moving into is much smaller than what we have here."

"That's good. It will force me to get rid of some of the stuff I've collected over the past seven years."

Not a bad idea, thought Sophie. Bram collected "stuff" faster than dust collected on her favorite cloisonné eggs. His study had become dangerously packed with all the "valuable" junk he couldn't bring himself to throw away.

"What are you thinking?" he asked, ruffling her short, reddish-gold hair.

"I'm wondering how big a Dumpster we need to order."

"Very funny."

The clock on the mantel chimed the hour. "Hey," she said, pulling away. "We've got to be over to the Maxfield by ten."

"We?" he repeated, looking confused. "I thought your parents didn't need to leave for the airport until noon."

"True. But Lavinia's planning a big surprise for the D.O.S.S. breakfast meeting this morning."

"So?"

"We're both invited."

He took a sip of coffee and inspected the invitation for hidden meanings. "Why does she want both of us there?"

"She's probably just being nice."

"If you ask me, that woman's a little too full of surprises for her own good." He ticked them off on the fingers of his right hand. "First, a new husband. A complete secret to everyone, I might add. And thirteen years younger."

"A woman can't marry someone younger?"

"You don't think thirteen years is a little much?"

She shrugged. "Men do it all the time."

"Second," he said dryly, ignoring the amused gleam in her eye, "during the reunion last night she casually lets it drop that an old friend of yours was murdered. Will she elaborate? Of course not. That would make life too simple. Not to put too fine a point on this, Sophie, but did it ever occur to you that your friend is a drama queen?"

"It takes one to know one."

"Hey!"

"Look, she simply didn't want to elaborate until she has all the facts."

"Sophie, think. Someone doesn't just let something like that slip. She did it on purpose. And she had a reason."

Sophie held the coffee mug to her lips, thinking it over. "Like what?"

"How should I know? They're your friends. Anyway, third." He continued counting. "Lavinia has planned another surprise for this morning's breakfast meeting."

"I'm sure the Zephyr Club will serve us something fabulous to eat. When the meeting's over, we'll both take Mom and Dad to the airport."

"My day off is looking better all the time."

"Oh, don't be such a spoilsport. The meeting could be interesting."

"With Lavinia in charge, I have no doubt you're right."

Ethel chose that moment to peek her head around the doorway. A tennis ball rolled out of her mouth as she gave a deep yawn.

"Poor thing," said Bram, watching her slump into the room and ease her old bones down on the rug next to him. He bent down to give her a pat. "She spent a good half hour outside this morning, watching the ants crawl across the cement. Exhausting work."

Ethel smacked her lips. It was just another day in paradise.

"She won't have any ants to watch when we move to the Maxfield," said Sophie, frowning thoughtfully.

"She'll survive."

Ethel's sad eyes rose to Sophie's. The loose folds of skin around her forehead made her look perpetually worried. Today, however, Ethel had chosen to add a slight baring of the front teeth to her image.

"Look, sweetheart," said Sophie excitedly. "She's smiling at me. I just love it when she does that."

In silent dignity, Ethel sniffed Bram's socks. Sometimes life threw you a curveball. If you were lucky, it was green and bounced. If you weren't, well . . . you could always pretend an expensive leather wingtip was a chew toy.

Life had its compensations.


"Everyone, please. If I could have your attention, I'd like to call this meeting to order." Lavinia stood behind the head table, tapping her fork against her water glass. "Perhaps we should give the wait staff another minute or two to clear away some of our dishes before we begin."

Sophie and Bram watched from their own table as they finished breakfast. Bunny had joined them as soon as they'd walked in the door, introducing herself to Bram with characteristic gusto and announcing that Cindy would be along any minute. They'd grabbed a spot in the back and waited, but for some reason, Cindy never appeared. All during the meal, both Bunny and Sophie kept glancing at the door, but still no Cindy.

The rest of the room was packed with at least ninety excited, boisterous conventioneers. From what Bunny had said, this business meeting was a command performance for all the D.O.S.S. officers. As national treasurer, Cindy was required to attend.

Lavinia looked remarkably elegant today in a red-and-black linen suit. Peter was with her. He seemed terribly solicitous of her needs, pouring water and coffee and generally making sure she had anything and everything she needed. Sophie was so curious about their interactions, she found her eyes sliding in their direction more often than good taste would allow.

Before Lavinia called the meeting to order, Peter had left the room briefly. He'd returned a few minutes later carrying a small plastic box. Sophie saw some people whispering about it, even pointing, though no one seemed to know what it was.

"What's she got up her sleeve now?" said Bunny, stabbing at her last bite of eggs Benedict. "She's giving me an ulcer."

Bram nodded his sympathy. "You have no idea what this morning's surprise is all about?"

"None. Except that it has something to do with the convention. After last night I shudder to think what she's done now." Bunny pushed her plate away and folded her arms over her chest in a gesture of uneasy resignation.

"Shouldn't she consult you on business matters?" asked Sophie. "After all, you've always been one of the driving forces behind the organization."

Bunny gave her a sour look. "Tell *her* that."

It was only now that Sophie noticed the hint of acrimony in her friend's voice. She wondered what it had been like, living in Lavinia's shadow all these years.

"Could you believe what Lavinia said about Ginger last night?" continued Bunny, watching the waiters pour a last round of coffee. "What the hell was she thinking?"

"You know," said Sophie cautiously, "I've really been remiss about keeping in touch with all of you. Just my usual card or letter at Christmas. But you two are still so close. It seems odd to me that Lavinia would keep something as important as this to herself." As soon as she said the words, she regretted them. By the wounded look on Bunny's face, Sophie could tell Lavinia's lack of openness had hurt her deeply.

"If I could have your attention now," called Lavinia again, tapping the fork against her glass several more times. "We need to start, otherwise some of you will be late to your panels." She waited for complete silence.

Bram caught Sophie's eye and whispered, "Show time."

"Before we begin the business meeting," continued Lavinia, her eyes sweeping over the crowded room, "I'd like to introduce all of you to my new husband. Peter, will you stand up, please?"

Looking self-conscious, Peter rose from his chair and grinned boyishly at the assembled group.

The surprised murmurs began almost instantly.

"After a whirlwind romance, Peter Trahern and I were married two months ago in a private ceremony. I must tell you, these last few months have been the happiest of my life." She grinned at him. "You'll all have a chance to talk to him a little later. Thanks, honey." As he sat down he motioned to a young woman standing in the back. A moment later the same young woman pushed a large-screen TV set and attached VCR into the room. As she plugged in the power cord Lavinia continued, "I have something I want to show all of you. It's a video Peter and I produced together, and needless to say, I'm not only very excited about it, but also very proud of what we've done. Before we start, let me tell you that this will be on sale at the D.O.S.S. information booth, right along with the newest edition of my cookbook."

As Lavinia switched off the overhead lights the screen came alive with music and sound. At first it seemed the video might be a tour of Lavinia's new house in California. It was a beautiful interior, open and airy, with high ceilings and expensive modern furniture. Also, it appeared to be right on the beach. The voice-over—Peter's voice—talked about California living. Health. Sun. And, interestingly enough, fitness. As the camera moved upstairs to a small room off the master suite, Lavinia suddenly appeared, huffing and puffing as she jumped rope to the sound of the Beach Boys. She was dressed in fashionable exercise clothing, a sweatband around her head.

"Oh, my God," whispered Bunny, her mouth dropping open. "What the . . . she couldn't—"

The music ended as Lavinia began to explain the importance of the warm-up.

"It's an exercise video?" said Bram, looking confused.

"It's *grotesque*," said Bunny, not even trying to keep her voice down. No one would ever accuse Bunny Huffington of beating around the bush, especially when it came to expressing an opinion. Several of the women at a nearby table turned around to glare.

The music swelled again as Lavinia began a series of aerobic dances.

"Don't you see?" said Bunny, leaning close to Sophie and whispering with an urgency that bordered on rage. "This is completely against what our organization stands for. For years we've been trying to get women to *stop* dwelling on their bodies, on how they look. This just buys into the same cultural narcissism we've tried so hard to fight against."

Sophie did see her point. Then again, it wasn't wrong to be physically fit.

"Shhh," said one of the women at another table. She gave Bunny a nasty look and then returned her attention to the front.

"Can she do this?" asked Bram. "Without anyone else's knowledge or approval?"

Sophie gave him a helpless shrug. She had no idea.

"Someone's got to stop her," said Bunny.

For one frightening moment Sophie had the distinct impression Bunny was about to do something violent. From the limited contact she'd had with her over the years, Sophie knew that she felt passionately about the philosophy behind the organization. And why shouldn't she? She'd formulated most of it.

Bunny watched for a few more seconds in smoldering silence and then abruptly threw down her napkin, pushed back from the table, and got up. Without so much as a backward glance, she grabbed her briefcase and stomped out of the room.

"Boy," said Bram, touching his fingers to his tie. "I'd sure like to be a fly on the wall when those two finally talk."

Sophie gave him a sickly smile and then pressed her fingers

against the side of her forehead. This reunion weekend was starting to give her a splitting headache.

# 12

Adelle gazed listlessly around the crowded Lindbergh Room, her eyes rising to the fresh flower arrangement she'd ordered for the stage. Sabbath services were about to begin. Folding metal chairs had been set up by the hotel staff to accommodate the church members now filing quietly into the room. As hotels went, she supposed, this one wasn't bad. The Maxfield had a certain gangster charm. But a hotel was a hotel. As far as she was concerned, she'd spent too much of her life living out of suitcases. This year, if she'd had her way, she and Hugh would have celebrated Tabernacles Week at home.

Oh, well, she thought to herself with an ennui born of far too many Sabbaths spent away from her friends and family, it would be over soon. Besides, this decision to spend the week in St. Paul might just turn out to be downright fortuitous.

As befitting his status, Hugh had chosen seats for them in the front row. He was sitting next to her now, intently reading through the general announcements he'd make right after the opening songs. Adelle couldn't help but wonder what sort of special announcement Howell Purdis had on the agenda. From what Hugh had disclosed to her last night, Isaac Knox would no longer be in charge of the morning service, nor would he be giving the first sermon of Tabernacles Week—or any other week.

Hugh and Isaac had been friends since childhood. They'd both been raised in the church, both attended the same high school in Altadena, although Hugh was seven years older. Adelle knew that, ever since Isaac's late teens when his parents had died in a car crash, Hugh had taken him under his wing, thought of him as a younger brother. As a young man, Isaac had been passionately committed to the teachings of Howell Purdis. That commitment, it would seem, had now ended. Isaac couldn't blame anyone but himself for the position he was in. To be on the safe side, however, Adelle wanted to point that out to him one more time.

Right after breakfast, while Hugh was in the bedroom praying, she'd called down to Isaac's room hoping to find him in. She was surprised when he answered on the first ring, and then disappointed as he explained that he couldn't speak to her right then. He was in the middle of an important meeting. By his abrupt manner and the general strain in his voice, Adelle assumed Howell Purdis had finally caught up with him. Since it was imperative that they talk, she insisted that he meet her in his hotel room at noon. Reluctantly, he'd agreed.

As Adelle touched the back of her red hair, she turned and noted that Roger Laybourn and his wife had taken seats on the other side of the aisle. Roger was in his early thirties, the pastor of the Milwaukee church. Leaning over to her husband, she whispered, "Is Roger replacing Isaac this morning?"

Hugh nodded, continuing to flip through his notes. "Father told me to arrange it."

"I thought he fired you yesterday."

Hugh peered over his bifocals, giving her a pained look. "Apparently I've been rehired."

As she was about to make another choice comment on her esteemed father-in-law's general mental disintegration, she saw Howell emerge from the rear of the stage, followed closely by Isaac Knox. Howell's jowly face looked unusually puffy and flushed.

"Look," she whispered, poking her husband's leg. "What's *he* doing here? I thought you said your dad was going to disfellowship him."

"He was. I mean, he is." Hugh removed his glasses and stared as the two men walked briskly toward the front. Once Howell had taken a seat on the other side of Adelle, Hugh glanced furtively at his wife, unable to hide his shock and confusion, and even, it seemed to her, a brief moment of panic.

This was not the way it was supposed to work. Normally, when a member of God's church was disfellowshipped, he was never again allowed to attend Sabbath services or mingle with the faithful. Yet here was Isaac, carrying his Bible, looking for all the world as if he was about to call for the opening prayer. This made no sense. Unless . . .

She snuck a quick look at her father-in-law, noticing that his hard, unblinking eyes were fixed straight ahead. Was it possible? Had Isaac changed his mind? Silently, Adelle began to weigh the possibilities.

From the very beginning of her marriage to Hugh, she had steadfastly refused to be drawn into church politics—all the changing alliances, who was in favor one minute, and who was the next. She simply couldn't be bothered. Over the past year, however, she'd begun to listen a bit more closely.

Adelle had slowly come to the realization that the church was fast becoming a hotbed of doctrinal dissension. There was no precedent for something as radical as disagreement in the Church of the Firstborn. From the very beginning, whatever Howell Purdis wrote in his pamphlets or preached from the pulpit was considered God-inspired truth. Recently, she'd begun to catch whiffs of this dissent in the most unlikely places. The president of the college women's club had wondered out loud about the necessity for third tithe. A local elder just in from the field expressed concern over the church's stand on certain child-rearing practices. The buildings-and-grounds manager suggested that Christ died on an almond tree instead of an alder. Everyone, it seemed, was challenging one or more of the church's long-standing beliefs.

Hugh had turned a blind eye to most of it, choosing

instead to be a force for unity. For good or ill, he'd spent the
last year flying from city to city, attempting to put a lid on
potential defections. He and Adelle didn't always see eye to
eye, but on this one point, they were united. It was their
son's legacy that Hugh was protecting—a legacy Joshua
wanted almost as much as they wanted it for him. Hugh had
never been particularly interested in assuming the top leadership role himself, though of course he would do so after
his father's death. Yet Hugh was sure he'd never be anything more than an interim leader. Eventually, he would
become an adviser to his son. Whatever problems and questions that might arise in the church right now needed to be
handled by the newly established doctrinal committee.
Hugh promised the field ministry that he would back this
committee with the full weight of his power and position.
He'd see to it that it continued to be a viable forum for doctrinal discussion, and thereby an alternative to defection.

To be honest, no one knew how much Howell Purdis was
aware of what was happening in the church. Lately, however, Adelle had begun to notice even more arrogance in the
way he behaved around the ministry. The question was, was
this change in behavior just an escalation of his normal arrogance, or was it in response to the problems? The answer to
this conundrum might well have direct bearing on what had
just happened this morning. That, thought Adelle, was the
best-case scenario. The worst case was too horrible even to
contemplate.

"It's time to begin," said Isaac, waiting a moment as
everyone found a seat. His voice projected just the right
mixture of authority and friendliness.

Adelle had to give him credit. Off the playing field, Isaac
Knox might seem like an ordinary enough guy, yet once he
took his position behind the podium, he became a player,
exactly the kind of quarterback Howell Purdis and those
under him had trained him to be. Perhaps *that* was why he
was still here, thought Adelle, her mood brightening consid-
erably. Maybe Howell had come to the same conclusion.

Isaac's loss would be far too big a blow for the church to bear. Except, as she thought about it, she knew it made no sense. The only person Howell Purdis saw as indispensable was Howell himself.

Isaac adjusted the microphone and then smiled his easy, confident smile. He was putting on a good performance. Adelle knew he couldn't really feel all that relaxed after the run-in he'd just had with God's apostle. Yet this outward show of confidence worried her. And it should be worrying Hugh, if he was paying attention. Isaac hadn't bothered to glance in their direction yet. She wondered if that omission was significant in some way.

"I believe Pastor Laybourn is going to lead us in our opening prayer," said Isaac, moving away from the podium.

Next to her, Adelle could feel her father-in-law stir in his chair. She wondered if he was looking for his songbook. "Did you misplace your hymnal?" she asked, noticing that, as his eyes rose to Isaac he began to clench and unclench his fists.

"Dad, are you all right?" asked Hugh, leaning in front of her and touching his dad gently on the arm.

"I'm fine," said Howell, shoving his son's hand away. "Mind your own business."

"But, Dad," said Hugh, lowering his voice even further, "what happened with Isaac? I thought you were going to fire him."

"I . . . haven't decided yet."

"But—"

"Shut up, Hugh." He spoke out of the side of his mouth. "And be still. If you do, you'll feel the hand of God."

"What do you mean?" asked Adelle, knowing they had barely moments before the prayer began.

"I've cursed him, that's what I mean."

"You've what?" said Hugh, swallowing back his surprise.

Howell fixed his son with a penetrating stare. "May God strike him down."

"Father!"

"And if He doesn't"—he closed his eyes and bowed his head—"I will."

# 13

Sophie gazed upon the Maxfield Plaza with new eyes. She'd just put her parents on a plane to Helsinki, and now, finally, it felt real. It was all hers, she thought to herself as she entered through the front glass doors, admiring the bold Deco lines, the decorative bronze grilles, and the dramatic open staircase that led up to the second floor. Walking into the lobby was much like returning to the Thirties, when a sinister presence like John Dillinger or Kid Cann might be sitting right next to you at the bar. They'd all visited the Maxfield. The famous and the infamous.

As she approached the front desk she noticed Hildegard emerge from her office accompanied by a burly-looking man dressed casually in a red sport shirt, light blue slacks, and white shoes. He looked like he was headed for a round of golf.

From the serious expression on Hildegard's face, Sophie could tell something was wrong. She approached them cautiously, wondering what was going on. She'd come back to the Maxfield this afternoon to spend a few hours observing the various operations. From there, she could start learning specifics. She wasn't the kind of woman to let grass grow under her feet.

"Sophie, hello," said Hildegard. She smiled, though somehow, the smile didn't quite reach her eyes. In her right hand, she held a file folder.

"Problems?" asked Sophie.

"I'm afraid so." Hildegard glanced uneasily at the man standing next to her. "This is . . . Mr. Clausen. The head of hotel security."

"Nice to meet you," said Sophie, extending her hand. She was still amused by Hildegard's somewhat excessive need for formality, though she knew it would get old pretty fast.

"Ms. Greenway is Mr. Tahtinen's daughter," added Hildegard quickly. "And the new owner."

"Is that right?" he said, raising a bushy eyebrow. "Well then, the name's Jack. I'll look forward to working with you." He didn't smile.

"So, what's up?" she asked, glancing from face to face.

Hildegard seemed to be weighing something in her mind. Finally, she said, "This is a rather delicate matter. Am I correct in assuming that you and Lavinia Fiore are quite good friends?"

"More or less. We went to college together."

"She hasn't mentioned any of this to you?"

"Any of what?"

Hildegard opened the folder and handed Sophie a photocopy of a typed note.

Reading down the page, she found that it was a short letter from a man named Morton. Apparently Lavinia had stood him up last night. Even though it carried no overt threat, the wording suggested a certain menace. "Does this mean what I think it means?" asked Sophie. "The police were waiting for him when he arrived?" Having St. Paul's finest milling around the lobby must do wonders for business.

Hildegard nodded. "This Morton fellow saw *them*, but they never saw him. I can only assume he never got out of his car. We have a sketch," she said, opening the folder once again and paging through the contents. "Yes. Here it is." She handed it over.

Sophie looked at it, but didn't recognize the man. "I've never seen him before."

"Count your blessings," said Jack Clausen. "He trapped Ms. Fiore in the service elevator yesterday. Wouldn't let her go until she promised to have dinner with him. This note," he said, tapping it with his finger, "makes me think he's going to try something else—some sort of payback. We've posted men around the building, but so far, no sign of him."

"Does this sort of thing happen often?" asked Sophie.

"With celebrities, occasionally. It certainly wasn't the first time Ms. Fiore has had an admirer."

What a stupid, insensitive way to put it, thought Sophie. "You think stalking is the same as admiration?"

He ignored the question. "Nothing usually comes of it."

If he intended to put her mind at rest, he'd failed. Miserably. "Can I keep this?" she asked, holding up the sketch.

"Good idea," said Hildegard. "I've handed copies out to everyone on staff. If he shows up again, he's going to get caught."

Sophie couldn't help but wonder what sort of precautions Lavinia normally took to ensure her safety. As Jack said, this wasn't the first time.

"So," said Jack, hooking a thumb over his belt, "if I could have that copy of Morton's note?"

Sophie handed it over.

"The police have the original," said Hildegard. "They wanted to check it for fingerprints."

Clausen's eyebrows knit together. "All I can say is, I hope they'll have something for us by tonight. In the meantime," he said, giving them each a quick nod, "I'll be in touch." In his haste to leave, he nearly knocked down a bearded man who'd just come out of the bar. Instead of excusing himself, he kept on walking across the lobby and out the front door.

"Is he . . . good at what he does?" asked Sophie. She wasn't impressed.

"Oh, yes. Your father's used his company for years."

"You mean this hotel doesn't employ its own security staff?"

"Oh my, no. You know your dad. He was a maverick when it came to certain standard practices. CSS—Clausen Security Systems—is quite a large concern. Mr. Clausen hires and trains his own people, and they're paid by him as well. I guess you could say he handles it all. Even as we speak there are no less than two security people in the lobby. Our Mr. Clausen is determined to catch his man."

That did make Sophie feel a bit better. Even if "Our Mr. Clausen" was Mr. Insensitivity in his private opinions, he at least had some professional smarts. "Well," she said, noticing that the man who'd come out of the bar was now reading the paper in the lobby. He was rubbing his right shoulder, the spot where he'd collided with Clausen. She didn't much care for his looks. The dark beard couldn't hide his unattractive face any better than the raincoat hid his unkempt appearance. "I hope this Morton fellow gets caught. Although if I were him, the Maxfield is the last place you'd find me."

Hildegard nodded in silent agreement. "Oh, look who's here," she said suddenly, her face brightening.

Sophie turned as Rudy, dressed in his white chef's uniform, emerged from the rear service elevator. He was pushing an empty kitchen cart.

"Hey," he said, giving them a wave. He parked the cart next to the wall and then walked over, wiping a hand across his forehead. He looked hot and tired.

"Hard at it?" asked Sophie, pleased to see him. "Say, weren't you supposed to have Saturday and Sunday off this week? You've got that paper to write for your Cultural Studies class."

He gave a weary nod. "Yeah, but my boss asked me to work, and I couldn't say no. The church is having a banquet here tonight, and I'm the only one in the kitchen who knows anything about their dietary laws."

"But . . . what about your paper?" She didn't want to sound like a nagging mother, but his schoolwork had to come first.

"I thought I'd do it tonight. I hope Bram doesn't mind if I borrow his computer again."

"I'm sure it won't be a problem."

"Great." He turned to Hildegard, flashing her a smile. "And how are you, Ms. O'Malley?"

Sophie could tell he'd picked up on the older woman's preference for formality. You had to give the kid credit. He certainly knew how to turn on the charm.

"Why, I'm just fine, Rudy. It's kind of you to ask."

As they continued to talk about some of the upcoming

events at the Maxfield, Sophie's eyes dropped once again to the sketch in her hand. She scrutinized the face for several long, thoughtful moments. Studying it now, it struck her that something about it seemed vaguely familiar.

"Is something wrong?" asked Hildegard.

"What? Oh, no," she said, brushing the question away. She kept her attention focused on the drawing. She'd seen that man recently. Very recently, in fact. But where?

"What's up, Mom?" said Rudy, touching her shoulder.

Suddenly it struck her. "He's here," she said, whirling around.

"Who's here?"

"It was the beard that fooled me."

"What beard?" asked Rudy. "What are you talking about?"

"This!" she said, rattling the sketch under his nose.

The man was still there, sitting in the lobby, reading the paper. Clausen had bumped right into Morton and failed to see the likeness. So much for his professional instincts. And the security guards, wherever they were, were every bit as worthless.

Rudy leaned close to Sophie and whispered in her ear, "Is that man over there the same guy who's been hassling Lavinia?"

She gave a tight nod. "Where are the security men?" she asked, looking pointedly at Hildegard.

Hildegard gave a perplexed shrug.

Sophie wasn't sure what to do next. "If we call the police, he could be gone by the time they get here."

"Don't worry," said Rudy. "I'll handle it."

Sophie felt a moment of panic as she watched him walk away. "Wait," she said, but he ignored her plea.

Straightening his uniform, Rudy approached the man's chair. They spoke for only a moment and then Morton got up and removed the wallet from his back pocket. Before he knew what hit him, Rudy had wrestled him to the floor and was straddling his legs, twisting his arm painfully behind his back. "Call the police," he shouted.

Two stunned and embarrassed security guards shot out of the bar. While one took over for Rudy, the other pulled a cell phone from his pocket.

"Whatever we pay these idiots," said Sophie dryly, watching the first man fumble and then drop the key to his handcuffs, "it's too much."

Hildegard nodded. "Your point is well taken, my dear."

As Rudy approached, brushing himself off, Sophie rushed up to him and gave him a hug.

"Stop it, Mom," he said, self-consciously, pulling away from her and then smiling sheepishly. He looked around the room to see if anyone was witnessing his embarrassment.

"Can't a mother hug her son, especially when he's a hero?"

"Oh, Mom, please."

"What did you say to him?" asked Hildegard curiously.

Rudy shrugged. "I just asked him if he wanted something to drink. He saw my chef's uniform and thought I was a waiter, so he ordered a beer. I told him he'd have to pay me up front. I've been in enough student theatre productions now to recognize a fake beard when I see one. So, when he got up, I jumped him." He allowed himself a small smirk.

Sophie didn't care. She hugged him again.

"Mom!" he said, blushing.

"You're just going to have to put up with me."

"Jeez," he said, a slow grin forming. "I can see that."

# 14

Lavinia pulled her rental car up to the curb and sat for a moment, stuffing the map—the one Peter had given to her right after the breakfast meeting—into the glove compartment. She knew she was a complete airhead when it came to directions, especially in an unfamiliar city. So, sweetheart that he was, Peter had patiently highlighted all the roads she needed to follow in order to get to the bar. As she turned off the motor she could see the lights of the low, rather seedy-looking building nearly a block and a half away. She'd driven past it first, just to make sure it was the right place. Parking spots were at a premium, as Peter warned they would be. He hadn't been to the bar himself since the last time he visited his parents, two years ago, but he said that on Saturday nights the building was always jammed to the rafters. Much to Lavinia's occasional embarrassment, it was just the kind of tacky, glitzy environment she loved. And northeast Minneapolis was far enough away from the convention site to allow her complete privacy.

Once inside McDivot's Nordeast Lounge, Lavinia grabbed the first available table and ordered a Ramos fizz, her favorite bar drink. Adelle should be along any minute. Lavinia had left a note for her at the front desk earlier in the day. Adelle had responded with her own message shortly after one P.M. saying she wasn't sure how she could help Lavinia in her effort to find the truth behind Ginger's death, but she'd be happy to join her for a drink later.

Lavinia was delighted by this small piece of good luck. She was sure she'd be able to jog Adelle's memory, get her to see what had really happened. If she could get a church member in her corner, she was halfway home.

"That will be three bucks," said the waitress, setting the Ramos fizz down in front of Lavinia. "You want me to start you a tab?"

"Good idea." She nodded, her eyes scanning the crowded room. She didn't know a single soul, and just as she'd hoped, no one seemed to be paying her any attention either. In an effort to disguise her looks, she'd wound an Indian silk scarf around her head. With her trademark mahogany tresses covered up, she'd be even harder to spot.

As the waitress stepped over to another table Lavinia glanced at her watch. It was almost ten. Surely Sabbath services hadn't gone this late. If she remembered correctly, on the first day of Tabernacles Week there would be both a morning and an evening sermon. Sermons in the Church of the Firstborn weren't fifteen minutes of uplifting fluff, like some churches she'd attended in the past few years, but instead, two to three hours of intense biblical exegesis during which the faithful were supposed to take notes for further study. "Prove all things," said the Bible. "Hold fast to that which is good." It wasn't that she disagreed with the sentiment, but remembering how Howell Purdis had used it as a battering ram to push his own agenda, well, even now it still had the power to give her a bad case of heartburn.

She remembered one minister who once spoke for six hours straight before finally quitting. He was a self-appointed traveling evangelist who thought of himself as the Church of the Firstborn's great interpreter of biblical prophecy. Nobody wanted to attend his sermons. Even the other ministers thought he was a little cracked, but since he was a personal friend of Howell Purdis, he was tolerated, even venerated. In her mind's eye, Lavinia could still see him, bobbing and dipping behind the pulpit, grasping the Bible with fire in his eyes and flinging it in the air, gesticulating wildly about the "little horn" of Daniel chapter eight, verse nine. She laughed to herself, realizing it was all still engraved on her memory. So long ago, but still so impossible to forget. Then again, so was the verse that said, "Those that walk in pride, He is able to abase." With a little help from Adelle, that's just what she'd come to the Twin Cities to facilitate.

As her gaze traveled restlessly over the smoky interior, Lavinia spotted Adelle standing in the doorway. She was fidgeting with her purse, looking for all the world as if she'd just entered a den of iniquity. Lavinia doubted her old friend spent much time in bars. Oh, well, she thought to herself, standing up and waving her over, she could cope this once. Nothing bad would happen to her. And anyway, it wasn't as if the consumption of alcohol presented some big moral dilemma.

"Did you have trouble finding the place?" asked Lavinia. Adelle made herself comfortable at the table before responding. "Not really." She touched a hand lightly to the side of her hair. "Your directions were fine."

"Good."

After ordering a Scotch and soda, Adelle gave herself a moment to absorb the surroundings. "Quite the dive."

"Peter suggested it. I wanted to go somewhere where we wouldn't be disturbed."

"You don't find this atmosphere the least bit . . . disturbing?" Her lips thinned in distaste as she nodded to a young man in tight leather pants with his hand halfway up some woman's dress.

"Oh, come on. Turn off the criticism for a little while and just chill."

"Chill?" she repeated, giving Lavinia a slow, deeply amused smile.

Lavinia ignored the sarcasm and instead took a sip of her Ramos fizz. "We need to get down to business."

"All right." Adelle leaned into the table with the kind of exaggerated patience she no doubt reserved for lunatics and very small children. "I told you in my note that I haven't the slightest idea what would possess you to think Ginger's death was anything other than natural."

"That's what I wanted to talk to you about." Lavinia paused for maximum dramatic effect. "I have Ginger's diary."

Adelle's eyes narrowed. "What diary?"

"Ginger kept a diary the year we were banished to Terrace Lane for our sinful appetites."

"Don't be so snide, dear. You could still stand to lose a few pounds."

"And you look like you've been on bread and water ever since you married Hugh."

Adelle folded her arms over her chest and stared down her nose. "You know, insulting me isn't going to get you anywhere."

She was right. "Come on, girl. Expressing a little attitude every now and then has made both of us rich and famous."

Adelle gave her a pained look. "You're incorrigible,

you know that. But let's get back to the diary. I'm ... intrigued."

Lavinia could tell Adelle was playing it cool, though she was clearly curious as hell. "Well, if I may summarize, it talked a lot about the six of us. Things we did together. And it also mentioned one other rather striking point. Ginger was in love." This was the stuff of disaster for a sophomore at Purdis Bible College. A student wasn't allowed to get serious about another student until the second semester of their senior year. Any romantic attachments that developed prior to that point were grounds for expulsion.

"With who?" asked Adelle, her expression skeptical.

"The diary doesn't say. You'd have to read it in context to get the full meaning. But there are only a couple of possibilities." She waited while the waitress set a bowl of popcorn down on the table, followed by a napkin and Adelle's drink. Selecting a single kernel, Lavinia popped it into her mouth and gave Adelle a look pregnant with meaning.

"And so, if we can cut to the chase here, who do you think murdered her?"

"The person she fell in love with."

"I don't get it. Why?"

"To cover up a very big secret."

"What secret?"

"You tell me."

By the end of this exchange, Adelle's expression had turned decidedly frigid. "I don't like games, Lavinia. You're going to have to be a lot more specific if you want me to comment. Who are you accusing?"

"Did Ginger ever confide in you about her love life?" Lavinia chose her words carefully. Adelle was probably completely in the dark, though there was a remote chance she knew everything. Either way, Lavinia had to tread carefully.

"Of course not." Then, hesitating, she added, "That is, I mean—"

A half-dozen guys in black leather jackets pushed noisily into the room. As Lavinia turned to see what the commotion was all about, she noticed two familiar faces bounce in behind them.

"Oh shit," she said, her shoulders sinking in exasperation as she watched them press through the crowd toward the table. Until she knew what was going on, she decided it was best to hide her frustration behind a forced smile. "What are you two doing here?"

"We could ask you the same thing," said Bunny, dumping herself into a chair. Cindy sat down next to her, looking ill at ease, as if she wanted to be anyplace else.

Bunny was trying to appear casual, though Lavinia saw through the act. Running into them tonight was no coincidence. "You followed me," she said, bristling.

"No, I didn't," said Bunny defensively. "Adelle told Cindy that she was meeting you here around ten. I thought it might be fun to crash the party."

"Did it ever occur to you that I might not want your company tonight?"

"Did it ever occur to you that I don't care?"

They held each other's eyes for several long seconds before Lavinia switched her gaze to Cindy.

"Don't look at me," said Cindy, flustered. "I didn't know it was a secret."

"Look, both of you," said Lavinia, attempting to rein in her impatience. "Adelle and I are having a private conversation here. We don't want an audience."

"Tough," snapped Bunny. "We've got to talk."

From the moment Bunny had entered the room, Lavinia had sensed some incredibly hostile vibes coming from her, though to be honest, she didn't have a clue what it was all about. "Talk about what?"

"The exercise video!"

"Oh." Her curiosity evaporated. She dismissed the issue immediately, letting Bunny's anger slide past her.

"You put me off all day. I won't be put off any longer! That video you and Peter made is a travesty!"

"Do you really think so?" said Lavinia, clearly stunned. She knew Bunny might not like the fact that she'd kept it a secret, but surely she saw its value. "Oh, come on. You're just jealous because you didn't think of it first."

"Like hell I am," said Bunny, slamming her fist down hard on the table.

"Calm down," said Adelle.

"Butt out," demanded Bunny. "This has nothing to do with you."

"You're right. It doesn't. And I'd prefer that you two have your fight someplace else. I'm not interested."

For a moment Bunny seemed to be at a loss for words.

"Not to change the subject," continued Adelle, "but before you arrived, Lavinia and I were having an interesting conversation about Ginger."

"Really?" said Cindy, her expression growing cautious. "What about Ginger?"

"She kept a diary the year we all lived together in Terrace Lane."

Lavinia couldn't believe Adelle had spilled the beans so blithely.

"A diary?" repeated Bunny, scrutinizing Adelle's face. "Is this true?"

"Yes," said Lavinia curtly. "It is."

"But where did you find it?" asked Cindy. She pulled her chair up closer to the table, though her bulk prevented her from getting as close as she might have liked. The country-western music had been cranked up several decibels since the addition of the six leather jackets.

"Apparently, someone decided to clean out Windsor basement," said Lavinia, gazing down into her empty glass.

Windsor Hall was the largest women's dorm on campus. Most of the girls stored their trunks in the basement. At the end of their senior year, every coed was supposed to remove her belongings. Most did. But, every now and then, something was left behind.

"Of course," said Adelle, the light dawning. "I remember. It was last year when the building committee decided to renovate it. Everything had to be moved out by the end of spring term."

"They found a trunk with Ginger's name on it," continued Lavinia, deciding there was no point in keeping it a secret any longer. "You know how that cavernous basement used to fill up. There was no system. People would forget they'd stored stuff down there. After twenty years of forgetful coeds, I'm sure the place was a nightmare of polyester blouses and silly scarves."

"But I still don't understand," said Bunny. "How did you get your hands on the diary?"

"I received a letter from an elderly woman in the registrar's office. It seemed she remembered Ginger and me, and also recalled that we were best friends. She contacted me through my publisher—she said she used my cookbook all the time—and asked if I'd like the trunk. What could I say? Ginger didn't have any other family. It seemed kind of cold to tell her to dump it in the trash, so I said, sure, send it along. I'd be happy to pay the freight."

"And inside the trunk you found the diary?" asked Cindy. Lavinia nodded.

"You know what?" said Adelle, stirring uncomfortably in her chair. "I hate to interrupt this stroll down memory lane, but I have to use the women's room. I wonder where it is."

"I saw it when we came in," said Bunny.

"Great. You lead the way." She stood.

"But—"

"Come on, Bun. I refuse to go alone. You're the college professor. You're used to these Hell's Angels types. I'm not."

"Excuse me?"

Adelle yanked on her arm.

Reluctantly, Bunny rose. "Don't say anything else until we get back. Oh, and see if you can catch one of the wait staff. I want a Gibson. Make it a double." All her concern about the exercise video seemed to have evaporated.

Once they'd disappeared into a wall of sweating bodies, Lavinia and Cindy fell into an awkward silence. Cindy looked Lavinia's way once, and then looked everywhere else.

After several unsuccessful attempts, Lavinia finally flagged down the waitress and placed the orders. One double Gibson and another Ramos fizz. Cindy passed, saying she didn't like to drink and drive.

"Didn't you and Bunny drive over together?" asked Lavinia, attempting to break the ice that seemed to have formed between them.

"No," she said softly. "Bunny had some D.O.S.S. business she had to take care of first. So she asked me to meet her here. She wanted my support when she talked to you about your video. I'm . . . ah, really sorry I didn't get to see it this morning. I had sort of an emergency."

Lavinia nodded. "But you do need to file your financial report with the national secretary."

"I know."

Lavinia suddenly remembered the phone call she'd received from Cindy right before breakfast. "Say, what did you want to talk to me about this morning?"

"Oh, well," she said, playing with a button on her blouse, "I just wanted to tell you about the emergency."

"No one in your family, I hope."

"No, nothing like that. It's just . . . I've done something . . . I mean—" She seemed to be searching for the right words. "Actually, I do need to talk to you, Lavinia. Only—" She smiled nervously. "This is hard. I know if you'd give me some time, you'd understand."

"Understand what?"

"Well, you remember that awful prank Ginger played on me back in college?"

"Sure. She made you look like an idiot."

"I know. Ginger was my friend. I hated her for what she did. As much as I tried to forgive her, I couldn't."

"So," said Lavinia, realizing she was a bit confused, "you wanted to talk to me about *that*?" Out of the corner of her eye she saw Bunny and Adelle weaving their way back through the tables.

Cindy saw them, too, and immediately clammed up. "Not

now," she whispered. "Later. Maybe when we get back to the hotel."

"What are you two plotting?" asked Bunny, lowering her sturdy frame into her chair. "And what's happening back at the hotel later?"

"I'm taking a shower and going to bed," announced Lavinia. "Wanna come watch?"

Bunny gave her a nasty look. "Okay. So, let's get back to our conversation about Ginger."

"I thought you wanted to attack me about the video."

"I do. But first things first. You said something last night that I can't let pass."

"You mean that Ginger was murdered, she didn't die of cancer?"

"Exactly."

"That's what I believe."

"On what basis?" asked Cindy, tilting her head back as the waitress leaned across her to serve Bunny her Gibson.

"On the basis that Ginger was in love. Her lover killed her."

Bunny nearly spilled her drink. "Do you realize how crazy that sounds?"

"I suppose it does."

"So what did Ginger say in her diary? Who was she in love *with*?"

"She doesn't give a specific name."

"This is ridiculous," said Bunny, throwing her hands in the air. "If the diary doesn't name a name, where's your proof?"

"I don't have any," said Lavinia flatly. "I told you that last night. But I want you all to think. Think back to the weeks before she died."

"She wasn't feeling well," said Adelle. "We all know that."

"But think harder. Examine what you know. And then, even if you haven't come to a firm conclusion, think about the night she died. What she said. How she looked." Over the rim of her glass, she watched her friends' reactions, wishing she could get inside their heads.

"This is ludicrous," said Bunny finally, tossing her napkin down on the table. "Are you accusing one of *us*?"

"Don't be ridiculous," said Cindy. "We're all women."

Bunny shot her a disgusted look. "I'm a dyke, remember? If Ginger was in love with a woman, I'm the likely candidate."

Lavinia's look was noncommittal. The truth was, she was getting a certain pleasure out of watching Bunny squirm.

"Well, I for one refuse to sit here and act like I'm talking to a sane woman," said Bunny. "I've had about as much of this idiocy as I can stand for one night. Lavinia, I think you've lost your marbles. First the video, and now this. I can see that now isn't the time or the place, but we *will* talk." She reared back from the table, got up, and stomped out.

"If you ask me," said Adelle, looking worried, "you two sure don't act like good friends. You know her temper, Lavinia. What are you thinking? Somebody better go after her and calm her down before she does something stupid." She tossed some cash next to her empty Scotch glass, grabbed her purse, and left.

Feeling her mood sour almost instantly, Lavinia stared across the table at Cindy. "So," she said, with another forced smile, "I suppose you're going to leave now, too."

"Yeah, I think I better," she said tentatively. "But I promise. I'll think about what you said."

"If you stayed we could have that private talk you wanted."

"No. I don't think so. Not now." She got up and backed somewhat clumsily away from the table. "I think I better call it a night."

Lavinia had no more energy left to argue. She gave Cindy a dismissive wave, and then sat back in her chair and closed her eyes, allowing the boozy laughter of dozens of loud conversations to soothe her weary soul. What a mess. Not at all what she'd planned. It would be just her luck that anything else that could go wrong tonight would.

# 15

Bram closed the front door and then leaned against it, folding his arms over his chest. "You aren't tired, are you?" he asked, eyeing his wife seductively.

Sophie started to laugh. "We should have those neighbors over more often."

"Yeah," he agreed, pulling her against him. "A rousing game of Trivial Pursuit always gets me in the mood." He nuzzled her hair. "So?"

"You don't want to try some of that chocolate cake first?"

"What chocolate cake?"

She stared up into his eyes, giving him a knowing look. "Mary Beth brought over some of her famous chocolate cake. The kind with the gooey fudge frosting. We were too full after dinner to eat it."

"Who was too full?" he asked indignantly.

She ignored the question. "I may be wrong, but I think our pieces are still sitting on the kitchen counter."

"You know, Soph, if you're trying to present me with a terrible dilemma, it's not working."

"You're a man who knows what he wants."

"That's right. First us. *Then* the cake."

"Priorities," she said, feeling his strong arms slip around her. Sometimes she wondered if he even knew how much she loved him. Maybe tonight was a good time to make sure. And besides, he was probably right. The cake could wait—briefly.

"Your room or mine?" he asked, whispering in her ear.

"Oh, well," she said, warming to the proposition, "since they're one and the same, why don't you pick?"

"My room," he said, smiling. He grabbed her hand and together they shot up the stairs.

As soon as he'd closed the bedroom door, the phone rang.

"Damn," he said, sitting down on the bed and glaring at the clock. "It's almost eleven. Don't you think that's kind of late for a phone call?"

Sophie's mother instincts moved into high gear. "It's probably Rudy. I hope he's all right." Instead of working on his paper tonight, he'd gone to a movie with John. She walked over and sat down on the other side of the bed, picking up the extension. "Hello?" she said tentatively.

"Sophie? Is that you?"

She recognized the voice immediately. "Lavinia. Hi. You're the last person I expected to hear from tonight."

Bram flopped on the bed next to her, heaving a resigned sigh. "Make it short," he mouthed.

"I didn't know who else to call."

"Why? What's wrong?"

"The right front tire on my rental car is flat. Wouldn't you know? I called the company, but they said it would be at least an hour before they could get anyone out here to help me. Maybe more."

"Where are you?"

"Well." There was a moment of silence. "I can't remember the cross streets, but I just came out of McDivot's Northeast Lounge."

"Just a sec," she said, putting her hand over the mouthpiece. She tapped Bram on the shoulder. "Ever heard of McDivot's Northeast Lounge?"

"*Nord*east," he corrected her.

"All right," she said with exaggerated patience, "*Nord*east. Do you know where it is?"

"Sure. Is that where she is? It's a dump. And it's not a very good part of town. Is she alone?"

Sophie shrugged. "Are you alone?" she asked.

"Afraid so," said Lavinia. "Adelle and I were having a

drink together when Bunny and Cindy showed up—sort of unexpectedly. But they left. It's too bad, too. If they hadn't all taken off, one of them could have given me a lift back to the hotel."

"Where are you calling from?" asked Sophie.

"It's a gas station across the street. I had to park about a block and a half away from the place. Actually, this whole area's kind of creepy. There's only one guy in the station. To put it bluntly, I don't think I'll be turning my back on him anytime soon."

"Tell her to take a cab," said Bram, running his hand lazily up Sophie's leg.

She slapped it and then said, "What can I do to help?"

"Well," said Lavinia, a hint of embarrassment creeping into her voice. "I know this is pretty pathetic, but I don't have enough cash with me for a cab. I suppose I could make the driver wait once we get back to the hotel while I run up to my room, but the truth is, I'm kind of freaked. A couple carloads of teenagers have already driven past, honking and yelling at me. I just want to get out of here. I tried calling Peter at his parents' house, but his dad said he was out for the evening." More silence. Then: "I don't suppose you'd consider picking me up. I know you live in Minneapolis, although I have no idea how far away you are."

Quite a ways, thought Sophie. The last thing she wanted was to leave right now. "Okay, here's what you do. Go back to your car, get inside, and lock all the doors."

"Right."

"It should take me, oh, about—"

"Wait."

Sophie could hear Lavinia put her hand over the mouthpiece and shout at someone. Even though the words were muffled, she could clearly hear the delight in her voice.

"What's happening?" asked Bram, propping a pillow behind his head.

Sophie put a finger to her lips. She was trying to hear Lavinia's conversation, but could only pick out a word or two here and there.

Finally, Lavinia came back on the line. "Everything's fine, Soph. But I gotta run."

"What's going on?"

"You won't believe this, but I got a ride. Great luck, huh?"

"Yeah. But—"

"Talk to you in the morning," she said, rushing to get off. "Remember, we're supposed to meet for brunch. Ten A.M. at the Fountain Grill. Just you and me, okay? I've got some important information we need to talk over."

"Sure. But—"

"The light's about to change. You're a doll, Soph. Give my love to that handsome hunk you married."

"I will."

The line clicked.

"What happened?" asked Bram. He swung his feet over the end of the bed and sat up next to her.

Sophie gave a perplexed shrug. "She got a ride."

"With who?"

"I don't know."

He took her hand. "You look upset."

"No," she said, shaking her head. Not upset, exactly. Relieved was more like it. Yet she couldn't help but worry whether Lavinia would make it back to the hotel safely.

"She's a big girl," offered Bram. "She wouldn't take a ride from someone she didn't know."

"True . . ."

"So. There you have it," he said with finality, stretching his arms over his head. "Case closed."

He was probably right. She could stop worrying.

"And now, where were we?" He brought her hand up to his lips and nibbled her thumb.

"Well . . ."

They both looked at each other and then grinned. Almost in unison, they said the words, "The cake."

"Are we getting old?" asked Bram, following Sophie down the stairs.

"Probably."

"I love you." He smiled, stopping her for a moment to give her a kiss.

"And I love you, too."

"Good. You know," he said as they continued on into the kitchen, "maybe we should consider chocolate cake a new kind of foreplay."

# 16

Sophie sipped from her morning mimosa and scanned the crowded restaurant, her eyes returning again and again to the front entrance. Lavinia was late, though if there was a better place to while away a few extra minutes on a pleasant autumn morning, Sophie couldn't think of one. The Fountain Grill was a popular spot for Sunday brunch not only because of its famous buffet, but also for its sleek, silvery Art Deco interior. Oversized windows threw bold geometric frames around the most picturesque part of downtown St. Paul. Soft Thirties and Forties era jazz played from hidden speakers. And, of course, the fresh-brewed French roast, and the bottomless orange-juice-and-champagne cocktail didn't hurt.

Sophie remembered the first time she'd brunched at the Fountain Grill, the Maxfield Plaza's famous second-floor eatery. It was 1963, the same year her father decided to purchase the hotel. At the time the entire building was pretty run-down, a pale image of its former glory. The Zephyr Club, the posh restaurant near the top of the south tower, and Scotties, the first floor bar, had both been named in honor of F. Scott Fitzgerald, one of St. Paul's most famous onetime residents. Indeed, Jerrod Beck, for years the driving force behind the Maxfield's culinary wizardry, was a lifelong friend of Scott and Zelda's. Sophie met Chef Beck that day, but by then he was an old man, no longer at the top of his game. Years later she discovered that he'd actually designed the Fountain Grill's interior. He was a man of many talents.

Thankfully, Sophie's father didn't believe in the worst forms of visual modernization, though some renovation, of course, was necessary. After purchasing the Maxfield, he'd set out not only to restore it to its former greatness, but to steadfastly preserve its architectural integrity. In that sense, Henry Tahtinen had been a visionary. He'd been adamantly opposed to the razing of the magnificent Metropolitan Building in downtown Minneapolis in 1961. It was torn down at the height of urban renewal fever in the Twin Cities. Henry often said that he'd be damned if another famous Minnesota landmark would be put on the block. As a matter of fact, the preservation of history was the main reason he bought the Maxfield. The desire to become an innkeeper was only secondary. Yet Henry had made a go of it. The irony was, the Maxfield's current success had come as a direct result of its historical significance. While other, newer hotels struggled through the Seventies and Eighties, Henry was building on the image of 1930s elegance. Add to that impeccable service and clean, beautiful accommodations, and you had a winning combination.

And now it all belonged to Sophie. She still couldn't believe it. She was just beginning to feel the weight of the responsibility that had landed squarely on her shoulders. This landmark, this charming piece of history, had to be cared for. Nurtured. No wonder her father had wanted to pass it on to someone in the family—someone he knew would love it the same way he had. It was a sobering thought, yet it did nothing to dampen Sophie's enthusiasm. First thing tomorrow morning, she planned to march into the office of Hilyard Squire, the publisher of *Squires Magazine*—and her friend and boss—and tender her resignation. Two weeks from now, if all went as planned, she would start learning the hotel business full-time.

As she sat fingering the stem of her wineglass, gazing

somewhat aimlessly out the window, she heard a throat being cleared behind her. Sensing it was meant to catch her attention, she turned and saw a tall, bearded, distinguished-looking gentleman staring at her with a look of mild confusion. At first she didn't recognize him. Then it hit her. "Isaac Knox?" she said, her voice tentative.

"That's right," he replied, his lips curling into a satisfied smile. "And you're Sophie—" He paused, searching his memory for the correct last name.

"Greenway," she prompted him.

"Yes, I thought it was you." His expression brightened. "I'm usually good with faces, not so good with names."

"My maiden name was Tahtinen. I married Norm Greenway right after graduation. We were divorced many years ago."

The divorce-and-remarriage doctrine was the only one on which Howell Purdis had ever changed his mind. In the early years of the church, he taught that an individual was married for life. If you separated from your husband or wife, you had to remain both celibate and single. After his own wife left him in the late Seventies, Howell began to allow the faithful to divorce, but only if the mate in question had been unfaithful. Even though there was no proof Howell's wife had engaged in any sort of extramarital affair, Howell quietly let it be known that she was an unregenerate slut, worthy of eternal damnation. After less than a year he proposed to his twenty-six-year-old secretary, but in a moment of rare insight, withdrew the proposal. As far as Sophie knew, he'd lived alone in his mansion ever since.

Isaac Knox stared at her, trying to put it all together in his mind. "I seem to recall something about—you and Norm had a child, didn't you?"

"A son."

"Yes, that's right. I met him once. At a ministerial conference. It was shortly after Norm remarried. The boy was pretty small. Reddish-gold hair—a lot like yours."

She smiled. "He's twenty now."

"Really." He glanced toward the door, then at his watch.

She assumed that, like her, he was waiting for someone. "Would you like to sit down for a minute? I'm waiting for a friend, but she's late."

"Thanks," he said, easing into the other side of the booth.

He'd accepted her invitation so quickly, Sophie figured he wanted to talk. Her curiosity piqued, she waited for him to get comfortable and then said, "You know, I almost didn't recognize you." Her eyes rose to his bald head.

"Yeah"—he smiled—"I guess age eventually gets to us all."

"Did your wife come with you? I roomed with her my freshman year." Funny how easily it all came back to her.

He shook his head. "Not this trip."

"I was more than surprised to see Howell Purdis the other day. That part of my life seems so long ago." And so far away, she thought to herself, gratefully.

"You're no longer a member of the church, then?"

She shook her head. "Although, to be honest, I've been thinking about the time I spent at Purdis Bible College quite a lot the last few days."

"Really?" He pulled a saltshaker in front of him and began to examine the top. Not looking at her, he asked, "May I ask why?"

"Four of the women I roomed with my sophomore year are in town right now. Three of them are part of a group called the Daughters of Sisyphus. The other—"

"—is Adelle Purdis," he said, finishing her sentence.

"That's right. We had a reunion on Friday evening."

"Yes . . . I knew about it."

Interesting. Adelle must have told him. "Actually, I'm waiting for Lavinia Fiore. We were supposed to have brunch together this morning, but she's"—she looked at her watch—"almost half an hour late."

His eyes darted away. "She was late to our meeting, too."

"You met with her?"

"On Friday morning."

Strange that Lavinia hadn't mentioned it. "Something to

do with the church?" she asked conversationally. She knew it was none of her business, but didn't care.

"Actually—" He seemed to grow ill at ease. "Lavinia made some rather startling accusations."

"About what?"

"Another old friend of yours. Ginger Pomejay."

Of course. Why hadn't she put it together before this? Deciding to go on a little fishing expedition, she continued, "Well, you *were* the dean of students the year Ginger died."

He eyed her cautiously. "Then she's talked to you about it, too? This ridiculous idea of hers that Ginger was murdered?"

Sophie nodded.

"But . . . she's just making noise, right? It's not true."

"I don't know."

"Do you believe her?"

"I have no reason not to." He seemed unusually interested in a wild opinion he'd just said was ridiculous.

Leaning into the table, he lowered his voice. "Is that all she told you about the matter? She didn't elaborate any further?"

"No, not really."

"You have to understand, an accusation of murder, even if it happened many years ago, is a very serious charge. And you're right. I was the dean of students that year. It was my watch. If there was a problem, I should have known about it."

"But you didn't."

"I knew of Ginger's family history of cancer. We'd talked about that several times. But the idea that someone would intentionally try to hurt her, well, it's preposterous. Absolutely impossible."

By the intensity in his voice, Sophie was pretty sure he was telling the truth, at least the truth as he knew it. That didn't necessarily mean that Lavinia hadn't come across some information he didn't know anything about. As a matter of fact, it was one of the matters Sophie intended to bring up at this morning's brunch. That is, if Lavinia ever got here. She looked at her watch again. It was now nearly a quarter to eleven.

"Here comes my party," said Isaac, pushing quickly out of the booth.

As Sophie looked up she recognized three portly evangelist-rank ministers striding purposefully into the restaurant. This must be some big-time powwow. Usually, only two or three top ministers were at any given holy-day site. Isaac Knox, Howell, and Hugh Purdis filled that bill, so what were these guys doing here?

"It was good talking to you," said Isaac, pointing the men quickly to a booth near the bar.

"I'm sure we'll bump into each other again before you leave," said Sophie to his retreating back. Charming fellow. Impeccable manners.

A few feet from the table he stopped abruptly and turned around. "I thought that fat women's convention was over today. Aren't you leaving?"

Sophie winced at his choice of words. And she couldn't let it pass. "I'd say the fat men's convention is about to begin." She nodded to the evangelists.

He stiffened.

"Besides, you misunderstand. I'm not a guest here. I own the hotel." That felt good. The poor and the meek might be praised from the pulpit, but it was power and money the Church of the Firstborn truly valued. She could see his eyes light up.

"This hotel? You own the Maxfield Plaza?"

She nodded.

He looked at her as if seeing her for the first time. "How . . . wonderful for you."

"Yeah, it's a great place."

"Well," he said with a slight bow, "perhaps we will talk again."

Not if I can help it, asshole. She nodded a less than sincere goodbye.

As she watched him walk away she waved at her waiter, attempting to catch his attention. "Would you bring me a phone?" she mouthed, holding her hand to her ear. She wanted to call up to Lavinia's room. Perhaps her friend was still in bed. Whatever the case, Sophie wanted to get the show on the road. It wasn't like Lavinia to miss an appointment.

The waiter finally arrived with the phone, as well as more fresh-squeezed orange juice and champagne. Sophie turned the latter down. Since food would not be immediately forthcoming, she didn't want to get any happier than she already was. She dialed the front desk and asked if she'd received any messages. After being informed that there were none, she asked to be connected to Lavinia's suite.

Seven rings later the hotel's voice mail picked up. Leaving Lavinia a message seemed pointless.

Well, she thought to herself, tossing a tip on the table and easing out of the booth, there was only one way to find out what was going on. She'd have to go up to the room herself. If Lavinia wasn't there, then Sophie would have to admit the obvious. She'd been stood up.

# 17

Sophie rode the service elevator up to Lavinia's floor and headed quickly into the north tower. As she rounded the corner near the stairway she saw Bunny step onto the main elevator at the other end of the hall. So that was it, thought Sophie. Bunny had waylaid Lavinia, most likely demanding to talk to her about that exercise video. Lavinia should have called down to the restaurant to let her know she was going to be late.

Feeling a bit annoyed, Sophie walked up to her door and gave it several solid raps. Then, slinging her sack purse over her shoulder, she waited for Lavinia to answer. When there was no response, she knocked again. After another full minute she leaned close and called, "Come on, Lavinia. Open up. It's me. Sophie."

The door remained locked, the suite behind it silent.

As Sophie pressed her ear against the smooth wood, listening for signs of life, she noticed a DO NOT DISTURB sign hanging from the knob. What was going on? Was it possible her old friend was still asleep? Bunny had clearly come calling, yet had she been turned away by the silence, too?

Seeing one of the hotel maids emerge from a room several doors away, Sophie waved and then raced down the hall to talk to her. Thankfully, she knew the woman, and more important, the woman knew her. Frances Lester had worked at the Maxfield for as long as Sophie could remember. She was now the weekend housekeeping manager, in charge of the staff in both towers.

"Sophie." Frances smiled, shutting the door behind her and making sure it was locked. In the past year her tightly permed salt-and-pepper hair had turned a rather brilliant shade of orange. All part of the aging process, Frances assured everyone with a broad wink. She held a clipboard in one hand, her reading glasses dangling from a cord around her neck. "How's tricks, kiddo?" She always chewed gum and knew how to snap it at just the right moment.

"Great," said Sophie, returning her smile.

"Hey, I hear congratulations are in order." She elbowed Sophie in the ribs and gave a loud snap. "You're my new boss."

Sophie doubted Frances thought of anyone as her boss. Even so, she was one of her father's favorite employees. "Thanks."

"Don't mention it." She pulled a pen out of her pocket and made a notation on the chart. "So, what can I do for you?"

"Actually, I need to get into Room 1432. Do you have a master passkey with you?"

"Right here." Frances patted her pocket.

As they approached the door she said, "Are you sure you want to go in there?" She raised a cautionary eyebrow and tapped the DO NOT DISTURB sign.

"Yes. Very sure."

"All right. It's your funeral. But just remember. The room hasn't been made up yet. Ms. Fiore called down to the front desk last night for a noon wake-up call."

"She did what?" Had Sophie heard her correctly? *"Noon?"*

"Says right here on my chart," said Frances. She shoved it under Sophie's nose and drew her finger down to the room number. "See? Noon wake-up call. She phoned from her room last night at exactly ten to midnight. By my watch"—she glanced at it—"she's still got another hour of snoozing to do."

"But—" Was it possible that Sophie had mixed up her days? No, Lavinia had reminded her of the date just last night. *And* the time. How could she have forgotten? An inner sense was beginning to sound an alarm. "Open it," she said, feeling her heart beat faster.

Frances slipped the card into the computer lock, waited for the light to change from red to green, and then pushed the heavy handle all the way down.

Inside, the curtains were drawn, the room dark.

It took a moment for Sophie's eyes to get used to the dimness. When they did, she let out an involuntary gasp. "My God," she cried. The room had been completely trashed.

Frances flipped on the wall switch. "This must have been some nasty slumber party."

"We've got to call the police," said Sophie, her eyes taking in the destruction. Drawers were pulled out and tossed aside, the contents dumped on the floor. Chairs and tables were upturned, pillows flung in every direction. Unfortunately, the doors into the bedroom were closed. An icy fist of fear squeezed Sophie's insides as she contemplated what might be hidden from view.

"I'll make the call," said Frances soberly, backing out of the room.

"No," said Sophie, grabbing her arm. "Don't leave . . . I mean, don't leave just yet. I want to check out the bedroom first. I don't want to be alone."

"I understand," said Frances, her eyes scanning the room warily.

Screwing up her courage, Sophie pushed through the doors into Lavinia's inner sanctum. The living-room lights illuminated another scene of destruction, yet as she searched through the rubble Lavinia was nowhere to be found. "She's not here," called Sophie finally, taking a moment to digest the scene. If she were a betting person, she'd lay odds that the bed hadn't been slept in last night. The sheets and pillowcases were still smooth, still perfectly pressed, although the bedspread was missing. She tried the closet door, but found that it was locked.

"I'm going to check the bathroom next," she called, taking a deep breath and kicking open the door. Again, no sign of Lavinia. All the towels were tossed in the bathtub, the contents of the storage area under the sink scattered on the floor.

"I think I should call the police now," said Frances uneasily. "What do you say? I'll just phone from in here."

"No," said Sophie, rushing out of the bathroom. "Don't touch anything. Call from the housekeeping station, okay? And alert hotel security. We've got to get to the bottom of this right away."

"Right," agreed Frances. She hesitated. "Where do you think your friend is?"

"I don't know," said Sophie, biting her lower lip and steadfastly refusing to entertain the worst-case scenario. "But if she's not here now, maybe she wasn't here earlier, when the place was ransacked."

"Good point," said Frances, snapping her gum thoughtfully. "I'll go make that call."

As soon as she was alone, Sophie's thoughts turned to the phone call she'd received from Lavinia last night. Who had picked her up? If she'd been having a drink with Bunny, Cindy, and Adelle, it seemed likely one of them had driven past that phone booth and offered her a lift back to the hotel. Except, if Sophie recalled correctly, Lavinia had said they'd all left before she had.

Walking silently through the mess, she began to examine the contents of the room for clues. A half-filled glass of some amber-colored liquid—she sniffed it and decided it was brandy—was still sitting upright on the bar. Perhaps Lavinia had poured it last night. But that meant she had to have been here. And if she was here, why hadn't she slept in her bed?

Sophie scanned the bar area and then the floor, but this glass seemed to be the only dirty one around. She also didn't see Lavinia's purse. She took that to be a good sign. If the purse wasn't here, then perhaps Lavinia was somewhere safe. The thought struck her that maybe her friend hadn't come home last night at all. But if she hadn't, where had she gone? And where was she now?

As she mulled this over an idea struck her. Of course. Why hadn't she thought of it before? When she'd talked to Lavinia last night, Lavinia had said that she'd called Peter's parents' house looking for him, hoping he could give her a ride back to the hotel. But his father had said he was out. Perhaps it was Peter who'd driven by the booth. Sure. And instead of waiting, impetuous people that they were, they drove straight back to Edina and broke the good news to his parents right then and there. And *that's* where Lavinia had stayed last night. Simple.

Sophie heaved a sigh of relief. That is, until she remembered that Lavinia had called from the room late last night for a noon wake-up call. That didn't fit. Instantly, her relief turned into even greater concern.

She moved resolutely into the bedroom. As she bent down to examine the contents of one of Lavinia's many suitcases, now jumbled into a big heap on the floor, she heard a deep male voice. Then another. A second later two police officers entered the suite, followed closely by Frances.

"I'm glad you could get here so quickly," said Sophie, hurrying into the living room. "I assume Frances filled you in on the details?"

"She has," said the shorter of the two officers. "I'm Sergeant Wilhelm. And this is Patrolman Green." He nodded to the other man. "We were just down on St. Peter when we got the call. I suppose you know about the mini-marathon."

Sophie vaguely recalled something about a ten-mile run through the city ending at the state capitol.

Both officers had portable radios hooked onto their belts, quietly blasting static into the air. As Wilhelm pulled out a notepad and pen he explained that he needed to stay in contact with what was happening down on the street. He'd spotted a gang of rowdy teenagers a few minutes ago and these kids clearly worried him. Watching him walk around the room, making notes and asking questions, Sophie could tell his main concern was elsewhere.

Patrolman Green disappeared inside the bedroom. "Does the housekeeping staff have a key to the bedroom closet?" he hollered, stepping back and glancing down at a snarl of clothes next to his foot.

"Sorry," replied Frances. She chewed her gum nervously. "They take those old-fashioned skeleton keys. Mr. Tahtinen likes to maintain that old-fashioned feeling whenever he can. I can run down to the locksmith's office and probably find one. We've only got twelve suites like this in the hotel."

The patrolman rattled the knob. "Not a very good lock," he mumbled, giving it one last yank. "But good enough."

The portable radio on Wilhelm's belt started to squawk. "Eddy," called a voice. "We got a situation developing. Find Green and get back here right away."

The patrolman spoke into a microphone attached to his shirt collar. "That's a Roger."

"There's no sign of a struggle," said the sergeant, moving more quickly now. "I'd say whoever was in here was looking for something. It might have been a robbery, or they could have been looking for something specific." He paused, then asked, "Do you have any idea what that could be?"

"None," said Sophie, touching her fingers to her temples. "No idea at all."

"Well, they obviously had a key. Or—" He paused again.

"Is it possible Ms. Fiore did it herself? Sometimes we over-look the most obvious."

Sophie couldn't imagine what would cause Lavinia to wreak this kind of havoc on her own belongings.

"Since there was no forced entry, there's not much we can do," said the sergeant, returning his notepad to his pocket and crossing quickly to the door. He glanced at his watch. "You might want to alert hotel security."

"I did," said Frances. "I wonder where they are?"

Where indeed, thought Sophie sourly. "I've got one last question before you go. I believe you arrested someone yesterday named Morton. He'd been stalking Ms. Fiore while she was here for her convention."

"Is that right?" said the sergeant. "I'd have to check on that."

"Do you think it's possible this Morton fellow had some-thing to do with . . . this?" She nodded to the mess.

Wilhelm removed his cap and scratched his head. "There's always a possibility. Although, if this guy's in cus-tody, it would rule him out."

Just what she wanted to hear. At least he was one person they didn't have to worry about. "Thanks for coming so quickly."

"If I were you, Ms. Greenway, I'd find Ms. Fiore. You said she was in town for a convention?"

"Yes. The Daughters of Sisyphus. They're meeting over at the St. Paul Civic."

"Well, then maybe that's it. She's over there. When you locate her, tell her to check her belongings carefully. She can call us later to file a report if anything's missing." He motioned to the patrolman to follow him.

"Thanks," said Sophie. "I'll pass that on."

"Oh, and one other thing." He leaned close and lowered his voice to a confidential whisper. "I saw one of your secu-rity guards downstairs in the bar. I could be wrong, but I'm pretty sure I recognized him from the last time we were here. If I were you"—he winked—"I'd fire his ass."

"Sergeant," said Sophie, giving him a knowing nod, "I believe you just read my mind."

# 18

Remembering that the phone in her parents' apartment hadn't been disconnected yet, Sophie let herself in, grabbed a pad and pencil from a drawer in the kitchen, and made herself comfortable on the living-room couch. She had some people she needed to track down right away.

First she called Bram to let him know what had happened. She also explained that unless she located Lavinia soon, their plans for the rest of the day were off. They were hoping to drive to an orchard near Stillwater, a small town on the St. Croix River, where they often picked apples in the fall. Even though he sounded disappointed, Sophie could tell her husband shared her concerns. And he wanted to help. He said he'd change his clothes and be right over.

In the meantime Sophie tried to contact both Bunny and Cindy—with no luck. She left messages for each of them to call her as soon as possible.

Next she tried Adelle's suite. On the third ring, a deep male voice answered. "Hugh Purdis here."

"Hi," said Sophie. Though she obviously knew he was staying at the hotel, she was still a bit startled to be talking to a man she hadn't seen in over twenty years. "This is Sophie Greenway. You may not remember me, but I'm an old friend of Adelle's."

"Of course," he said. His voice sounded distracted, as if he were only half listening.

Sophie could hear a clicking noise, like someone typing onto a computer keyboard. "Is Adelle there?"

"No, she's out doing some shopping." More clicks.

"What time do you expect her back?"

"Well, she'll have to be here by six or so. Bible study starts at seven."

"I see." This was so frustrating. She needed answers and no one was home. "Look, I wonder if you could tell me what time Adelle got in last night."

The clicking stopped. "Why do you ask?"

"She met with Lavinia Fiore at a bar in northeast Minneapolis. I was just wondering what time she got home."

"To be honest," said Hugh, hesitating only briefly, "I couldn't say. I went out last night, too. Some old friends invited me to dinner. I got back around midnight—maybe a little after—and Adelle was already in bed, asleep."

Not what Sophie wanted to hear. She decided to press a little further. "Did Adelle happen to mention anything to you this morning about giving Lavinia a ride back to the hotel last night?"

"No. Nothing."

"Okay," she said wearily. "But will you do me a favor? When Adelle gets in, have her give me a call." She repeated her parents' number. "I need to talk to her."

"Sure thing," said Hugh. The clicking resumed. "Nice talking to you."

Sophie dropped the phone back on the hook, feeling completely thwarted. Three strikes and you're out.

Half an hour later Bram breezed through the front door waving a shopping bag. He was wearing old jeans and a well-worn flannel shirt. Bending down to give her a kiss, he said, "I'm still hoping we can drive over to Stillwater. I've got your apple-picking duds in here." He held up the sack.

She grabbed his arm and pulled him down on the couch, laying her head on his shoulder. A little TLC was just what the doctor ordered.

"That bad?" he asked, drawing her close.

"Worse. I can't get anyone on the phone."

"We could walk over to the Civic, see if she's there."

"I already asked Elvis, one of the bellboys, to run over."

"And?"

"He's not back yet."

Bram nodded, smoothing back her hair and kissing the top of her head. "You know who else you could call?"

"Who?"

"Why not try her new husband?"

Sophie sat up straight. "Jeez, sometimes I'm so thick I appall myself." She jumped up and ran to the kitchen, returning a moment later carrying the Minneapolis White Pages. "What was his last name?"

"Trahern," said Bram, waiting as she scanned down the page, then flipped to the next.

"There's only one Trahern in Edina. On Morningside Drive. Edward M." She picked up the phone and dialed the number.

After two rings a woman's voice answered. "Hello?"

Sophie assumed it was his mother. "Hi. I wonder if I could speak to Peter?"

"I'm not sure if he's here," said the woman. "Just a minute."

Sophie waited, leaning back into the couch cushions and chewing the top of her pen. Finally, a male voice answered, "This is Peter."

"Hi," said Sophie, heaving a sigh of relief. At last she'd found someone who might have some answers. "It's Sophie Greenway. We just met at—"

"I remember you," he said with a smile in his voice. "You're one of Lavinia's old college buddies."

"That's right." She was grateful she didn't have to do a five-minute reintroduction. "I was wondering . . . do you know where Lavinia is?"

"I assume she's over at the Civic. Let's see. It's almost one. I think she was supposed to chair a panel that started at twelve-thirty. It runs until three. After that, the convention's done. She should be packed and over here by five."

If it could only be that simple. "You didn't by any chance see her last night."

After a pause he said, "No, she was having a drink with a friend."

"Right. At a bar in northeast Minneapolis. But she called me around eleven. Seems she had some car trouble and needed a way home."

"Really. That's the first I've heard of it."

"She called you at your parents' house, but you weren't there."

"No, I . . . wasn't."

Interesting, thought Sophie. Why the hesitation? She wanted to ask him where he was, but since he wasn't being particularly forthcoming, she thought it might seem too intrusive. "Have you talked to her this morning?"

"Actually, no. I left her a couple of messages, but she hasn't called me back yet. I figured she'd be pretty busy on the last morning of the convention." He paused. "Is something wrong? You sound worried."

There was no point in keeping secrets. "Lavinia and I were supposed to meet for brunch around ten. She never came. So I had someone let me into her suite and—" She stopped herself. Why hadn't she anticipated how difficult it would be to tell him her fears?

"And what?" he prompted.

"Well, the place was trashed."

Silence.

"Everything was upturned, tossed around."

"But . . . I don't understand. Who did it?"

"I don't know."

"What did Lavinia say? She must have some idea."

"That's just it. I . . . don't know where she is. I was hoping she was with you."

More silence. "She's not."

"Look, Peter, I think it was probably a pretty straight-forward burglary attempt. Except that—"

"Except what?"

"Whoever got into the room must have had a key."

"What the hell's going on over there?" Suddenly he sounded angry.

"But the police said there was no evidence of a struggle," she reassured him, feeling more clumsy with each passing second. She was saying all the wrong things in all the wrong ways. She glanced over at Bram for moral support. "But maybe Lavinia was called away early and forgot about our brunch. While she was gone someone must have gotten into the room. Except—"

"Tell me!" he said, his voice rising in frustration.

"Well, her bed doesn't look like it was slept in."

"This is ridiculous. I'm coming back there right now."

"Sure, but—"

There was no goodbye. Only the click of a broken connection.

"Pretty upset, huh?" said Bram, watching her drop the receiver back on its hook. He eyed her with concern.

"Yes," she conceded. "He was."

"You did your best to put a positive spin on it."

"Did I?" She was thoroughly disgusted with herself. She'd acted without thinking. She should have spent a few moments figuring out how to break the news to him, but instead, she'd blithered her way through the entire conversation, making everything worse.

"Don't be so hard on yourself," said Bram, giving her hand a squeeze.

His attempt at kindness only made her feel worse. She shouldn't be let off the hook that easily. She was angry. At herself, at her friends for not being there when she needed to talk to them, and at Lavinia. "I've got to get to the bottom of this," she said, feeling incredibly awake, plugged in, ready for action. Yet there was nothing to *do*!

The buzzer sounded.

"Maybe that's Elvis," she said, hurrying over to the door. Sure enough, when she swung it open, the bellboy stood outside.

"Hi, Ms. Greenway." He flashed her a friendly smile. "Mr. Baldric." He nodded to Bram.

"Come in." Sophie held the door for him while he entered.

"Actually, I should get back to my station," he said apologetically. "But I did check out the convention, just like you asked."

"And?"

"She's not there. Or at least, nobody's seen her. One of the women at the information booth said she was supposed to be in charge of some panel, but she never showed up. I guess another woman had to fill in for her. People were really upset."

Sophie could feel her heart beat faster. This was *not* good news.

"But," continued Elvis, "on my way up here I ran into my supervisor. We got to talking in the elevator and he said he was pretty sure he saw Ms. Fiore leave the hotel sometime around eleven."

"Pretty sure?" repeated Sophie.

Elvis shrugged. "That's what he said. He's seen her a few times in the hotel lobby, so I assume he knows what he's talking about."

"Was she alone?"

"Yup. She got off the elevator and walked straight out the front door."

Sophie felt the muscles in her back relax. At last, something positive. "Thanks, Elvis. I really appreciate your help."

"No problem. Well, I gotta go." He tipped his cap and made a speedy exit.

"So," said Bram, watching her. "That's good news, right? Lavinia must be around somewhere."

Sophie shut the door and then leaned against it, mulling it over. "If it actually was Lavinia."

"Who else could it be?"

"Think about it for a minute, Bram. Lavinia and Cindy still look a lot alike, especially when Lavinia has her hair up. If you didn't know them all that well, you could easily get them mixed up."

"Oh."

"*And*, if she left around eleven, why didn't she make it to the convention for her panel?"

"That's a good question. So, what do we do next?"

Wasn't that the sixty-four-thousand-dollar question? "Come on," she said, grabbing her purse.

"Where are we going?"

"Back down to Lavinia's suite. Who knows? Maybe I missed something the first time. We'll never know unless we give it one last shot."

# 19

"You were right," said Bram, entering Lavinia's suite a few minutes later. "This really is a mess. I'm glad your mom and dad aren't here to see it. It would have sent your dad's blood pressure right through the roof."

Sophie stepped over to the far wall and drew back the dark brown curtains. Bright afternoon sunlight streamed in through the windows, making the room look even worse.

"Are we allowed to touch?" asked Bram, moving cautiously over to the bar. "Or did the police suggest we leave it alone until Lavinia gets back?"

"As far as I know, the police just wanted her to look through her belongings to make sure nothing was missing."

Bram leaned his elbow on the polished marble counter. As he gazed at the once beautiful interior he lapsed into a kind of depressed reverie.

Sophie flipped on the light in the bedroom and opened the blinds. She needed light before she could begin any kind of examination. She had no idea what she was searching for, she was merely proceeding on the assumption that there might be a clue she'd missed, one that might tell her where Lavinia had

gone. If the police hadn't viewed this mess as anything more
dastardly than a simple hotel burglary, why should she?

She paused in the doorway and glanced at her husband,
who was now down on his hands and knees searching
through the contents of one of the larger suitcases. She was
glad he was here, even if he didn't bring any more answers
to the table than she did. "Honey?"

"Um?"

She wasn't sure she wanted to ask the question that had
been gnawing at her for the last hour. "How long does
someone have to be gone before the police consider them a
'missing person'?"

Bram looked up. "I think it's a little too soon to hit the
panic button, Soph. Let's give it some more time."

"But . . . what if she doesn't come back by tonight?"

"Then—" He sat back on his heels. "We'll notify the
police."

"But what if she's in trouble *now*?"

"Sophie, you're going to drive yourself nuts if you keep
asking all these questions. We'll just have to wait and see."

Not a good enough answer, thought Sophie, yet it was the
only one they had. As she sat down on the only part of the
sofa still intact, she noticed a paper plate sticking out from
underneath a section of the morning newspaper right next to
her foot. Curious what Lavinia had been eating, she kicked
the paper aside. "What's this?" she said under her breath.
She bent down and picked up the plate, uncovering several
small lumps of what looked like her once famous bite-sized
cream cheese balls.

"What is it?" asked Bram. He stopped his own search to
see what she'd found.

"Remember those cheese balls I used to make?"

"You mean your old college recipe?"

She nodded, then pointed to the lumps. "When I served
them the other night at the reunion, everyone said they
hadn't eaten them in years."

"Maybe Lavinia took some with her."

"Nope. We ate them all." She poked one of the lumps.

Bram came over to take a closer look. "So what's it mean?"

"It means," said Sophie, tapping a finger against the side of her face, "that someone made a batch yesterday."

"You mean Lavinia?"

"Possibly."

"Why not probably? They're in her room. Unless she made them herself, where else would she get them?"

Sophie shrugged. "Bunny, or Cindy. Even Adelle. They all had the recipe. I xeroxed each of them a copy of my old cookbook. If you could make them in a dorm room, you could certainly make them in a hotel. Maybe someone decided to whip up a batch and share them around. You know, just to be friendly."

Bram leaned close to the floor and sniffed the lumps. "Whew, they stink."

She took her own sniff. She had to admit, they didn't smell quite right.

"What was that?" Bram's head shot up.

"Someone's at the door," said Sophie. Right now neither one of them had nerves of steel. "Come in," she called, getting up. "It's open."

Frances Lester, the housekeeping supervisor, popped her head inside the room. "I finally found a key for the closet door. Thought I'd bring it up." She dangled it off the end of her finger.

"Thanks," said Sophie, slipping it into her pocket.

"Have you heard anything from Ms. Fiore?"

"Not yet."

"I'm sure you will soon. If you ask me, whoever burgled her stuff should be boiled in oil." She gave the room a nasty glance. "Well, if you don't need me anymore, I've got some work to do in the south wing."

"I'll let you know what happens," said Sophie. "And thanks again for the key."

After she was gone, Bram asked, "The closet door is locked? You mean, no one's checked to see what's inside?"

"Not yet."

"But . . . doesn't that strike you as funny?"

"Doesn't what strike me as funny?" She hurried into the bedroom.

Bram followed. "I know these old locks. Any guy with a modicum of strength could snap it open in a flash. How come the burglar didn't do it? There might have been valuables inside just ripe for the picking."

"That's a good question," said Sophie. One neither she nor the police had considered. "Maybe the burglar was a woman and the lock was too strong for her."

"A sexist comment if I ever heard one."

Sophie pushed the key into the lock, twisted it, and opened the door. Inside, everything was jumbled together on the floor. Dresses. Shoes. Coats. Hats. Nothing was where it should be.

"Hmm," said Bram, staring at the mess. "I guess we were both wrong. The burglar did get in." He kicked some of the clothes aside, revealing a corner of the bedspread.

"Hey," said Sophie. "I wondered where that went. But . . . what's it doing in here?"

Bram leaned down and tried to yank it free. It wouldn't budge. He pulled several coats and sweaters off the top to get a better grip.

Sophie took some of the clothes and placed them carefully on the bed. Lavinia would just be sick when she saw how wrinkled everything was.

"What the—" He was on his hands and knees now.

"What is it?" asked Sophie, moving back to the closet.

As Bram looked up she could see that his face had lost some of its color. "We've got to call the police," he said, scrambling to his feet.

"Why?"

"It's Lavinia." He gripped her shoulders and looked her square in the eye. "Sweetheart, she's . . . dead."

It took a moment for his words to sink in. When they did, her knees nearly buckled. "You're . . . sure?"

"Positive."

"Anybody home?" called Peter, pocketing his key as he breezed through the door and entered the suite.

Sophie seized Bram's arm. This was the worst possible timing.

"What are you two doing in here?" he demanded, seeing them emerge from the bedroom. His blond hair was wind-blown. As he stood glaring at them he tried to rake it back into place.

"I'm afraid—" began Bram, but Peter cut him off.

"You're afraid what? What the hell's going on here?" He surveyed the room in one long, defiant glance. "I want some answers."

"It's Lavinia," continued Bram.

"What about her?"

"We . . . found her in the closet. I'm sorry, Peter."

He bumped past them into the bedroom. In an instant he was by her side, checking her pulse, his fingers gently smoothing back her hair. "Get somebody! Call someone! There's got to be something we can do!"

Bram squeezed Sophie's hand. There was no way to make this easier for him.

And no way on earth to change what had happened.

# 20

As Sophie walked into the bar, she looked around for a dark booth where she could sit unnoticed and alone. Fourteen stories above her, a homicide detective had taken over Lavinia's suite and was interrogating Peter. Since she and Bram had discovered the body, they'd spoken with the officer first, giving their statements as clearly and concisely as possible.

Unfortunately, Bram had scheduled a six o'clock taped interview with a state senator over at WTWN and couldn't get out of it, not even to stay and help Sophie come to terms with the loss of an old friend. They would spend some time together later, back at their own home, attempting to make sense of what, on the face of it, seemed an utterly senseless murder.

For now, Sophie was on her own. She didn't want to leave the Maxfield until she'd made an attempt to contact the other members of her old group. So, instead of hiding in her parents' apartment, she decided to go downstairs and use the bar phone. That way she felt more connected to what was happening, and ultimately, less isolated by her own thoughts.

The convention had ended hours ago. By now, Bunny and Cindy should have returned to the hotel. The odd thing was, when she'd checked her parents' voice mail a few minutes ago, there were still no messages.

Easing onto a stool, Sophie caught the bartender's eye.

"Hey, Ms. Greenway," called Sherman. He was pouring a drink at the other end of the bar. "Be right with you."

Sherman Watts was an institution around the Maxfield. He'd been the main bartender at Scotties for almost thirty years. Perhaps he might find this an unflattering observation, but Sophie'd always thought he looked like a jockey—small, tough, wiry. All that was missing were the silks and the horse.

She waited for him to finish, absently popping several peanuts into her mouth. They tasted like sawdust. Pushing the bowl away, she folded her hands on the table and gazed at her own reflection in the etched mirror that ran the length of the back counter. She looked every bit as depressed as she felt.

"Can I get you something?" asked Sherman, running a damp cloth over the counter as he approached.

"Why not?" said Sophie. "Make it a whiskey sour." She watched his experienced fingers prepare the cocktail. "And I need to use the bar phone."

"No problem." He set the drink on a napkin in front of her

and then reached under the counter and grabbed a small cell phone.

"Thanks." She was about to move over to a booth with it when she had a thought. "Say, Sherm? I was wondering. Do the hotel security guards spend a lot of time in here? Drinking? Shooting the breeze? Eating peanuts?"

"Well, not drinking *alcohol*," he said somewhat sheepishly. "But yeah, they drink a lot of Coke."

"I thought so," said Sophie. She hesitated. "Did my father know about it?"

He shook his head. "When they saw him coming, they always took off out the back."

"And you didn't want to rat on fellow employees by informing my dad that they were worthless deadbeats."

"Something like that, Ms. Greenway. Being a management mole isn't part of my job description." He said the words soberly, yet she could see a certain twinkle in his eye.

"Thanks, Sherm."

"No problem." He picked up a glass and began polishing it. "Oh, by the way, the security boys were in here a little while ago, but they left before you came in. They must have radar."

"No, actually, we had an ... incident upstairs. That's where they are now."

"Same thing as yesterday?"

"What happened yesterday?"

"That man who was stalking one of the guests. The police took him into custody yesterday afternoon."

"Oh, right. No, that guy's in jail, thank God."

Sherman stopped polishing. "No, he's not."

"Of course he is. The police arrested him."

"Not according to what one of the security guards told me just a few minutes ago."

Sophie stared at him. "Explain."

"Well." He leaned across the bar and spoke more confidentially. "The police took him in and questioned him, but they didn't have evidence to make an actual arrest."

She was aghast. "You mean he's out on the streets?"

"Don't shoot the messenger, Ms. Greenway." He held up his hands. "That's just what I heard."

This was terrible news. How could they let someone like him go? "Thanks for the information."

"This guy . . . he didn't hurt anyone, did he?"

Dropping her gaze to her drink, she said, "I don't know. We'll just have to wait and see."

She was glad he didn't push any further. Moving the phone and her glass over to a booth, she made herself comfortable and then dialed the number of her boss at *Squires Magazine*. Even though Hilyard Squire worked weekends, she doubted he'd be in the office this late. It was now nearly six P.M. Most sane people were home being scandalized by *60 Minutes*.

After a couple of rings the answering machine picked up. Sophie listened to the brief message and then began one of her own. "Hilly, it's me. It's Sunday evening and—"

"Sophie," said an energetic voice. "What a nice surprise. I was just getting ready to leave."

"Sorry to bother you so late," she apologized.

"How's the birthday girl?" he asked cheerfully.

"Well . . . that's kind of a long story."

"I love long stories—if they're good ones."

"Oh, this is. But . . . actually, I was calling to ask a favor."

"Ask away."

"Well, a friend of mine just died."

"Gosh, sorry to hear that, Sophie."

"Thanks, Hilly."

"And you need to attend the funeral."

"Something like that."

"When is it?"

"That's just it, Hilly. I don't know. Is it possible I could take this coming week off?" Before he could say no she added, "I know I'm asking a lot, and I wouldn't if I didn't think it was absolutely necessary."

After several long seconds he said, "Well, I suppose we could swing it—just this once."

"Great. You're a doll, Hilly."

He grunted. "Tell that to my wife."

"I will. And . . . when I get back, I'll tell you the amazing story of my birthday party."

"Why does that sound ominous?"

Sophie allowed herself a private grin. "It's all a matter of perspective, Hilly."

"Isn't everything?"

"So I'll see you a week from Monday?"

"Bright and early," he said wearily. "I'm sure your desk will be buried by then."

If Sophie hadn't fully comprehended it before, she did now. Just thinking about the same-old-same-old of her routine at that magazine was enough to turn her stomach. As she said goodbye she gave a silent cheer. She needed a change in her life and her father and mother had dropped one right in her lap.

Taking a sip of the whiskey sour, she sat back in the booth and spent a few moments admiring the room—the green glass-block bar and chrome stools, the framed photos of famous stage actors hanging on every wall. Strange that the pleasure of sitting here now was mixed with such sadness.

Several police officers were standing near the bar entrance locked in private conversation. As she continued to sip her drink she saw a familiar face enter the room and walk quickly up to the counter. For a moment her heart stopped. Lavinia! she said under her breath. As the woman turned to look for a vacant table, Sophie could see she'd made the same mistake the bell captain supervisor had made earlier in the day. It wasn't Lavinia at all, but Cindy.

"Over here," called Sophie. By the dour look on her friend's face, Sophie wondered if she'd already heard the news.

Cindy waved and then waited as Sherman drew her a beer. Hurrying over to the booth, she settled her bulk into the seat across from Sophie. "Have you heard what just happened?"

Sophie gave a gloomy nod.

"A man in the newspaper kiosk told me." She lowered her voice. "Everyone's talking about it."

Sophie grimaced. She knew she had a lot to learn about

managing negative hotel information. This obviously wasn't the kind of publicity the Maxfield wanted or needed, yet she failed to see what she could do about it now.

Cindy stared straight ahead at nothing in particular. "I can't believe it. I just can't believe it."

"Peter's upstairs talking to the police."

"Why? Do they think he had something to do with it?"

Sophie noticed a certain eagerness in Cindy's expression, an eagerness that repulsed her. "I don't know. No one knows anything yet."

"Well, I wouldn't be surprised. Most murder victims know their murderers."

Thank you for that *Reader's Digest* moment, thought Sophie. "There are a lot of people in town this weekend who knew Lavinia."

"Meaning what?"

"Just that there could be a lot of potential motives."

"I certainly hope you're not talking about me," she said indignantly.

"No, Cindy. I'm not talking about you."

"I should hope not." She took a gulp of beer. "I still can't believe it. It's like . . . a horror movie. It can't be real. I wonder if Bunny knows."

"I left messages for all of you to call me. So far no one has."

"I haven't been up to my room yet, Soph. I just got back from the Civic a few minutes ago."

"Is Bunny still there, too?"

"I don't know. I haven't seen her since this morning. Funny, she'd just come back from Lavinia's suite."

"What time was that?" asked Sophie.

"Oh, let me think. Probably around eleven."

"Did she say she'd talked to Lavinia?"

"No, only that she'd knocked on her door. Lavinia never answered."

Sophie mulled this over.

"I wonder who found her?" asked Cindy, pulling the bowl of peanuts in front of her.

"Bram and I."

Her eyebrow raised. "Gee, I'm really sorry. Was it . . . was she—"

"Yes, she was already dead. But before I say any more, I'd like to hear what the police have to report." Sophie could feel Cindy's eyes boring into the side of her head. Feeling incredibly uncomfortable, she decided to ask a few questions of her own. "I heard that you, Bunny, and Adelle met with Lavinia in a bar last night. Some dive in northeast Minneapolis."

"It wasn't my idea," said Cindy quickly. "Bunny made me go."

She sounded more like a high-school sophomore than a grown woman.

"I agreed to come along as long as we got home early."

"Did you drive together?"

"No," said Cindy, lifting the beer to her lips, "I met her there."

"You didn't by any chance give Lavinia a lift home, did you?"

She stopped, set the glass carefully back down on the table, and then replied, "She had her own car, Sophie. Why would I do that?"

"Lavinia phoned me around eleven from a pay phone outside the bar. One of her front tires had gone flat."

"Really." She turned the glass around in her hand. "First I've heard of it."

"What did all of you talk about last night?"

"You should have been there, Soph. It was something else. Lavinia announced that she had Ginger Pomejay's diary—one she apparently kept the year we all lived together in Terrace Lane. Lavinia brought it with her to the convention, God knows why." She crunched a peanut thoughtfully. "Actually, I've been thinking about Lavinia's murder theory—the one she mentioned the other night at the reunion."

"You mean that Ginger didn't die of cancer?"

"Exactly. Apparently, in this diary, Ginger said she was in love."

"So?" said Sophie. "We all had crushes."

"Right, but Lavinia said the person Ginger loved was the one who murdered her."

Sophie's head jerked up. "Why? I don't understand."

"Me either. All Lavinia would say was that there was some big secret. Ginger was killed to keep her from spilling the beans—or words to that effect."

Cindy was right. This was an amazing story. "So who was this mystery person?"

"Lavinia said she didn't know for sure. Although, if you ask me, I think she suspected someone pretty strongly. She said there were only a couple of people it could be. That's when Bunny got pretty uptight. She accused Lavinia of suspecting one of us."

"Excuse me?" said Sophie.

"Yeah, I know." Cindy laughed, draining her glass. "That would mean Ginger was in love with a woman. Hardly likely."

But it would have been quite a secret, thought Sophie, rolling it around in her mind. No wonder Bunny got hot under the collar. She was the only lesbian in the group. Still, so much was missing from the story, it made no sense. "Did Lavinia suggest the method of Ginger's murder?"

"Sorry, that's all I know." Cindy pushed her empty glass away. "Maybe we'll find out more later."

Sophie couldn't imagine how. With Lavinia dead, the subject would no doubt die with her. Unless? "Where's the diary now?"

"I assume it's up in her room."

A lightbulb went on inside Sophie's head.

"Where else would it be? Say, Sophie." Cindy examined her fingernails with a studied casualness. "Since you own the hotel, will the police give you a full report about Lavinia's death?"

"I hope so. This is all kind of new to me." She tapped her chin in thought. "You know?" she said after a long moment,

"I know this is a lot to ask, but would you do me a big favor?"

"Sure. Anything."

"This has been kind of a rough day. Would you mind passing the information about Lavinia's death on to Adelle and Bunny. I don't think they should hear it from a stranger, and I'm afraid I really need to get home."

"Don't give it another thought," said Cindy, patting Sophie's hand. "I'll take care of everything. A good night's sleep will fix you right up."

Sophie was a bit startled by the shallowness of the comment, but let it pass. Death did that to you. She'd had enough experience with the Grim Reaper to know that reactions became out of whack. The concerns of everyday life seemed like worthless trivia, just as the people who went on with their normal lives—or who appeared to grieve less than you did—seemed shallow.

And yet, life did go on. For everyone, that is, except Lavinia.


# 21


Searching for her car keys inside her purse, Sophie stepped off the elevator into the subbasement of the parking garage across the street from the Maxfield Plaza. The dank concrete ramp had been built in the late Sixties. Although the lighting was up to code, it always struck her as dim.

As she walked toward her car she glanced over her shoulder several times to make sure she wasn't being followed. Perhaps it was a reflex. Too many women had been attacked in parking ramps in the last few years for her to feel entirely comfortable. Or maybe she was just feeling jumpy. After what had just happened, she had good reason.

The security in this part of the building was tight. Since no one could get into the basement and subbasement without a passkey furnished by the hotel, the lower two floors of the building weren't as busy as those open to the general public. And that's the way it was tonight, thought Sophie. Quiet. The kind of quiet that got inside your bones and made you walk a little faster, breathe a little harder.

Her heels clicked on the concrete as she hurried toward the far wall where her car was parked. Somewhere in the distance, she heard a car door slam. Then footsteps echoing away. She pulled her thin coat more tightly around her body and looked in every direction, but saw no one. Feeling more isolated and vulnerable than she dared admit, even to herself, she opened the car door. She had to calm down. She'd been in this garage a hundred times and nothing had ever happened before. As a matter of fact, this was one of the safest ramps in the city. Nothing was going to happen tonight either. She'd go home, take a long hot shower, and—

"Excuse me," said a voice from behind her.

Her head snapped up. Stiffly, she turned, seeing a man standing in the shadows about ten feet away. He was holding what looked like a thick envelope in his left hand. His stance was casual, yet something about the way he looked frightened her. She had to admit, in her present state of mind, the sight of any stranger would have caused a moment of panic. "Did you say something to me?" she said, clearing her throat.

"Yeah." He leaned against a Jeep. "Just chill, okay. I ain't here to hurt you."

How good of him to point that out up front.

"Did you just come from that hotel over there?" His eyes flicked in the direction of the Maxfield.

"I did," she said slowly.

"I heard . . . I mean, somebody told me that . . . you know, a lady got hurt over there. Is it true?"

She saw no reason to lie. "Yes. It is."

"Um." He nodded. "But I mean . . . how bad's she hurt?"

He was a sleazy-looking fellow. How on earth had he gotten into the Maxfield's section of the parking garage? "Very badly," she replied.

"But she'll be okay, right? She ain't gonna buy it or nothing like that." He seemed highly agitated. She couldn't tell if he was angry or scared.

"I'm sorry, Mr.—" She waited for him to say his name. When he showed no sign of a pending response, she continued, "I'm afraid that's all I can say." She started to get in her car.

"No!" he said, moving quickly toward her. "I gotta know."

He was fast, but Sophie was faster. She slid into the front seat and slammed the door, pressing the automatic door locks.

In frustration, he beat on the driver's-side window with his fist. "Tell me!" he yelled. "Was it Lavinia Fiore?"

His face was close to her now. So close, she finally realized who she was addressing. The police sketch had captured him perfectly. Feeling a shiver of adrenaline shoot through her system, she started the motor and backed the car up.

Morton held on to the door handle, trying to yank it open. "Just tell me," he demanded. "I gotta know." Smashing both hands against the window, he inadvertently flattened the envelope he was holding against the glass. The open flap revealed a thick bundle of cash.

Sophie stared at it for just a moment before her eyes rose to his.

He reeled back as if her expression were a terrible accusation, dropping the money to the ground. "It ain't what you think," he shouted. "I never hurt no one."

Jamming the gearshift into drive, Sophie pressed down hard on the gas and sped away from him. The last thing she saw in her rearview mirror was Morton, down on his hands and knees, stuffing the bills back into the envelope.

# 22

Adelle felt dizzy when she sat up in bed the following morning, rubbing her sore eyes awake. Hugh had already gotten up and left. He'd scheduled a meeting with Isaac Knox and a couple of the other evangelists for nine o'clock. Not wanting to be late, he'd set the alarm for seven. Adelle had planned on getting up with him, but as soon as she'd opened her eyes, she realized her headache was immense. There was no use fighting it. Mumbling something about seeing him later, she'd turned over and gone back to sleep. She hated herself when she drank too much, but if there was ever a time when it seemed appropriate, it was last night.

Cindy and Bunny had knocked on the door to her suite just after she'd returned from her shopping trip to Dayton's. They brought with them the news of Lavinia's death. Thankfully, Hugh allowed her to bow out of the Bible study. It was usually a command performance during Tabernacles Week, but tonight, even *he* saw the wisdom in allowing her the night off.

After a two-hour walk down memory lane with her friends, she'd finally gotten rid of them. She'd spent the rest of the evening in her bedroom, nursing a ten-year-old bottle of Scotch. It seemed a fitting tribute to an old friend, as well as a quick way to dull the pain. She was a little surprised at how philosophically both Bunny and Cindy were taking Lavinia's death. But then, they didn't know what she knew.

Many years ago, long before Lavinia had come upon the

diary, Adelle suspected Ginger's death hadn't been due to cancer. Yet she'd kept her mouth shut. To be sure, Ginger hadn't confided in her, but then, she didn't need to. Adelle had witnessed the truth. And then she'd mutely witnessed the consequences. Her silence had been her shame, and had remained her shame to this very day.

Easing her legs out of the bed, she sat forward, one hand on her stomach, the other pressing against her forehead. She felt rotten in so many ways, the alcohol was the least of her problems. Still, she wondered if she should go get some aspirin. Church members weren't allowed to take drugs, though she knew her father-in-law always traveled with a small apothecary. Sleeping pills. Cold medications. At heart, he was a rather silly hypochondriac.

"Adelle? Are you up?" called an angry voice from the other room. A moment later Hugh burst into the bedroom. When he saw the look on her face, his angry expression turned more tentative. "I'm really sorry about what happened yesterday. If there was any way I could change things—make it easier for you—"

"There isn't."

Early in their marriage, she'd wanted so much for them to be happy, to be deeply in love. She'd playacted the role for years, but the reality had never materialized. The one good thing to come from their union was their son. That had become the ground on which they were finally united. At best, she thought of Hugh now as a friend. Maybe, in the end, that was the greatest gift marriage could give anyone.

She would have preferred to marry a stronger man. But then, if Hugh had been that stronger man, he might not have married her. She hadn't been easy to live with, she knew that with absolute certainty. Sometimes, she even felt sorry for him, though that was rare. He'd made his own bed, as she had, and they were going to lie in it together until the day they died. They'd both made a bargain with the devil. While trying to serve God, they needed to please Howell Purdis. More often than not, it was a difficult—even impossible—task. But that's the way God worked. He used human beings, fallible, weak, even headstrong human beings. And in the end, somehow, the job got done.

Adelle rose, careful not to jar her aching head, and walked into the bathroom, where she spent a moment splashing cold water into her face. Then, grabbing a hand towel, she returned to the bedroom. "What's wrong?" she asked, seeing the anger return to her husband's face. "What happened at your meeting this morning?"

Hugh sat down, resting his elbows on his knees. "It's Isaac."

"Of course it's Isaac. It's always been Isaac. Tell me something I don't already know."

"He's going to be the death of me."

"You've got to stop protecting him, Hugh. Why you feel a sense of loyalty to someone who's done nothing but betray you, I'll never know."

His eyes rose to hers, and then looked away.

"So what did he say?" she asked, stepping over to the mirror above the dresser and examining her face for signs of damage.

"He finally dropped the bomb."

She stopped and turned around. "What?"

"Do I have to spell it out for you?"

She stared at him. "But he promised—"

"All bets are off. He wants something now. He's like a dog with a bone. No one's going to take it away from him."

She ordered herself to breathe. After giving herself a moment to regroup, she said, "You're a fool, Hugh. You always have been. God knows why you ever befriended that man. He's done nothing but use you and abuse you from the time you were boys."

"That's not the way he sees it."

"Of course not. Isaac is a selfless man," she said sarcastically. "A loving man. What he does, he does for the good of others."

"That's what he thinks he's doing now."

"By breaking up the church? Destroying what we've worked so hard to build?"

"He wants me to join the new group he's putting together."

"Your father will destroy him! And he'll destroy you, too."

He got up and began to pace. "We've got to put a stop to all this wrangling once and for all. It's tearing the church apart."

"Isaac's tearing the church apart!"

"He doesn't see it that way. He thinks Father is being completely unreasonable because he won't even discuss matters of doctrine. What he's taught for years is God's truth and that's it. Period, the end."

"This is news?"

"No, but the ministry is sick of it. They refuse to believe everything is set in stone. Do you know what happened yesterday when the great Howell Purdis tried to disfellowship Isaac? Isaac threatened to take seventy percent of the ministers with him if he left. And that means most of the membership. He must have scared my dad pretty good, because he backed off."

"I wondered what he'd done. But, you mean your dad believed this insanity?"

Hugh shook his head. "It's not insanity. That's what the meeting was about this morning. Isaac really does have the backing of most of the top ministers."

Feeling dazed, Adelle sat down on the edge of the bed.

"Don't you get it?" said Hugh, sitting down next to her and dropping his head in his hands. "If I stay with Father, our son will be presiding over an empty church. But if I throw in with Isaac, there's still a chance Joshua will one day assume the leadership role."

She turned her head and glared at him, amazed by his ignorance. "You're living in a dreamworld if you believe that. You're a weak man, Hugh. You've only survived this far because you were Howell Purdis's son. Without him, you're lost."

"I've never cared about power."

"That was your first mistake."

"Maybe. But what about all the good people out there who support our ministry? I care about *them*. And I care about our son. Think about it. If I stay with my father now, Joshua is lost. Do you want that? Do you!"

"No!"

"Then you tell me what I should do."

As much as she hated to admit it, even to herself, he had a point. "Just give it more time, okay. Don't give Isaac your answer right away."

"He's allowing me two days."

She stared back at him, her mind racing. "All right. Then take it. Who knows? Your father's still a player in this game. He won't go down without a fight."

Hugh rose and looked down at her with a coldness she found chilling. "This may surprise you, Adelle, but I'm not going down without a fight either. Don't count me out just yet."

He slammed the door on his way out.

# 23

Sophie spent all day Monday waiting for an official police report on Lavinia's death. She tried to stay busy, calling real-estate agents and setting up a couple of appointments. The house needed to be appraised, and since she had some free time, she decided she might as well get the ball rolling. Yet her concentration was constantly broken by the image of her friend lying silently amid the rubble of her closet.

By lunchtime, the day was really beginning to drag. Finally, around four, a Lieutenant Riley from the homicide division of the St. Paul Police Department called with an initial report. As the man spoke in his calm, almost matter-of-fact voice, Sophie sat down at the kitchen table and took notes, asking him about certain points, not wanting to forget any of the information.

"I really appreciate the call," she said, hurrying to squeeze in one last question. She could tell he was busy and wanted to get off. "Did you find a diary when you searched through Lavinia's belongings?"

He paused for a moment, rattling some papers. "We found a daily appointment calendar."

"No, that's not what I'm talking about. This would have been an actual diary—lots of personal writing. That sort of thing."

"Can you describe it?"

"Sorry. I've never seen it."

"Well, there's no mention of a diary in this report, Ms. Greenway. Why do you ask?"

Sophie saw no point in keeping the information from him. She quickly relayed the story of Ginger's death, and of Lavinia's contention that the diary, one she brought with her on her trip to Minnesota, contained information that pointed to a murderer. She also mentioned that many of the people who knew Ginger back in the early Seventies were in town right now—most of them staying at the Maxfield Plaza.

"You mean to tell me Lavinia Fiore had proof of a murder?"

"No," said Sophie. "She was careful never to say she had the actual proof—just suspicions."

"So why would this diary—assuming there is one—be important?"

"Because it pointed to a specific person," said Sophie, exasperated by his inability to grasp the obvious. "I may be wrong, but I think that's why her room was ransacked. Someone was looking for it."

"Why didn't you tell us about this yesterday?"

"I didn't know about the diary until after Bram and I gave our statement. If you want to follow it up, you'll need to talk to Bunny Huffington, Adelle Purdis, and Cindy Shipman."

Again, he rattled his notes. "You mean the same women who had a drink with the deceased on Saturday night?"

"Exactly. All five of us were old friends of Ginger's. We lived in the same dorm the year she died."

There was silence on the other end. She assumed he was writing it all down. "This may have nothing to do with Ms. Fiore's murder, but we'll check on it. In the meantime, if you come up with anything else that might have a bearing on this investigation, please give me a call." He repeated his phone number.

She copied it down, assuring him she would.

After she said goodbye, she immediately called Bram. They had to talk right away. Since it was a beautiful autumn afternoon, temperatures in the mid-seventies, they agreed to meet at a favorite restaurant on Lake Harriet in south Minneapolis.

Half an hour later Sophie was ushered to one of the Lyme House's nicest outdoor tables. She sat down next to the wood railing, delighted by her view of the bandstand on the far shore. She'd been a restaurant reviewer for so many years, everyone knew her face and tended to pander to her well-known likes and dislikes. At least in the culinary biz, she was a local celebrity, a status she heartily enjoyed. She was also a friend of the restaurant's owner, Jane Lawless.

Bram arrived a few minutes later, eager to talk. Over a bottle of California Merlot, Sophie recounted what the lieutenant had explained to her. Lavinia's death had been ruled a murder. The cause of death, poisoning.

"What kind of poison?" asked Bram, leaning into the table.

"They haven't done an autopsy yet, but they've analyzed that small cheese ball nugget we found on the floor."

"And?"

"The cream cheese had small bits of oleander flower in it."

"So?"

"It's highly toxic," said Sophie, staring down into her glass. "Death was immediate."

They both sat silently for a few minutes, digesting the information.

Finally, Bram asked, "Where would the murderer get oleander flowers?"

She shrugged. "Any garden store. Or—" She shifted uncomfortably in her chair.

"Or what?"

"Well, the Maxfield's garden—the one between the two towers—has several pots."

"You think the murderer used some of *that*?"

"I hope not. I'd hate to think the Maxfield provided the murderer with the murder weapon. You know," she said, swirling the wine around in her glass, "it's surprising how many ordinary plants are poisonous. Lily of the valley. Rhododendrons. Even azaleas."

"When did you become such a font of gardening trivia?"

"Right after Rudy was born. I never wanted any of them in the house."

"You amaze me sometimes, Sophie. You really do." He reached across the table and took her hand. "But let's get back to the police report. Do they know when she died?"

Sophie checked her notes. "The medical examiner estimated the time of death at somewhere between eleven P.M. Saturday evening and four in the morning on Sunday."

"She died in her hotel room?"

"That's what they think."

"And do they have a suspect?"

"Well, not exactly. They've talked to Peter twice. Once yesterday afternoon, and once again this morning."

"That sounds kind of ominous. What's his story?"

She squeezed her husband's hand and then pulled away. "According to what the detective told me, he wasn't at his parents' house last night, but maintains he has an airtight alibi."

"From eleven until four in the morning? What the hell was he doing?"

"That's just it. He won't say. If push comes to shove, he told the police he could produce a witness who would place him well away from the scene of the crime during those five hours. But for now, that's all he'll say."

"You know," said Bram, his gaze wandering to a distant

dock where a lone woman stood feeding the ducks, "in a case like this, the police usually look at the husband pretty hard."

"But why would he want to hurt Lavinia? He loved her, or at least he said he did. They both seemed genuinely happy."

"Don't be so naive, Soph. It could always be an act. Lavinia was a rich woman. He no doubt stands to inherit a sizable estate."

Sophie didn't believe it was an act, not that she was a perfect judge of character. Nevertheless, she prided herself on having a pretty good sense of people. "You really think he could do something that hideous just for money?"

"Don't give me that scrutinizing stare," said Bram, straightening his tie. "I didn't say he *was* guilty, I'm just examining potential motivations."

Sophie sat back as the waiter arrived with a basket of freshly baked bread. After handing each of them a menu, he moved on to the next table. Lowering her voice, she continued, "All right. I admit I could be wrong. But I think we should consider other motivations as well."

"For instance?" he said, placing the menu squarely in front of him.

"The room was searched, right? Someone was looking for something?"

"A fair assumption."

"Remember the diary I told you about last night?"

"The one Lavinia thought pointed to Ginger's murderer? *If* she was murdered," he added impatiently, "which is only speculation. Besides, that was a long time ago. What possible bearing could it have on today?"

"I don't know," said Sophie, angry at herself for not having an answer. She took several sips of wine, looking glum.

"I think we have to stick with motivations in the here and now."

"You mean Peter."

"Yes, for one."

"Who else?"

"Well, what about Bunny? She was certainly upset with Lavinia for making that videotape. Correct me if I'm wrong, but I believe I saw steam coming out of her ears on Saturday morning. She could have strangled Lavinia right then and there."

"Strangled, maybe. But *murdered*, I just don't buy it."

"Look," said Bram, folding his hands calmly over the menu, "from what you've told me, Bunny's never received the attention or acclaim she deserved—the kind Lavinia always drew to herself. And yet wasn't Bunny the brains behind the Daughters of Sisyphus Society? Maybe her jealousy finally got the better of her. In a moment of rage she—"

"Whipped up a batch of cheese ball nuggets using just the right amount of poisonous flowers? It wasn't a moment of passion, Bram, it was premeditated murder. It's also exactly the kind of weapon someone would use if he or she didn't have a gun, or wasn't brutal enough to use a knife or a baseball bat."

"You *have* been thinking about this, haven't you?" he said, eyeing her uncertainly.

"Of course I have! Virtually everyone who might be implicated in this mess is someone I know. I may be way off base, but I think if we find that diary, we'll have a much clearer picture of who murdered both Ginger and Lavinia."

"You think it was the same person?"

"It's possible. Or at the very least, I think we'll find a connection."

"But," said Bram, pouring them each more wine, "the diary's been found. Whoever ransacked Lavinia's suite took it."

"Maybe," she said, a note of depression creeping into her voice. "On the other hand, maybe Lavinia outsmarted them. She hid it somewhere terribly clever and it's still around."

"Kind of a long shot."

She shrugged.

"And also, you've got to consider the fact that the diary might not have been what the murderer was looking for."

"I know that," said Sophie, meeting his eyes. "But if I'm wrong, all I'll be wasting is my time."

"I see. I assume that means you're planning to look for it."

She nodded.

"Am I going to be conscripted into this special forces team, too?"

She gazed at him languidly over the rim of her glass. "Kindly refrain from using your tasteless radio sarcasm on me, dear. The answer to your question is yes, I expect some help—if I need it, which I probably won't."

"Famous last words. You know, Soph, you can't go off half-cocked and get involved in an official murder investigation."

"I'm not getting involved," she said indignantly. "I'm just doing a little quiet checking around. I've done it before."

He shook his head.

"Look," said Sophie. "I told that detective all about Ginger and the diary. I'm sure they'll haul Bunny, Cindy, and Adelle in and talk to them. Who knows? Maybe it will take some of the heat off Peter. I hope it does."

"*If* he's innocent."

"Exactly. All I'm saying is that I want to look around the hotel for the diary. I'm not going to do anything dangerous."

He folded his arms over his chest. "But think about this. If one of your friends *is* a murderer, you could be in real danger."

"I'm aware of that. And I'll be careful."

He didn't seem convinced, but moved quickly on to his next worry. "What about this Morton character?"

Sophie'd been thinking about him ever since he'd frightened the wits out of her last night. "I don't know. I'm sure the police will want to talk to him again. But you know, I can't help but wonder about the money he had with him. Do you think he might have been in that parking ramp to get paid off? He didn't win the lottery, that's for sure."

"You mean someone hired him?"

"Possibly."

Bram's eyebrow arched upward. "To murder Lavinia?"

She gave a guarded nod.

"Listen, Sophie," he said, sitting up straight, "no more walking around in darkened parking ramps, okay? From now on I want you to have one of the bellmen get your car for you."

She'd already reached the same conclusion. "I promise. Believe me, I don't want to run into Morton any more than you want me to."

The waiter arrived to take their order.

"I'll have the grilled fresh tuna," said Bram, handing him the menu.

"And I'd like the black-bean cakes," said Sophie, handing hers over as well. She didn't feel much like eating, although sitting here with Bram, sharing a bottle of good wine, she did seem less anxious—even a little hopeful. After dinner they'd walk around the lake, maybe even take a stroll in the rose garden.

As the waiter returned to the kitchen with their orders, Bram sat back, shook his head, and sighed. "Why do I feel like we're the condemned couple about to eat a hearty meal?"

"Don't worry, darling. The health department consistently gives the Lyme House an A-plus rating."

"You're missing my point, *darling*."

"No I'm not," she said, patting his hand and smiling. "I'm just choosing to ignore it."

# 24

On Tuesday morning, after a less than restful night's sleep, Sophie drove over to the Maxfield Plaza to begin her search. Even though she had no idea where to look for the diary, she started with the assumption that the police had covered the suite with a fine-tooth comb. Consequently, she dispensed with that.

After spending several hours talking to all the bellmen, the staff at the front desk, and requesting that someone check the safe to see if there was anything inside with Lavinia's name on it, she returned to her father's office—now her office—and dropped with an air of failure into the leather desk chair. She hated to admit it, but perhaps Bram was right. Whoever had torn the suite apart had already found the diary. She was simply spinning her wheels.

As she gazed up at the oil portrait of her mother and father on the wall behind the desk, an idea occurred to her. What if Lavinia had given the book to someone for safekeeping? Sure. That was a possibility. But whom would she trust in a city where she barely knew a soul?

A name popped immediately to mind.

Lifting the Minneapolis White Pages from the bottom desk drawer, she once again looked up the number for Peter's parents' house in Edina. After punching in the numbers, a man's voice answered.

"Is Peter there?" asked Sophie, hoping she'd find him in.

"He's taking a shower," replied the man. Then, hesitating, he added, "Who is this?"

Sophie felt sorry for him. The last few days must have seemed like a nightmare for his family. Peter returns home for a visit, and a couple of days later the woman he's just married—and failed to tell them about—is murdered. "My name is Sophie Greenway. I was a friend of Lavinia Fiore." She decided not to mention that she was the one who'd called yesterday.

"I see," he said, his tone a mixture of reserve and relief. "I'm Peter's father. I thought for a second there that you might be with the police."

"No, no connection. But I would like to come over and speak with your son. Will he be around for a bit?"

"I'm sorry, I don't know. He's trying to plan a memorial service for the end of the week, but what with the police hounding him every minute, it's been hard to get anything done. I'm leaving in a couple of minutes myself. Would you like me to give him a message before I go?"

"That's not necessary. I'll just stop by and take my chances."

"All right." He hesitated. "He could use a friend right about now. You are . . . a friend, aren't you?"

"Yes, I am," said Sophie. She hoped that was true. After saying a quick goodbye, she sat back in her chair and gave herself a moment to plan her next move.

If Peter was in the shower, that gave her a little extra time. The freeway would be the fastest route. She'd been up so many blind alleys already this morning, what was one more dead end in the scheme of things?

Half an hour later she pulled up in front of a large, two-story brick house. Only one car was in the drive. It looked new, possibly a rental. And that meant Peter might still be home.

Easing out of the front seat, Sophie made straight for the front door. She rang the bell and then waited, glancing up at one of the second-story windows. The curtains parted briefly and then eased back together. Whoever was inside was being careful. She stood—quietly examining the shrubbery—for what seemed like an eternity before the door finally swung open. Peter appeared dressed in a gray-and-white-striped bathrobe, a towel draped around his shoulders. He didn't look surprised to see her, merely resigned.

"This is kind of a bad time," he began, making no move to ask her in.

"I know," said Sophie, nodding sadly. "I've heard about all the trouble you're having with the police. But I didn't come to talk about any of that."

"You didn't? Then why are you here?"

"I wanted to ask you about—" She hesitated. Lowering her voice she continued. "Something private."

"Like what?"

"Invite me in and I'll tell you." She hoped she'd piqued his curiosity.

"Oh, all right," he said, stepping back and allowing her to enter. "Come on," he said, leading the way through the kitchen to a three-season porch at the back of the house. After making himself comfortable on a wicker sofa, he said, "So what's up?"

Sophie sat down opposite him. He looked tired today, his good looks a bit frayed around the edges. He also seemed nervous, jumpy, fidgeting with the newspaper lying next to him on the couch, making as little eye contact as possible. She couldn't help but think it was a response to the hours of intense questioning he'd undergone at the police station. "First, let me tell you how sorry I am about what happened to Lavinia. We didn't get much of a chance to talk yesterday."

"Thanks." A small tremor passed across his face.

She watched him struggle to adopt a more impassive expression. "This may seem totally off-the-wall, Peter, but did Lavinia ever mention a diary to you? One that a woman named Ginger Pomejay kept back in the early Seventies?"

"Sure," he replied, his agitation easing just a bit as he saw that she really wasn't going to press him on the subject of his wife's murder. "The one who died back at that religious college you all attended. If I'm not mistaken, she brought the diary with her to Minnesota."

"Do you know why?"

"She wanted to confront someone with it. Someone she thought might have had a hand in Ginger's death."

"And do you know who that someone is?"

He looked away. "She asked me not to tell, not that I thought anyone would ever ask. She wanted to keep it a secret until she had a chance to talk to the man."

So it was a man, thought Sophie. Fascinating. "She didn't by any chance give the diary to you for safekeeping before she died?"

He shook his head. "Sorry."

"You have no idea where it might be?"

"None. Say, now that you bring it up, that's kind of funny. I saw a detailed list of her belongings in the police report this morning. They asked me to go through it and comment on what I thought might be missing. All I could see that was gone was her jewelry."

This was news to Sophie. The detective hadn't mentioned it. "You say her jewelry had been taken?"

"Every last scrap. But now that I think about it, someone must have taken that diary, too." He raked a hand through his clean, uncombed hair. "I loved her, Sophie. I've never loved anyone the way I did Lavinia. She was special. One of a kind. I felt so lucky when she agreed to be my wife. And now . . . why can't the police see that? Why would I want her jewelry? It makes no sense." He dropped his head in his hands and closed his eyes.

The pain on his face touched her deeply. She might be a romantic sap, but she had a hard time believing it was an act.

After almost a minute he wiped a hand across his face and looked up. "I'm such a pathetic fool," he whispered. "I deserve everything I get."

"Why would you say that?"

"Because . . ." His eyes slid past her.

He seemed to be having difficulty finding the right words. Sophie waited, then coaxed him by saying, "You can trust me, Peter. I believe you're innocent. I think the real reason Lavinia was murdered has to do with that diary."

"You do?"

She gave a grave nod.

"Then . . . if I tell you something, will you promise to keep it a secret—at least for now."

"You have my word of honor."

He got up and walked over to the far wall, turning his back to her. Placing a hand on the screen, he said, "The night Lavinia died, I wasn't home."

"Really?" Her instincts told her to play dumb.

"You have to understand. Mom and Dad didn't realize I was married. So, when an old girlfriend called a couple of weeks ago and asked for my phone number in California, they told her I was coming home soon. Without my knowledge, they arranged for her to come by on Saturday night as sort of a surprise. They even made reservations for us at one of my favorite restaurants. The entire evening was on them." He shook his head. "Mom's always wanted to see me married and happy. They like this girl a lot. Her name is Miranda. Since I couldn't exactly spill the beans and tell them I was married, I had to go along with it."

"You went out with Miranda."

He nodded. Turning around, he sat down on a wooden bench, folding his hands in front of him. "Miranda and I, well, we've always gotten along great. We've known each other since high school, even dated for a couple of years before I left for California. That night, she was really hot to renew our old relationship."

"She told you that?"

"Told me . . . and showed me."

A cold feeling grew in the pit of Sophie's stomach. "*Showed* you?"

He didn't respond immediately, but instead seemed to be weighing something in his mind. Finally, he said, "I don't know if you can understand this, but when Miranda and I broke up, she was the one who dumped me. What can I say? It was hard to take. It hurt a lot. When I saw her on Saturday night, the tables had turned. She wanted me back. It felt . . . good. Better than good."

"So you strung her along?"

He gave a guarded nod.

"Until four in the morning?"

His shoulders tensed. "We drove around for a while, then went back to her place."

"Did you sleep with her, Peter?"

"No! Absolutely not. We . . . kissed . . . and you know. Touched. I had way too much to drink. But I stopped it before it went too far."

A fine distinction, as far as she was concerned. She realized she was angry at him not only for what he'd done—betraying Lavinia's trust, abusing another woman's emotions just because he'd once been hurt by her—but also for trashing her own romantic notions of "true love."

"I left around four. By then I'd made it clear we weren't going to get back together."

"That was kind of you."

His eyes flicked to her and then away.

"Am I correct in thinking that this is why you don't want to give the police your alibi? If they call your ex-girlfriend for verification, she's going to verify a lot more than you want."

"I'll not only look like some sort of disgusting womanizer," he said, his eyes fixed on the floor, "but it will look as if I didn't love my wife."

"That's what I'd think."

"But it's not true!" he said, shooting off the bench. "I did love her. More than anything."

"But not enough to keep your hands off Miranda." She knew she was punishing him, but couldn't help herself.

"Okay, I accept what you're saying. It was wrong. *I* was wrong. No more excuses. But I didn't murder my wife. The police theory goes something like this. Because I'm going to inherit a lot of money—"

"Is that true, Peter? Are you going to inherit Lavinia's estate?"

He nodded. "They think I got rid of her for the inheritance. And now, if I have to produce a witness to prove I couldn't have done it, the witness will just make it look more and more like I didn't care about her. Like I really did have a motive. One of them even said, 'Hey, buddy, she was old and fat. You some kind of weirdo? If *you* didn't do it, maybe you had someone do it for you.' "

Sophie's eyes opened wide. She couldn't help herself—she thought of Morton. What if Peter had hired him?

"What?" he asked, staring down at her. "Something's upset you. What are you thinking?"

"Me? Nothing." He'd caught her off guard. Even so, she knew better than to voice her suspicions. "I, ah . . . I'm just listening to what you're saying."

"But you had a funny look on your face."

"I did?" She cleared her throat. "I guess I just don't like the word *fat*. It always rubs me the wrong way."

"Right," he said, nodding his agreement. "I understand. And I feel the same way. I could have decked that guy. We're way too stuck on looks in this country. Not that Lavinia wasn't a solid ten on the Richter scale—in my opinion."

Score one for Peter—that is, if he was telling the truth. She was no longer confident he was.

"But see," he said, sitting down across from her again, "if your theory is true, it gets me off the hook. Maybe you're right. Lavinia was pretty sure she knew who was behind your friend Ginger's death."

"Peter," said Sophie, choosing her words very carefully, "I don't mean for you to break a confidence, but it would help me a great deal if I knew who she suspected."

He wrung his hands together in front of him. "Well . . . I suppose. What the hell? The guy's name was Knox."

Sophie blinked her surprise. "Isaac Knox?"

"That's the one."

"But . . . how? Why?"

"I don't know. Lavinia never actually said. But she came here to confront him. She found out early last spring that he was going to be in the Twin Cities for a church holiday. That's why she insisted the D.O.S.S. convention be held here this year, instead of Chicago. She gave herself six months to find out everything she could on the guy, and then she was going to talk to him in person. She also thought someone in your old group might know something about it, so she finagled the reunion. She said the timing was perfect. She mentioned her suspicions last Friday night, right?"

Sophie nodded.

"I know she was planning to talk to all of you privately. Except . . . she never got a chance."

Sophie's mind was racing. What possible reason could Isaac Knox have had for hurting Ginger? Had she threatened him in some way? "Did Lavinia ever say *how* Isaac Knox did it? We all thought Ginger died of cancer."

His face drawn with fatigue, he replied, "I should have listened more carefully, Sophie. I'm sorry. I just don't remember."

Damn it all. If she could only find that diary!

"You believe me, don't you?" he asked, his eyes pleading with her for understanding. "I didn't hurt Lavinia. I couldn't. She was the best thing that ever happened to me."

In her youth, Sophie had often been a sucker for handsome and needy. Unfortunately for Peter, she'd grown up. "I'll promise you one thing," she said, rising and looking down at him. "I think that diary is important, and until I learn otherwise, I believe it played a role in Lavinia's death."

"You do believe me, then," he said, exhaling his relief. Rising quickly, he accompanied her to the front door. As he opened it he fixed her with his intense blue eyes. "Lavinia will be buried in New York, but I've planned a memorial service for her here, at Lakewood Cemetery, on Thursday evening. I hope you can come."

"Of course. I'll be there."

"Good. You know, Sophie, if I've only got one person in my corner, I'm glad it's you."

His handsomeness was seductive. So was his sincerity. Containing her ambivalence behind a forced smile, she nodded a quick goodbye and then walked back out to her car.

# 25

After returning to her office at the Maxfield, Sophie called Bram's private line at the radio station to give him an update. He picked up on the second ring.

"You'll never believe what I just found out," she said, her voice breathless with excitement. She settled into her father's leather chair with a growing sense that it now belonged to her.

"Hello to you, too," said Bram, a hint of sarcasm in his voice. "And yes, I'm fine. The show went well this morning, thanks for asking. I don't suppose you caught it?"

"No. Sorry."

"It was on crime in the Twin Cities."

"How timely," she said, matching his tone.

"I agree. And as Minnesota's revered radio lion, I was typically incisive, bringing great depth to the subject."

"I'm sure you did. But just listen, okay?"

"You have my full attention, my love. Shoot."

She doodled on a notepad as she talked. "I spent the last half hour talking to Peter. Get this. He said that the person Lavinia suspected of murdering Ginger was none other than Isaac Knox."

Bram whistled. "That *is* news. So what are you going to do?"

She'd been thinking about it all the way back to the hotel. "What can I do? Without the diary, everything I know is merely hearsay. The police certainly won't take it seriously. And I can hardly walk up to Isaac and say that I've *heard* there is a diary out there somewhere that *suggests* he may have had something to do with Ginger's death."

"Good point. I guess that means you didn't have any luck finding it this morning."

"None. Say, while we're on the subject of Peter, he said something else I found interesting. It seems the police accused him of hiring someone to murder Lavinia."

Another whistle. "What does that make you think of?"

"Exactly. Morton. The worst thing is, Peter's alibi for Saturday night is an ex-girlfriend. They were messing around back at her apartment until four in the morning."

"That guy's a total idiot. Do the police know?"

"Not yet."

"Jeez, Sophie. And you still think he's innocent? Not to put too fine a point on it, but sometimes your lack of cynicism drives me nuts."

"Meaning what?"

"That . . . you amaze me. After everything that's happened to you in your life, you still think the best of people."

"Is that so awful?"

"Yes. Because it makes you vulnerable. Forget Isaac Knox and the diary. Peter might as well plaster a bull's-eye on his shirt when the boys in blue find out he was cheating on his wife—now conveniently deceased. If he wasn't already their prime suspect, he soon will be."

In frustration, Sophie tossed her pencil on the desk, leaned back in her chair, and closed her eyes. Maybe Bram was right. Yet something inside her continued to resist the notion that Peter was a killer. "So where does that leave us?" she asked, her voice growing weary.

"Were we've always been," said Bram. "A couple of private citizens with a bad case of curiosity. Speaking of which, you weren't the only person this morning to ferret out some fascinating info. I had an enlightening conversation myself. It was during one of the hourly news breaks. You remember my buddy from the St. Paul Police Department? Al Lundquist?"

"How could I forget him. He punctuates every statement by cracking his knuckles."

"I've never noticed."

"Please."

"Anyway," continued Bram, "if you recall, Lavinia died somewhere between eleven and four in the morning. But . . . get this. Her room wasn't torn up until sometime after six."

"How on earth could they know that?"

"It seems that, while Lavinia was staying at the hotel, she'd ordered the *St. Paul Pioneer Press* to be brought up to her room every morning. The paper is delivered around six A.M. But on Sunday, the paper was already inside the room with some of Lavinia's belongings tossed on top of it. That means whoever ransacked the room didn't do it until *after* six on Sunday morning. They must have picked it up on their way in the door."

Sophie sat up straight. "That's . . . amazing."

"The police agree. It's an odd set of circumstances, but

undoubtedly significant. Did you know Lavinia's jewelry was missing?"

"Peter told me."

"Okay, so if the point of the murder was to get her out of the way so that the murderer could search the room for valuables, why didn't they do it right away?"

"I . . . don't know." She gave herself a moment to think it through. "Maybe they're separate issues—the killer and the thief weren't the same person."

"But it had to be someone with a key, Sophie. Other than Peter, the only person with access to one was Lavinia's murderer. He or she could have easily removed it from her purse after she was dead. Remember, there was no sign of breaking and entering."

This was fascinating, thought Sophie. And frustrating. "Lavinia called the front desk for a wake-up call around midnight."

"*If* it was Lavinia who made the call. Think about it, Soph. It could have been her killer who called."

She hadn't thought of that. "But why?"

"Simple," said Bram. "They needed more time. Lavinia asked for a noon wake-up call, right? That ensured that the hotel staff wouldn't make any attempt to clean the room until after lunch. It gave the killer all morning to get back and search the place—without someone going in and discovering a dead body first."

"This is incredible."

"I agree."

"But let's backtrack a second," she said, picking up her pencil again. "You mentioned that Peter probably has a key."

"Most likely."

"But if he was the killer, what was he searching the room for? It couldn't be the diary. He didn't kill Ginger."

"I don't have the answer."

She hesitated, and then continued. "Do the police really think she was murdered for her jewelry?"

"Al didn't say anything about that directly, but it hardly

seems likely. If you ask me, whoever took those jewels did it as a cover."

"So, we're stuck with the same question. The room was obviously searched. What was being sought?"

"I hate to admit it, Sophie, but your diary theory is, so far, the only one on the table that makes any sense."

"Bingo!"

"Don't get ahead of yourself, dear. I'm sure other theories will develop."

"Well," she said, tossing her pencil on the desk once again, "all I can say is, I've had about as much sleuthing as I can take for one day."

"Really? Why do I find that hard to believe?"

She let his annoyingly amused tone slide past her. "We're short one person on the front desk this afternoon. I think I'll spend the rest of the day helping out."

"A good way to put your finger on the pulse of the hotel," agreed Bram. "I'll see you at home later. We can continue our discussion over dinner."

"Fine. I'll pick up some take-out Chinese on the way. Oh, and don't forget to stop by the cleaners to pick up your shirts. They should be done by four."

"I need a wife."

"Me, too," she said, grinning. "But we can't afford one. They're *very* expensive. Later, sweetheart."

For the next two hours Sophie answered phones, checked guests in and out, and generally handled whatever problems came her way. Even as a teenager, she'd always liked working at the reception desk. Right now, however, she was particularly glad for this respite from the murder investigation. She needed some time to think, to mull over the facts of the case, at least as she knew them so far.

Around two, she saw a familiar face emerge from the elevator and head her way.

Isaac Knox, flanked by four gray-haired men in expensive business suits, approached the marble counter. Before another clerk could offer assistance, Sophie stepped up to them, a friendly smile on her face. It took a moment for the significance of his entourage to sink in. When it did, she realized she was facing four of the highest-ranking ministers in the Church of the Firstborn. She hadn't seen them in years, which probably accounted for why she didn't immediately recognize them.

"Good afternoon," said Isaac in his deepest register. "I'm sure you remember my friends here." He swept his hand to the men with more than a little grandiosity, almost as if he were introducing royalty.

"Of course," said Sophie, nodding pleasantly. It was a stretch. "How can I help you?"

"They each need a room for the next couple of nights."

She tried not to act surprised, though the more she thought about it, the screwier it all seemed. On Sunday morning, Sophie had seen three evangelists with Isaac Knox. Today, here were four more. Counting Hugh and Isaac, that made nine evangelists in one place at one time. She couldn't help but wonder why.

"Do you have rooms available?" asked Isaac, the impatience showing.

Sophie knew she better stop gawking and get down to business. "I'm sure we do," she said, typing the appropriate codes into the computer. Most of the members of the D.O.S.S. convention had left on Monday, leaving the hotel fairly open for the next few days.

"If you have suites available, that would be our first preference."

"Of course."

"Nonsmoking," he added, leaning toward her over the counter.

As she was about to suggest rooms on the tenth floor, she glanced over his shoulder and saw another familiar face enter through the glass front doors. Howell Purdis, wearing a pair of furry blue bedroom slippers with bright yellow tassels dangling off the tops, paused briefly next to the bell stand, waiting as three other men, each carrying several pieces of luggage, caught up to him. Making sure they were safely in tow, he steamed resolutely across the carpet, heading straight for the desk. Sophie recognized this new group as more evangelists. This growing assemblage of top brass at a single holy-day site was getting stranger by the minute.

Isaac squared his shoulders and straightened his back as Howell moved up next to him.

They glared at each other for several long seconds and then Howell turned to Sophie and announced, "I've already arranged for three more rooms. We're here to get the keys."

"Certainly," said Sophie. Since these ministers had known each other for years and were supposedly great friends, their lack of eye contact not only surprised, but baffled her. "I'll be done here in just a second."

Howell seemed more than aggravated that he had to wait.

As the men all stood staring straight ahead, Bunny approached the counter cautiously and leaned her elbow next to Sophie. "When you're done, maybe we could have a cup of coffee?"

"Sure," said Sophie, returning her attention to the computer. "I'd love to. Just give me a couple of minutes."

"No problem." She turned to one of the ministers, eyeing him curiously. When he glared back at her, her expression turned angry. "Sorry. Did I forget to wipe the triple-six off my forehead?"

A couple of the ministers glanced at her dismissively, but no one made a move to comment. Silence seemed to be the order of the day.

As Sophie typed away, getting everyone set up with a room, she was dying to know what was going on. Everyone seemed not only ill at ease, but also, interestingly enough, on different sides of some great divide. The four men Isaac had brought with him were careful not to connect in any way with the three men accompanying Howell Purdis.

After requesting some help from one of the other clerks, Sophie finished with all the check-ins, handing everyone a key.

"Thank you," said Isaac formally. He turned to Howell.

"Our meeting is scheduled for four tomorrow afternoon. We should be done in time to announce the results at Bible study."

"Fine," said Howell, his tone curiously subdued. "We'll be there." He padded doggedly off toward the elevators, followed at a suitable distance by his Three Stooges. Sophie knew it was an unflattering characterization, and she loved every inch of it.

"Looks like you're lining up for a battle," said Bunny, still leaning on the marble counter. Her casual body language was as much of a comment as her amused look.

Isaac's frown deepened as he muttered, "It's none of your business. Come on," he said to the four men standing next to him. "I need some fresh air."

The tension surrounding them traveled like a miasmic cloud, floating with them and disappearing out the front door as they made their hasty exit.

# 26

From two to four every weekday afternoon, the Maxfield Plaza served a proper St. Paul tea in the hotel's atrium, a rear court tucked snugly between the two towers, enclosed under an ornate glass-block-and-steel skylight. Small round tables were covered with the finest Irish linen. Amid the tinkling of teacups and soft classical music played by a young man seated at a grand piano near the garden entrance, the rich perfume of freshly baked scones and cakes wafted through the crowd.

Afternoon tea at the Maxfield was a St. Paul tradition. Though it was usually packed with Twin Citians seeking a respite from a hectic business or shopping day, the subdued conversations lent an easy, comfortable air to the open courtyard.

"With all these ministers milling around," muttered Bunny, making herself comfortable on one of the brocade armchairs, "I feel like I'm back at college. Except my face doesn't hurt from all that eternal smiling."

Sophie laughed as she sat down next to her, glad for the opportunity to talk. "Do you know what's going on? How come so many of the evangelists are in town right now?"

Bunny shrugged. "Adelle told me Isaac Knox is making a play to replace Howell Purdis as head of the church."

"You're kidding."

"Don't you think it's about time somebody challenged that old bag of wind?"

"Sure, but they're all cut from the same cloth—all those ministers spending their lives poring over ancient texts, strangling some new meaning out of two or three words. They've spent their whole lives boring deeply into twigs."

"Well put," said Bunny, crossing one leg casually over the other. "It's amazing, isn't it? That church is still going strong—still ruining people's lives."

"You really feel that way?" asked Sophie. Nobody had said much about the church at the reunion the other night, although she pretty much assumed Adelle's presence had caused the reticence.

"Of course I do. Don't you?"

"You better believe it. I don't have anything against morals and values, but the way Howell Purdis uses religion to control people's lives, well, all I can say is, it's destructive. I spent many years hating that man, and everything and everyone associated with the church."

"Especially after Norm got custody of your son."

Everyone in her old group knew the story. "I wanted nothing more than to have a hand in raising him, but Norm—in his infinite wisdom—wouldn't allow it. Since he'd been given full custody, he was in charge. As far as he was concerned, if I wasn't a member of the church, I was unfit to even be *around* Rudy."

"I'm really sorry, Sophie. It must have been terrible."

"It was. When a church plants itself between a parent and a child, I think it's wrong. Worse than wrong. It's evil. Adults can argue all they want about truth and error, but separating a mother from her child is unforgivable, and I've never—nor will I ever—forgive any of them."

"You know," said Bunny, her unblinking eyes holding Sophie's, "you did everything right. You knuckled under, succeeded in college, married a minister. Yet in many ways, you were screwed worse than any of us."

Sophie looked down at her hands. "It's only been the last few years that I've been able to talk about that time in my life with any degree of rationality. I suppose it's why I never wanted much contact with you, or any of the others from Terrace Lane. Keeping up with the gossip, rehashing old times—it just hurt too much."

Bunny nodded, looking up as a waiter arrived with a menu.

"I think we know what we want," said Sophie, forcing her voice to sound something other than grim. She was glad for the interruption, and for the change of subject she hoped it would bring. "By the way, tea is on the house."

"Hey," said Bunny, a delighted look on her face. "You don't have to do that."

"I know." Sophie smiled.

"What kind of tea would you like?" asked the waiter. "China or Indian?"

Bunny shrugged.

"Let's have the Indian," said Sophie. "And a mixed tray." As he walked away Sophie noticed Bunny examining the skylight with great curiosity. "Is this the first time you've eaten in the atrium?"

Bunny nodded. "I spent a little time in the garden the other day. I sat with Adelle and had a cup of coffee. But this is the first time I've been in here."

"Just for the record, teas are a lot like wines," said Sophie. "The soil, altitude, and climate influence the final flavor, and no two vintages are exactly alike. We have our teas blended by a local distributor to ensure a consistent quality and taste."

"You know something, Soph?" She folded her arms over her chest. "You haven't changed in over twenty-five years. You're still fascinated by anything that has to do with food and drink."

"At least I'm consistent."

"That you are." Bunny smiled. "As I think about it, none of us has changed all that much. Take Adelle for instance. She still has all the warmth and charm of a rattlesnake."

"But look where it got her," said Sophie. "She married the second most powerful man in the church."

"True. But is she happy? I may be way off base, but I don't think so." She removed her glasses and, for a moment, rubbed her eyes. "And then, of course, there's me. I just wanted to be left alone to think and read. It's perhaps an understatement to say I wasn't the minister's-wife type."

"Were you always attracted to women?" asked Sophie, hoping she wasn't asking too personal a question.

"As far back as I can remember. I fought it with every ounce of strength in me, but in the end, I couldn't stuff my sexuality back into the bottle, not even for God."

"I'm sure it must have been hard for you. I know it was tough for my son."

"You have no idea. A lesbian and an introvert among the fundamentalist elite. Talk about not fitting *anywhere*."

"None of us felt like we fit, Bun."

"Maybe. But you ... you always seemed to be exactly what they were looking for. On top of your studies. Committed. Good-looking."

Sophie's eyebrow arched upward. "I was?"

"Sure. You know, I never understood why the dean of women put you on the Terrace Lane diet. You were just round, what some might call voluptuous."

Sophie felt herself begin to blush. "I think I passed the voluptuous point long ago."

"That's nonsense. You look great. You're an only child, right?"

She nodded.

"That's what I thought. It's probably why you're such an overachiever."

"Coming from someone with a doctorate, I'll take that as a compliment."

"You should." Her smile was warm. "You know, it was as if Howell Purdis had this team he was building. All the guys had to be quarterbacks and all the women had to be cheerleaders. If you deviated from the image, you were either punished, or relegated to some menial position."

An apt description. "Are your parents still in the church?"

"Dad is. So are my two brothers. Mom died about ten years ago. She had a bad heart. Actually, she was sick pretty much all the time I was in college. In a way, I suppose, that's why I never left. I thought about it more than once, but I knew if I took off, the embarrassment and the worry would kill her."

The waiter arrived with the tea. He placed the china cups and saucers on the table in front of them and then lifted the round metal teapot onto a trivet. After lighting the spirit lamp underneath it to keep it warm, he set the milk and sugar in front of Sophie.

Bunny closed her eyes. "It smells wonderful."

Sophie poured. "When I have the Indian, I usually use milk and sugar. It has a rather hearty malt flavor."

"Just milk for me," said Bunny. "It's really amazing to think you own this hotel now. But . . . it must be awful for you—having Lavinia die here."

"Awful for me, but worse for her."

"Yeah. You know, I talked to the police this morning. They had some questions about Ginger's diary, among other things."

"Really. And what did you tell them?"

"The same stuff you probably did. Oh, they wanted to know if I was mad at Lavinia for anything. Apparently they'd already talked to Cindy. She told them I was furious about the exercise video."

"Weren't you?"

"Absolutely. I thought Lavinia had lost her marbles. I can't conceive of why she'd want to attach the D.O.S.S. name to something like that. I mean, our intent, as an organization, is to focus women's energy *away* from their bodies. Did you hear about that recent study McGill University did?"

Sophie shook her head.

"They took a hard look at people who lived their entire lives on low-fat low-cholesterol, controlled-intake diets. The researchers concluded that these people succeeded in extending their lives by only a few weeks."

"Fascinating."

"Now, of course, that's only one study. And it doesn't mean that I disagree about the importance of regular exercise. We should all try to lead healthy lives. But good health doesn't always conform to high fashion or culturally defined ideas of beauty. Lavinia knew there was already an overabundance of information on exercise and nutrition out there. *We* hardly need to provide more. What our organization does provide is a place where women can meet and socialize, and *not* obsess about how they look. It's amazing how often women lose weight when they focus on what they're really hungry for."

Sophie could tell she was on a soapbox, but she could also see her point. "Did you say any of that to Lavinia?"

"Why would I need to? How on earth could she not get the point?" She removed a pack of cigarettes from her blazer pocket and slipped one out.

"You can't smoke in here," said Sophie, reminding her gently.

"I know," she said gruffly. "I just need to hold one in my hand. It helps me think." Tapping it on the table, she continued, "I always knew Lavinia was philosophically shallow, but this video borders on the philosophically *obscene*."

"Why do you think she did it?"

"It was Peter's idea. It had to be. From what I can tell, he set the whole thing up. He stands to make a lot of money from the video, if it sells. And since both Lavinia's name and the D.O.S.S. are associated with it, it will."

"Do you dislike Peter?"

"I don't like fortune hunters," she said flatly.

"You think that's what he is?"

"Why else would he marry her?"

Sophie saw this comment as a bit of a double standard. "You mean Lavinia was older and less attractive than he was."

"Old and fat. How could a man like Peter be attracted to that?"

"But, Bunny, aren't you defeating your own principles with that kind of statement? Maybe he saw past the superficial and truly came to appreciate Lavinia for who she really was. Her humor, her playfulness, her energy."

"Right. And I'm Madonna."

The waiter appeared once again, this time carrying two smallish tea plates and a round, three-tiered silver tray. Setting it all down, he said, "The bottom tier contains the savories. Today we have an assortment of pinwheel sandwiches. The fillings are lobster salad, cucumber and cream cheese, smoked cod roe, and chopped egg and watercress. The top two tiers are the sweets. Dundee bread. Hot buttered scones, clotted cream, and strawberry jam. Peach tartlets. And of course, the Maxfield's famous homemade brandy cake. Enjoy, ladies." He bowed slightly and then moved on to another table.

"This is a feast," said Bunny, her eyes glowing as she examined the contents of the tray. "I don't know where to begin."

"Try a sandwich," said Sophie, selecting one herself. Her favorite—a Bengal spread made with butter, anchovy paste, chopped egg, curry powder, lemon, and cayenne pepper—wasn't on the menu today.

Bunny took several.

"So," continued Sophie, taking a sip of tea, "you and Lavinia never actually connected?"

"I was hoping to talk to her on Sunday morning, before the last day of the convention got under way. But I couldn't find her."

"You know, Bun, I haven't mentioned this before, but I

saw you standing outside her door on Sunday morning. It was around eleven."

She stopped chewing. "You did?"

"Lavinia and I had made a date for brunch. When she didn't show up, I thought I'd see what the problem was. So I took the service elevator up to the fourteenth floor."

"That's right," said Bunny. "I knocked and knocked, but she never answered. I guess . . . she was already dead."

"I suppose so. Did I tell you I talked to Peter this morning? I asked him if Lavinia had ever mentioned the diary to him."

"And?" she said, pausing mid-chew.

"She had. He even gave me the name of the person Lavinia suspected of murdering Ginger."

Bunny's eyes opened wide. It was either surprise or alarm, thought Sophie. She couldn't tell which.

"Who?" demanded Bunny.

"Isaac Knox."

She sat back in her chair and looked away, digesting this for some moments in silence. Then, bursting into laughter, she said, "Ginger wasn't in love with Isaac Knox."

It wasn't a response Sophie had anticipated. "It seems strange to me, too. On the other hand, without actually seeing the diary, it's hard to assess what Lavinia was getting at. Was Ginger in love with someone and Isaac found out about it? Made some move to put a stop to it and ended up by doing more damage than he'd intended. Or was she in love with him?"

"It's all nonsense," said Bunny with a dismissive wave. "I'll believe it when I see the proof, which, I should point out, no one has seen so far. When Lavinia brought up the subject of the diary at that bar the other night, she really had me going. I know this sounds crazy, but I thought she was suggesting the diary implicated *me* as Ginger's lover. Can you picture it? I was so deep in the closet back then, I couldn't have been found with six floodlights and a bloodhound. To think Ginger and I were in love—" She picked up her cigarette and began tapping it on the table once again. "Ridiculous."

Sophie picked up the pot and offered Bunny more tea.

Dragging the cup and saucer in front of her, Bunny took a deep breath, attempting to calm herself down. "I'm sorry," she said, running a hand through her short brown hair, "but these past few days have been terribly frustrating for me. I didn't like being mad at Lavinia, but sometimes she acted like such an ass. Even now, I find it hard to let my anger go."

"I understand," said Sophie. And she did.

"After her death became public knowledge on Sunday evening, what was left of the D.O.S.S. leadership—those who hadn't already left for the airport—called a crisis meeting. They asked me to attend. The upshot is, I was offered the presidency of the organization."

It was Sophie's turn to be surprised. "Did you accept?"

"Of course. How could I turn it down? Especially with the direction—or I should say, the lack of direction—of the past few years. Lavinia was turning the organization into her own private industry. She'd made millions off her cookbook, but that wasn't enough. Sure, she gave generously of her time and money to the organization, but the copyrights—and the title of the organization—remained hers. This new scheme—the video—would have netted many more millions. I intend to put a stop to it. We'll sue her estate for the sole right to use the name Daughters of Sisyphus Society. And we'll win."

By the determined look in her friend's eye, Sophie had no trouble believing it.

"Lavinia was misusing her power," continued Bunny. "Destroying something that took years to build. You talked about loving your child. Well, this was *my* child. And it was in trouble. There was no oversight committee, financial or philosophical. Nobody really knew what local chapters were doing or not doing. Lavinia's style was way too loose, too shoot-from-the-hip. I simply couldn't stand by and watch the chaos any longer."

Sophie found it an odd statement. "So what did you do about it?"

"Do?" she repeated, raising the cigarette to her lips, and then, realizing it wasn't lit, tossing it on the table. "I . . . took the head job when it was offered to me. What did you think I meant?"

Bunny sounded unusually defensive. "I don't know," said Sophie.

"Well, rest assured, I'm not going to allow these sloppy management practices to continue. Since most of the board members are staying in town for Lavinia's memorial service on Thursday, I called another meeting for tomorrow afternoon. It's funny," she added. "Cindy is the only one who isn't in sync on this. If you ask me, she's been acting strangely all weekend."

"In what way?" asked Sophie.

"Oh, I don't know." She picked at a piece of cake. "She seems . . . too quiet one minute, and too talkative the next. It's like . . . she's on stage and she's got a bad case of stage fright. She's more self-conscious than I've ever seen her. You know how she always likes to act confident, like she's in charge. As far as I can tell, she hasn't changed, but there's an edge to it now." She took a sip of tea and then pushed the cup and saucer away. "She can't exactly get out of this meeting, can she? She's the national treasurer."

"So I understand."

"She was supposed to present her financial report at last Saturday morning's breakfast meeting, but you know what kind of circus that turned into." She shivered with distaste.

"I assume that means you didn't buy one of the exercise tapes."

Bunny gave her a fish-eyed stare. "I left my wallet at home."

"That's what I figured."

"The video was the last straw, Sophie. Something inside me snapped when I saw it."

"Did it?"

"Yes," she said firmly. "But it's history now. A new day is dawning for the Daughters of Sisyphus Society. And I'm proud to be the one leading the way."

# 27

The doors opened and Hugh Purdis stepped onto the empty elevator. He needed to get out of the suite for a little while and take a walk, breathe some fresh air and work off some of his growing tension. There were no services this afternoon, only another Bible study tonight, and thankfully, he wasn't presiding. He was scheduled to lead the study tomorrow evening, and thinking about it now, he knew what he wanted to talk about.

The topic of predestination had always intrigued him, ever since he was a child. Did God have a plan for every human being's life? Was it all mapped out for you in advance, no matter how hard you tried to convince yourself you were the master of your own fate?

Hugh knew well his father's teaching on the subject. To be able to make moral decisions, humans must be allowed to exercise free will. The whole point of existence was to build godly character so that one day a person could join God as a member of His family.

Yet, was that really true? Was a man in charge of his own destiny? Hugh wasn't so sure anymore. As much as he wanted to believe the message he'd been taught—the message *he'd* taught others for over thirty years—his faith was faltering.

Time after time, the decisions he'd made in his life had been sabotaged, undermined, and ultimately—against his will—wrested from his control. Was an unseen hand at work? And if so, was it useless to fight against it?

As the small compartment sped downward Hugh moved next to the control panel, gazing up at the descending numbers above the door. On the sixth floor, the doors opened. Isaac Knox stood facing him.

"Is this going down?" asked Isaac, his voice cold.

Hugh nodded.

He stepped on.

After the doors closed, Isaac eased back against the opposite-side wall and stared directly at Hugh. He waited several seconds and then said, "I suppose your father told you I already have seven evangelists in my camp."

Hugh cleared his throat. "Yeah. Something to that effect."

Clasping his hands in front of him, Isaac allowed himself a small smile. "Remember, Hugh Abraham. I need your decision by tomorrow morning. The earlier the better."

"Don't call me that," he said gruffly. "You know I loathe my middle name."

"No? The father of nations? Your dad must have liked it. He probably thought it was your calling. Your destiny."

"Right," said Hugh under his breath. Something twisted inside him. Looking up at Isaac, he realized for the first time that what he was feeling was pure hate.

"Just remember. You've got nothing if you stay with your dad. Come with us, Hugh. This new church will be a fulfillment of the brightness of His promise. We'll all work together. We'll build something strong and decent. Not with domination and demands, but with love and brotherhood. Let no man take thy crown, Hugh. Not even your father."

Words, thought Hugh. Just words. Clenching his hands into fists behind his back, he replied, "You'll have your answer by tonight, Isaac."

"Really? That's wonderful." He seemed not only surprised,

but delighted. "I'll be at dinner until close to nine. After that, you can reach me in my room."

"Fine."

# 28

Rudy stuck his head inside Sophie's office door. "I thought I might find you in here."

"Hi!" She smiled, delighted to see him. She was sitting at the desk, gazing up at a computer terminal. Since she didn't have to be home for another hour, she'd decided to use the time to familiarize herself with her father's personal filing system.

Rudy was wearing his chef's uniform. By the looks of it, he'd been attacked by something large and red. "I dropped a can of tomato sauce," he said, looking somewhat embarrassed. He stood in the center of the room, sniffing the air. "Something's missing."

"Like what?"

He thought for a minute and then snapped his fingers. "The cigar. It seems so weird to be in here and not choke to death on secondhand smoke."

"Actually, I found a couple of Havana specials in the desk," said Sophie, giving him a mischievous wink. "Maybe I'll take it up—just so that you'll feel at home."

"No thanks." He crouched down next to her. "Have you found Grampa's computer solitaire game yet?"

"I haven't seen *any* games."

"That's because you don't know where to look."

She got up and allowed him to sit down in her place.

"See? It's under Stress Management." He clicked on an icon and a solitaire game popped up on the screen. "And look at this," he said, clicking to another screen. "Here's a record of his wins and losses. He told me he's been playing on the computer for three years, but before that, he played the old-fashioned way. It's all here. Every detail. How many games per day. His longest winning streak, and his longest losing streak. He's even got his old deck of cards in the bottom drawer of the desk."

Sophie could still see her father sitting at the kitchen table in her childhood home on Dupont Avenue in south Minneapolis, playing his card games after dinner. He always played for exactly half an hour—no more, no less. When he was done, they'd go for a walk, or sit down to watch something on TV. Henry Tahtinen was a disciplined man. He liked his routine. Before he became the owner of the Maxfield Plaza, he'd been a salesman—and a very successful one at that.

Sophie lowered herself into the chair on the other side of the desk, watching her son scroll through several more screens. It had taken her years to become comfortable with computers, but Rudy, like most young people, had grown up with them. "I'm stopping at the Ho Min on the way home to pick up some Chinese food. You want to join us for dinner?"

He clicked a few more keys and then sat back, a serious look forming on his handsome face. "Mom, I wanted to talk to you about something. It's kind of important."

She wasn't sure she liked the sound of that. "What is it?" she said, keeping her voice even.

"Well . . . actually, I was thinking of moving."

For a moment she was too startled to speak. "Moving? Why? Aren't you happy living with Bram and me?"

"Of course I am. You two have been great—more than generous. But . . . I just thought—" He rolled the chair directly in front of the desk and began again. "For the last few months things have gotten pretty serious between John and me. We've been dating for almost two years now. I just think that moving in together should be . . . you know. The next step in our relationship."

"What does that mean?"

"It means . . . we're planning a commitment ceremony. Sometime before Christmas."

Sophie wasn't sure how to respond. Sure, she knew they'd been dating—seriously dating. But Rudy was only twenty. Much too young. "Are you sure you've thought this all through?"

He gave her a slow smile. "If I'd been dating a young woman for two years, would you object to my marrying her?"

She hesitated. "Yes. I'd probably try to talk you out of it. It's too soon to settle down. You have your whole life ahead of you. Why rush it?"

"But you got married when you were my age. Could anyone have talked you out of it?"

"No," she said, conceding his point. "But we're not really talking about marriage here. You'd just be moving in together."

His smile faded. "Listen to me for a minute, Mom, and try to understand." Folding his hands patiently on the desktop, he continued, "I'm in love with John. Society thinks all gay men are promiscuous, that we can't commit. All we're interested in is one thing. Sex. We move from partner to partner as the mood strikes us. On the other hand, that same society refuses to allow us to marry—to commit legally. It's crap, Mom. We can't win. I know I'm young, but both John and I want to build a life together. Don't you think I know that there aren't any guarantees in my life—for anybody? But we're going to try as hard as we can to make this relationship work, with or without society's sanction. I hope we don't have to do it without yours."

"But . . . what about your degree?" She was grasping at straws, and felt foolish the moment she'd said it.

"I've only got a year or so left. Then I'll have a choice to make. I love working here. I think I'd make a pretty good chef, if I got some real training. And then, of course, there's acting. That will always be an interest. But lately, I've been thinking about something else."

She was almost afraid to ask. "What?"

"Entering the seminary."

Her expression froze. "You want to be a minister?" She knew her son was still quite religious. Though his upbringing had been in the Church of the Firstborn, he'd pretty much rejected most of that. But a seminary—this was something new. Something completely unanticipated.

"It's just an idea, Mom. I haven't made any decisions yet."

"Good."

His smile was gentle. "I know you feel bad that you missed so much of my childhood. But you won't lose me again. I'm in your life for good now—you couldn't get rid of me if you tried. But I can't go on living with you and Bram forever. I'm an adult. I want to get out on my own. I'm earning a pretty good wage at the hotel right now. And since I know the lady in charge, there might even be a raise in my future."

"Anything I have, anything you ever need is yours."

"I know that. But I don't want to be *given* my life. I want to go out and earn it—one that makes sense. I want a life that's filled with the same kind of love and contentment you and Bram have."

She couldn't argue with that. "Of course you have my blessing, Rudy. You already know how Bram and I feel about John."

"That means more than anything."

He was such a great kid. The sight of him could melt her heart.

"Thanks for letting me get that off my chest."

"I'm glad you did." At least she was *sort of* glad. She'd have to think about it a bit more before she'd be *really* glad, but that would probably come in time, too.

"So," he said, rolling the chair back in front of the computer and punching a few more keys. "Were you trying to find something specific in the hotel system?"

Sophie felt he was changing the subject a bit too quickly, but decided to go along with it. For now. "Yes. Actually, I've spent all day looking for a needle in a haystack."

"Can you be a little more specific?"

"It's a long story."

He checked his watch. "And I've got to get going. John's expecting me. But I'm intrigued. Just give me a clue."

"I'm searching for a diary, one that Lavinia Fiore brought with her to Minnesota."

"Hmm. I see."

She could tell he wanted to know more, but was torn. He hated being late.

"Have you checked the hotel safe file?" he asked, flipping to another screen.

"Not to change the subject, but how did you become so knowledgeable about the Maxfield's filing system?"

He shrugged. "Grampa showed me. Ever since I came to Minnesota, he's been wanting me to come work over here, you know that. I wasn't much interested in the front-desk job he offered, but when the cook position opened up, that was another story." He squinted at the screen. "Nope, nothing in the safe from Lavinia Fiore. Sorry."

It wasn't news. "Thanks for trying to help."

"No problem. Now, sorry but I gotta hit the bricks." He pushed out of his chair. On the way past her he leaned over and gave her a peck on the cheek. "I'll tell John we finally had a talk."

"You do that."

"Later, Mom." He closed the door on his way out.

Sophie resumed her place behind the computer. She only had a few more minutes before she had to leave herself, and there were a couple other areas of the system she wanted to check before she called it a day. As she gazed up at the list of guests who currently had stored valuables in the safe, a name caught her eye. Scrolling down, she clicked on the number opposite the name and found that a package had been entrusted to the Maxfield's care the previous Thursday evening by a Ms. Martha Finchley. No room number had been given.

This was too close to be a coincidence. Martha Finchley was the silly alias Lavinia had used to order pizzas from a local pizza joint the year they'd all lived together at Terrace Lane. If they got caught, it was her head that would roll. Consequently, she insisted on using a fake name to place the order. When she wasn't around, sometimes Sophie or Bunny would do it—but always in the name of Martha Finchley. Even now, Sophie continued to use the name when she wanted to remain anonymous. It was almost a reflex.

Her heart began to race. Could this be it? Had Lavinia stored the diary in the hotel safe after all? She buzzed the front desk and asked to have the package brought to her. Rising from her chair, she began to pace in front of the couch. No one on the hotel staff would have associated the two names—no one except her. Feeling the thrill of the hunt, she began to pace even faster. Moments later there was a knock on the door.

"Come in," said Sophie, taking the package from the young man's hand. "Thanks," she said, barely able to control her excitement.

She sat down at the desk, took a deep breath, and then opened the sealed manila envelope. She felt her heart skip a beat as a book about the size of a Bible slipped from the package into her hand. The word DIARY was stamped in gold letters on the front cover. She touched the leather reverently, feeling a sense of awe as she realized these were the thoughts of a woman long dead, perhaps even the key to her death. She held it a moment longer and then opened it. Inside were the printed words "This diary belongs to—" In purple ink, Ginger had written her name.

"Yes!" she shouted, thrusting a fist into the air. "Yes! Yes! Yes!"

Grabbing her purse, she switched off the computer and headed for the door.

She had some serious reading to do!

## 29

After dumping the cartons of take-out food on the counter, Sophie pushed her sunglasses on top of her head and sat down at the kitchen table. She removed the diary from her purse began to read. Most of it was fluff—easy to skim and dismiss. The real story didn't seem to start until midterm, when Ginger was offered a new job on campus. And then, nothing stood out as particularly important until early March. This was the point where Sophie began to read critically.

Half an hour later Bram breezed in through the back door. "Lucy, honey, I'm home," he crooned. He examined the small cartons briefly and then said, "Are we expecting company? You bought enough for an army." When she didn't respond, he walked over, bent down, and whispered in her ear, "Did you invite the Mertzes without consulting me first? If you did, you've got some serious 'splaining to do."

She patted the side of his face but kept on reading.

"What have you got there?"

"Ginger's diary."

"What!" He grabbed it out of her hand, examining the front cover. "Is this a joke?"

"Do I look like I'm joking?"

"But—" He seemed at a loss for words. A rare occurrence in the Greenway-Baldric household. "When . . . How—"

She plucked it back. "Sit down," she said, motioning him to a chair. "I'll read you what I've discovered so far."

"Let's go in the living room. I want to be comfortable when I hear this."

"Whatever you say, dear."

"My, aren't *we* in a pliant mood."

"You could say that," she said, brushing her lips against his as she got up.

Once ensconced on the couch, Bram put his feet up on the coffee table, leaned back, and clasped his hands behind his head. "Start with how you found it. I don't want to miss a thing."

Sophie briefly recounted the story. When she was done, she paraphrased the first hundred or so pages. "The diary actually begins on the first day of class. We were all staying in different dorms then—the same assignments we'd had for the previous year. The new assignments weren't posted until a few weeks into the new term. That's when we all found out we'd been banished to Terrace Lane. Nothing of much significance happens until Ginger is offered a new job right around the end of November. I think this is important, so I'm going to read it to you verbatim."

"Read away," said Bram, closing his eyes.

Sophie began:

Isaac Knox called me into his office this morning. I expected to be chewed out because I'd been tardy to class a couple of times, but instead, he offered me a secretarial job. Can you believe it? I'm going to be working for him! In the administration building. I'm so thrilled, I can hardly stop smiling, singing, praising God! This means a raise in my salary, too. And it means I won't have to walk all the way down to the press building every morning. Isaac is incredibly kind—and handsome! I suppose I shouldn't say something like that about one of the elders, but I can't help it. I also can't believe that out of all the coeds on campus, he chose me!

"She doesn't say anything else about the new job until several weeks later," said Sophie. "Oh, I should tell you that the only ministers who actually had offices in the administration building were Isaac Knox, Hugh Purdis, and Howell Purdis. All the other ministers had their offices in the annex about a block away. But, of course, they were in and out all the time."

I'm not sure I'll ever get used to being around so many ministers. Sometimes I feel so nervous, I could just crawl in a hole. But then I tell myself, God must have put you here for a reason. Just smile and act natural. The act-natural part is hard when Howell Purdis walks by your desk. I can hardly believe I'm that close to God's apostle. Yesterday he stopped and asked if I liked my new job. All I could do was nod. He must not mind tongue-tied young women, because he smiled at me for a long time, even sat down and told me about some church area he was going to visit next month. He doesn't like to fly. Can you believe it? God's apostle doesn't like to fly. I thought only people like me ever got scared, but I think that's so human—so real. Isaac has been helping me with my shorthand. I'm getting better. He even suggested that I come by after hours to practice.

"A come-on if I've ever heard one," snorted Bram.

Sophie'd wondered the same thing. She flipped a few more pages. "Most of this next part is about moving into Terrace Lane. I didn't realize it at the time, but from the first week, Ginger and Cindy were at odds. If it wasn't how the desks should be arranged, it was how to handle the leftovers. I just figured they liked to argue, but it was more than that. It was a very real personality clash. I'd forgotten this, but Ginger mentions how often Cindy complained about the way the women in the Bible were treated. At the same time Cindy always had all these big ideas about her future. Unfortunately, in the church, she had very few career options. That was the basis of the huge fight she and Ginger had toward the end of the term."

"I'm glad you brought that up," said Bram, absentmindedly scratching his chest through his shirt. "You alluded to their fight a couple of times before, but you never told me what it was about."

"Well, to make a long story short, Cindy wanted to work in the letter-answering department. Because of the radio broadcast and the Bible correspondence course, the church got lots of questions from people all over the country. The problem was, up until then, only men had answered letters. They weren't actually doing the job of a minister, so they didn't have to be a firstborn—"

Bram interrupted her. "You mean to be a minister in that church, you had to be a firstborn male?"

"Absolutely. In the Old Testament, God used the Levites as priests. But after Christ came, we moved into the New Covenant Dispensation. Jesus was Mary's firstborn son. Thus, he was firstborn of the flesh. And, he was God the Father's firstborn son. So he was also the firstborn of the spirit. He set the standard for the New Covenant. We believed—as a matter of faith—that the disciples were also firstborn males.'"

"You took it on faith?"

"It's what Howell Purdis taught."

"I see," he said, continuing to scratch his chest. "And if he told you the world was flat, you would have believed that, too?"

"I hate to say it, but yes, I probably would have."

"So, since Hugh Purdis was his firstborn child, he could be a minister."

"Exactly. But women, even if they were firstborn, weren't allowed to preach. There's a scripture somewhere in one of the Epistles that says women aren't allowed to speak in church. I don't remember where it is anymore, but it was Cindy's contention that it had nothing to do with answering letters. As long as she could prove she was qualified—that she had the requisite biblical understanding and the ability to write clearly—then she should be allowed to work there. As you might expect, since it had always been one of the men's jobs, the pay was better. So she petitioned Hugh Purdis—he was in charge of the department at the time—to work answering letters. She made her case in a short position paper. The next week during assembly, Hugh announced that he was going to allow Cindy to take the same test as the men. If she passed, she could start work immediately. Well, of course, Cindy was thrilled, but the controversy it created spawned a minor firestorm. Everyone on campus was taking sides. Some thought Cindy should be allowed in, some thought it was nothing short of blasphemy."

"So what happened?" asked Bram.

"Well, Cindy brushed up all weekend on church doctrines, and on Monday morning she took the test with the rest of the senior men."

"And?"

"Three days later the results were announced. She'd failed."

"That surprises me."

"It surprised all of us, including Cindy. She was completely devastated. She couldn't understand it, so she asked to see the test. It took a while, but she finally got it back. When she did, she realized immediately that something was wrong. All the tests were typed, so there was no way to tell who'd altered it, but none of the responses were hers. She told Hugh Purdis what had happened, but since she had no proof, he wasn't sure how to handle it. And then, when he suggested she take the test again, the men put up such a stink that he had to rescind the offer. They said it constituted 'special privilege.' "

"Bastards."

"I agree."

"But what's this got to do with Ginger?" asked Bram.

"Several weeks before she died, she told Cindy the truth. She'd been the one who'd altered the test. Since she worked in the dean's office at the administration building, she had easy access to it. She felt strongly that Cindy had no business trying to do a man's job. If Hugh Purdis wasn't going to be strong and deny her request, Ginger felt it was up to her to see that God's will be done."

"Nasty."

"Everyone at Terrace Lane pretty much agreed with that assessment. We all thought it was horrible. Maybe, deep inside, Ginger came to feel the same way and that's why she couldn't keep it a secret any longer. At the time I guess I thought her admission was prompted by her failing health. She hadn't been feeling well and we all feared the worst. I figured she was trying to come clean, to make some sort of amends."

"How did Cindy take it when she found out?"

"She was furious. She stormed around the apartment for days, even threatened Ginger physically a couple of times. Nobody believed she meant it, of course, but it was still pretty intense. Then, all of a sudden Cindy just shut down. At first she wouldn't talk to anyone. Later she directed the 'mute but smoldering act' only toward Ginger."

"You think it was an act?"

"No. She meant it all right. After she found out the truth, she took the story to Hugh Purdis. Unfortunately, by then, so many other senior women had come forward demanding to take the test, he'd called a halt to the whole thing. So, in effect, Ginger had won. And Cindy, I have no doubt, never forgave her."

"Do you think Cindy had anything to do with Ginger's death?"

"It never occurred to me, not even for a moment. I knew there was a lot of bitterness between them, and that Cindy refused to be in the apartment while Ginger was dying. But later, after the college doctor came and pronounced her dead, it was all forgotten."

"Why's that?"

"There was no point."

He turned his head and looked at her. "Meaning?"

"The church doctor established the official cause of death. We all saw it."

"Hey, I thought you didn't believe in doctors."

"We didn't, but it was a legality. You had to have an infirmary and a doctor on staff if you were going to call yourself a college. I don't know all the particulars, but that's what I was told. Our doctor's name was Harbaugh. He used to be a practicing GP before he joined the church. Howell Purdis hired him to look after sprains, minor injuries—that sort of thing. But he still kept his license. Every now and then he'd give someone a vaccination, but he'd barely scratch the skin. And then he'd rub a slice of lemon on it to suck anything out that might have penetrated. It was a joke."

"So, can I assume this doctor was in Howell Purdis's pocket?"

"I suppose a case could be made, although I'm not sure he would have lied for him."

"And what did the good doctor say was the cause of death?"

"Ovarian cancer."

"But if that's true, Lavinia's suspicions are groundless. Ginger died of cancer. End of story."

"*If*," said Sophie. It was a big word.

Closing his eyes again, Bram said, "So continue with the diary."

Sophie turned to the next page. "This is the first place that I felt the tenor of her writing had changed."

Sometimes I look at myself in the mirror and wish I were prettier. I know that's just female vanity. My body is the temple of the holy spirit, but sometimes I wish it wasn't such a big temple. But I'm working on that. I'm going to fast every other day until I lose fifteen pounds. *And no more popcorn!* Then maybe—oh, don't be so silly. Nobody's ever going to look at you twice until you're thin. Especially *him.*

"I guess that lets your friend Bunny off the hook. It was a guy."

"So it would seem," said Sophie. She continued:

We had lunch together today. Sort of a picnic. I don't think he wanted us to be seen, so we got in his car and drove down by the arroyo. It was sunny and windy, and our paper plates blew away. I chased them until I fell on the ground laughing. He touched my face, told me he thought I was beautiful. What's happening to me? I'm fat and ugly, and he says I'm just fine—that girls like me need to develop more confidence. He says he wants to help. He scares me, sometimes. He's so powerful, so filled with the holy spirit. And yet he's so gentle. I never think about our age difference. Sometimes I don't know what's happening to me. All I do is think about him. In class, at work, at dinner. Just listen to me. I'm acting like there's something between us, which, of course, there isn't. He was just trying to be encouraging. He likes me, but he called us friends. And that's what we are. Just friends.

"She's got it pretty bad," said Bram, his voice growing wistful. "I remember my first crush."

"Me, too," said Sophie, scanning several more pages. "How much older was Isaac than Ginger?"

"Close to eight years. She was twenty-two and he was nearly thirty."

"That's a big difference for someone her age."

"It's not huge, but it was definitely an issue, especially when it came to marriage. Howell Purdis taught that husbands and wives should be close to the same age. No more than five years' difference at the very most."

"That guy had a rule about everything."

She lowered the book slightly and stared at him over the edge. "You got it, darling. *Everything*." She read silently for a few more moments and then said, "The next ten or so entries all center on clandestine meetings with the mystery man."

"Young women do have a one-track mind."

She knocked him on the arm. "I want to cut to the chase," she said, scanning quickly. "Now, Ginger is careful never to mention a name. It looks as if she and this guy drive to the arroyo for lunch several times a week. Then, on February sixteenth, they start going for evening walks. I remember she was gone a lot that winter and early spring. It was kind of strange. Usually, by seven, we were all sitting at our desks, studying—except for the nights we worked. But Ginger didn't work evenings. I think I remember Lavinia telling me she'd spoken to Isaac Knox about her absences. Remember, he was the dean of students. All the dorm monitors talked to him if they had problems."

"How convenient," muttered Bram. "What did he say?"

Sophie scratched her head. "I don't really remember. It was so long ago. But he must not have been very upset about it because nothing changed. After a while Ginger was never at her desk in the evenings anymore. That much I do remember."

"Does the diary mention it?"

Sophie drew her finger down several more pages. "Not really. This is just more of the same. But you can tell she's really getting hooked by this guy—whether it's love or a crush, who can say? Now listen to this. It's March third."

It happened tonight. I don't know what to think. I knew it was coming—inevitable almost. I feel—how can I describe it? Womanly. And, at the same time, frightened. I know he loves me. I can hear it in the way he says my name. Am I crazy? Is this really happening? *My Lord*—I called him that tonight. He got mad—but then I explained, and I think he understood. He said that women don't understand how much a man needs to be close to a woman's body. It's like an ache. And yet now, I have a secret. I don't want to be separated from my friends, but what can I do? I can't tell them. He says what we did isn't really wrong. If anyone should know about right and wrong, he should. Sometimes I think he knows everything.

"Hmmph," said Bram, his tone disgusted. "If I didn't know better, I'd say she was talking about Howell Purdis. He's the know-it-all."

Sophie looked up. "Howell?"

"Sure. Why not?"

She entertained the idea for a moment, then rejected it. "I don't think so. Howell had his share of personal problems, but seducing coeds wasn't one of them."

"You're sure of that?"

At this point Sophie wasn't sure of anything. "He was married, Bram. In his early sixties." Then again, his wife was ill. Had been for years. And she'd always been highly Victorian.

"So? He could have been sleeping around all of his adult life and just been discreet about it." Poking her knee, he said, "Just keep reading. Maybe we'll find an answer."

"Okay, let's see. She stops writing a couple of days later and there isn't another entry for more than a month."

"That's strange."

"Not if you think about it. If she *had* entered into a sexual relationship with an older man—which is what I think she was referring to—writing about the details might have seemed too scary. What if someone found the diary?"

"Did you know she kept a diary?"

Sophie shook her head. "I kept a journal of sorts myself, but I only wrote in it when I was inside one of the prayer closets. It was the only place I had any real privacy. I hid it under my mattress."

"Not very original."

"I was nineteen, Bram. It took me several more years before I hit my creative stride."

"So, what's her next entry?"

"The nineteenth of April. It's pretty short."

I can't afford to get the flu. I have a midterm tomorrow in his class—and later we're riding out to the pier.

"Did Isaac teach a class?" asked Bram.

"Sure," said Sophie. "Most of the ministers did. Let's see. That would have been Ginger's junior year. Isaac taught a class on the Pauline epistles. She would have been eligible to take it."

"Do you know if she did?"

"I can't remember. Then, of course, Hugh Purdis taught third-year Bible. Every junior had to take that. And Howell taught Marriage and Family Living, another third-year requirement. There were other electives, but nothing comes to mind." She turned the page. "This is dated May the ninth. Hey," she said, sitting up straight. "Listen to this."

Still throwing up in the mornings. I'm beginning to get worried. I missed my period last week. What if I'm—I'm too scared to even write the word. I can't talk to him about this. I'd die! It's the last thing he needs. He says he loves me, but the disgrace would ruin him. What do I do? There's no one else to turn to. Without him, I'm all alone.

Sophie let the book fall to her lap. "She was pregnant," she said under her breath. "I never knew. She never told any of us."

"Keep reading," said Bram. When she didn't respond fast enough, he snatched the book out of her hand and picked up where she left off. "The next entry is three days later. The twelfth of May." Clearing his throat, he began:

> I.K. is right. We have to take care of it.

"Isaac Knox," whispered Sophie, her gaze colliding with his.

Bram continued:

> He's going to set it up. This A.M. Harbaugh looked at me and confirmed. Nearly eight weeks. Tomorrow we'll drive to a place he knows about—a guy who does it in his basement. He says we have to take care of it now. It's the only way. I have to be strong and trust him. I do. And there's no other way.

"Jeez," said Bram. "That was 1971, right?"

Sophie nodded.

"Abortions were illegal back then. I can't even imagine what it must have been like. Going to some backstreet abortionist, not being sure he knew what he was doing. She was so young."

"And," said Sophie, her face hardening with anger, "at the mercy of some sexual predator who put his career and his reputation before everything else. There's no doubt about it now. Isaac was Ginger's lover."

"Except," said Bram, his eyes dropping to the book, "if we're going to get technical, it never actually says that."

"Sure it does," said Sophie.

"No," said Bram. "It doesn't. Not directly. If this were the only record and it was argued in a court of law, a good attorney could drive a truck through the ambiguity."

"Maybe the diary says something else. What's the next entry?"

"That was the last," said Bram, slipping his arm around her shoulder.

Of course, thought Sophie. The twelfth of May. Ginger died the next day.

"And wasn't that precisely Lavinia's problem?" continued Bram. "This diary is incriminating, but not crystal clear."

"It's clear enough for me."

"Okay, maybe you're right. But even if it's all true, the only thing Isaac was guilty of was buying an illegal abortion. The fact that it was botched—and what Ginger potentially died of—wasn't his fault."

"Of course it was," said Sophie, anger rising in her throat. "She needed medical attention. He murdered her just as sure as if he'd put a gun to her head."

"But your church didn't allow physicians to treat members."

"But . . . *something* should have been done. He could have taken her to a hospital. Someplace far away from campus where nobody knew them. I mean, he slept with her out of wedlock. *That* wasn't allowed. He fathered a child with her and then convinced her their only option was an abortion—none of that was allowed either. It didn't bother him to break the rules when it was to his advantage."

"You're right."

"It *was* murder," said Sophie, staring straight ahead. "The real reason he didn't get her to a doctor was because he wanted her to die. With her out of the way—and some stooge doctor to falsify the medical records—he was home free. No one would ever know what he'd done."

She got up and walked over to the mantel, pausing to collect her thoughts. Staring into the cold hearth, she said, "Don't you see? We've finally found the answer to everything that's happened here this past week. Isaac hasn't changed. He still needs to hide what he did. If Howell or Hugh Purdis found out, they could use that knowledge against him." She turned to face him. "I didn't mention it before, but it looks like Isaac is trying to gain support from the evangelists for some sort of battle against the Purdis family. I don't know the specifics, but some of the evangelists appear to be on Isaac's side, some on the Purdis's. If the word got out that he'd fathered a child by a student back in the early Seventies and then had it aborted, his credibility would be ruined."

"It's an interesting theory."

"It's more than that," said Sophie, not even attempting to hide her frustration at his reticence. "Once again, it's self-interest, pure and simple. Isaac still needs to protect his position in the church. It's his whole life. So what does he do? He poisons Lavinia."

"But . . ." Bram hesitated. "This may sound kind of picky, but how did he know she liked those cheese balls? And where did he get the recipe?"

"How should I know? We need to concentrate on the main points. Lavinia was the only one who'd seen the diary—the only one who knew for sure what had happened back at college. She came here to talk to him—and talk to him she did. He told me as much on Sunday morning. Except, I'll bet he denied everything."

"It didn't matter," said Bram. "If she had the diary, she was still a threat."

"Exactly. If I know Lavinia, she probably told him she was going to find out the truth, no matter how long it took. And then she was going to hang him with it."

"But, Sophie, just take a breath and think for a moment. All of this sounds plausible, I agree, but you're constructing a house of cards based on only one comment. Two small initials. Let's say they *were* his initials. All it really says is that he took her to an abortionist. It never says he was her lover."

Her eyes shot fire. "You're being willingly obtuse."

"No I'm not," he said firmly. "I'm just trying to step back and see if your theory holds water."

"Of course it does." She glared at him.

Attempting a placating smile, he said, "All right. Fine. I don't want to fight. What do you say we continue this discussion over dinner? I'll pop the food into the 'wave, uncork some wine, and—"

"I'm going upstairs," she said abruptly, stomping over to the couch and grabbing the diary. "If I have to read it through ten times, I'm going to prove to you I'm right."

"But—"

Marching resolutely out of the room, she called over her shoulder, "Don't forget to feed Ethel. I hope the two of you have a perfectly scintillating evening."

# 30

By the time Sophie and Bram went to bed that night, Sophie had come to the rather painful conclusion that her husband's reticence was justified. While the diary clearly stated that Isaac Knox was the one who'd taken Ginger to the illegal abortionist, nothing—not one word—specifically named him as her lover. Sophie had simply jumped to the same conclusion Lavinia had. Not that Isaac wasn't still the prime candidate. He saw Ginger every day that winter and spring. And, interestingly, after the first few days at her new job, she never again mentioned him by name. For Sophie, that fact alone seemed highly suspicious.

Then again, she couldn't dismiss the fact that two other ministers had offices in the administration building. Howell Purdis and his son, Hugh. If there *were* other candidates besides Isaac, these two men were at the top of her list. The bottom line was, all three of these men had motive, means, and opportunity. They all had a car, so they could easily whisk a coed off campus. And they all saw Ginger nearly every day. The motive was the clearest of all—casual sex with a naive young coed, someone who was already impressed by their power and position, and ultimately, easy to manipulate and seduce.

As Sophie tossed and turned, unable to shut off her mind, she couldn't help but wonder if Ginger's weight had also played a part in her seduction. The message the women at

Purdis Bible College received was clear. Unless you looked and acted a certain way, no man would ever be attracted to you. If you were fat, forget it. Ginger's self-esteem was in the toilet, as was pretty much the case with everyone who lived at Terrace Lane. Consequently, when a man finally did show interest—a minister to boot—she must have been dumbfounded, amazed, and ultimately thrilled by her good luck. That growing attachment probably provided her with a kind of vicarious self-worth—the worst kind, in Sophie's book.

After finally dozing off around three A.M., Sophie slept until shortly after nine. Bram had already left for the station, propping a note next to her alarm clock. Rubbing her eyes, Sophie sat up in bed and opened it.

Dearest Sophie:
After last night, Ethel and I have called it quits. We're filing for divorce. I suggested "irreconcilable differences," but she insists on "alienation of affection." She thinks I'm in love with another, and pathetic man that I am, I had to tell her the truth. The one I love was upstairs, reading and sulking, while I was downstairs, watching Ethel do her "ball of energy" routine. By the way, Ethel doesn't like Chinese food—way too many vegetables. But she did enjoy her fortune cookie. It said: "Let there be magic in your handshake." She spent the evening pondering the meaning. Mine said: "A man's character is his fate." Care to get together later and discuss it?
                                                                Bram

Sophie smiled to herself, glad that he wasn't angry at her for the way she'd behaved last night. She'd taken her frustration out on him, which wasn't fair. He was just trying to be cautious. Somewhere around midnight she'd finally admitted to herself that she was still so angry at the Church of the Firstborn she was willing to believe the worst about anyone and everyone associated with it. And *that* kind of knee-jerk reaction wasn't exactly fair either.

After taking a shower and slipping into her favorite

sweater and jeans—she didn't intend to work officially today, just putter behind the scenes—Sophie dashed downstairs to make herself a pot of coffee. As she was drinking her second cup she noticed her purse on the kitchen counter right where she'd dumped it last night. Fishing quickly through the contents, she withdrew a folded piece of paper. It was a copy of the note Morton had left for Lavinia the day after she'd stood him up.

In thinking about the entire situation last night, something about that note struck her as wrong. She read through it quickly, instantly seeing what she'd missed before. The problem was the *way* it was written. Even though she'd only talked to Morton once, she had no trouble remembering that his grammar was terrible. He wasn't an educated man. Yet this note was flawless—spelling, punctuation, and English usage all perfect. It seemed impossible to her that Morton could have produced it. So, if not Morton, who? Did that mean he had an accomplice? Or, as she suspected the other night, had someone paid him to stalk and perhaps even murder Lavinia? She had a hunch where she might find the answer.

First, however, she had something more pressing to do. Picking up the phone, she stood in the kitchen and dialed the hotel's main number. She needed to meet with Isaac Knox as soon as possible. After what she'd learned last night, she had to look him in the eye and demand an explanation. If he really had poisoned Lavinia and then torn the room apart looking for Ginger's diary, he needed to know it had now been found and was safely in the hands of the St. Paul police. She'd drop it off at the station on her way to the Maxfield. Since it was still early, she hoped she'd find Isaac in his room.

After being connected, the phone rang six times before the hotel's voice mail picked up. She left a quick message, asking him to call her at her hotel office as soon as he got in. She made it sound urgent, allowing his imagination to fill in the blanks. Then, grabbing her purse and patting Ethel on the head, she headed out the back door.

Forty-five minutes later, after making a short stop at the police station, she was seated behind the desk in her office,

ready to get started on her newest theory. Much to her
growing frustration, the police were now treating her like a
busybody, incapable of anything other than annoying them
with ever-more-ridiculous, unsubstantiated ideas. It didn't
matter that she'd found the diary all by herself and dropped
it right in their lap, the investigating officer let her know—
politely but firmly—that he viewed it as peripheral to their
central investigation of Peter Trahern.

As far as Sophie was concerned, if the cops couldn't see
the connection—if they wouldn't help—screw 'em. Two
days from now everybody who'd once been associated with
Purdis Bible College would be gone. The murderer, whoever he was, would return to his normal life, leaving Peter
holding the bag.

Switching on the computer, she began to check the phone
logs from three of the Maxfield's rooms. First, she tried
Howell Purdis's suite. He'd made several long-distance
calls, but nothing local. Unless Morton lived out of town—
something she felt was unlikely—or unless Howell made
his calls to him from a different phone, there was no connection between the two of them.

Next, she checked the connecting suite, the one
belonging to Hugh and Adelle. Again, there were a number
of long-distance calls, the bulk of them going to San Diego,
where their son was now a preaching elder. One number,
however, did appear to be local.

Sophie copied it down and then punched it into her
phone. After only one ring a rather breathy woman's voice
answered. "Hello, is that you?" She sounded excited, as if
she'd been expecting the call.

"Good morning," said Sophie pleasantly. "I wonder if I
could talk to Morton?"

"Who is this?" she demanded. "How did you get this
number? It's unlisted."

"Well, I—"

"There's no Morton here. And you've got to get off the
line," said the woman impatiently. "I'm expecting an
important call." The line clicked.

So much for "Minnesota Nice," thought Sophie, dropping the phone back in its cradle.

Okay, she'd struck out twice. Maybe the third time would be the charm. Popping up Isaac Knox's phone records on the monitor, she studied the list of numbers. He'd made at least twenty calls. A few were local, most were long distance. Interestingly enough, there was a local number that he'd called four times during his stay. Sophie felt her pulse quicken as she picked up the phone.

On the second ring, a child answered. "Hello?"

Sophie couldn't tell if it was a boy or girl, not that it mattered. "I wonder if I could talk to Morton," she asked slowly.

"Dad!" called the child, a hand placed partially over the receiver. "Phone."

Sophie's heart skipped a beat. So she'd been right! Isaac *was* connected with Morton—if it was the right Morton, and she was sure it was. Sophie had saved Isaac's room records for last because she still thought he had the best chance of being not only the one who'd taken Ginger to see the abortionist, but also her lover. Bram could be cautious all he wanted, as far as she was concerned, this was proof positive.

She had to think fast. She needed to talk to him in person, but she had to do it somewhere public, someplace where he couldn't possibly bring a weapon or threaten her in any way. Bram would be hysterical when he found out what she was doing, but she couldn't stop herself. She was too close to the truth now to allow a small degree of danger to get in her way.

"Yeah, hello?" said a deep voice. "Who's this?" Even though she'd only spoken with him briefly the other night, it wasn't a voice she'd soon forget.

Lowering her own voice to a whisper, she said, "I know about you and Isaac Knox. I'll trade my silence for some information." She knew she sounded like a bad TV show, but on such short notice, it was the best she could do. She hoped he'd take the bait.

"Hey, who is this?" he demanded. She heard a door slam. He probably didn't want to be overheard.

"That doesn't matter. We have to meet."

"Listen, lady, I'm not meetin' with nobody. Not unless I know who I'm talkin' to and what it's all about. I ain't never heard of—what did you say his name was? Isaac Knox?"

"I don't believe you," she said flatly. "And I already told you what it's about. You have two choices. Either you talk to me, or I talk to the police. What's it going to be?"

"Hey, hey, just slow down." His voice lost some of its bluster. There was a long silence. Then: "Yeah, I suppose we could meet. I ain't admittin' to nothin', though."

"Fine." She gave him a time and a location. "Do you know where that is?"

"Listen, lady. I been livin' in the Twin Cities all my life. I think I can find my way."

"Then I'll see you in two hours."

"Right—but, I mean, what do you look like? How will I find you?"

"I'll find you, Morton. Don't be late."

Sophie hung up the phone and then took a deep breath. What on earth was she getting herself into?

# 31

Standing in front of the mirror in her bedroom, Sophie selected a black wig, tight black jeans and boots, and Bram's old motorcycle jacket. On the drive back home from the Maxfield, she'd come to the conclusion that it might be wise to disguise herself for her meeting with Morton. Since she dressed in disguise on a regular basis in order to visit restaurants anonymously for later review in her food column, she had many costumes from which to choose. This was one of Bram's least favorites. He called it her "Betsy the Biker Moll" look.

An hour later, after leaving her car in the short-term parking lot, Sophie entered the main airport terminal, ready as she'd ever be to talk to Morton. She walked quickly to the nearest security station, where she was eyed somewhat warily by the guard on duty. Once past this checkpoint, she took up a position across the lobby and waited. The airport was the only place she could think of where she had a guarantee that Morton would be searched by an expert before they met. It was also about as public a place as she could imagine.

Realizing she had a good fifteen minutes before Morton was supposed to arrive, she stepped over to a pay phone, sat down, and punched in her number at the Maxfield. Much to her disappointment, Isaac still hadn't returned her call. He probably had a lot on his mind, especially if there really was some sort of evangelical war brewing. Whatever the case, the message she'd left hadn't moved him to contact her and she was starting to get annoyed. The least he could do was acknowledge the call, even if he didn't have time to talk to her right then.

As she contemplated leaving him another—more specific—message, she saw Morton saunter into the terminal. He'd already come through security, so unless he was some sort of slick foreign terrorist, he was unarmed. She watched him walk slowly over to the Burger King counter, speak to the woman taking the orders, and then wait as he was given an empty cup. He handed her some change. Moving over to the drink area, he filled the red Coke cup before finally heading off toward the red concourse.

Sophie got up immediately and followed him, keeping a good distance between them as she made her own way toward Gate 28. As she neared the spot where she'd asked him to wait, she saw him sitting in one of the seats directly across from a ceiling-mounted TV set. At least he could follow directions. She stood next to a vending machine and slipped in some change for a cup of coffee, noticing that he was reading a newspaper, his drink on the floor next to him.

Every few seconds his eyes would dart over the top edge of the paper, examining the people moving down the concourse. He didn't seem exactly nervous, but wasn't taking any chances either. No one was going to sneak up on him unobserved.

Sophie waited a few more minutes, sipping her coffee and going over in her mind the questions she intended to ask. Finally, after removing a pair of dark glasses from her pocket, she slipped them on and crossed into the waiting area.

Morton looked up as she sat down one seat away from him. She could see the question in his eyes, and then a certain loss of focus as he seemed to put it together.

"So, you're the one who called," he said, lowering the paper to his lap. He studied her for a moment, then picked up his Coke. "I wanna make this fast. I got other stuff to do."

She glanced up at the TV set. It was an all-news channel, and the local news was just about to begin. "All right." She lifted the coffee casually to her lips, then regretted it immediately when she saw her hand was shaking.

Since no planes were arriving or departing from this gate, she decided that if they kept their voices down, they didn't need to move. "Tell me why Isaac Knox hired you to stalk Lavinia Fiore." She might as well put it on the table.

He glared at her a moment and then his eyes drifted toward the windows as a plane roared down the runway. "Listen, lady. I don't have to tell you shit about—"

"You're right. You don't. So let me tell you what I know. You were questioned by the police last Saturday afternoon after you were picked up at the Maxfield Plaza for stalking."

"The police didn't have no proof of that," he protested. "They let me go."

"True. But what I know and the police don't is that Isaac Knox called you at least four times this past week—and that he paid you off quite handsomely on Sunday night, *after* Lavinia was murdered."

"Shit," he said, accidentally spilling the Coke on his pants. "I knew I shouldn't have talked to you that night."

Her eyes opened wide. "You . . . mean you recognize me?"

"Sure. You're Sophie Greenway."

"You . . . know my name?"

"It's a secret or somethin'?"

Her shoulders sank as she realized her stab at anonymity had fallen flat.

"Like I told you, I lived in this town all my life. I used to drive a cab up to a couple of years ago. I seen you goin' and comin' at that fancy hotel lotsa times. I maybe even had you in my cab once or twice. I mean, you dyed your hair and all, and you're dressin' better, but I saw it was you right away—just like the other night."

Sophie looked past him to a 757 moving slowly up to a far gate.

"Listen," he said, brushing some of the liquid off the end of his knee, "how come you're so interested in all this?"

Realizing there was no point in keeping it from him now, she said, "Lavinia Fiore was an old college friend of mine. Isaac was the dean of students the year a friend of ours died."

"Purdis Bible College?" he asked curiously.

"Yes. How did you know about that?"

"You ever meet someone there named Russell? Tina Russell."

"You mean Isaac's wife? Sure, I knew her."

"She's my sister-in-law. My wife's sister."

She digested this for a moment. "You mean—you're related to Isaac?"

"Guess so." He took a sip of Coke.

"Then—" She shook her head. "I don't understand."

"No, lady. You *don't* understand."

"But—"

"Look, I don't have to tell you none of this. I did what I did, and I can't change it. But, I mean, after what's happened—maybe I'm feelin' kinda sorry I got mixed up in it. I can't talk to the wife, even though . . . see, it wasn't like Isaac hired me to do nothin' illegal." He shifted as far away from her as he could without changing seats.

"Then what was it?"

"See, my wife and her sis are still pretty close. And Isaac and I, we been buddies for years. I taught the guy everything he knows about huntin' and fishin'. He brought his family to Minnesota nearly every summer and fall for the past eight years. Maybe you don't think a guy like him could like a fella like me, but you'd be wrong. We was great pals. He liked to get away from all the churchy stuff and just hang out with regular folks sometimes. He said it relaxed him. I got to know him pretty good. I respected him a lot." He squinted, then looked away. "Loved him, even," he said under his breath.

Sophie waited, hoping he'd go on with the story without being prodded.

"So, one day last week I get this call. He's in town on business and he tells me some lady from his past is buggin' him, threatenin' to tell his boss about somethin' he done when he was way too young to have any sense."

"Did he tell you what that something was?" asked Sophie.

He gave a guarded nod. "He, ah, helped some girl get an abortion."

Fascinating. Isaac really *did* trust this guy. "Did he tell you why?"

"No. And I don't butt in where I ain't asked."

"But you had a theory."

He shrugged. "Maybe." Swirling the Coke around in his glass, he said, "You know how things are sometimes. Maybe he got her pregnant."

"And so how did you get involved?"

"Well, he asks me could I mess with Lavinia a little—keep her off balance. You get the picture. Until he figured out what to do next."

"And you agreed?"

"Sure. Why not? If a buddy can't help a buddy, what good is he?"

"But . . . Isaac wrote the note, right?"

He scowled. "What note?"

"The one you supposedly sent Lavinia after she stood you up."

"Oh, yeah. I never seen it until the police showed it to me. Was I glad he didn't threaten her. I could of been in deep shit if he had. I guess he dropped it off by her door on his way to breakfast—least that's what he told me later."

"After the police hauled you in."

He nodded. "But I never killed no one. Neither did Isaac I got no idea what happened to that lady."

"Isaac told you that—he didn't poison her?"

"Absolutely. Swore up and down."

"He *swore*?" said Sophie, repeating his word. She knew full well that Isaac would never *swear* to anything. It was completely against what the Bible taught. She still remembered the verse. Matthew 5:34. "Swear not at all; neither by heaven; for it is God's throne: Nor by the earth; for it is his footstool."

"Yeah," he said, warming to his story. "Isaac said, 'Morton, I swear to you on this Bible and on the life of my wife and children that I didn't hurt no one.' And I believed him."

This, thought Sophie, was a lie. Perhaps Isaac did explain to Morton that he hadn't murdered Lavinia, but he would never have said it in that manner. And of course, this left her with a dilemma. What else had Morton lied about? Thus far, she'd believed him. Had that been a mistake? "So," she said, coaxing him to continue, "on Sunday evening, Isaac paid you off?"

"Cripes, you make it sound so . . . dirty." He cleared his throat, took a sip of Coke, and then began again. "See, it wasn't like the way you're paintin' it. Isaac asked me to do him a favor and I done it. No questions asked. And then, well, you know how hard it is to make a buck. He knew I got laid off from my job three weeks ago, so he gave me some money to tide me and the family over. That's all. I ain't done nothin' wrong." He glanced up at the TV set, batting at his cheek with the back of his hand.

Was that a tear? wondered Sophie. An odd reaction. "All right," she said, picking up her coffee cup but rejecting it when she realized it was lukewarm. "I appreciate your time. I'll be talking to Isaac later today. One way or the other, I intend to find out who murdered Lavinia Fiore."

"You *what*?" he said, staring at her as if she'd lost her mind.

She was unnerved by his sudden intensity. "I said . . . I intend to find out—"

"No no," he said, shaking his head. "The part about Isaac."

She realized she was growing impatient with him. "That I hope to meet with Isaac later in the day. Actually, I'm sure by the time I get back to the hotel, I'll have a message from him."

"You talk to angels, lady?"

"Excuse me?"

He flicked his eyes to the TV screen.

As Sophie looked up she saw the beginning of a news clip showing the police surrounding a parked car. The voice-over said, "An early-morning runner found a man dead in his car at Boom Island Park in downtown Minneapolis. Police later identified the man as Isaac Knox of St. Louis, Missouri. While the initial cause of death was thought to be a heart attack, the police later discovered a computer diskette in the man's pocket containing a suicide note. Knox was in the Twin Cities for a church convention."

Sophie felt as if a firecracker had gone off inside her head. She was dazed—stunned. Unable to move.

"The wife's been cryin' since they announced it on the morning news," said Morton softly. "She wouldn't even let the kids go to school. I had a hell of a time gettin' out of the house. She's been on the phone to her sister off and on all day."

"I . . . didn't know," said Sophie. "I'm sorry." It was about all she could squeeze out of her paralyzed brain.

"Yeah. Thanks. Anyway," he said, folding his arms over

his chest and returning his attention to the TV. "It's a hell of a mess."

# 32

When Rudy worked afternoons, he often took a break around two and walked for a while in the Maxfield's garden. Today, as he entered through the spiked wrought-iron gate, he saw Hugh Purdis sitting on a far bench, his arms resting on his knees, his eyes staring straight ahead. He looked like a man deep in thought, someone who wanted to be left alone.

As Rudy wove his way through the gravel-lined paths, he made a quick decision. He'd been wanting to talk to Hugh Purdis ever since he'd learned that the Purdis family was going to be staying at the hotel. This was the first time he'd seen Hugh by himself, instead of surrounded by a mass of people all vying for his attention.

The gravel crunched softly under his feet as he slowed his pace, hoping he wasn't interrupting something important. He didn't like to be bothered when he was deep in thought either, but this couldn't wait. It might be his last opportunity to catch him alone. The church festival ended day after tomorrow. As far as he was concerned, it was now or never.

Clearing his throat, he said, "Mr. Purdis?"

Hugh stirred from his reverie. "Yes?"

Rudy could tell that Hugh was looking at him, but not really seeing him. "You may not recognize me. I'm Rudy Greenway. Norm and Sophie Greenway's son."

Confusion creased his eyes. "Oh, sure. I remember you. Nice to see you again."

Rudy wasn't certain he did remember. He'd been pulled

back from someplace far away and the response felt like a simple reflex. "I wonder if I could talk to you for a minute."

"Well . . ." He took Rudy in for the first time. "You said you were Norm Greenway's son?"

"That's right."

"Well, sure I remember you. You were a lot younger the last time we met."

Rudy smiled. "It was at the church summer camp. I was fifteen."

"Right." He returned the young man's smile, then moved over so Rudy could sit next to him. "How's that dad of yours? I haven't seen him since—" He seemed to recall something unpleasant.

Easing down next to him, Rudy said, "I haven't seen my dad in a couple of years. I left the church when I came to Minnesota to attend the U of M."

He nodded. "Norm told me. I was sorry to hear about it."

"There's no need to be sorry. I hope you won't take this the wrong way, but I'm pretty much through with totalitarian religions, Mr. Purdis."

Hugh gave a weary laugh, glancing at Rudy with a wry smile. "Are you now? Well, you know, all religions are more or less totalitarian, son. It's in their nature."

"I guess that's where we disagree."

"Do we? How so?"

"Well, it seems to me that the Bible gives us standards, tells us what's right and wrong—what's of value, and what's of no value. But it doesn't attempt to do our thinking for us, doesn't demand that we give absolute allegiance to any man—to his thoughts, his opinions, his tastes, and especially his whims."

Hugh seemed surprised. "Is that how you saw the Church of the Firstborn?"

"I'm afraid it is, sir," said Rudy, feeling his stomach tighten. This wasn't easy for him. For most of his life he'd believed that the Purdis family headed the only true church on earth. Father and son were holy men. "Since I've left, I've slowly come to see the kind of damage some of your doctrines have done."

His smile faded. "For instance?"

"I had a friend die because she wasn't allowed to go to a doctor. I've seen two very fine women beaten and brutalized by men they couldn't leave because the church told them that when they married, it was forever, for better or worse. They would never be allowed to divorce."

"But we changed that doctrine," said Hugh. "I agree with you, it was too harsh."

"But how much damage did it cause before it was changed? And *why* was it changed, Mr. Purdis? Because you saw the error of your ways, or because, before your mother died, your father was thinking of divorcing her?"

Hugh looked off in the distance, choosing not to respond.

"You know," continued Rudy, "my dad gave a sermon once on corporal punishment—how a father had a right to discipline his child the way he saw fit. The next day one of my buddies came to school with welts all over his back. I told my dad about it, but he wouldn't even go talk to the guy's father. He said it was none of his business."

"That was wrong, Rudy."

"I agree. But it doesn't change what happened, or a church philosophy that says that a man is the king of his castle. What he does within its four walls is no one's business but his own."

Hugh focused his attention on a distant hedge. "What else upset you?"

"Well, in 1989, the year Howell Purdis said Christ was returning to earth, I saw people quit their jobs and sell their houses in preparation for the Second Coming. They sent all their money to headquarters and then waited and prayed. When Christ didn't return, they asked for the money back and were told it wasn't possible. These people ended up on welfare, Mr. Purdis. Their lives were ruined."

"Matters were mishandled, I agree," said Hugh. "We should never have set a date."

"Set a date? What about the money you never gave back?"

"We're human, Rudy. We make mistakes."

"I never saw much of that humility from the pulpit," said Rudy indignantly. "And I've been listening all my life."

Hugh was silent for a long moment. Finally, he said, "No, maybe not."

Rudy was a little amazed at the passive way Hugh was taking all this in without getting angry. "You know, Mr. Purdis, I was taught that I belonged to the one true church—we were the only ones who knew the truth. The rest of the world was steeped in error, but we," he said, emphasizing the word, "were special. We were small and persecuted by the larger Christian denominations, but that's the way the Bible said it would be. It didn't matter what lies people spread about us because we knew that only godless heathens would go to church on Sunday, instead of the true Sabbath. Only heathens wore makeup and celebrated pagan holidays like Christmas and Easter. As far as I can see, all our so-called knowledge did for us was give us permission to be arrogant, self-righteous, and intolerant. Sure, we were told to despise the sin and not the sinner, but in my experience, that's a pretty tall order. It's a mental trick most people can't perform. In the end I think all we got was the message that it was not only okay to feel superior, but it was all right to hate."

Hugh lifted his head and stared straight ahead. "I'm sorry we failed you, Rudy. Maybe what you never understood is that we're just men. Fallible. Imperfect."

"No," said Rudy, trying hard to control his own anger. "I think you guys in the ministry are the ones who forgot that."

Hugh turned to look at him, then his eyes slid away.

"Look," said Rudy, "I didn't come over here to beat you up, although the church has caused me and my family a great deal of pain and I refuse to hide that any longer. My mother was prevented from seeing me most of my life. My dad felt that since she was an unbeliever, she'd be a bad influence on me. So he kept our contact to a minimum. When we finally reunited a couple of years ago, it was tough. Mom was so angry—I don't even think she saw how angry she was. Over the years she's pretty much rejected Christianity because of what happened to her in the church, and in a way, I can't blame her. But for both of us, I suspect, it wasn't all bad. Some of the best times I had were at that church summer camp. And you, Mr. Purdis, were the best part of that."

"I was?" said Hugh, looking both stunned and confused.

Rudy nodded. "You were so great with us kids. I remember a conversation we had once when we were paddling a canoe toward Bird Island. I thought, this is the kind of man I want to be when I grow up. You didn't talk about God all the time, like my dad did. You weren't always quoting the Bible. And you didn't condemn us when we failed. Instead, you encouraged us. I could tell you cared deeply about your beliefs, but you were so much fun to be with. So alive and interested in what I thought about stuff. You really listened. I remember feeling jealous of your son. He had you around all the time."

"Norm is a good man, Rudy. You mustn't forget that."

"Oh, I know. And I always knew he loved me. But he's a hard man to be around. A hard man to please. I haven't heard from him since the night I called and told him I was gay."

Hugh was about to respond, but stopped himself.

Rudy guessed he was going to offer his condolences.

"I didn't know," said Hugh finally.

Rudy figured it was about as noncommittal a statement as he could devise on such short notice.

"Does your mother know?" asked Hugh.

"Mom? Sure. She's fine with it. So am I. I'm not asking permission anymore to be who I am. But you know what? I still want to be a man like you. Oh, I don't want to be straight—I'm perfectly happy the way I am. It's who God made me, and I don't think it's a mistake. I also don't believe the way you do anymore. But I want to help people the way I saw you helping the kids at summer camp. I want to be of some use in my life. And at the end of it, I want to be able to look back with the conviction that I tried hard to do what was right."

Hugh closed his eyes and leaned back, sucking fresh air deeply into his lungs. "I wish you luck, son."

"Thanks," said Rudy. He waited until Hugh opened his eyes and then he stuck out his hand. "I really mean that, sir.

Thanks for being such a decent guy to a crazy kid you hardly knew."

Hugh tightened his grip. "You're welcome. You don't know how much that means to me right now, Rudy."

Their eyes locked for a brief moment and then Rudy headed quickly back to the hotel. As he slipped inside the garden door he turned to take one last look.

Hugh had risen from the bench and crouched down next to an oleander bush on the other side of the gravel path. As Rudy continued to watch, the older man's face reddened and he broke into tears.

# 33

Sophie removed the black wig and floozy makeup in an airport rest room and then drove immediately back to the Maxfield. It was after three when she arrived at the front entrance, leaping out of her car and asking one of the bellmen to park it for her. She knew the boots and motorcycle jacket were a bit of a fashion stretch, but figured Hildegard could cope this once. She had to call Bram right away. She needed to tell him not only what had happened to Isaac, but also what she'd learned from Morton.

Rushing into the lobby, she saw several police officers standing near the front desk. Another officer had paused in front of the elevator, waiting for the doors to open. As she hurried past the bell captain's stand Hildegard marched grimly out of her office, blocking her forward progress.

"I've been calling your house for hours," she said, her voice hushed and tense. "Did you hear what happened this morning?"

"If you mean Isaac Knox, yes." Sophie wished the woman would get out of her way.

"It was a suicide, you know." Hildegard cast a furtive glance at some of the hotel guests sitting around the lobby. Pursing her lips, she added, "Two deaths in one week. The papers are going to have a field day." She drew Sophie aside. "The police gave me a list of people they want assembled in the Fireside Room ASAP. They're going to question all of you after they get done looking at Mr. Knox's room."

"All of *us*?"

"Yes, you're on the list. I've gathered everyone except the Purdis family. I haven't been able to reach them by phone, and no one seems to know where they are. I don't suppose you do?"

Sophie shook her head, noticing Hildegard's eyebrow raise ever so slightly at the motorcycle jacket. "It's a Versace original," she said offhandedly. "You know how much he likes to design with leather."

"Really?" Hildegard touched a worn spot. "I didn't know you went in for such . . . high fashion."

"Oh, always. I'll let you borrow it sometime if you're good."

The older woman hid her distaste behind a forced smile.

"Do you think I've got time to make a phone call first?" asked Sophie.

"I think it might be better if you joined your friends. I don't think they're too happy."

"All right." She unzipped the jacket. "If anyone wants me, they know where I am."

Entering the Fireside Room a few minutes later, Sophie found Bunny sitting morosely in a chair. Cindy was pacing silently in front of the cold fireplace. Neither seemed to be in a very talkative mood.

"I suppose you already heard," said Bunny. She was seated under an ornate oil portrait of G. S. Osgood, the Maxfield's first owner. The dark paneled walls were filled with portraits of his family.

"Yes," said Sophie, walking up to the hospitality table

and popping a grape into her mouth. She hadn't eaten since breakfast and the sight of so much fresh fruit and such a tempting array of muffins caused her stomach to growl. "I saw it on the news."

"Will you *please* stop pacing," said Bunny, shooting a disgruntled look at Cindy. "You're getting on my nerves. In fact, you've been getting on my nerves all week. If there's something you want to say, just say it."

Cindy made a small grunting noise, but kept moving.

"Has anyone heard what Isaac said in his suicide note?" asked Sophie.

Before anyone could respond, Hugh and Adelle Purdis walked glumly into the room, followed by an angry and snarling Howell.

"This is preposterous," barked Howell. "This isn't a police state. I demand to know what's going on."

"You don't know?" said Sophie, grabbing another couple of grapes. She knew eating at a time like this was gauche, but couldn't help herself.

"All we were told was that the police wanted to talk to us," said Hugh. "Except for a late lunch break, we've been in a private meeting most of the day."

"I think someone owes us an explanation," said Adelle, her tone distinctly icy.

"I'm going to call my lawyer," agreed Howell, looking around for a phone.

Cindy's clear, high voice cut through the air like a knife. "It's Isaac Knox. He's dead."

No one spoke for almost a minute.

Howell was the first to recover. Walking slowly toward her, he said, "You better explain yourself, young woman. He was supposed to be here to address the ministry in less than an hour."

"Well, he's not coming," said Sophie. "His body was found this morning at a park down by the Mississippi. The police think it was a suicide."

"They know it was," said Bunny. "The cop I talked to

earlier told me all about it. Seems Isaac admitted to poisoning Lavinia."

Adelle gasped, covering her mouth with her hand.

"Why?" demanded Howell, his bulky frame looming over Bunny.

She gave him a disgusted look. "You can save the theatrics for the faithful. It doesn't work on me anymore. The fact of the matter is, Isaac got a friend of ours pregnant back in college. Ginger Pomejay. Remember her?"

Howell glared. "How should I recall a name from that long ago?"

"I suppose names do get mixed up in that aging goo you call your brain. Allow me to refresh your memory. Ginger was a senior the year it happened. It seems Lavinia found a document that proved Isaac got Ginger pregnant and then tried to cover his tracks by arranging an illegal abortion. Ginger died the next day. He thought he'd gotten away with it—that is, until Lavinia appeared a few days ago and informed him he hadn't. I guess, in the end, Isaac couldn't face what he'd done to either of them, so he took the same poison he used on Lavinia. It's all in the note."

"I think he deserves everything he got," said Cindy, sinking into a chair.

"What is this so-called document?" demanded Howell.

"Ginger's diary," said Sophie. "The police have it now."

Howell turned to face her, a flush climbing his jowly cheeks. "And ... are you telling me this so-called diary actually says Isaac fornicated with a coed? That he fathered a child and then had it aborted?"

"Well, not ... precisely."

"Then what does it say!"

Gazing up at him now, Sophie was struck by how much Howell Purdis resembled a throbbing neck vein. His pomposity was only rivaled by his bad manners. "It said that Ginger was in love. And that Isaac arranged an abortion."

"You've actually seen it?" said Bunny.

She nodded.

"But ... where did you find it?" asked Cindy.

"It's a long story." She didn't feel like getting into it now.

Howell walked off stroking his chin. "So," he said, stopping directly in front of Hugh. "This just proves my point. Isaac was an unprincipled man. His actions were completely in character."

"Oh, Father, leave it alone," said Hugh, pushing his hands deep into the pockets of his suit coat. "We can't know what really happened if all we've got is a note."

"But, it's all we *need*," said Howell, a glimmer of triumph in his eyes. "Don't you see?"

"I see nothing but tragedy," said Hugh sharply.

Howell ignored him. Walking over to the food table, he helped himself to a cup of coffee. As he returned his attention to the assembled group, he seemed pleased, even expansive. "Isaac's been discredited, just as I predicted he would be. When the fellows hear this, they'll see I was right."

Sophie remembered that Howell always referred to the ministry as "the fellows." And wasn't that exactly why he was so delighted by the news of Isaac's untimely demise? The battle Isaac was leading against the Purdis family might now be over.

Sophie couldn't help herself. She decided to toss in a note of doubt, just to make him squirm. "Well, you know, Howell, the diary doesn't actually say Isaac was Ginger's lover. He might have just been assigned the dirty work—cleaning up someone else's mess."

Bunny shook her head. "If you ask me, that's neither here nor there, Sophie. In my experience, the *fellows* aren't up to much critical thought. If Isaac arranged the abortion, he's already committed an unforgivable offense. Whether or not he fathered the child is secondary."

"But he did father the child," said Adelle, moving farther into the room. She'd been standing near the door, listening. Now, with these few words, she'd instantly become the center of attention. Walking slowly over to a love seat, she sat down, her hands twisting together nervously in her lap. "I'm afraid everything that's been said about Isaac is true." She glanced from face to face. "I should have said something a long time ago, but . . . I didn't."

"Meaning?" said Bunny, her voice a mixture of surprise and impatience.

Adelle asked Hugh to get her a glass of water. After she'd taken several swallows, she said, "I know what I did was wrong. I know I should have said something right after Ginger died, but I was frightened. Confused. And then . . . when Hugh and I started dating, how could I tell him? Isaac was one of his dearest friends. A man he thought of as a brother. I couldn't tell him what kind of man Isaac really was. The scandal would have devastated him, and hurt the entire church."

Hugh crouched down next to her, taking her hand. "You don't have to do this," he said softly.

"No, I do," said Adelle, wiping a hand over her eyes. "I share his guilt because I knew what was happening and I didn't try to stop it."

"Don't worry about that now," said Bunny, urging her on. "Just tell us what you remember."

Taking another sip of water, Adelle looked up pointedly at Howell and then continued, "I knew Ginger was falling in love with Isaac. I'd seen them together a couple of times in his office at the administration building. It was after school hours, so she had no business being there. A woman can tell when there's sexual tension in the air. Oh, Ginger denied it when I asked her about it later, but it didn't matter. I knew.

"Several months after I caught on to what was happening, Professor Dahlburg let me borrow his car so that I could drive over to baby-sit his kids while his wife took a Lamaze class. Their third child was due in a few months, and she wanted to brush up on some of the information.

"As I was backing out of the parking space, I saw Ginger and Isaac come out of the administration building and get in his car. I guess I was curious where they were going in the middle of the day. Since I had some extra time before I had to be over to the Dahlburgs', I followed them. The Dahlburgs' house was in Alhambra, so the drive through south Pasadena wasn't completely out of the way. After parking in front of a rather nondescript rambler, they got out and went inside. I waited for a few minutes, but when nothing else happened, I drove to the Dahlburgs', where I baby-sat the kids for the next two hours.

"When Mrs. Dahlburg returned home after the class, we sat for a while and talked about her kids, and then I packed up my books and headed back to campus. Out of curiosity, I drove past the rambler again. Isaac's car was still there. I parked down the street and just sat and watched. I was about to give up and leave when the front door opened and Isaac and Ginger came out. Another, older man was with them. He was tall and thin, with square dark-rimmed glasses—a lot like Bunny's—and wispy white hair. I could see immediately that something was wrong. Ginger was all stooped over, and she was walking quite slowly. The two men had to help her into the front seat. I couldn't help but wonder what was going on. She was fine when she went in.

"Later that night when I got back to the apartment, Lavinia met me at the door and announced that Ginger was sick. Instead of eating dinner, she'd gone to her room to lie down. I went in right away to talk to her, to ask her where she'd been earlier in the day, but she was asleep. She looked so pale I didn't dare wake her. After that, I never had a chance to talk to her alone again. She died the next evening."

Adelle took a tissue out of her purse and wiped her eyes, giving everyone a moment to reflect.

Sophie had absolutely no idea anyone knew what had really happened, yet now, finally, it was beginning to make sense. Adelle must have lived with a terrible burden all these years.

"How did you know he'd taken her to an abortionist?" asked Bunny. "I mean, I assume there weren't any signs on the man's house."

"No," said Adelle, catching her sarcasm. "No signs. But my gut instinct told me I was right. It all fit. And then, less than a month later, I saw a picture in the *Pasadena Star*. It was the same man I'd seen help Ginger out to the car. He'd been arrested the day before for performing abortions. No matter how much I might have wanted to resist the truth, I finally had my answer."

"But," said Cindy, looking uncertain, "didn't the college doctor sign a form that said Ginger's death was a result of advanced cancer?"

Adelle nodded. "And that was my problem. If I called the doctor a liar, I had to have proof—and I had none. It was my word against Isaac's. I suppose I could have informed the police, but that never crossed my mind. I'm ashamed to admit that I simply took the easy way out. I put it out of my mind. But I never—*ever* had any sense it would come to this."

As she pressed her thumb and forefinger to her temple, Adelle's eyes moved cautiously from face to face. "I can't change what happened, or what I did—or didn't do. But I won't keep it a secret any longer. I should have told Lavinia the truth the night we met at that bar, and I might have if it had been just the two of us. But when Bunny and Cindy arrived, I got cold feet. And then, the next day, she was dead. It all happened so fast. I wondered if Isaac had something to do with it, but then I found out the police thought Lavinia's new husband was responsible. So, once again, I let it go." Her gaze came to rest on her husband. "Hugh, can you ever forgive me?"

"Forgiveness isn't necessary," said Howell, plunking himself down next to her on the love seat. "My dear, rest assured, this story of yours is one many will be interested to hear."

Slowly, Adelle turned her head until she was staring straight at him.

Sophie wondered if the others in the room were catching the look of absolute revulsion on her face.

"So, where are the authorities?" said Howell, raising a hand to smooth the side of his white hair. He seemed completely unaware of the daggers being shot at him. "We've got business to attend to. First, I'll make an announcement to the ministers about Isaac, and then I'll need to prepare a general statement for the Bible study later tonight. I think I'll lead it." Glancing at Hugh, he said, "Tell whoever you assigned that they've been bumped."

As Howell continued to issue orders a police officer

entered. Sophie recognized him as one of the men who'd
answered the hotel's 911 call on Sunday morning.

Resting a hand above his gun, he surveyed the group
briefly and then said, "By now you all know what happened.
Lieutenant Riley will question each of you individually
about the matter. It shouldn't take long. We'll start with
you, Ms. Greenway." He nodded to Sophie.

All Sophie wanted now was to get through this and go
home. She needed some quiet time to process what had happened, to put it all in perspective. Since Isaac had already
admitted to Lavinia's murder, she assumed the police would
want to search through his hotel records with a fine-tooth
comb. That meant they'd find out about his connection to
Morton. She couldn't help but feel sorry for the guy. She
might not know the legalities involved, but assumed he was
in a lot of trouble.

Following the officer out of the room, Sophie experienced
a surprising sense of relief. It was finally over. By bringing
that diary to Minnesota, Lavinia had begun a chain of events
that no one could have predicted. And even though Sophie
didn't feel all that great about how matters had turned out, at
least she had the answers in her hand now and could begin to
put the events of the past—and the present—to rest.

# 34

"That's quite a story," said Bram, resting his hands
against the top of his rake. He stood knee-deep in a pile of
maple leaves.

Sophie was standing next to him, stuffing the leaves into
a plastic lawn bag. "And you remember the jewels stolen

from Lavinia's room? The police found them in Isaac's suit-coat pocket. According to the suicide note, he took them to throw the authorities off the track."

"Clever, but no prize," muttered Bram, pulling up a lawn chair. "He didn't fool anyone. The thing I can't understand is, the night Lavinia called you from that bar in northeast Minneapolis? How did she get home?"

Sophie stopped and looked up at him. "I don't know."

"If you ask me, the whole thing felt like a setup. First the flat tire. Then someone swings by just at the right moment and offers her a lift back to the hotel."

"Must have been Isaac."

"Hardly. She wouldn't have gotten into a car with someone she'd just accused of murder."

"True. As I recall, when we were talking on the phone that night, she sounded pretty happy to see whoever it was who drove up." She took a twist tie out of her pocket and wound it around the top of the sack.

"Exactly my point," said Bram. "Maybe one of your friends picked her up. That's the most likely story."

"Not unless someone's lying. They all said they drove back to the hotel alone."

"Then, what about Peter?"

"Again, unless he's lying, he was nowhere near the bar. And anyway, what difference does it make how she got back to the hotel?"

"Because," said Bram, giving her a frustrated look, "it just does. It's a loose end. Whoever drove her back could have followed her right up to her hotel room and murdered her. And if they didn't murder her, maybe they saw some-thing important."

"I suppose it's possible," said Sophie, "but we already have Isaac's confession."

Bram shook his head, kicking a branch away from his foot. "You don't find that just a little too convenient?"

To be honest, she did. And since Isaac was dead, he couldn't be questioned about any of the details.

"You say the police found the suicide note on a computer disk?" asked Bram.

She nodded. "It was in his pocket with the jewelry."

"No handwriting to verify. Nothing except words on a screen. Anyone could have typed the note."

Sophie stared at the pile of leaves in front of her. She knew he had a point.

"Didn't the police even consider that the note might be phony?"

"Riley did say there were some holes in the investigation, points they needed to clear up. He even mentioned Peter again like he was still a suspect. If you ask me, that Riley's got a one-track mind."

"Maybe he knows something we don't," said Bram, fanning air into his face with his work gloves. "And another thing. Why did Isaac murder Lavinia, leave, and then come back the next morning to search the room? He already knew about the diary. Why didn't he search for it that night? Why take a chance that someone might see him entering or leaving her suite the next morning?"

"I . . . don't know," said Sophie. She was becoming more confused by the minute.

"Maybe all that diary stuff was just a cover. Who knows, Soph? Someone else could have used the situation for their own purpose. What if Lavinia's death had nothing to do with the diary? Isaac's suicide makes it *look* that way, but what if that's just another part of the cover-up. Sure, the note places all the guilt on him—it seems to fit, but what if it's wrong?"

The cordless phone on the screen porch started to beep.

"I'll get it," said Sophie. She drew back the door and rushed inside, retrieving it from under a magazine. "Hello?" she said, nearly tripping over Ethel. She was curled up next to one of the redwood chairs. It would never occur to her to move simply because someone was about to break their leg.

"Sophie? Is that you?"

"Yes," she said, not recognizing the voice.

"It's Peter Trahern."

"Oh, hi." She sat down, pulling a leaf out of her hair. "How are you?"

"I've been better. This has been a pretty awful week. I assume you've heard the news about Isaac Knox."

"Yes. I talked to the police this afternoon."

"Just between you and me, I think I came pretty close to being arrested."

"But . . . you had an alibi, Peter. Your ex-girlfriend."

His laugh was bitter. "Right. The only problem is, she was about to throw me to the wolves."

"Meaning?"

"She refused to verify my story. Privately, she told me she didn't care what happened to me. It was her way of getting even for what happened that night."

"That's kind of an overreaction, don't you think? You could have spent the rest of your life in jail."

"Tell me about it. You don't know Miranda, Sophie. When she's mad at you, she makes sure you get hurt."

Sophie had a hard time understanding people like Peter's ex-girlfriend.

"This past week has felt like a nightmare. Anyway, the reason I called was to remind you about tomorrow night. Lavinia's memorial service is scheduled for seven-thirty at Lakewood Cemetery. I hope you can come."

"I'll be there," said Sophie.

"Great. Your husband's invited, too. If you feel moved to get up and say something, you're welcome to do so. I've already extended the same invitation to Bunny, Cindy, and Adelle."

"Thanks," said Sophie. "I'll probably just sit in the audience."

"Sure. Whatever you want. Well, I've still got quite a few people yet to phone, so I better make this brief. See you tomorrow night?"

"You will. Thanks for calling."

After they said goodbye, Sophie glanced out through the screen at her husband. He'd resumed his raking and was now all the way on the other side of the yard. Pushing out of her chair, she called, "Honey?" She waved at him from the porch door. "Would you mind finishing up by yourself? I want to run up to the attic and check on something."

"No problem," he shouted back, patting his stomach. "It's good for me to work off some of that dinner you made."

She gave him a grateful smile and another wave, and then disappeared inside the house.

Half an hour later Sophie sat amid a pile of college memorabilia. She'd opened her college trunk last weekend looking for her old cookbook, but before that, she hadn't rummaged through any of it in over twenty years. After she lost Rudy in the divorce, the memories were too painful.

Most of what she'd saved were class notes and school yearbooks, but there were also shoe boxes full of prayer lists, letters she'd received from her parents and friends, and the exuberant miscellany of four years of college life. But what she was really looking for was a journal she'd kept sporadically, one she'd completely forgotten about until last night when she was talking to Bram about Ginger's diary. Hers was only a simple spiral notebook, not an official leather-bound volume. After digging to the bottom of the trunk, she'd finally located it under a pile of church pamphlets.

Bram had talked earlier about loose ends. Sophie decided that she had a rather major loose end of her own. She hoped the journal might help her tie it up. As she read through all the religious blither she couldn't believe she'd ever been that person. Her comments struck her as not only painfully young but incredibly judgmental and moralistic—so much so that she had the distinct urge to toss it in the garbage. It was hard paging through the writing, yet she was searching for something specific and she couldn't stop until she found it.

About a third of the way through the notebook, she came across a section she'd written the day after Ginger's death. She'd jotted down some notes about the last words Ginger had spoken the night she died. At the time they'd struck her as odd. Now she wondered if she couldn't find a specific meaning in them—something she'd missed way back when because she hadn't understood the full story. Bram might not believe Ginger's death had anything to do with present events, but Sophie couldn't shake the feeling that it was all related.

She pressed a finger to the page and read silently to herself,

> I have to write about this because I'm still so upset. Ginger died last night. God didn't answer our prayers— or maybe He did. He just said no. Ginger's asleep now, awaiting the resurrection, and I know I should put it to rest, too, but I still wish I understood what she was trying to tell us last night. As best I can remember it, here's what she said. First, "He's coming!" She sounded terrified. If she really *was* talking about the Second Coming, as someone suggested, she wouldn't have been frightened. Next, she talked about the fire and the wood. And a ram. I thought she might be referring to an Old Testament sacrifice. And then she said the word *Moriah.* Mount Moriah, I assume. I know what sacrifice took place there, but I can't think what it would have to do with anything. Then she shouted the name Isaac, mumbled something about not caring about . . . stars. We all assumed she meant Isaac Knox, so we called him and he came right over. But was it really the fever talking? Was she out of her head? That's what Mr. Knox said, but I'm not so sure. I saw her eyes. Her words meant *something*, I'm sure of it. I've been thinking about it ever since, but I can't figure it out. I talked to Bunny this morning, but she says to let it go. I know she's right. Except first, I thought I'd write it all down. Maybe one day I'll understand.

Sophie looked up from the notebook. The quiet in the attic pressed down on her, forcing her to confront the image in her mind. She could see Ginger's feverish body lying on her bed, the bloody sheet pulled up around her middle. She could smell the cinnamon tea, hear the prayers of classmates in the next room, feel the same fear and helplessness that had overwhelmed her that night.

"Moriah," she whispered, feeling the word escape her lips like an ancient breath, one that had been trapped inside her far too long. In that one moment, in a flash of absolute clarity, she saw it all—what she'd missed so many years ago, and what she was missing now. Ginger *had* been talking about a sacrifice. She'd given up her child. Writhing on that bed, she'd desperately wanted to turn back the clock—to have the ram take its place. And the stars. What did Ginger care about God's promise of nations and multitudes? Without her child, it was all meaningless.

Sophie understood the emptiness. Deep in her soul, she'd felt the same longing. And wasn't that the irony? Tears welled in her eyes as she realized how much they'd *all* lost. Everything was there in those few tortured words.

Even the identity of the man Ginger had once loved.


# 35

"Lake Avenue Real Estate," said the woman's voice on the other end of the line. "May I help you?"

"This is Sophie Greenway. I'd like to speak to Earl Sullivan." It was Thursday morning and Sophie was seated in her office at the Maxfield Plaza, the phone propped between her chin and her shoulder.

"Mr. Sullivan is on another line right now, Ms. Greenway." The receptionist sounded busy. "Would you like to hold, or leave a message?"

"I'll wait," said Sophie, drumming her fingers impatiently on the desktop.

She'd arrived at the Maxfield about an hour ago, the realization she'd come to last night still gnawing at her. Over breakfast, Bram had made the rather lame suggestion that she call the police. They both knew that when Lieutenant Riley asked for proof, all she could give him were Bible verses, church doctrine, and her latest "new" theory. Riley would laugh in her face.

The good lieutenant's sense of humor notwithstanding, Sophie knew that this time she was right. There was no question that Isaac had a strong motive for wanting Lavinia out of the way. That connection had fooled her at first. Yet there was someone else who had even more to lose. Someone with a bottom line far more compelling than Isaac's, one she hadn't appreciated until last night. The problem was, even though she'd racked her brains trying to come up with a way to get the proof she needed, she'd come up empty.

"Sophie, hi." Earl Sullivan's voice boomed. "What can I do for you?"

Sophie was jolted back to the moment. Picking up a pencil, she pulled a notepad in front of her. "I need to know if you've taken a look at the house yet? We want to get an idea of the market value as soon as possible."

"Of course. Yes, I did drive by yesterday. Even got out and walked around the property. Most everything looks like it's in good shape—at least as far as I could tell. We'll have to hire someone to do the Truth in Housing inspection, of course, but that shouldn't take long to set up. I saw only one real problem."

"And that was?" said Sophie, steeling herself for the bad news.

"Well, it looks to me like you've got a hole in your facia board near the top of the gable on the south side. There's a tree branch covering it, so I suppose that's why you haven't noticed it. I'd say if you don't already have a nest of squirrels up there, you soon will."

"Squirrels!"

"Have you seen any evidence of them in your attic?"

"Absolutely not." She was appalled. If Ethel went upstairs and came face-to-face with a squirrel, the poor thing would have a stroke. Come to think of it, so would she. Hearing a knock on the door, she put her hand over the mouthpiece and said, "Come in."

Hildegard O'Malley hurried into the room. "You've got to come right away," she whispered. "We've got . . . a situation."

Sophie wondered what constituted a *situation*, but wanted to finish her conversation with the agent first. "I'll talk to my husband about it tonight."

"Good. The sooner you take care of it, the less damage the little critters can cause. Let me know when someone's going to be home, and I'll come by for the interior appraisal. After that, we'll find ourselves an inspector, sign some papers, and we'll be off and running."

"Thanks," said Sophie. "I'll talk to you soon." As she dropped the phone back on the hook, she could tell Hildegard was about to burst. "What is it?"

"It's that friend of yours—I didn't know what to do. We sent two security guards up there, but she threatened to jump if they didn't leave."

"Slow down. Which friend? Up where?" Then, realizing the significance of Hildegard's words, Sophie added, "What do you mean *jump*?"

"Cindy, is that her name? You know the one I mean. She looks a lot like Lavinia Fiore."

Sophie shot out of her chair.

"She's on the roof," continued Hildegard as they rushed toward the elevators. "One of our workmen was up there fixing something when he saw a head peak out the security door. Before he knew what was happening she was standing near the edge. He tried to explain that nobody but maintenance was allowed on the roof, but she wouldn't listen. I think she scared him pretty badly, so he called security. Two of our men tried to reason with her, but she said if they didn't leave her alone, she'd jump."

Several minutes later, after consulting briefly with the secu-

rity guards, Sophie stepped onto the roof herself. She had no
idea what she was going to do or say, she just knew she had to
act. Cindy might not want to spill her troubles to a stranger,
but perhaps she'd talk to a friend. Their connection was no
longer strong, yet that might just work to her advantage.

It was a sunny, cloudless, windy morning. Cindy was
standing next to a roof vent several yards in from the edge,
her yellow skirt billowing in the breeze, her eyes fixed on
the Mississippi River eighteen stories below.

Glancing at Hildegard and the two security men, Sophie
stepped slowly away from the door. She'd never liked
heights, and didn't much care for the gusts of wind flat-
tening her clothes hard against her body. Stopping a fair distance away, she called, "Cindy?"

Cindy turned, her eyes struggling to focus. After a long
moment she said, "What do you want?" Her voice held
nothing but coldness.

Walking a few paces closer, Sophie replied, "To talk."

"Just go away. This . . . isn't what it looks like. I just
needed a quiet place to think."

"Why don't you come down to my office, then. You can
think down there much more comfortably. We can talk, or
I'll leave you alone. Whatever you like. I'll even have
someone bring you a breakfast tray. You'll feel much better
after you've had a good meal." She knew it was a pathetic
attempt, but she didn't know what else to say.

Cindy held Sophie's eyes for a moment, then looked back
down at the river. "Just go away. This is no concern of
yours."

"Maybe not," said Sophie, inching closer to the edge.
"But I know *this* isn't the answer."

"I told you." Her voice grew insistent. "I just need some
time to think things through. I'll be down in a few minutes."

"I don't believe you."

Cindy's head whipped around. "Look, we don't know
each other anymore, Sophie. If this past week has taught me
anything, it's that. Adelle is the only one I've stayed close
to, even though I've always thought our friendship was kind

of odd. She has that entire church at her feet and yet who does she confide in?" She answered her own question. "Me."

"She *confides* in you?" said Sophie cautiously. She waited a moment and then continued, "Did she ever confide in you what really happened to Ginger back at college?"

"You mean the abortion?" She shook her head. "We never talked about that. I was as surprised by what she said yesterday as you were."

Very softly, Sophie replied, "I'm not convinced she told us the truth."

This time, Cindy turned completely around. "What do you mean?"

"Do you remember what Ginger said the night she died?"

"I wasn't there, Sophie. Remember? Ginger and I hadn't spoken to each other in weeks."

"Oh . . . right." How could she have forgotten?

"Besides, I'm bored with the subject of Ginger Pomejay. Whether or not Isaac was responsible for her death has very little meaning to me now. I've got"—her eyes moved away—"problems of my own."

Sophie recalled Bunny's words the other day at tea. She'd insisted Cindy had been acting strangely all week. Sophie had seen it, too. Behind her outward calm, Sophie had sensed a nagging fatigue. "But, Cindy, this isn't the way to solve your problems. There's got to be something you can do short of jumping off a roof." She knew what she lacked in tact, she made up for in sincerity. And anyway, there was no point beating around the bush. They both knew why Cindy was standing five feet from the edge of a precipice.

Cindy gazed at Sophie, lifting her hand to shield her eyes from the sun. Then, touching her fingers lightly to her forehead, she said, "Do you remember what they told us in college? The first sin, the oldest sin, was eating? It was a joke, of course, but in a strange way, I always knew there was a nugget of truth in it. Anybody who couldn't control their weight—any *fat* woman—was Eve's sinful daughter. Remember how the ministers used to revile her? If it hadn't been for Eve and her pathetic lack of self-control, we'd all still be in Eden. She ruined everything for man. Sometimes I wonder if that isn't the basis for all the woman-hating I see around me."

Sophie wondered what this had to do with Cindy's present predicament. "What are you trying to say?" she asked cautiously.

"Just that it wasn't eating that was the sin, Sophie, it was appetite. Female appetite. Eve wanted knowledge. The serpent offered it to her. When she indulged her appetite and ate the apple, her eyes were opened. She finally got the point."

"What point?" asked Sophie.

"That women weren't supposed to *have* appetites. That's man's sphere. Women have no business wanting to control the world, to make their mark, to feed and expand, to grow heavy with power, knowledge, and authority. Instead, they're supposed to stay home, be small, soft, quiet, obedient. The only problem is, we all bear the mark of Eve in our souls. We're torn. We want to be good little girls, please our daddies, our husbands, our moral leaders. Yet we want more than we're supposed to have. We try to convince ourselves we're happy with the status men and the God they created in their own image have allotted us, but in our hearts we know we're still Eve's daughters. And it's not enough."

"That's quite an interpretation. And I don't disagree," said Sophie, feeling a gust of wind knock her slightly off balance. "But what's it got to do with jumping off a roof?"

"Just that I overstepped my bounds . . . again."

"Meaning?"

Wiping a hand across her mouth, she said, "You want to lend me a hundred thousand dollars?"

"Excuse me?"

"I'll take that response as a no."

"Cindy, you're going to have to explain—"

Cutting her off, Cindy continued, "Do you remember the fight Ginger and I had in college?"

"Sure. Vividly."

"Do you remember what it was about? I wanted to push the boundaries. Do something no woman had ever done before."

"You were always . . . ambitious," said Sophie, choosing her words carefully. She didn't know where Cindy was headed and didn't want to upset her any more than she already was.

"Ambitious. Good word. You always were a diplomat, Sophie. I remember that now." Resting a hand against the vent, she looked off in the distance. "I've worked most of my adult life as a secretary. Since I graduated from Purdis Bible College, I had—as one of God's elite—a lot of biblical expertise, but I didn't know how to make a living. I see that as a rather glaring omission in their program, don't you? Anyway, for one reason or another, I never married. Never had any kids. No life, really, when you think of it. Just my nine-to-five jobs. Then, five years ago, when my dad got sick and needed someone to step in for him at his trucking company for a few months, he called and asked if I was interested. I don't know why he called. Maybe he figured he could control me better than the guys he had working for him. Whatever the case, I got the nod. While I was there something happened that neither of us ever anticipated. I realized I was good at the job. As his cancer got worse I took over more and more of his responsibilities. He died last year. When it came time to read the will, I discovered to my immense surprise that the old man had left me the business."

"You told us about it at the reunion."

"But what I didn't tell you was that the longer I was there, the more I realized how deep the financial troubles were. Mainly, we needed some new rigs. The ones we had were breaking down all the time. That lost us both time and money. So, the year I was appointed treasurer of the Daughters of Sisyphus Society, I decided to do a little creative accounting."

"You mean—"

"I took money from the organization. I figured the coffers

were full. Nobody would miss it and I'd be able to put it back before anyone got wise. I had confidence in my ability to make Shipman Trucking the best in the Southwest. That's our slogan."

Sophie felt a *but* coming on.

"But," said Cindy, "it didn't happen the way I planned. Just like what happened at college, my . . . ambition, as you call it, got me nowhere. The economy slowed. We took a couple of bad financial hits because of it. Then some of the men started to quit on me. They didn't like working for a woman. One thing led to another until last month, I had to file for Chapter Eleven."

"Bankruptcy?"

"Afraid so. I came to this conference hoping I could talk to Lavinia about it. Get her to see why I'd done what I'd done. I knew I could make her understand. She's taken a lot of risks in her own life. But . . . it just seemed like every time I tried to talk to her, she was either too busy, or I'd get cold feet. I even went to her room the night she died."

"You did?" said Sophie. This was the first she'd heard of it. "Do you remember what time?"

She shrugged, leaning her shoulder against the vent. "Eleven-thirty, maybe. I got back to the hotel a little after eleven, but I knew I couldn't sleep until I'd had it out with her. It took me a good half hour and several shots of vodka before I screwed up enough courage to go up to her room."

"Was she there?"

"Sure. But it was just my luck that she wasn't alone. I listened at the door before I knocked and heard her laughing. That laugh of hers could shatter glass."

"Do you know who she was talking to?"

She shook her head. "I didn't stick around long enough to find out."

"She may have been talking to the person who murdered her."

Another shrug. "I guess I figured it was her husband and I had no business interrupting."

"So, what did you do then?" Sophie knew instinctively

that if she could keep her talking, there was a chance this might end in something other than tragedy.

"Well, as soon as I saw there was no chance of connecting with her that night, I went back to my room and got quietly drunk. I didn't know what else to do." She turned back toward the river. "Bunny's completely different from Lavinia, you know." Her voice was now muffled by the wind. "She'll never understand. She wants order. Clarity. Rules. Unlike Lavinia, she's going to whip the D.O.S.S. into shape. And she will, too. She's a tough old broad. Unfortunately, in the process, what I've done will be discovered and I'll be sent up the river." Inching closer to the edge, she looked down into the watery abyss and added, "I figured it might be easier if I saved everyone the middleman."

Sophie heard a noise behind her. She turned just in time to see Bunny step out of the door onto the roof.

"Cindy!" called Bunny, her voice echoing off the metal vents.

Cindy dropped her head but didn't turn around. "Oh, God. What are you doing here?"

"I heard most of what you said." She walked up next to Sophie and stood, hands in the pockets of her jeans, her light cotton jacket flapping in the breeze. "You may think I don't understand, but I do. And I want to help. We can work something out, Cindy. I'm sure of it. I can't tell you exactly what, but I give you my word—I swear to you on the friendship we once had—we *will* work it out."

Sophie and Bunny exchanged quick glances.

"You mean that?" said Cindy, resting a tentative hand on the roof vent as she turned around.

Bunny nodded. "I don't give my word lightly."

"Because, you know, I'd be willing to do almost anything. Who knows, maybe I can even beat the odds. Turn my company around."

"Come away from the edge, Cindy, and we'll talk about it."

"I just *can't* go to jail." As she stood staring at them her lower lip began to tremble. "The idea of being locked up in some tiny room—some horrible dank place with bugs and rats. Open toilets. No privacy. Nothing to look forward to but a day just like the last. It terrifies me! And my family. They'd think I ran Dad's company into the ground because I didn't know what I was doing. I was just another stupid, useless woman who was in over her head. I'd rather *die* than have them think that."

Bunny held out her hand. "You don't have to die, Cindy. But you do have to come away from there. It makes my knees weak to see you standing so close to the edge."

Cindy moved hesitantly toward them. "Are you sure?"

"Positive," said Bunny. She gave her an encouraging smile.

Cindy seemed beaten, weary, and yet immensely glad that someone had cared enough not to leave her alone in her pain.

Sophie and Bunny each took one of Cindy's arms and slowly, carefully, they walked her back inside.

# 36

On Thursday evening, the memorial chapel at Lakewood Cemetery was packed with mourners, women mostly, paying their last respects to Lavinia Fiore. In the last two decades of the twentieth century, Lavinia had touched a deep chord in women's lives with her message of physical acceptance and personal courage. She would not be soon forgotten.

Sophie and Bram arrived early and sat near the back, watching people quietly file down the center aisle. Normally, the cemetery was closed at this time of night, but

Peter's parents had pulled some influential strings. Lavinia had been a national figure, and on this one special night, rules were made to be broken.

Bunny and Cindy arrived together, nodding a subdued greeting to Sophie and Bram as they took seats on the other side of the aisle. It was a good sign that they were together, thought Sophie. She didn't know how Cindy's legal problems would be resolved, but the look on her face told Sophie that, at least for now, all was well.

Hugh and Adelle Purdis came through the front door shortly before the service was to begin. Both looked exceedingly tired, as if they hadn't slept well in days. Much to Sophie's surprise, Howell Purdis, dressed in a dapper navy-blue suit, red silk tie, and matching scarf, accompanied them.

"Look who's here," said Sophie, elbowing Bram in the ribs.

He turned to see. "Hey, the wolf arrives."

"Adelle probably insisted, although I can't imagine why."

Bram leaned close and whispered, "It makes him look innocent. Not too many murderers come to pay their last respects."

And, thought Sophie, Adelle played right along because she had her own vested interests.

Since the only seats left were in the last row, that's where they sat. Hugh wedged himself in between Howell and Adelle—a stalwart book between two hostile bookends. Sophie felt a moment of cosmic depression settle into her bones as she realized Lavinia and Isaac's murderer was about to get off scot-free. The gall it took for the Purdis family to show up at this memorial was nothing short of monumental.

Sophie knew that Howell Purdis loathed anything that smacked of traditional Christianity. Indeed, in his view, any religious edifice was part of Babylon the Great—the name he reserved for all things Protestant or Catholic. This particular chapel, one which most everyone found incredibly lovely, was probably giving Howell a bad case of spiritual indigestion. He undoubtedly felt that the delicate, brightly colored mosaics took the depiction of angels from the sub-ime to the ridiculous. Sophie watched him examine the chapel's interior, silently condemning everything he saw.

Returning her attention to the front, she sat in frustrated silence as the service began.

Peter spoke first. He seemed truly shaken and, occasionally, on the verge of tears as he read from prepared notes. Sophie was touched by the amount of time and thought he'd put into his short comments. She'd never really doubted his love for Lavinia, and tonight he spoke of that love eloquently. Next came Lavinia's sister. She talked only briefly. Her comments were unprepared, but heartfelt. She was followed by two elderly women who'd flown in from New York. Both had known Lavinia since she was a child.

Finally, a Lutheran minister took the podium for some closing words. He was a dry speaker attempting, in Sophie's humble opinion, the impossible: defining for the newly bereaved not only the meaning of life, but the significance of death. Sophie tuned him out.

As her eyes traveled aimlessly around the room, rising finally to the golden dome above her head, Bram slipped his hand over hers, giving it a reassuring squeeze. She assumed that he, too, was finding the minister a little hard to take. Checking her watch, she saw that it was going on eight-thirty. Outside, the twilight was deepening into night. The service would end soon.

Stifling an impatient sigh, Sophie glanced over her shoulder at the Purdis family one last time. Howell's chin had sunk to his chest, his eyes closed. What a respectful tribute from one minister of God to the next, mused Sophie. Her thoughts were full of acid, but she didn't care. Watching him a moment longer, she was surprised to see a familiar face enter through the rear of the chapel. Morton, his Twins baseball cap sticking out like a sore thumb, moved quietly into the crowd of onlookers standing near the back. Catching Sophie's eye, he held up a manila envelope, nodded to the exit, and silently mouthed the words "Meet me" as he eased into a shadowy corner.

A jolt of adrenaline shot through her system. What had he

brought with him? And why did he want to show it to her? It had to be something important, otherwise he wouldn't have driven all the way down from Brooklyn Center. As her gaze moved back to Howell she saw that he was staring at her now, his expression stern. Hugh was watching her, too. Realizing that she was the only one seated in the pews not listening to the minister, she quickly returned her attention to the front.

Ten minutes later, after several songs and a final prayer, the service ended. Sophie'd been silently debating with herself whether or not she should tell Bram that Morton was here. If he insisted on coming to meet with him, Morton might not feel quite as free to talk. She couldn't take that chance.

"Honey, I think we should stick around for a few minutes and mingle," said Sophie, slipping her arm through his.

"You mean, you want to talk to Bunny and Cindy."

"Well . . . yes, I do."

"Fine. I'll be over talking to Brad Johnson. Just come get me when you're done."

She eased her arm around his back and rested her head against his chest. "You're a dear man, do you know that?"

"Shhh," he said, bending close to her ear. "Don't let my radio audience hear you say that. It would ruin my curmudgeonly image."

She gave him a hug and then said, "I won't be long."

Glancing over her shoulder, she saw Morton duck out. She moved quickly to the other end of the pew, burrowed through the glut of people standing in the vestibule, and followed him.

As she stepped into the chilly night air she saw only a trickle of people making their way to their cars. Most everyone was still inside. To her immediate right was a gravel path that curved around to a stone arch on the north side of the building. When the service was a funeral, and not a memorial, that's where the hearse usually parked. She started down the path but stopped when she heard someone whisper, "Mrs. Greenway, over here!"

She turned, squinting into the darkness. Morton stood at the south end of the chapel. The soft, undulating hills of Lakewood Cemetery stretched out behind him, a faint glimmer of dusk still visible in the western sky.

She accompanied him around to the back of the building. Stopping in front of a door marked FLOWER ROOM DELIVERY ENTRANCE, Morton put a finger to his lips. He looked carefully over both shoulders and then said, "I knew I'd find you here. The six o'clock news said there was going to be a memorial tonight. I gotta talk to you. I been thinkin' about this all day."

"Thinking about what?" asked Sophie, seeing a look of tension cross his face.

He drew her closer to the door. "Here," he said, handing over the envelope. "Isaac gave me this last week. He asked me to keep it for him. I didn't tell you about it the other day 'cause it was a secret."

"What is it?"

"It's stuff he planned to use against the Purdis family if he needed to. He was plannin' to leave that church and take as many folks with him as he could. Did you know that?"

"I suspected it."

Running a nervous hand over his unshaven face, he continued. "He told me not to look at it, just keep it safe. And then he made me promise not to tell no one about it. Not even the wife."

Sophie wished she had a flashlight in her purse. She had everything else. In the darkness, there was no way on earth she could read.

"But I broke my promise," said Morton, shaking his head. "Do you think that was wrong?"

"No," said Sophie. "Isaac's dead now. Who knows? He might even have wanted you to open it."

"Yeah, that's what I thought, too. So I took all the stuff out and looked at it. You're never gonna believe what I found." Snatching the envelope back, he reached inside. "Remember I told you Isaac helped some girl get an abortion once? Well, I was wrong about part of it. He didn't get her pregnant, another guy did."

"Do you know what guy?"

"Sure. It was the head honcho's son. Hugh Purdis."

Just as Sophie had suspected. "And you've got proof?"

"Shit, yes. That's what's in the envelope. There's a prayer list that belonged to the girl. All it talks about is Hugh *this* and Hugh *that*. Poor kid, she really had it bad for him. Then there's some legal crap—a notarized letter from some doctor. The sleaze admits he lied about how the girl died. Way back when he said it was cancer. This paper says he takes it all back. She died from a botched abortion."

Sophie couldn't believe her ears. This was incredible luck. "Anything else?"

Morton shoved an audiotape into her hands. "That," he said angrily. "I played it on my kid's box this afternoon. There's a label on the plastic case that reads 'May twelfth, 1971,' and then the words 'Counseling session with Ginger Pomejay.' When Isaac worked at that college, did he, like . . . counsel people?"

"That was one of his primary responsibilities," said Sophie.

"That's what I figured. He must've taped the sessions. On this one, the girl admits she's pregnant, and that Hugh Purdis is the father."

It was everything Sophie needed, all neat and tidy and ready to hand over to the police. They'd have to listen to her now. "But why are you giving it to me?"

"I want you to pass it to the cops."

"But . . . why don't you?"

"Hell no, lady. I ain't no fool. The cops don't know about me and Isaac, and I ain't gonna tell 'em. Besides, if they get enough on someone else, they won't come lookin' for me."

So, thought Sophie. The police hadn't connected them yet.

"Look, you can make up some sort of story, can't you? Tell 'em someone mailed it to you or somethin'. Use your imagination. But, yeah. The main reason I brought it to you was so you could help clear Isaac's name. I'll bet you anything he didn't have nothin' to do with Mrs. Fiore's death. It was probably that Purdis guy. And the more me and the wife thought about it, the more we figure Purdis murdered Isaac, too."

Sophie's thoughts exactly. Stuffing everything back into the envelope, she said, "I'll do my best."

Morton stuck out his hand. "Thanks, Mrs. Greenway. And—" He hesitated, jamming his hands into his pockets. "Remember, don't mention my name."

"They won't find out about you from me," Sophie assured him.

"Great. Will you call if you get any news?"

"I will. And thanks, Morton. This will make all the difference."

He gave his cap a yank and then took off running around the side of the building.

Sophie stood for a moment, her eyes rising to stars just beginning to appear in the night sky. A harvest moon sat directly over one of the mausoleums on the hill, shining a brittle light down onto its triangle facade. All around her, the graveyard was silent and empty. Peaceful, in its own way. For the first time all week Sophie felt truly hopeful.

Remembering that Bram was still inside, she tucked the envelope under her arm. As she rounded the corner she walked straight into Adelle Purdis.

"We need to talk," said Adelle, her body blocking the narrow path.

Sophie was startled, but tried to hide it. Adelle was the last person she wanted to run into right now. "If you don't mind—" She tried to push past her.

"I do mind," said Adelle, standing her ground. She took her right hand out of her raincoat pocket and pointed a gun at Sophie. "I'll take that."

"I beg your pardon?"

Adelle grabbed the envelope. "I've been looking for this all week. It was kind of you to find it for me."

"You mean—"

"Yes. I heard everything. Lucky for me I followed you out here."

Sophie's eyes dropped to the gun barrel. "Adelle . . . wait. Just think for a moment." She knew, even as she said the words, that it was hopeless. "You have to be reasonable. The police will find out what Hugh did sooner or later. Save yourself now—and your son."

At the mention of her son, Adelle leveled the gun at Sophie's stomach and said, "Walk."

"But . . . where?"

"Down that hill," she said, pushing her forward. "I'm right behind you, so don't make a sound."

Sophie tripped and stumbled. Scrambling to her feet, she said, "Adelle, this is crazy."

"Shut up."

"But . . . what are you going to do?"

"Just keep moving."

# 37

Sophie perched precariously on a gravestone, easing off her right shoe and rubbing her ankle. She'd twisted it as they'd run down the hill. Attempting to keep her voice calm and steady, she asked, "Where are we going?"

Adelle stood over her, breathing hard. Glancing up to the mausoleums at the top of the hill, she said, "I don't know. Maybe up there."

"But . . . why?"

"I don't know!" She spun to her right and walked over to the gravel road. "Where does this lead?"

"The road? It crisscrosses the cemetery. It doesn't really lead anywhere."

"Then . . . how do you get out?"

"Through the front gate."

"But . . . there are guards on the front gate!"

"Then I guess you take your chances with the spiked wrought-iron fence."

Adelle whirled around, looking wildly in every direction. Sophie could feel her confusion, and her desperation. "Look, Adelle, can we talk for a minute?"

"Shut up and let me think."

"I want you to know that I understand. You're guilty of nothing more than wanting to protect your husband and your son."

"Get up."

Sophie tried to put some weight on her foot but stopped when a searing pain shot up her leg. "I can't. I think I sprained my ankle. Let me rest just a minute more."

"Look, you either cooperate or I shoot you right here." She leveled the gun at Sophie's head.

Sophie didn't really believe she'd do it. Adelle wasn't a killer, but she was frightened. "All right," she said, hobbling to her feet. Right now she didn't see that she had any other choice.

"Walk in front of me." Adelle directed her through the darkness. The streetlights from Dupont Avenue shed some light on their path, though instead of staying close to the street, Adelle pointed them deeper into the graveyard. Sophie felt certain that Adelle didn't have a clue where they were going, they simply had to keep up the appearance of movement. Yet when the pain in her leg became so terrible that she couldn't stand it another minute, she eased onto another gravestone. "Let me rest here, Adelle. Please."

Adelle leaned against a tree, catching her breath. "Okay, maybe . . . maybe I need some time to figure this out." Looking back at the chapel, she said, "We've got to get out of here, but to do that we're going to need a car. Howell will eventually get impatient and want to leave. He'll send Hugh out to look for me." Walking a few paces away from the tree, she announced, "We're just going to have to wait here until he comes."

Bram would discover that she was missing, too, thought Sophie. She had to hold on to the hope that he'd find them first.

"You know," said Adelle, "this is all your fault. Cindy told me you thought I lied yesterday. If you'd minded your own business, none of this would be happening."

"But Ginger was my friend," said Sophie indignantly. "So was Lavinia."

"Just . . . shut up."

"Look," said Sophie, slipping off her shoe. The ankle was starting to swell. "I understand why Hugh did what he did. I was part of the church once myself. I haven't forgotten the doctrines."

"Meaning what?"

"Your son, Joshua. He could never become the head of the church if Hugh had fathered a child before him. Even if that child didn't live, it meant your boy wasn't Hugh's first child—there would always have been a question whether or not he was Hugh's first son. And that, in and of itself, would have disqualified him to be a minister."

Adelle dropped the hand holding the gun and just stared at her. "Amazing, Sophie. This is so true to form. Why don't you stay out of matters that don't concern you?" She sank down onto a gravestone.

"But . . . I wanted some resolution about Ginger—about what happened to her. And then, about Lavinia, too. I understand what your life's been like. I've been there myself, seen the kind of isolation you live with as a minister's wife. Only, I'm sure with Hugh, the isolation was ten times worse. It's tough always having to set the example, be the role model. You're never allowed to form any real friendships because you have to keep so much hidden."

"Tell me about it."

"But, Adelle, you can talk to me. I won't judge you."

"How generous."

"I need to understand. I need to hear it from you." She took a chance. "I was right, wasn't I—about Hugh's motive for Isaac's murder?"

"Oh, don't feel sorry for Isaac. He was a complete bastard. He's been dangling that little tidbit of knowledge over our heads for the last twenty-five years."

Of course, thought Sophie. Isaac must have wielded a great deal of power. "If he told Howell what he knew—"

"Howell would have hit the ceiling. He'd have tossed Hugh and me out of the church. And Joshua, well, he could forget being a minister."

"But Isaac arranged the abortion. He couldn't exactly deny it."

"Which is why I never worried all that much about him talking. We all had something to lose. I figured it was a standoff. That is, until this week. I realized too late that the balance of power was about to change."

Sophie nodded. "I knew something was up when I saw all those evangelists checking into the hotel."

"Yes, you would have recognized them, wouldn't you?" She got up and walked back over to the tree, holding the gun stiffly at her side as if she were almost afraid of it. "The fact is, Howell finally found out what Isaac had been doing behind his back all these months. He intended to toss him out, and that's exactly what he would have done except for one small point. Isaac threatened to take half the church and most of the ministry with him. Howell pretended to reconsider, but only to test the waters, see who was still on his side.

"Isaac wasn't stupid. He knew his days were numbered, so he forced a showdown. He had nothing more to lose. So, in a masterstroke, he decided to blackmail Hugh into joining his side against Howell. Hugh would have been the final zircon in his fake diadem. No matter what my husband did, he couldn't win. If he threw in with Isaac, Joshua was lost. He'd never become the head of the true church because Isaac was hell-bent on destroying it. He was changing doctrines, Sophie. He no longer believed abortion was wrong. Since most of the ministry agreed with him, he had nothing to fear from his past. Hugh, on the other hand, did. And in Isaac's new church—well, guess who was going to lead that? On the other hand, if Hugh stayed with Howell, Isaac threatened to spill the beans about Ginger. Either way, Joshua was lost, and so was the church. There was no other way."

Sophie saw it all much more clearly now. "But . . . why did Lavinia have to die? She was nowhere near the truth."

Adelle shook her head. "She was near enough. Lavinia told me that her next move was to talk to Howell Purdis. Howell would have smelled a rat and gone to Isaac to demand the truth. And Isaac, honorable man that he was, would have given it to him."

Sophie winced as she tried to take a step on her foot. "But . . . surely murder wasn't the answer."

"It was the *only* answer," said Adelle bitterly. "How could we tell Joshua he wasn't a firstborn child? It's who he *is*. How could I look him in the eye and tell him his father had slept with someone before we were married? Joshua adores his dad. It would have devastated him personally, professionally, and spiritually. Joshua would have been the one to pay the price for all of *our* sins!"

Sophie recalled that Old Testament verse, "I, the Lord thy God, am a jealous God, visiting the iniquity of the fathers upon the children unto the third and fourth generation."

"You of all people should understand, Sophie. I had to take the sin back and place it on *my* head, where it belonged. What did it matter what happened to me?"

"But Hugh was the one who slept with Ginger. You didn't do anything wrong."

Adelle looked up at the moon. "You were right, Sophie. I didn't tell the truth yesterday. It wasn't Isaac's office I saw Ginger in all those years ago, but Hugh's."

Sophie assumed as much. "Okay, so you lied. That's not the end of the world."

"I did much more than that." She sat down on a grave-stone closer to Sophie this time. "After I found out about the abortion, I came to Hugh, told him I knew everything. I used that knowledge to insinuate myself into his life. I convinced myself that I wanted to provide him with a sympathetic ear. I never suggested I'd tell on him, but the threat was always there. He knew it. I knew it. After a while he gave in, opened up to me. He was so lonely, so devastated by Ginger's death. He loved her deeply and would have married her in a second if he'd known about the child. But the sad fact was, no one ever told him."

"He . . . didn't know?" said Sophie. This *was* news.

"Come on," said Adelle, her voice resuming its former coldness. "I don't know why Hugh hasn't come looking for me yet, but we can't just sit here."

"Please . . . just one more minute," pleaded Sophie. "My ankle really hurts."

As Adelle stood she glanced back toward the chapel. "People are starting to leave. Where *is* he? Get up!" she ordered, yanking Sophie to her feet.

Sophie's foot hurt even worse now. She felt something snap every time she put any weight on it.

"Move," said Adelle, shoving her toward a more wooded section.

Sophie limped along valiantly, attempting to keep the conversation going. If she could only reach Adelle, get her to see that her position was hopeless. "Isaac probably thought he was doing Hugh a favor by arranging Ginger's abortion. He was taking care of a nasty task for a friend. Maybe Ginger thought she was doing what Hugh wanted her to, saving him from a scandal."

"That's right," said Adelle, motioning her between two large headstones. "I have no doubt that, for Ginger, Hugh would have found the courage to defy his father's wrath. Even though she wasn't thin and perfect the way Howell insisted a minister's wife should be, Hugh was in love."

"But he loved you, too," said Sophie.

"He never loved me." As Adelle came to a stop, scanning the moonlit darkness for her husband, Sophie stumbled over a metal flower holder sticking precariously up out of the ground. She fell against a gravestone.

"Has anyone ever told you you're clumsy?" said Adelle, staring down at her.

Sophie decided the question was rhetorical. Rubbing her head, she said, "My ankle is killing me."

"Oh, all right. We're more hidden here. We might as well stay put. For now. If Hugh doesn't come, we'll have to wait until the cemetery closes down for the night."

"And then what?"

"Just . . . shut up."

Hoisting herself onto a gravestone, Sophie pulled off her shoe. This time she tossed it away. She took the other shoe off and did the same thing. High heels were a menace in a place like this. "I can't believe Hugh never loved you, Adelle."

"Why should he?" She turned her back to the chapel and sat down. "I manipulated him into marrying me. The idea of becoming the wife of Howell Purdis's son was pretty intoxicating back then. Women don't have many opportunities for power and status in the church and I've always been vain enough to want that. I was sure I could make it work. I lost weight, attended to clothing and appearance the way I never had before. But while both Hugh and I tried hard to keep up appearances, our union was never anything but a sham. That's been my cross to bear all these years, Sophie. I thought I could make him love me, I thought I could make myself love him. But in the end, I couldn't. Joshua was the one who finally brought us together. He's always been our first priority. I couldn't allow him to get hurt because of our stupidity. Any mother could understand why I did what I did."

"What you did," said Sophie, her pulse quickening as she noticed movement in the distance. It looked as if someone was running down the hill to the south of the chapel. Adelle didn't notice it because her back was turned. "If I didn't know better, I'd think you were saying *you* poisoned Lavinia and Isaac. Not Hugh."

Looking up pointedly, Adelle said, "I thought that's what we've been talking about. Of course I did it. Hugh doesn't have the guts."

Sophie was startled into silence. Up until this moment she hadn't truly appreciated the danger she was in. She thought she'd be able to talk to Adelle, get her to see reason. But now she knew better. "You know, Adelle, I . . . won't tell anyone what I know. I promise, I'll keep my mouth shut." It was a desperate stab.

"Really? How wonderful! All my problems are over."

"No, I mean it. I understand. I have a son, too."

"You can cut the act."

"Adelle, killing me isn't going to help you. For starters—" She thrashed around in her mind for something to say. "What would you do with my body?" It was a gruesome thought.

"I don't know," she said, looking down at the gun as if seeing it for the first time. "With Lavinia and Isaac, I had time to plan."

Sophie saw a figure moving steadily toward them. Holding her breath, she waited as the moon moved out from behind a cloud. Her heart sank as she saw that it was Hugh.

Adelle turned as he approached. "It's about time."

"Where did you get that?" said Hugh, stopping dead in his tracks when he saw the gun.

"From the glove compartment of Isaac's car."

"Adelle, what are you thinking?" His frightened eyes shot to Sophie.

With a gesture of triumph, Adelle held up the envelope. "Here's the proof Isaac had on you and Ginger. He wasn't lying."

"But . . . where did you get it?"

"From her. She knows everything."

Pushing past his wife, he walked up to Sophie, gazed down at her, and said, "You're sure?" He was still speaking to Adelle.

"Completely," she answered. "Now listen. This is what you need to do. First, I want you to go back to the chapel, find Bram Baldric, and tell him that Sophie and I needed to talk. Tell him I'll drop her back home later. Next, I want you to take Howell back to the hotel."

"Slow down, Adelle." He rubbed the back of his neck. "This just gets worse by the minute. Everything you do just digs us in deeper."

"Me? Look who's talking!"

"I never wanted you to poison anyone!"

"So? What was I supposed to do? Let Isaac walk all over us?"

"Yes," he barked. "Don't you think that's preferable?"

As they continued to rail at each other Sophie saw the chance she'd been waiting for. Hugh was mere inches away. He and Adelle were both so caught up in their argument, they weren't paying any attention to her. The problem was, running might be impossible. On the other hand, she didn't have a choice. Steeling herself against the pain, she waited for the right moment.

It came as Hugh turned his back on her to confront his wife about the gun one more time. Sophie shot off the gravestone and pushed him as hard as she could. As he fell forward he knocked Adelle down, too. Both of them hit the ground with a thud.

In a flash, Sophie was up, lumbering clumsily across the grass as fast as her damaged foot would take her. Her ankle was already swollen to the size of a grapefruit, but she couldn't give in to the pain.

Just as another cloud covered the moon she lunged behind a clump of trees.

"I don't see her!" shrieked Adelle. She was disoriented from the fall.

Sophie peeked out from behind one of the larger trunks and saw the two of them scrambling to their feet. Fortunately, at their age, it was an awkward process.

"She went that way," said Hugh, pointing.

It was the wrong direction.

"I don't think so," said Adelle, weaving unsteadily toward the trees.

"What does it matter? Give me the gun." His voice had grown hoarse.

"Why?"

"Just give it to me."

"Not until I know what you're going to do with it."

"It's over, Adelle. It stops right here."

"Are you crazy?"

"I'd be crazy to let this go on any longer. I'm sick to death of people cleaning up after my disasters. Nobody ever consults me first, they just act on my behalf."

"That's because you're weak, Hugh."

"That's not true!"

"Of course it is. Who was the only one who ever disciplined Joshua? You were never there for the hard parts, only the easy, touchy-feely parts. You've never had the courage to do what's necessary. Not in your career, and not in your personal life. If I didn't do it for you, it didn't get done!"

Sophie could see him grimace, as if he'd been slapped across the face. It took him a moment to regroup. "Maybe that was true in the past. But it's not true now."

"Wonderful," shouted Adelle, flinging her hands in the air. "And for your very first act of courage you're going to ruin everything I've tried to do to save the church and our son."

"Be reasonable," he demanded.

Sophie backed up and began running again. As she dove behind a far bush she felt an arm grip her around the stomach and then a heavy hand clamp over her mouth. Her first instinct was to scream.

"Cool it, Soph," came a familiar whisper. "It's me."

She looked up into Bram's beautiful green eyes, knowing that if she lived to be a hundred, she'd never be happier to see him than she was at this moment. She held on to him for dear life.

Bram lifted a finger to his lips.

"You haven't saved anyone," bellowed Hugh, calling to Adelle from one of the gravestones. He sat dejectedly on the edge.

"Just shut up and help me," she pleaded, easing around a tree, the gun held rigidly in front of her.

Through the brush, Sophie could tell that she was headed

away from them. She settled against Bram's stomach, feeling his strong arms hold her tight.

"You're just like Isaac," shouted Hugh. He sounded exhausted now. At the end of his rope. "You've done nothing but make matters worse. And then, just like him, you have the gall to want me to thank you for it!"

"Help me find her," she demanded, parting the bushes with her free hand.

"Why? So you can poison someone else? Do you travel everywhere these days with oleander flower?"

"You're pathetic, do you know that?" She rushed toward him, her face burning with anger. "You had a chance to say all this to me back at the hotel. Why didn't you?"

"Maybe you're right. Maybe I am a coward. But where's it going to stop, Adelle? Are you going to poison the whole world?"

Sophie lifted her head at the sound of a police siren. It was coming this way. "Did you call the police?" she whispered, turning around to look at her husband.

"Of course I did," he whispered back. "I believe in backup."

"How—"

"Morton saw Adelle hiding in the shrubs after the two of you were done talking. He heard what she said, saw her pull the gun. That's when he came in to find me."

"Thank God," said Sophie.

Bram nuzzled the side of her face. "Thank Morton."

"A siren?" said Adelle, whirling around just in time to see two squad cars roar down Dupont Avenue. "They're coming this way!" she called, her voice full of panic. "What are we going to do?"

"Come here," said Hugh, his voice oddly calm.

"Why?"

"Just come here." He held out his hand.

Adelle stared at him. Hesitating, she moved closer. "What are we going to do?"

In one quick movement, he grasped her upper arms,

looked her square in the eye, and said, "We're going to call it a day, Adelle."

"No!" She hit his chest, struggling to get away.

He held on. "What do you suggest we *do*? There's nowhere to go. No place to hide. This is it, Adelle. It's over."

"But—"

"But what?" He crushed her against him, holding her tight until she stopped struggling and dropped the gun. It didn't take long.

"I'm sorry," she cried, burying her head in her hands. "I didn't know what else to do."

"I know," he said, stroking her hair.

They held each other for nearly a minute. Then, still holding hands, they sank to their knees as the squad cars roared over the rise and sped straight for them.

Sophie couldn't hear their words now, but she could see their faces twisted with pain. They looked like two sad statues, heads bowed, their hands pressed together in a gesture of supplication. Were they seeking their God's forgiveness, or merely waiting for the inevitable? She would probably never know. Yet the irony was inescapable. The destructive doctrines of a destructive church had, in the end, destroyed the lives of two of its truest believers. For a moment Sophie almost felt sorry for them.

Then, as she knew it would, the moment passed.

# 38

"Are we comfy?" asked Bram.

"Reasonably," said Sophie.

"Want me to fluff your foot pillow again?"

"No, but a little more martoonie would be nice." She held up her martini glass, feeling a mellow buzz settle into her aching muscles. Her ordeal in the graveyard two nights ago had left her bruised and sore.

Bram leaned around behind him and grabbed the pitcher.

"Are there any more olives?" Sophie held the glass on her stomach as he poured.

"We've cleaned out your parents' stash."

"They aren't martoonie drinkers."

"No, but they had all the liquid fixings."

Sophie and Bram were lying in the middle of the hardwood floor in their empty apartment at the Maxfield, pillows tucked under their heads, another pillow propped carefully under Sophie's injured ankle. It was Saturday evening. Outside, the light was fading slowly over downtown St. Paul.

After a busy day spent talking to housing inspectors and real-estate agents, Sophie and Bram made a spur-of-the-moment decision to spend the night at the Maxfield, sleeping in Sophie's parents' apartment. The evening's agenda, however, wouldn't have been complete without a visit to their future apartment.

"Where's Ethel?" asked Sophie.

"I think she's in the kitchen sniffing the mop boards."

"You know, I realize I'm genuinely tired when Ethel seems to have more energy than I do." She lifted her head and took a sip.

"This is nice, isn't it?" said Bram, clasping his hands behind his head. "Maybe we should forget the furniture. Live . . . simply."

"You mean uncomfortably."

"I thought you said you were comfortable."

"I said I was *reasonably* comfortable. I'd be *more* comfortable on a couch or a bed."

"But . . . furniture would destroy the minimalist aesthetic I'm trying to achieve in my life right now."

"Right. You should write the book. 'The Pack-Rat Minimalist.' You could sell it at garage sales. Junk stores. Flea markets."

"Now you're making fun of me."

"No, dear," she said, patting his hand. "I'm just drinking my martoonie and enjoying a quiet evening at home with my husband."

"But it's not our home yet. And I'm not entirely kidding. I like these high ceilings, the bare walls—the feeling of space. I look out the living-room windows and see downtown St. Paul stretching out before me—it makes me feel like I'm in a castle looking down on my kingdom."

"Well, first, dear, I understand there are cures for megalomania these days, so don't panic. We'll get you some help. And second, this may be your castle, but without furniture, you'll be living in it by yourself."

He turned over on his side, resting his head on his hand. "I'd never want to live without you, Sophie."

The sudden fierceness with which he said the words startled her. "Gee, I didn't realize I had such power. As I think about it, if you don't do all the laundry—*and* the dishes—from now on, I'm outta here."

He grinned, touching her face with the tips of his fingers. "With all the money we'll be saving on rent, we'll get a maid. Don't all castles have maids?"

"You think you've got an answer for everything, huh?"

"Not everything," he said, lowering his eyes. "You know, I ran around that graveyard for ten frantic minutes the other night before I spotted you."

"Thank God Adelle didn't see *you*."

"Oh, I never gave it a thought. A radio personality learns early in his career to live by stealth. Move in quick, and get out before the audience can find shotguns and form a posse."

She laughed, reaching up and smoothing the hair away from his forehead. "I knew you'd come, you know."

"I know." He leaned down and kissed her cheeks and her eyes, and then her lips. "I'm just glad it's over. Adelle Purdis will be put away for the rest of her natural life, and that's okay by me." Rolling over on his back again, he continued, "Come to think of it, you never did explain the precise significance of Ginger's words the night she died. You just gave me the biblical-illiterate overview."

"Are you sure you're interested?"

Ethel lumbered out of the kitchen, her green tennis ball clamped between her teeth. Pausing next to one of the ornate metal floor vents, she dropped the ball on top of it and then watched to see what would happen. When it didn't roll, she nudged it with her nose. These days Ethel lived for scientific investigation.

"I'm all ears," said Bram, pouring himself another drink.

Sophie fortified herself with a sip of her own and then began, "In Genesis, we find the story of Abraham."

"I know that."

"Don't interrupt. Now, when he gets to be a hundred years old, he and his wife, Sarah, have their first child. They name him Isaac. One day God decides to test just how loyal Abraham is. So He orders him to take his son and go to the land of Moriah. When he gets there, he's supposed to offer the boy as a burnt offering."

"You mean, a human sacrifice?" said Bram. "He was supposed to kill his own son? I don't remember that part."

"That's exactly what I mean. But Abraham doesn't tell his son what's going to happen—at least not right away. After they place the wood on the altar and get everything all set up, Isaac asks his dad where the ram is, the one that's going to be sacrificed. That's when Abraham explains to him that he, Isaac, will be the offering. God has commanded it. So Abraham ties him up, places him on the wood, and then pulls out this big knife. But as he's about to plunge it through his son's chest, he hears God's voice telling him to stop. Because Abraham was willing to obey, to sacrifice his only child, God says He believes now that Abraham truly fears Him. The upshot is, God says he will bless Abraham by making his descendants as numerous as the stars of heaven."

"Okay," said Bram, patting Ethel's stomach. She was lying on her back next to him now, all four paws thrust limply into the air. "So how did you put that together with Ginger's last words?"

"Well," said Sophie, pausing to collect her thoughts, "the night Ginger died she mumbled something about a ram. And then she said, 'The fire and the wood.' All of this pointed to an Old Testament sacrifice. The word *Moriah* was another tip-off. It suggested a specific sacrifice. The next thing she did was cry out for Isaac. Back then, we all thought she was referring to Isaac Knox, that she was sick and in pain and wanted a minister to come and pray over her. As the dean of students, Isaac was a logical choice. The problem was, we had no context in which to place her words. We didn't have a clue that she'd just had an abortion. But now I believe that in her feverish state, she was mixing up two different stories."

"You mean hers, and the biblical story of Abraham and Isaac."

"Exactly. I think, in her mind, she'd conjured up the image of Abraham sacrificing his son, Isaac, because, in a very real sense, that's just what *she'd* done. The emotion was genuine. She wanted her child back. Putting Hugh first, protecting him at all costs, doing what Isaac Knox probably convinced her was the only honorable thing to do, had been the wrong choice. You have to understand, most of her words were garbled. But when I read in my notes that she'd said, 'I don't care about the stars,' it finally struck me what she meant. She didn't care about God's promise to Abraham if it meant losing her child. The parallel between the two stories is striking, except in her mind, she was making the opposite choice from the one Abraham had made. She wanted to put her child first—before obedience to the dictates of God's ministry. Unfortunately, it was too late. I believe it was that struggle, that realization—that *agony*—which consumed her final hours."

"How awful for her," said Bram, stroking Ethel's ear.

"Actually, there was one other comment Ginger made in her diary that I wondered about when I read it. She said that she called the man she loved 'Lord.' After I began to form the theory that Hugh might have been her lover, and not Isaac, it all fit. Hugh's middle name was Abraham. There's a verse somewhere in the New Testament—don't ask me where anymore—that says Sarah, Abraham's wife, called him *Lord*. Ginger probably fantasized about marrying Hugh. If she was a normal human being, she was no doubt impressed by his rank within the church. Calling him Lord probably occurred to her because of that verse. I think it's also fair to say that she may have envisioned the two of them as modern-day versions of Abraham and Sarah. From the words she spoke the night she died, she certainly saw her child as Isaac. It all makes sense."

"Poor kid," said Bram. "But, as a guy, I've got to say I feel kind of sorry for Hugh. If your church hadn't had all these do's and don'ts associated with marriage—who you could marry, what age your potential partner had to be, how your future wife had to look—somebody might have simply told the poor schmuck the truth, and then he and Ginger could have tied the knot. In the end, all the cover-up got any of them was death and ruined lives."

"Then, as well as now. By the way, since we're on the subject, I should tell you I got a phone call from Lieutenant Riley before we drove over here tonight."

"Where was I?"

"Cleaning the garage. I didn't want to disturb you on the off chance you might actually be throwing something out. I knew we'd have a chance to talk about all this later."

"So talk," said Bram. "I'm all ears."

"Well, Riley said that, after consulting an attorney, Adelle has now decided to cooperate. They've already interviewed her a couple of times. Her lawyer is negotiating some sort of plea bargain."

"As long as she's put away."

"She will be."

"Say, did Riley say where Adelle got the oleander flower?"

A frown formed on Sophie's face. "Yes."

"The hotel garden?"

"Afraid so. It was a convenient—and quiet—murder weapon. Adelle found out the make and model of Lavinia's rental car, and then, the night she drove to that bar in northeast Minneapolis to meet with her, she slashed a tire before she went in. That way, she could drive by later and offer Lavinia a ride home."

"So it was Adelle who came by when Lavinia was on the phone with you."

"That's right. And when they got back to the hotel, Adelle suggested they have a nightcap together in Lavinia's room. Surprise surprise. She even had a snack to offer, one she knew Lavinia couldn't resist."

"The cheese balls."

"Exactly. Thanks to that old college recipe book I handed out at the reunion, she had the recipe right at her fingertips."

"But," said Bram, thinking it over, "what about the wake-up call? Why did Adelle come back the next morning?"

"Simple. She promised Hugh that she'd be back by midnight. He was going out with friends that night himself. He told her he was being dropped back at the hotel around twelve-fifteen. She wanted to be in bed with the lights off by the time he got home. That way, she could lie about what time she got back from the bar. Since she didn't have time that night to search the room, she called down for the noon wake-up call so that she could come back the next morning and finish the job. Her big mistake was picking up the morning newspaper. The police never could quite figure that out."

"Neither could we. But, I mean, are you telling me Hugh never suspected what she was up to?"

"I guess not. At least, not at first. He pretty much bought the rumor circulating around the hotel that Lavinia's husband was responsible for her death. Then, when Isaac turned up dead with a suicide note that named him as Lavinia's murderer, I guess Hugh finally smelled a rat. He knew Isaac was on the verge of realizing one of his greatest dreams—becoming the head of his own church. It simply wasn't logical that he'd commit suicide. I suspect," said Sophie, slipping her hand over Bram's, "that right from the beginning Hugh wondered about Adelle's involvement. I'll bet he feels guilty that he didn't do more to prevent a tragedy."

"The story of his life."

"Yeah, you could say that."

"What about Isaac?" said Bram, prying the tennis ball out of Ethel's mouth.

"You mean how did she poison him? Well, she informed him sometime Wednesday afternoon that if he wanted Hugh's support in the fight against Howell Purdis, he needed to talk to her. She was the real power behind Hugh's throne."

"And he had no trouble believing that?"

"From what Adelle told the police, none. She suggested they meet at Boom Island Park. It was far away from the hotel, easy to find, and provided them with complete anonymity. After he arrived, she joined him in his car with a thermos and some food she was snacking on. Being the polite sort, she offered him some. He was dead in a matter of minutes. She knew Hugh's laptop computer was the same as Isaac's, so she'd typed the message onto a disk before she left the hotel. She slipped it into his pocket along with the jewelry she'd taken from Lavinia's room. Before she left, she grabbed a gun from his glove compartment."

"The awful thing is," said Bram, examining the tennis ball for teeth marks, "Adelle might have gotten away with it if it hadn't been for Morton."

"That's true. I guess you could say he saved the day."

"I think you saved the day, sweetheart," said Bram, bringing her hand up to his lips. "You were the one who kept pushing to discover the truth. However, I hope this is the last time you'll get mixed up in anything this dangerous. My nerves can't take any more of your unpaid detective work."

"Don't worry," said Sophie with a sigh. "I'm just a boring old innkeeper now."

"Good."

"You know," she said, reflecting a moment more. The

alcohol had taken the edge off some of her more painful emotions, and yet nothing could dull the enormity of what had happened to her this past week. "These last few days have been the biggest roller-coaster ride I've ever been on. From inheriting the hotel, to losing Lavinia, then Isaac, and then Adelle. Cindy nearly jumps off the roof. And finally, to top it off, Rudy's big announcement."

"What's that?"

"He and John are moving in together. They're planning a commitment ceremony next Christmas."

Bram tossed the tennis ball in the air. "I know "

"You know?"

"Sure. Rudy tells me lots of things before he tells you. I think he figures if he has me on his team, he's got a better chance convincing you."

"Am I that hard to deal with?"

"Your love, and your approval, mean a great deal to him. Sure, he gets nervous sometimes. He's just a kid."

"That's my point."

"Give him some credit, Soph. He's got a good head on his shoulders. He's a lot like you."

She could hardly argue the point.

Catching Ethel's attention, Bram bounced the tennis ball a few times in front of her face and then tossed it into the dining room.

Ethel lurched to her feet and glared down at him as if he'd lost his mind.

"You don't *throw* tennis balls anymore, honey," said Sophie, giving Ethel's head a sympathetic pat. "They're only for chewing, guarding, and falling asleep in front of. Not chasing."

"Since when?" he said indignantly.

"Since we were at the park two weeks ago. We were playing fetch in the bushes and somehow or other the ball disappeared down a hole. I doubt I will ever be forgiven my cavalier approach to tennis-ball ownership."

"Life is full of peril."

Ethel raised her eyes with great dignity and smacked her lips. Her thoughts exactly.

"Well, all I can say is, I hope the worst problems we have in the next few years revolve around lost tennis balls." Bram drained his martini glass.

"Here's to that." Sophie drained hers as well. "I think running this hotel will be a lot of fun."

"You're not worried about owning a hotel that has . . . you know. A curse on it?" he asked.

"Hey. I'd forgotten about that."

"So had I. Until just this minute."

She turned to look at him. "I don't believe in curses."

He turned to look at her. "Me neither."

"Howell Purdis doesn't have the power to curse a hotel."

"A bed-and-breakfast, maybe, but nothing this large."

"Well put."

They stared at each other.

"I wonder how you get a curse removed," asked Sophie.

Bram thought about it for a moment and then leaped to his feet. "I'll get the Yellow Pages," he said, hurrying into the kitchen.

# Excerpts from the Terrace Lane Cookbook

## Sophie's Infamous Cheese Ball

The Original Cheese Ball:

2  8-oz. packages cream cheese
1  cup shredded cheddar
1/4  cup minced green top (spring) onions
1/8  tsp. cayenne pepper (optional)
2  tsp. Worcestershire sauce

Mix all together in a bowl. Shape into a large round ball, or small walnut-sized nuggets, or one long cheese log. Roll in chopped walnuts. Serve with crackers and crudités.

The Olive Cheese Ball:

2  8-oz. packages cream cheese
1/2  cup chopped pimento-stuffed (green) olives
1/2  cup chopped black (ripe) olives

Mix all together in a bowl. Shape into large round ball, or small walnut-sized nuggets, or one long cheese log. Roll in chopped almonds.

The Date-Nut Cheese Ball:

2  8-oz. packages cream cheese
1  cup chopped dates
1/2  cup crushed pineapple (remove as much juice as possible)

Mix all together in a bowl. Shape into large round ball, or small walnut-sized nuggets, or one long cheese log. Roll in chopped pecans.

## Bunny's Favorite Chicken-Stuffed Mushrooms

The chicken salad:

*3   cups chopped roasted chicken, white meat only*
*1/2 cup chopped toasted walnuts*
*1/2 cup chopped celery*
*1/2 cup sweet red seedless grapes, slivered or chopped*
*1/8 cup chopped green top (spring) onions*
*1   tsp. Hidden Valley Ranch Buttermilk Recipe Ranch Salad*
     *Dressing Mix (dry)*
     *Mayonnaise*

Mix ingredients in a bowl and add enough of your favorite mayonnaise to bind all together. Some may like more mayo, some less. The amount is up to you. Prepare at least a dozen large stuffable mushrooms by removing the stems and cleaning out the interior carefully with a spoon. Heap the chicken salad onto the prepared mushroom and sprinkle with paprika and fresh chopped parsley. Can be prepared several hours ahead and refrigerated until ready to serve.

## Tahtinen Family Cold Torsk Salad, Northern Minnesota Style

*1   16 oz. fillet of torsk (or cello cod) baked, cooled, and flaked*
*3   hard-boiled eggs, chopped*
*1/2 cup celery, chopped*
*1/4 cup green top (spring) onion, chopped*
*1/4 cup chopped watermelon pickle with juice*
*1   tsp. fresh lemon juice*
     *Salt and fresh ground pepper to taste*
     *Mayonnaise*

Mix ingredients together in a bowl and add enough mayonnaise to bind (can use low-calorie mayo). Chill at least three hours to blend flavors. Serve salad in a large bowl decorated with lemon slices and fresh parsley. The Tahtinen family often served this on hot summer nights accompanied by dark pumpernickel crackers and ice-cold beer.

## Spinach & Boursin Cheese in Phyllo

2  10-oz. packages frozen chopped spinach, thawed and
   squeezed dry of liquid
1  5.2-oz. Boursin cheese
1/2 cup chopped parsley
1  egg, raw
1/4 cup chopped green top (spring) onions
   Fresh ground pepper

Mix ingredients together in a bowl.

Thaw one package of phyllo dough. Use according to package directions. Cut dough into two sections. Place a rounded tablespoon of the spinach mixture at the bottom. Brush thin sheet of phyllo with butter. Fold both sides over the center. Brush with butter again. Roll into cylinders. Brush the outside of the rolls with butter.

Bake at 350 degrees for 15 minutes—or until golden brown.

Serve hot with mustard dill sauce if desired.

## Mustard Dill Sauce

1  cup sour cream (or low-fat sour cream)
1/4 cup stone-ground mustard
1  tsp. dried dill weed

Mix together and chill.

## Oriental Chicken Salad

For the dressing, combine and mix well:

3   T. sugar
1/2 cup vegetable oil
3   T. white-wine vinegar
3   T. water
1   T. sesame oil
2   T. light soy sauce
1   tsp. grated fresh ginger

For the salad:

1   (3 oz.) package Ramen soup noodles, uncooked
4   cups thinly sliced green cabbage
2   cups thinly sliced red cabbage
2   T. thinly sliced green top (spring) onions
2   cups cooked shredded chicken (1 whole breast)
1 1/2 cups toasted, slivered almonds
2   cups pea pods, blanched
1/2 cup shredded carrots

3   oz. rice (Mai Fun) noodle/oil

Open Ramen noodles and save envelope of seasoning for a future use. Marinate the noodles in the dressing until tender (about 2 hours). In the meantime, combine the cabbage with the onion, carrots, chicken, and almonds in a bowl. When noodles are tender, pour noodles and dressing over salad and mix together. Place in the center of a decorative plate. Arrange pea pods around the edge.

Heat oil until hot. Toss rice noodles into oil a little at a time until puffed and light. Remove with slotted spoon to paper towel. Crumble and spread over salad.

## Milk-Chocolate Raspberry-Jam Torte

1/2  cup butter (1 stick)
4    eggs, separated
1    cup sugar
1/4  lb. milk chocolate
1    cup cake flour
1/4  cup soft raspberry jam

Icing:
1/4  cup milk chocolate
2    T. butter

Cream butter and sugar together. Add yolks one at a time. Beat until light. Melt chocolate in a double boiler. Cool slightly. Add to egg mixture. Add flour. Beat egg whites until stiff. Fold into batter. Pour into greased and floured 8- or 9-inch spring-form pan. Bake approximately 1 hour at 350 degrees. Cool. Frost top with soft jam. Melt chocolate and butter in top of double boiler. Frost over jam. Decorate with whipped cream.

*Meet another Minneapolis sleuth, restaurateur Jane Lawless, in these mysteries by Ellen Hart*

Published by Ballantine Books.

"Ellen Hart is a writer to watch and so is her lesbian sleuth." —Sandra Scoppettone

# HALLOWED MURDER

The police think Allison drowned, but her sorority sisters think it was murder. That's when Minneapolis restaurateur and sorority advisor Jane Lawless steps in to find the truth and risk everything to ensnare a cunning killer.

# VITAL LIES

An old friend invites Jane Lawless and her irrepressible sidekick, Cordelia Thorn, to her Victorian inn to celebrate the winter solstice and investigate a murder from years before. Upon her arrival, Jane is plagued by malicious pranks that lead to a much more timely and malicious murder.

# STAGE FRIGHT

Jane Lawless must come to the aid of her theater-manager sidekick, Cordelia, who is undone by backstage pranks that escalate into murder.

# A KILLING CURE

Jane discovers membership can be a deadly affair when she uncovers dark secrets at a prestigious women's club.

# A SMALL SACRIFICE

When Jane accompanies Cordelia to a college reunion, she has no clue murder is on the menu. Long-simmering jealousies and secrets that have been stewing for more than twenty years explode into murder, with Jane and Cordelia caught in the crossfire.